The elf felt about in the pocket of his coat as he continued to run. His fingers found the carved mosaic stone from the burial ground. I must tell Goldmoon, he thought as he raced toward her tent.

Tell her what? the spirit interrupted his thoughts.

Gair couldn't see the Que-Nal, but somehow he knew the spirit was at his shoulder.

Finish the task!

"No!" I must tell Goldmoon.

Tell her that you dabbled in something she had oft refused to teach you? Tell her that you abused the skills she shared with you? Tell her you've breathed life into a ghost? What would your teacher think of you?

NOVELS

BRIDGES OF TIME SERIES

DragonLance® NOVELS

THE SILVER STAIR

JEAN RABE

For the Ladies of Ottawa:

Edna and Jo
Lucille, Geraldine, Denise, and Marge
Dolores and Arliss
and
Dee and Crystal

Cover art by Jeff Easley
First Printing: January 1999
Library of Congress Catalog Card Number: 98-85778

9 8 7 6 5 4 3 2 1
21315XXX1501

ISBN: 0-7869-1315-0

U. S., CANADA,	EUROPEAN HEADQUARTERS
ASIA, PACIFIC, & LATIN AMERICA	Wizards of the Coast, Belgium
Wizards of the Coast, Inc.	P.B. 34
P.O. Box 707	2300 Turnhout
Renton, WA 98057-0707	Belgium
+1-800-324-6496	+32-14-44-30-44

Visit our Website at **www.tsr.com**

Chapter 1

The Hope of Kothas

The thick iron chains were uncomfortably heavy. Beneath the manacles, sores festered that the creature could not scratch. He did his best to ignore the pain and concentrated instead on the cries of the gulls circling overhead. With each breath, he pulled as much fresh air as possible into his lungs. The air was crisp, almost brittle, on this late fall morning, and it was laced with the scent of sea bass that had been caught a number of hours ago and was now threatening to spoil. It carried with it a worse and all-too-familiar odor—the stench of his captors. The creature growled softly and gritted his teeth as a whip struck his back.

"Move!" A grim-faced sea barbarian cracked the whip again. "Faster, you stinking beast!" There were other words that were more vicious-sounding, an unending stream of expletives that the barbarian thought the creature could not understand and that he rattled off for his own pleasure. "You're the slowest of the lot! Move!"

The creature called himself R'vagho, and had stated his name repeatedly to his captors. They thought the word was only a growl.

Another lash.

Reluctantly he sped up his pace, chains clanking

sonorously above the snap of the billowing sails. Bow to stern and back again, across a deck that had become deeply scarred by the chains dragging over it, the walk was achingly brief and monotonous, but it was far better than staying forever in the stuffy, urine-reeking hold. It gave the creature some semblance of exercise so his muscles would not atrophy—and so he could fetch a better price.

Thirty-odd creatures rested in the belly of the cog currently called *The Hope of Kothas*. The ship had changed its name twice since it had taken the creatures on as cargo, and it had flown a dozen different flags. All of that subterfuge was lost on the beasts.

The creatures were to be sold as slave labor for an inland mining company within the week in a port called Goodbay. R'vagho had never heard of Goodbay, or of Abanasinia, the country in which it rested. He only knew that they were heading south. The rising and setting sun told him that much.

At one point there had been more than a hundred and fifty of the beasts crammed into the hold. Most had been sold in small ports to the north, along with chests containing relics from the Blood Sea, always at night, when the palms of sentries were filled with enough steel coins so they would look the other way. The barbarians' merchant captain, whose face was always hidden by a voluminous hood, had an accomplished sorcerer under his command. The sorcerer, also obscured by his expensive, billowy clothes, kept the creatures in line and waggled his fingers to magically put to sleep any on the docks who might object to the slaving operation.

"Move!"

The walk ended all too quickly, and the creature was returned to the hold. Another captive was taken up top, then another. R'vagho and his fellows passed the day in the close darkness of the ship's belly as they always did—eating the barbarians' scant leftovers, listening to the timbers creak softly, and trying to remember just how long they had been gone from their home.

Sleep came with difficulty, as usual, and the creatures were rudely roused from it. R'vagho felt the ship lurch wildly. He stood, only to be driven to the hold's floor as the cog rose and fell with what must have been an especially large wave. His breath was knocked from him as one of his fellows stumbled into him, then the pair scrabbled to their feet. Another bucking motion, and the creature was tossed against the hold's side, his head striking the rough timbers. He grabbed at his stomach in a pointless attempt to keep it from giving up his meager dinner.

A storm. They'd been through several during the trip. Some had been worse than others, but this felt like an especially bad one. The creature clung to a beam and tried to shut out the growling complaints of his fellows. He picked through the noises, trying to sort out what was going on above.

The timbers were groaning, as they always did during strong winds. The sound was different this time, not the gentle, almost soothing sound he had come to consider pleasant. If the timbers were living things, the creature would have believed these were groans of pain. Straining his ears, he heard the faint snap of the sails, but this, too, was different. He heard the crash of waves across the deck, the fearful bellows of the barbarians, the creak of the masts—louder than in the previous storms, if R'vagho's memory served him.

The wind whistled shrilly, and the sound grew to a keening wail as the minutes passed and the others in the hold finally grew quiet and listened to the sounds of the storm. A rumbling started, at first soft, like the growling of an empty stomach, then within the space of a few breaths becoming so thunderous it fairly overpowered their senses. It brought lightning with it, the cracks sharp and frightening. The ship rocked with an ever more frantic pace, wildly rising and falling and lurching unpredictably from side to side.

R'vagho barely made out the voice of the captain. He was shouting orders, panic clearly evident in his voice. Feet pounded across the deck, though amid the crescendo of the storm, the footfalls sounded faint.

The largest of those in the hold, a tall, hulking brute, was making his way to the ladder that led up to the hatch. The brute's thick chains thudded dully against the rungs as he climbed.

R'vagho steadied himself and made his way to the ladder. He grabbed another beam and doubled over as the bucking motion of the ship caused him to lose his balance and retch.

More of the creatures were surging around the brute on the ladder who was now slamming his fists against the door of the hold. The wood was slowly giving way, just as the previous hatch had done during an earlier unsuccessful escape attempt.

R'vagho numbly watched them. When they broke through the hatch, they would be severely beaten, as they had been following the earlier attempt. Perhaps this time the brute would be scorched by the sorcerer's horrible, tiny lightning bolts or maimed by the frightening fire-magic. Maybe the creatures would be keelhauled.

More pounding fists echoed against the hatch. Growls of encouragement came from those clinging to the ladder beneath the brute. The faint cries of the sea barbarians drifted down from the deck. Then finally the sound of wood splintering cut through the chaos. Success! The brute scrambled through the broken hatch and onto the deck. The others followed quickly up the ladder behind him.

R'vagho let out a deep breath, closed his eyes, and waited for the sound of the sorcerer's terrifying spells and the thuds of his fellows falling to the deck in fiery death throes.

Instead, all the creature heard was the howl of the storm. The wind and the thunder rose eerily louder now, the broken hatch carrying a chill gust into the hold where it echoed like a maddened ghost. The rain was coming with it, a driving sheet that spattered in a staccato rhythm against the hold's floor.

His brethren would be lashed by whips and put to sleep by the magic they all loathed or else they would be killed. Still, R'vagho was curious, and joining his fellows on deck would be better than staying down here in the foul hold.

The creature pushed away from the beam, staggering as the ship continued to pitch wildly. He fell twice before he made it to the ladder, and he clung to the rungs to steady himself before he began a slow ascent.

Despite the black sky overhead, it was somewhat lighter on deck. Dark gray clouds were intermittently illuminated by lightning. The wind was fierce. It had broken the rear mast, which lay amid torn sail and rigging and the unmoving bodies of a several barbarians. The captain ordered the mainsail to be taken down.

Men scurried here and there, tightening down everything, lashing water barrels together. The first mate tied himself to the wheel, and the sorcerer was near him, waggling his fingers and casting a spell at the ship's bow. The wind had blown back his cowl, revealing a startlingly white face and a shaven head. Lips the color of cinders were in constant motion, spilling out the phrases of the enchantment.

There was chaos everywhere. The sea was roiling like

a pot of boiling soup, sending waves taller than the ship's mainmast crashing across the deck. The water was icy cold and immensely powerful, driving everyone in its path to his knees and threatening to pull the cog under the water's surface.

Through the cacophony, the creature heard a sea barbarian shout that a dragon had birthed the storm, and that the great beast would swallow any survivors.

"We'll all die!" It was the same barbarian who had whipped R'vagho that morning on deck.

"Aye, and you'll die even sooner if you don't help Gristen at the wheel!" The captain bellowed to be heard above the howling wind. The storm had revealed his dark face, which was surprisingly youthful.

R'vagho spotted the brute, who was motioning the creatures forward. A handful of sailors rushed toward them, fumbling at their waists for belaying pins and whips. The men hollered and gestured toward the hold, but the brute growled and defiantly shook his head.

No one was going back down there. Freedom was within the creatures' reach, even if it might be short-lived in this raging storm. R'vagho saw the brute raise his shaggy arms, flailing his thick chains in the face of the nearest sailor. The brute's followers were quick to copy the gesture, overcoming the barbarians before they could use their weapons.

Faintly through the rain and wind, the creature heard the snap of bones and the splash of human bodies being tossed overboard. He heard the captain shouting more orders as his crew tried to deal with the rebelling beasts and keep the ship intact.

Lightning flashed from the sky at the same time miniature bolts shot from the sorcerer's fingertips. The small bolts struck one of the creatures squarely in the chest, and he crumpled atop a barbarian he'd been trying to rend. More bolts flew into the pack, slaying another two of the rebels, and the sorcerer returned his attention to the bow.

The sails were down from the mainmast now, and the brute and another three creatures were there grabbing up lines and wrapping them around cornered barbarians. A pair of creatures picked up a water barrel and were using it as a shield against the bosun's mate. The man slashed at the barrel with his sword even as the creatures drove him back against the railing. Suddenly the ship rode a large crest and plunged downward. A wave washed across the bow, and all three were swept over the side.

R'vagho was doing his best to stay on his feet, but the erratic movement of the ship was making him nauseous and dizzy. He lurched toward the capstan, sliding clumsily across the water-slick deck and falling. He managed to wrap his long arms around the base of the capstan and took a deep breath. The ship climbed again, and this time it seemed to hang suspended in the air for several heartbeats before it fell with a deafening, bone-jarring crash. A wave thundered across the deck, sending several more creatures and barbarians into the sea.

R'vagho continued to hold tight and blinked furiously, trying to get the salt water out of his eyes so he could see what was going on. When the ship crested another wave and dropped again, a barbarian who was charging toward the creature slipped and fell. His sword flew from his grasp and clattered to the deck close to R'vagho as the man was washed overboard.

The creature awkwardly wrapped his clawed fingers around the small pommel and tried to shut out the confusion around him, tried desperately to ignore the bucking of the ship. The best he could manage was to fight off the nausea. When the unsettling wave in his stomach subsided, he jammed the blade's tip into a chain link just above his ankle. The link was rusty, and although he had tried unsuccessfully in the hold to pry it apart with his hands, maybe with this blade . . .

The storm continued to hammer mercilessly at the deck, and the waves threatened to sweep the creature overboard, but still he concentrated on the link of chain. The tip of the blade snapped, but he continued to pry at the link with the blunted sword. R'vagho gritted his teeth as he heard a loud snap and glanced up to see what had made the noise. The railing to his right snapped free, taking more of his fellows and some of the barbarians into the swirling sea with it.

He continued to work on the link and was finally rewarded when it snapped free from the manacle. The creature took another deep breath. The air was bitter. He smelled blood mixed with the overpowering scent of the saltwater.

He turned his attention to his other ankle and began to worry at a link there. The blade snapped again, leaving several inches of steel protruding from the hilt. He tried to be more careful now. There was still enough metal left to slip into the seam of the link. His big hands worked feverishly, and he grunted with satisfaction when the chain fell away, freeing his feet. The manacles remained, but he would deal with those later—if there was a later.

R'vagho peered over his shoulder. Beyond the creatures' forms, he spotted two sea barbarians. Unarmed, it appeared they were trying to surrender. R'vagho started to work on the chains affixed to his wrists. His frenzied fellow captives killed the men.

After what seemed like an eternity, a link separated from one manacle, then from the other. He dropped the broken weapon, scooped up a length of chain, and edged away from the capstan. Feet spread wide, knees bent, he braced himself as the ship crested a wave. As the bow rocked forward, he slid across the deck, heading toward the wheel. The first mate was still there, battered by the waves and looking oddly like a broken doll. The barbarian who'd whipped him this morning stood unsteadily nearby.

R'vagho raised his lips in a snarl as he lashed the chain about like a flail. It cracked hard into the face of this morning's tormentor, breaking his cheekbone with a sickening snap and sending the man to the deck. The creature lashed out at him again and again. Blood pooled about the man's unmoving form. Another wave crashed across the deck, washing the blood and the man away.

The first mate could not flee from the creature. His waist was firmly lashed to the center of the wheel, and his right hand was tied about the king's spoke. The remainder of his crewmen could not help him. The few remaining on deck were busy trying to fend off the brute and the other creatures. The captain was nowhere to be seen, nor was there any trace of his booming voice. The sorcerer was perched on the sterncastle above and behind the wheel, somehow surefooted in this gale, hands faintly glowing, face fixed on the bowsprit, trying to use his magical powers to keep the ship afloat.

R'vagho kept a nervous eye on the sorcerer and braced himself as the ship bucked beneath a huge wave. He felt himself flying forward. His arms thrashed about wildly, and he found something to grab on to—the wheel. He held tight until the water receded, then found himself staring right into the face of the first mate. The lightning was coming even faster now. The sharp cracks of thunder that followed reminded the creature of the crack of the barbarians' whips.

The first mate's steely eyes seemed to challenge

R'vagho. He winced as a bolt of lightning struck near the ship, then again as another and another shot down from the turbulent sky. His gaze drifted up from the creature's fierce visage, and his eyes widened. R'vagho turned to see what the first mate was looking at.

One of the bolts of lightning had struck the main-mast. It stood teetering, the wood wailing a final protest. It seemed to dangle like a marionette on invis-ible strings, then toppled toward R'vagho, the first mate, and the wheel.

The creature leapt to the port side, where the rail was still intact. His arms circled the posts just as the mast struck the deck, splintering the timbers. The creature held on as a wave surged above *The Hope of Kothas* and engulfed the deck, threatening to capsize the now mastless ship. As the water receded, R'vagho shook the saltwater from his eyes.

The first mate dangled lifelessly from what remained of the wheel. The wheel itself was broken, a tangled mess of spokes. Part of the mast was sticking out of a hole in the deck, and two of R'vagho's fellows were desperately hanging on to it.

The brute skirted the hole. He had somehow man-aged to get out of his chains, and he was stuffing swords into a belt he'd appropriated. His jowls were red with blood, and he threw back his head and howled in victory. Caught up in the blood frenzy of the slaughter, he leapt onto the sterncastle and grabbed a fistful of the sorcerer's robes. The human uttered a string of unintelligible words that somehow cut through the bedlam of the storm. Miniature red light-ning bolts shot from the sorcerer's fingers and struck the brute, dropping him to his knees. The brute some-how survived the magical attack and pulled the sor-cerer down with him. Clawed fingers found their way to the human's throat and squeezed with savage force.

The sorcerer was dying, and the ship seemed to shudder in response. The groan of the timbers was louder now, drowning out the sound of the wind and the driving rain. The waves continued to batter the ship, and the hole caused by the broken mainmast widened as the ship listed to port.

The brute cast the sorcerer's body from the sterncastle and howled in triumph, though his cry was a whisper amid the rush of the waves and the wind. R'vagho caught his attention and gestured toward the longboats. There were two on the starboard side that had miraculously escaped heavy damage. The brute roared and slammed his fists against his seared chest and nodded.

The creatures hurriedly gathered clothes and weapons—belaying pins, swords, daggers, and anything else that might prove useful—as they lumbered toward the longboats. Eight occupied the first longboat, which was quickly lowered into the water and was propelled away from the ship by a swelling wave. R'vagho scampered into the crowded second boat just as the brute joined him and sliced through the ropes that held it to the cog.

Wave after wave threatened to overturn the tiny longboat. There was no food left in R'vagho's stomach, but the nausea persisted and burgeoned. His head pounded in time with his heart, and he tried to occupy himself by levering a dagger into the fastenings of his manacles. Others copied him, with varying degrees of success, as the brute continued to howl in victory.

The storm broke shortly before dawn. In an impossibly short time, the sea was like blue glass, mirroring the sky and hiding the evidence of its recent fury. There was no sign of the other longboat or the crippled cog. There was no sign of anything but sky and water.

For days the creatures drifted, seeing no other ship

and no other life other than an occasional seagull. Their bellies grumbling loudly for food, their skin blistering and cracking from the pitiless sun, they drank what little rain fell into the bottom of the boat and hungrily eyed the smallest among them who could put up little fight against the brute's claws. After several days of incredible suffering, they spotted land to the south. They awkwardly headed toward it, not knowing how to use the oars in concert, but they lost sight of the shore as darkness fell. In the morning, they spotted land again—closer, but still miles away, and the current seemed to be sweeping them beyond it. The brute stood on the narrow longboat seat and stared longingly at the land. He growled softly, then dived over the side and started swimming toward the distant land. One by one, the other creatures followed.

Swimming such a distance was a daunting task at best, but it was made worse by the chill fall air and the cold water. It took them the better part of a day—those who survived—to reach land. The sun was starting to set by the time they pulled themselves up onto the beach. The sand was coarse, and the air that coursed over their tired, aching bodies nipped cruelly at them. Trees beckoned several yards away, green pines and maples that sported a riot of color made more intense by the last of the sun's rays.

The brute crawled toward the pines, nose quivering in search of food, legs moving sluggishly and begging for rest. The others trailed behind him, their limbs like lead from the cold water and the long swim. They plodded slowly but relentlessly, deeper into the forested grove. As they traveled, the woods darkened around them with the gathering shadows of twilight. The mature trees cut the brunt of the wind and hid all trace of the accursed sea. The brute leaned against a thick trunk and grunted as he caught his breath. His nose continued to quiver, bringing a myriad of scents to him—the headiness of the loam, a trace of game. He took another deep breath and gestured with a shaggy arm, staggering forward, the rest of the creatures shuffling after him.

The stars were out by the time they neared a clearing, and he motioned for them to stop. A small herd of deer was grazing beyond the thinning line of trees. The brute crouched as the others moved closer, their jaws slavering with the prospect of food. They crept around the bushes and toward the edge of the clearing and the oblivious deer, crept silently . . . and froze. The wind rustled the branches, revealing something near the deer, a thin, glowing construction that twisted upward from the ground, climbed into the wispy clouds far overhead, and disappeared from view. Nothing supported it, and it reeked of magic. Unnerved, the hairs raising on the backs of the creatures' necks, they plunged headlong away from the clearing and deeper into another section of the woods, not stopping until they were far out of sight of the unnatural thing.

Chapter 2

The Celestial Ladder

"These insects! For each one I swat, a hundred arrive to take revenge!"

The dwarf chuckled at his companion as he tromped clumsily through a tangle of tall grass. "So what d'ya expect, Gair? It's summer, an' we're in the woods, miles and miles from any city or village or anythin' else for that matter. Out in the middle of nowhere. 'Sides, I'd think you'd like it."

"Like insects?"

"The woods. Elves're supposed to like the woods, ain't they?" The dwarf's voice was deep and craggy, but not unpleasant. He paused and pretended to tug thoughtfully at his short russet beard before he repeated a little louder, "Well, ain't they?"

"And dwarves are supposed to like the mountains, or so I've heard. There's not a single mountain on this island." Despite his gruffness, the elf's words sounded silky and musical and soft, like the faint rustling of the leaves.

"Ah, by Reorx's beard, I do like the mountains, but the woods are just fine."

The elf sighed and batted futilely at a swarm of gnats

wreathing his head. "I like the woods 'just fine,' too, Jasper, when there is enough of a breeze to keep the insects—and this appalling heat—at bay, that is. It's hours after sunset, and it's still insufferably hot. My clothes are drenched with sweat."

The dwarf chuckled again and resumed his tromping. "We could stop for the night. Tired?"

"No." The elf grimaced as he flicked a large shiny beetle off his shirt. "We might be close, if we're not lost."

"Close? Do you really think so?" There was hope in the craggy voice.

"No. I believe we are lost."

"Gair, I think you just like to complain."

The pair presented a sharp contrast. The dwarf was thickset and ruddy complected, looking a bit like a tree stump bedecked in an age-worn ginger-colored shirt with sleeves pushed up past his elbows and bright green pants that were stuffed into the tops of faded leather boots. He had brawny limbs and stubby fingers that flitted playfully across the array of ferns that spread alongside the overgrown path. His hair was uncharacteristically short for one of his race, and his blue eyes, from which the hint of a few smile lines sprouted, sparkled mischievously. His face was broad and careworn, his nose slightly bulbous and a little off-center. His wide teeth were even, practically perfect, and as he grinned they glimmered like polished pearls in the light of the full moon that cut through gaps in the canopy.

"I don't complain, my dwarven friend, not at all. As a matter of . . ." The elf frowned and mumbled a string of foreign-sounding curse words as a thorny branch snagged his voluminous sleeve. "I was only making conversation," he added more softly.

"An' you don't argue, either, do you, Gair?" The

dwarf sniggered, half under his breath. "An' I bet you *really* don't like the woods. All you like are books and magic."

Gair was tall for an elf at nearly six feet. He had to duck frequently to keep from getting smacked by low-hanging tree branches that the dwarf easily passed under. His eyes looked black-shiny—like wet stones—nearly matching the shade of his impeccably pressed and recently purchased trousers and shirt. Were the light better, however, his eyes would show themselves to be a rich shade of purple flecked with bits of gold. There were muscles rippling in his lithe frame, a hidden strength, and he carried himself gracefully, like a dancer, despite the large pack on his back. His skin was pale, a scholar's complexion, and his face was slightly gaunt, yet handsome, his expression serious. His hair was shiny silver-white like the moon, and as he walked, it fluttered back from his firmly set jaw and teased his narrow shoulders.

"Jasper, to be honest, I've just never enjoyed the Raging Fire all that much, or all these insects that come with it. It's just too hot to do much of anything. Too hot to think. Too hot to . . . it's just too hot."

Raging Fire was a plainsman term for the warmest month of the summer. The elf and the dwarf found themselves in the heart of an especially sweltering evening.

"I've never minded the Raging Fire—the Dry Heat." The latter was the dwarven term for the same month.

"You don't mind anything."

"Ah, Gair, the key is not to mind it but to *appreciate* it." The dwarf watched the elf nimbly avoid an exposed sweet bay root while he struggled to tug his own boot free of it. "Just look for somethin' enjoyable—the sounds of the crickets, the song of the owls, the feel of the new leaves beneath your fingertips. Mmm . . . the heat of the summer against your skin. All the things you don't care for just run right off your shoulder like rainwater, forgotten."

The elf sighed again. "At least it quit raining."

The pair lapsed into silence and continued down the twisting path, allowing their keen vision to separate the shadows so they could find their way through the dark woods. An owl hooted, long and soft, its call muted by distance. Closer, a hawk cried shrilly to its mate. A startled whippoorwill took flight, its wings beating against the leaves as it climbed and sending a cloud of finches rising and chittering in its wake. Around the elf and the dwarf, a symphony of crickets and frogs swelled, stopping for only an instant when Jasper stepped on a fallen branch, snapping it loudly beneath his heavy foot.

It had rained briefly earlier in the day. The moisture had long since burned off the foliage in the late afternoon sun, leaving the ground smelling rich and sweet. There were few spots where something wasn't growing on the forest floor—mushrooms, moss, creeper vines, a variety of grasses, wildflowers that gave off a faint, fragrant scent, and trees and more trees. The rising moon revealed an amazing diversity of the latter—junipers, willows, flowering pears, shaggybarks, hardwoods, nut trees, ginkgoes, poplars, wild cherries that had given up their fruit months ago, cedars, and some broad-leafed trees that were somehow hardy enough to handle the island's winters. When Krynn was much younger and colder, floes of ice pushed seeds from the far north and the far south to this place, resulting in the present remarkable mix of trees and plants. The Cataclysm further altered the land, crushing the spiraling mountains that once formed a jagged spine down the middle of the island, leaving instead gently sloping hills—and inadvertently giving the foliage more places to grow.

"Are you sure this is the right path?"

The dwarf nodded.

"Are you sure we didn't miss a fork somewhere?"

The dwarf nodded again and noted sadly that the crickets had stopped their serenade.

"Then we must be close. We should have caught up to her by now."

Jasper made a huffing sound. "She's got better'n two hours' start on us, Gair. Wanted a little time alone. Remember?"

"I never should have let her go." The elf waited for the dwarf to agree. Getting no response, he continued. "She's far from a young woman, Jasper Fireforge, and unless she turned off on another path to rest somewhere, we should have caught up to her by now."

Again no response.

"Maybe something happened to her. She could be lost, hurt. We should have talked her into searching in the morning."

"Can't find what she's lookin' for in the daylight."

"We should have—"

"Wouldn't've done any good."

"We could go back and retrace our steps, see if she—"

"Goldmoon can take care of herself, Gair. She's all right." The dwarf's voice was confident. Inwardly he worried a little.

Gair stopped on the path and ran a sweaty hand through his hair. The leaves of a willow teased the top of his head. "We should have followed right away, not waited. She's taking far too many chances for someone her age."

"And you take far too few," the dwarf whispered too softly for the elf to hear.

"She could have gone some other time. She's human. She can't see in the dark like we can. She . . ."

The dwarf made a clucking sound as he stepped in

something squishy. He kept his eyes straight ahead, not wanting to discover what it was. "We're the students, Gair. She's the teacher. 'Sides, I've known her a little longer'n you, an' I know she can manage. She'll be all right, you'll see, an' we'll catch up soon enough." He huffed. "An' then I can get some sleep."

"I hope you're right, my friend, but I am not happy about this." His voice dropped to a whisper. "And I have the oddest sensation prickling at the back of my neck."

"Like we're bein' watched?" the dwarf asked in a hushed tone.

"Yes."

"I think someone's been watchin' us for quite some time."

*　*　*　*　*

Goldmoon picked her way through the woods, using a small lantern to guide her. The oil was burning low, so she tried to increase her pace, not wanting to be caught alone in complete darkness. The aging healer was tired, long decades and the heat of the Raging Fire had taken their toll. Her aching legs suggested she rest awhile, but her will was much stronger than her body, and she refused to give in. She'd come too far to stop now.

She inhaled, slowly and deeply, and ran her sleeve across her forehead to wipe away the sweat. "Beloved Riverwind, I remember when we shared many Raging Fires together. I miss those years desperately. The heat was tolerable with you at my side. Everything was somehow . . . better."

She continued along the overgrown path, seemingly talking to herself and musing about what brought her to Schallsea Island in the middle of the New Sea—a need to find a purpose for however many years she had left on the face of Krynn. Goldmoon wasn't convinced she would find the answer here, though something in her heart urged her to search here. If she didn't find what she was seeking, she would travel somewhere else, maybe back across the New Sea to Abanasinia and the Qué-Shu tribes, her people, or perhaps far to the south, in the Plains of Dust. There were many mystical sites dotting that arid land, places where the magic of the gods was still rich and pulsing, where the Raging Fire would be even more intense. She was looking for just such a mystical site now.

"Where is it, my beloved?" Goldmoon had consulted a cartographer a few days ago in the island's small port town. She was on the correct path, she was certain of it, and she could sense that many others had traveled this way through past decades. Indeed, the cartographer had told her people from town still wandered out occasionally to take a look at the site, though almost always when the weather was more pleasant and always in respectable numbers to insure their safety. There were wild animals on the island, he said.

"Where? It can't be much farther."

Through gaps in the shaggybark branches, she saw the stars winking into view in a purple-black sky. Their light was mimicked by the fireflies that danced around her lantern. The constellations were far different now than they had been when her husband Riverwind was alive and at her side. That was a time when the gods still maintained a presence on Krynn and when magic came easily. After the gods left Krynn following the Chaos War, the stars changed, and the three familiar moons vanished. Now only one cold, pale moon hung in the sky, competing with the stars for her attention.

"I wish you were here to search with me, my beloved. I wish . . ." Her thoughts trailed off. The trees before her

were thinning out, giving way to a clearing. The grass
was tall and brittle-looking from the summer's heat,
and the ferns that grew haphazardly amidst the grass
were stunted. But something rose in the center, stretching taller than the oldest of trees. Goldmoon gasped,
and the lantern slipped from her fingers.

"By the memory of Mishakal," she breathed. The
healer stared wide-eyed, not daring to blink, her feet
rooted to the spot. She was called a Hero of the Lance,
had fought dragons in her youth, brought healing
magic to Krynn, witnessed unbelievable wonders—
things that common folk didn't even know to dream
about, but all of those things paled beside this.

"It's . . . it's beautiful," she whispered after several
moments. She could find no other word to describe it,
yet beautiful seemed woefully inadequate.

Like a curling strand of hair, the stairway spun
down from a faint, wispy cloud, glimmering like dia-
monds and shaming the stars. She stared in disbelief
for several long minutes until her legs tingled from
lack of movement. She held her breath, closed her
eyes, and slowly opened them again. The stairs were
still there.

Goldmoon risked a step forward, then another. She
let her pack fall from her shoulders, followed by her
cloak, not hearing either drop to the ground. Scarcely
breathing, tentatively edging closer, she kept her eyes
on the spiral. The steps shimmered faintly, inviting and
haunting and looking as insubstantial as strips of gossamer glimmering with some undefinable inner radi-
ance. They twisted up until their light looked as pale as
a slender moonbeam, disappearing into the wispy
clouds far overhead.

"The Silver Stair," she whispered. "By the sacred
memory of Mishakal, why did I wait so long to travel
here?"

Her words were the only sound in the clearing. No insects chittered, and the faint breeze through her sweat-soaked graying hair scarcely rustled a blade of grass. She could hear her heart, the breath coming in and out of her lungs, the sounds as oppressive as the heat. Her chest felt tight, whether from fear or from awe or perhaps from both. Her fingers trembled as she moved closer to the construction, and she bit down on her lower lip until she tasted blood. She had not fallen asleep on the trail. She was not dreaming.

The light intensified as she came closer still, filling her vision as she moved to stand in front of the spiral. It glimmered like sun specks caught on the surface of a still sea, winked and sparkled and made her breath catch in her throat as she stared at the bottom step. The steps looked fragile, like the wings of a butterfly, and she could see through them to the ground beneath.

She bent over to touch the bottom step, half worried that it might burn her with its magic, half afraid that it would pop like a soap bubble. Her fingers tingled as they traced a pattern of shimmering lights, felt the magical energy that suffused the step and likely the entire staircase. Goldmoon couldn't discern what the stairway was made of—not enchanted wood or steel, certainly not glass. This was truly a mystery, a creation of the vanished gods. She laid her palm flat against it, reveling in the pulsing sensation, then pressed hard against it to be certain it would hold her weight.

The cartographer had told her that people came out here to look at the stairs, yet none within his memory had dared to climb it, though he admitted they might not have told him about it. She edged out of her sandals, feeling the coarse grass against the soles of her feet. She put one foot and then the other on the lowest step, steeling herself as the tingling energy pulsed against her skin and crept up her legs. She didn't want to miss even one sensation, and she feared that even the thin leather of her sandals might mute this experience.

She wished Jasper and Gair were here to share in this, regretted a little that she had plunged on ahead of them. However, Goldmoon had wanted—*needed*—some time alone, and there was some consolation that her favorite students would not be too far behind. She glanced down at her discarded sandals, swallowed hard, and took another step, then another. There were no handholds, no landings that she could discern, just this seemingly never-ending spiral of steps so narrow that her heels hung over the edge.

Goldmoon continued to climb, the hot summer air cocooning her and making her sweat even more profusely. The sweat-slick skin of her feet made her ascent more precarious, but she wasn't about to turn back and retrieve her sandals. She guessed she was at least a dozen feet above the earth when she paused to catch her breath. Her sailcloth tunic clung to her body, and her leggings were as wet as if she'd been wading. If she climbed higher, she knew that one careless footfall would bring certain death, but she wasn't afraid of dying. She had lived long enough, outlived, in fact, all those who had been closest to her. Perhaps it was past time for her spirit to join theirs.

She steadied herself as a faint wave of dizziness washed over her, and she concentrated on the tingling of the steps against her feet. The healer's legs ached. She'd pushed herself hard to reach this place by nightfall, and she was pushing herself harder still. There were limits to her aging body, and she had just about reached them. She would not give in to the infirmity of her years just yet. Goldmoon glanced to the south as she climbed higher, thrusting the soreness in her legs to the back of her mind and focusing instead on the faint lights of the port city of Schallsea. She climbed higher still, until her feet felt numb, her legs felt stiff like wood, until those lights almost disappeared, looking as tiny as fireflies. Higher.

The heat was gone from the summer sky, replaced with a chill breeze this high above the ground. She climbed higher still, wishing she'd not abandoned her cloak. It was cold now, and the wind was increasing in intensity. She forced herself to continue.

Goldmoon shivered as the wind whirled all around her. Trails of fire and ice raced in and out of her with each step she took. Her lungs burned from the climb and froze from the thin, cold air she was taking into them in ever more ragged gulps. Her feet tingled, not the interesting, magical sensation any longer. The energy of the place seemed stronger the higher she climbed, and the tingling was causing her feet to throb almost painfully.

"Not much farther," she said to herself, though in truth she didn't know how much higher the stairway went. She still couldn't see the top of it. She entertained no thoughts of giving up, but she mentally berated herself for not seeking this site much earlier in her life, when her body was as strong as her mind and when she was confident she would have been able to reach the top. She wasn't completely certain she had the physical strength left to tackle this, at least not this night.

As she continued to ascend, more doubts about her capabilities crept into her mind. It took a considerable effort now to lift her legs to attain the next step, and there were so many steps left to go. She didn't want to give up, wouldn't willingly give up, but she recognized that no matter how strong her mind was, her body would not permit her to go much farther, perhaps not any farther.

As well, there was the climb down to consider.

Goldmoon knew the Silver Stair was the only surviving Celestial Ladder on all of Krynn. At one time, there had been two others, and each was said to take those who dared to climb them to the home of a god of magic. The Silver Stair was reputed to be the link to Solinari, the god of good magic. The other two ladders, the Star Stones in Neraka and the Moon Steps in Northern Ergoth, were said to have led to the homes of Nuitari and Lunitari respectively. Both those stairways had collapsed during the Chaos War.

Goldmoon glanced down. She no longer saw the firefly lights of the port town of Schallsea, nor could she see the ground—only blackness, cut through by the moonbeam of glistening silver steps winding away below her. Higher, she demanded of herself . . . just a little higher.

The fact that this one Celestial Ladder remained, Goldmoon thought, surely was a sign that good would ultimately triumph in the dragon-plagued world. Now if she could only triumph over the limitations of her body and reach the top before she froze to death.

A few more steps and a mist swirled around her head. Clouds, she guessed as she reached deep inside herself to summon the very last of her strength, climbing higher still. Suddenly the mist swirled all around her, and she could no longer make out the stairway above or below her—even directly beneath her feet. Her pace slowed to a crawl as she forced herself on, edged one foot up at a time, feeling for the next step. It was so terribly cold here, and the air was incredibly thin. It hurt just to breathe.

"Not much farther." Please, she added to herself, please don't let it be much farther. There had to be an end to the stairway, didn't there? It couldn't continue on to infinity.

She felt as if she couldn't move another inch when

her head poked above the clouds and the last few steps came into view. "Not much farther," she stated with more conviction as she slowly struggled up the remaining few steps, her legs so sore it felt as if tiny needles were being jabbed into them.

Balancing carefully on the top step, she gazed out at a majestic sea of stars spread out like a blanket before her. She sucked in her breath, overwhelmed by the stark resplendence. Abruptly the stars were gone, the cold gone. The stairway beneath her feet had faded. In a heartbeat, stretching out before her was an arid plane.

"By the vanished gods," she breathed in hushed disbelief. The air grew instantly warm around her, night turned to bright day, and waves of heat drifted up from the parched ground. The waves quavered and caught her attention, coalescing to form an image of a beautiful woman.

"Mishakal," Goldmoon whispered. Her fingers fluttered up to touch an ornate disk hanging around her neck, the symbol of Mishakal, the goddess of healing magic whom she revered and had dedicated her life to so many years ago. "Mishakal?" Goldmoon somehow found a new reserve of strength. She took a step forward and another, experiencing a moment of panic so intense it felt as if her heart were being squeezed. This is an illusion, she admonished herself. You're standing on the topmost step of the Silver Stair, and if you move another inch you'll fall a very long distance.

The goddess floated backward, her arms beckoning Goldmoon to follow. She seemed so incredibly real.

"It's an illusion," Goldmoon stated aloud. Nevertheless, she edged a foot out. The ground, cracked like a scorched riverbed, felt solid enough beneath her bare feet, and it felt genuine—dry and jagged and unpleasant to walk upon. The tingling of the stair was gone. She tentatively took another step, and then another and another. As she neared the goddess, the air grew warmer, as hot as a blistering day during Raging Fire.

"Mishakal," Goldmoon said in a strong voice, staring into the diaphanous face of the goddess. "Where are you? Have you truly left Krynn? Am I only imagining you?"

As if in answer, the effigy faltered, and Goldmoon stretched out a hand to touch it, hoping to hold on to some part of the goddess, and therefore some part of the faith she once fervently had in her and in all of Krynn's deities. "Mishakal? No!"

The image wavered until it was so transparent she could hardly make it out, then it grew until it towered over Goldmoon and the plateau. It darkened and thickened, taking on a new visage.

"Chaos." The word sent the color draining from Goldmoon's face.

The God of All and of Nothing opened his maw and laughed at the insignificant healer so far below him. Goldmoon thrust her hands over her ears to blot out the sound. Instead, she heard the laughter more clearly. As it grew louder, it became distorted, sounding like the roar of a great fire one moment, next like the booming thunder of a storm. The sound receded, but it did not disappear entirely, as other noises came from the god's mouth—snarls and battle cries. He opened his maw wider, and tiny dragons fluttered out in a blur of racing colors.

The soft thunder of his laughter was gradually drowned out by the cracks from bolts of lightning that came from blue dragons. As those dragons grew larger and started circling the god's head, Goldmoon made out Knights of Takhisis astride their backs. The dragons passed close so the riders could jab lances at the god's eyes. Silver dragons joined the blues, Solamnic knights mounted atop them. Their small swords glimmered like stars.

The plain beneath Chaos's feet rippled, and from the ground sprouted more knights and dragons, all fighting the God of Everything and of Nothing—and all to no avail. Goldmoon guessed she was seeing the Chaos War in the Abyss played out before her.

The fight continued for what seemed like hours, though she sensed only minutes had passed. Nothing seemed to faze the god. Nearly hidden behind the god's leg, Goldmoon saw the diaphanous image of Mishakal once more, and near her a kender who plunged a knife into the god's boot.

The laughter stopped, and the great form of Chaos seemed to tremble. The god inhaled deeply then, drawing back into his mouth the forms of the dragons and knights—and the form of Mishakal, who spiraled around his body and then slipped inside his mouth as his teeth clamped closed.

"Chaos took the gods with him," Goldmoon stated softly. "When he left Krynn, he bade them to follow." She stared at the great image, which trembled more noticeably now. As Goldmoon continued to watch, his form began to shrink and then to melt. She stepped backward as a god pool formed on the plateau, red with the blood of Chaos and those he had slaughtered. The pool bubbled like lava, adding to the heat of the place, and Goldmoon's eyes grew wide as the bubbles rose above the pool and collected into the images of the great dragons now plaguing Krynn.

They flew toward her, diving and passing through her like phantasms, so fast that they were a blinding blur of red and white, black and green and blue. She blinked and trembled in disbelief as the dry ground rippled, the lava becoming a bright green now and covering the land, the bubbles thinning and forming tall blades of grass. Trees sprouted at the edge of her vision, circling her as the sky darkened again. She stood in a clearing now, and before her was the Silver Stair, its steps glimmering invitingly as they had when she first saw them. Minutes ago? Just this instant? Waiting to be climbed.

"I . . ." For a moment Goldmoon wondered if she had ever climbed the stairs in the first place, if she had instead fallen down from exhaustion and merely imagined the arduous climb and the images of Chaos and Mishakal at the top. There was no cloak on her shoulders, and no sandals at the base of the steps that twinkled several yards away. She glanced behind her: no discarded lantern.

She took a tentative step forward and considered climbing this new stairway, though she doubted she could manage more than a few feet. Another step.

"Ouch!" Bending down, she saw a nail. There was a small pile of them, and a hammer nearby—Jasper's hammer. The nails and hammer hadn't been there a heartbeat before. When she again looked up to see the stairs, the land had changed once more. Hedges, carefully trimmed, circled the steps and flowed outward like spilled ink. She skittered back several steps to avoid being overrun by the bushes. Springing up around them were large pearls.

Not pearls, she realized as she stared longer and the globes grew to dwarf her. Buildings. They ringed her and the hedges and the stairway like a bracelet. As she tried to take it all in, she heard voices. Coming from all around her, they were talking to her, though she saw no one, only shadows moving about within the globes.

"Teach me." The voice was young and feminine.

"I want to help others." An elderly man's voice.

"Teach me."

"I don't understand this . . . this power of the heart. Is that what you call it?" This was a coarse voice, sounding almost dwarflike.

"Teach me."

"I want to make a difference." The young, feminine voice again. "Show me how."

"Teach me. Please."

"Teach me . . . teach me . . . teach me." The words repeated like the persistent buzzing of a bee. More and more shadows flitted inside the globes, pressing themselves against the glass, looking out at her, whispering to her, asking her to teach them. "Teach me." It had become a resonant mantra.

Goldmoon could almost make out faces.

"I . . . I will teach you," she heard herself say. "All of you. I will . . ." Her words trailed off as the globes melted into the ground, and the grass ran like water away from her in all directions. The stars winked into view again, gemstones on velvet, and the Silver Stair that had seemed several yards away was now beneath her feet, the topmost step tingling with magical energy. She was impossibly high above the earth once more.

The air was cold again, and the breeze whipped her silver-gold hair madly about her face. She brushed away the strands, carefully pivoted on the balls of her feet, and slowly made her way down the waiting stairs.

* * * * *

"Goldmoon! Are you all right?" Gair was at the edge of the clearing where he had picked up her lantern. Concern was etched deeply on his young face. Jasper tromped past him as fast as his stumpy legs would carry him, his eyes locked on to the shimmering stairway, mouth open in amazement, all thoughts of whatever or whoever had been watching them instantly discarded. The dwarf mumbled a greeting to Goldmoon as he brushed by her and approached the celestial ladder.

Goldmoon knelt to retrieve her cloak, slipped into her sandals. "I'm fine, Gair," she answered. "I feel . . . well." The ache was gone from her legs and she breathed easily, as if she hadn't undertaken the laborious climb up the magical staircase or the long walk to reach the clearing. "I'm just a little tired. It's been a long day."

Goldmoon watched as the relieved elf left her side to circle the staircase. The dwarf stood unmoving, like a rock, about a yard away from the base of the Silver Stair and was mumbling something in his native tongue. The elf couldn't contain his curiosity, touching the steps, feeling the energy tingle beneath his fingertips. He climbed up the first half-dozen steps, craning his neck toward the stars above, then scampered down, his cautious nature winning out, and nearly knocking Jasper over.

"You climbed it," Gair began as he rushed back to her side. "I saw you coming down just as we got here. You looked like you were walking on air. Did you go all the way to the top?"

Goldmoon nodded, a smile playing gently across her lined face as she saw the dwarf finally move. He inched closer, knelt in front of the stair as if it were an altar, prodded at the bottom step with the scrutinizing eye of an engineer. "What's it made of?" she heard him ask. "It's not metal. Amazin'."

"I can't even see the top," the elf interjected. "What's up there, anyway?"

The aging healer drew her lower lip into her mouth. It still tasted faintly of blood. "I'm not sure, Gair. Everything. Nothing. You must climb it and find out yourself."

The elf was clearly fascinated by the structure, as he was with magic in general, drawn to it like a moth to light. Again he scampered up the first few steps, nearly trampling Jasper's questing fingers. He craned his neck upward and narrowed his eyes. The dwarf continued to prod at the lowest step.

"Truly amazin'," Jasper said in a hushed tone.

"Tales say the Silver Stair only shows itself by the light of the moon," Goldmoon explained as she glanced around the clearing. She thought she'd heard a twig snap somewhere nearby.

"Wish my Uncle Flint were alive to see this." Jasper cocked his head. "Hmmph. On second thought, maybe he did. He traveled quite a bit. Amazin'." The dwarf looked up at his elven friend, rooted on the seventh step, still staring at the stars and trying to see the top of the stairway. "Go ahead, Gair."

The elf didn't budge.

"Well, you gonna climb it?"

The elf shook his head and leapt nimbly to the ground.

"Ah, the wariness of youth," the dwarf grumbled. "You never take chances."

"Some other time," Gair replied. "I'm sure we'll return here. I'll climb it then."

"Return?" Goldmoon stopped her survey of the clearing. "Gair, Jasper, I'm not leaving, not for a long time. Perhaps not for the rest of my life."

Behind the elf, Jasper chattered happily to himself. "Well, at least I won't have to climb the stairway tonight then. There'll be plenty of time later. An' then maybe I can figure out what it's made of. Not metal, that's for certain. Tomorrow night, I think, I'll climb it. Maybe I can get some sleep now." He tromped a few feet away from the Celestial Ladder and settled himself on the ground, cradling his head with his folded arms, his face pointing toward the magical structure.

"Not leaving?" The elf's mouth gaped open, then he quickly regained his composure and presented his serious face. "You're going to stay here? But Gold-moon, what about your students in Abanasinia? You've so much to offer them, and they have so much yet to learn."

"We'll send word for them to join us." She reached into her pack and retrieved a thin blanket, carefully spread it on the ground near the base of the stairway, and lay down. She arranged her pack to use as a pillow. Despite the warm night air, she pulled her cloak over her. "I'll teach them here."

The elf scanned the clearing, remembering the prick-ling sensation on his neck. The sensation was gone now, and whatever or whoever had been watching them was likely gone with it. Maybe it was just a forest animal. He vowed to look for tracks in the morning.

As he considered the situation, a chorus of crickets rose around him, accompanied by the sonorous tone of Jasper's snoring. He turned to glance again at the mag-ical stairway, stepped closer, and bent to touch the bottom step. Energy pulsed through it, and he felt a tin-gling sensation against his slender fingers. He ran his hand along the edge of the step, then along the under-side.

"All right," the elf pronounced to himself as he con-centrated on the tingling energy that continued to pulse through his fingertips. "I suppose I could get used to the woods again. We can stay here for a while, anyway." He swatted at a mosquito with his free hand and stared up the spiral staircase. "So beautiful."

Chapter 3

Camilla

"It's so beautiful." Camilla Weoledge stood on the bow of a small carrack as it eased up to the dock.

"Indeed it is a most lovely town, Commander."
The Solamnic lieutenant at her side snapped to attention as Camilla strode past him down the gangplank and onto the dock, not waiting until the ship was properly moored. Her boot heels clicked rhythmically over the weathered wood, and her lieutenant hurried to catch up.

The port town of Schallsea was waking up around them. Merchants were on their way to their shops, bundled in coats on this early winter morning, walking with shoulders hunched into the wind, the ends of their scarves waving behind them like colorful pennants. Outwardly, they paid the knights little heed—that is, until they were safely past and could gawk from a respectful distance.

Chimneys were puffing smoke, tingeing the air with the scent of wood and cinnamon and bacon. Camilla inhaled deeply, finding the scents pleasing. Someone nearby was baking bread, and it sharply reminded her she hadn't eaten since early yesterday.

"Willum, I've visited many port towns, but . . ." The

commander found herself at an unaccustomed loss for words as she stood on the shore and glanced up and down the streets that radiated outward from the docks like spokes on a wheel.

"But seldom one so tidy, Camilla."

"Tidy. Yes, Willum. Schallsea is quite tidy. I like that."

The port was large enough to accommodate warships, even several at a time. Steep granite cliffs protected the bay from storms. The buildings closest to the docks were made of stone with thick slate roofs, designed to keep the occupants safe from invading armies. The population of Schallsea had burgeoned during the War of the Lance. A large group of settlers had been the Solamnics' dark-armored enemies who used the port as a base for raids, primarily against Abanasinia and Southlund.

The streets of the walled city were remarkably clean. They were not of dirt or gravel as in most port towns in Ansalon's southern hemisphere. They were made of cobblestones, a mix of gray and rose stones, all of them looking as if they'd just been scrubbed. The storefronts were in good repair, with no peeling paint on shutters, no debris out front. The bright colors of the buildings seemed to complement each other.

As Camilla and Willum walked southwest through the town, two dozen knights marching behind and nearly a hundred soldiers trailing them, they noticed the residences were tidy and well maintained, from the modest cottages of the shopkeepers to the handful of sprawling manses with manicured lawns and sculpted evergreens.

"The citizens obviously take pride in this place," Willum observed. "It's an honor to be stationed here, Commander."

Camilla did not reply. She pointed at a keep perched on a hill at the southern edge of the bay. It was the most notable landmark in Schallsea.

"Our home," she said tersely. "At least for however long the Solamnic Council decrees we stay here."

"Quaint." Willum drew his lips into a narrow line and squinted. "Look there! Complete with ballistas and catapults to protect the harbor."

"Let's hope we won't need them." Camilla stared at the structure. The masonry had been severely weathered by the salt air. "Krynn has seen too many wars, Willum. I hope we never see another one in my lifetime."

"The battle here went well enough for us."

"I suppose, in the end, but that was a long time ago."

Willum made a humming noise in his throat. "The Dark Knights were kind enough to leave us a place to stay. It's defensible for certain."

Camilla nodded. "The Sentinel, it's called."

"Unfortunate for us they didn't finish it. Look there! Only three sides to the rear section."

She shook her head. "Actually, I consider it most fortunate they were not afforded the opportunity to finish it, Lieutenant." Camilla knew well the history of the Sentinel, eventually abandoned by the besieged Knights of Takhisis in the year 352 A.C., one year before the War of the Lance officially came to an end.

Willum adopted a cheerful tone. "Well, Commander, perhaps we will have a chance to finish it. We could import some stone, obtain the services of some builders. It's rather small, after all. Certainly not up to the usual Solamnic standards. I would think if we—"

"I have other things to worry about than bricks and mortar just now, Lieutenant."

Willum's lighthearted demeanor turned instantly serious.

"Have the men unload the arms and equipment, then get them settled in their barracks." She eyed the rank of knights and selected six of them. "You and I and these

men will visit our charges. I'll meet you at the northern
edge of the city in one hour. Make sure everyone gets
something to eat. We've a hard march ahead of us."
Camilla acknowledged the salute of her knights and
pivoted sharply on her heels. She had just enough time
for a quick tour of the port town. She heard Willum call
that she should get breakfast herself, but she had other
concerns. She suspected that food would only further
upset her already churning stomach.

She walked purposely up and down the side streets,
noting that there did not seem to be a single empty res-
idence. A few clipped questions confirmed that all the
boarding houses were full. An abandoned temple had
been recently turned into an apartment building, and a
kindly woman outside the entrance said many of those
rooms would be filled with the next boatload of newcomers. Did she need accommodations? Camilla shook
her head and moved on.

The knight commander saw that despite the cold
Schallsea's carpenters and masons were doing a booming business, scrambling to finish a new row of houses
before winter set in. At the edge of her vision, stakes
and ribbons hinted that other streets were planned,
extending eastward into the heart of the island. Gray
and rose cobblestones were piled nearby, indicating
they would be improved soon. Schallsea was growing
rapidly, perhaps too rapidly. A shiver danced down her
spine.

She paused outside an establishment called The Cozy
Hearth, a sunny-looking hostel with butter-colored
eaves and shutters painted seafoam green. A sign
rested against the windowpane: *Pilgrims Welcome.* In
smaller print, it announced, *Comfortable beds, Rates reasonable, no one refused. Iryl Songbrook, proprietor.* The
knight's scowling image was reflected in the window.

Camilla's hair was boyishly short, her tight

mahogany curls looking like a cap. Her nose was slightly hawkish, her cheekbones high, and her eyes a bit too large for her face. She wasn't unattractive by any means, but in her opinion she was a little too tall and hardly beautiful. She did little to improve her appearance or to make herself look feminine or appealing. She had more important things to address. She let out a long breath, turned away from the window, and continued her tour.

It was easy to see which buildings had stood since the War of the Lance. They were of thick stone, squat and looking a bit like the shells of tortoises. The newer buildings, mostly farther from the harbor, were two and three stories tall and were made of a combination of stone and wood. Most had sod roofs. Though the majority of the businesses were close to the harbor, other establishments were scattered here and there along the side streets: bakeries, weaponsmiths, clothiers, grocers, leather workers. They were practical businesses, catering to people's needs, nothing prone to much extravagance such as a jeweler's, florist's, or an art gallery. It was a simple town. The larger Schallsea grew, the more it would change.

Camilla hurried toward a stable at the northern end of town, realizing her tour had taken much longer than she expected. It was one of the new buildings, judging by the men still painting it, and considerably larger than the stable near the docks. She spied Willum talking to a thickset man with red paint smudges on his shirtsleeves. Her knights, their duffel bags at their feet, were leaning against the corral, admiring the horses snorting in the chill air.

"Commander!" Willum snapped to attention when he spotted her, and the knights immediately drew themselves away from the horses and formed a line behind the lieutenant.

She nodded curtly to them and started walking down the path that led out of town. Willum rushed to walk at her side, awkwardly shouldering two packs. The knights followed in single file.

"I've made arrangements for the horses coming with the next ship," he began. "The stable near the harbor was—"

"Already full," she finished for him.

He made a humming noise in his throat. "Yes. Well, it looked like there was a stable at the Sentinel—rather run-down, however. If we are stationed here long enough, perhaps we can repair it and keep most of the horses there."

"*If* we're here long enough."

He made the humming noise again. "I took the liberty of having your belongings placed in the Sentinel's tower room. It has a nice view of the harbor and the docks, and I unpacked a few things for you."

"Thank you, Willum."

"The people in town say it is a few days' walk. Bread?"

She took one of the satchels from him and effortlessly slung it over her shoulder, and he passed her a roll. Obviously it had come from one of the town's bakeries. She paused as if inspecting it, then ate it slowly as they fell into an easy gait. The town of Schallsea grew smaller behind them.

The clank of the knights' armor drowned out the whistling of the cold breeze as they made their way along the winding path leading northward. A rut ran down the middle, the original trail that led out of town. As more and more people had used it, the path had widened and pushed back the vegetation. There was evidence of wagon wheels and shod horses at the outer edges. Some of the tracks were very recent, making slight impressions despite the winter-hard ground. A

mix of pines and shaggybarks sheltered the inland side
of the trail. Low bushes, their leaves long since chased
away by the cold, were set back from the western side
of the trail, and through gaps in the scrub the knights
spotted the sea in the distance.

The sky was gray, the color of Camilla's eyes, and she
cast her head back to watch a lone gull fly to the west
and drop toward the water. The air was crisp, laced
with the scent of salt water and pines, and the clouds
overhead hinted of snow. The padding beneath her
armor, coupled with her red wool cape, kept her warm,
though her fingers stung a little from the cold air. She
flexed them in time with the knights' steps and watched
as her breath formed a misty cloud in front of her face.

Willum walked with a stoic gait at her side, his face
twitching. He hummed in his throat and concentrated
on the trail ahead.

They paused briefly at noon, then resumed their trek,
stopping again at sunset to set up camp. In the morning, Camilla afforded little time for breakfast before
they were off again at a brisk march. Two hours into
their journey, a scream cut through the wintry air.

Camilla sprinted ahead. Willum and the rest of the
knights trailed after her, the clamor of their armor practically drowning out what sounded like a battle ahead.
She dropped her pack and churned her legs faster,
rounded a turn in the trail, drew her sword, and
instantly assessed the situation she saw ahead.

One man lay dead at the side of a large wagon, a
thick spear protruding from his chest. A thin elven
woman was at his side, glancing furtively into the trees
on the inland side the path. A dwarf stood with a
hammer held high in one hand, the reins of a quartet of
dappled horses in another. He was trying to keep the
animals from bolting and taking the wagon with them.
Near the dwarf was another elf, this one a lanky man in

black who was weaving a sword back and forth in front
of him and peering intently into the trees. On the sea-
ward side of the wagon, more than a dozen townsfolk
crouched for protection.

There was no immediate sign of the enemy, save for
several spears lying on the ground. The attackers must
be keeping to the trees. As Camilla closed the distance,
the knights coming fast behind her, another volley of
spears streamed from the trees, followed by the
screams of frightened townsfolk. Three spears landed
several feet short of the wagon, a fourth cleared the
wagon and elicited another scream from a young
woman when it fell near her. The last two spears shot
toward the dwarf, who was still trying to keep the
horses under control. At the last moment, the dark-clad
elf knocked the dwarf aside. One spear lodged deep
into the elf's thigh and pinned him to the ground. The
other bit into his shoulder.

"Gair!" the dwarf hollered as he dropped the reins.
He started toward the downed elf just as the lead
horses reared. The dwarf cursed himself and made a
grab for the reins, but the horses were already charging
forward, the wagon clattering behind them.

The elven woman left the dead man's side and
rushed toward the other townsfolk, yelling at them to
get down, pushing them onto their bellies.

At the same time, Camilla cut toward the dwarf,
motioning for her men to follow. Arrows rained from
the trees, most of them striking the ground or bouncing
off the knights' armor, but some finding their marks
among the townsfolk.

"I don't know where you Solamnics came from, but
praise the memory of Reorx that you're here!" the
dwarf huffed above the cries of the townsfolk. He was
on his knees next to the male elf, who was trying
futilely to push him away.

"Jasper," the elf groaned. "I'm all right. See to the others." His dark eyes were demanding. "I can heal myself. Help them."

"Don't have to tell me," the dwarf grumbled as he pushed himself to his feet and whirled to see two men with arrows in their shoulders. The female elf was ordering the others to keep their heads down.

"They'll live!" she called to the dwarf. "Look out!"

A second volley of arrows came from the trees, one striking the female elf in the leg. Jasper rushed toward her as more arrows arced from the trees.

"They've got us pinned down," the dwarf called to the Solamnics. "Can't see 'em. Don't know how many there are."

Camilla could barely hear him. She was charging toward the trees, feet pounding, armor clanking, peering into the shadows as she ran, trying to locate the archers. Willum and the other knights were fast on her heels, spreading out and batting away arrows with their shields.

She hollered, "Find the archers! If we can engage them, they can't fire on those people! Move!"

Camilla and her knights thrashed through the woods, sending a cloud of birds erupting from the trees. The knights were shouting, but the noise of their armor and the breaking branches muffled their words.

"They move fast! Can't make them out!"

"Find them!" This came from Camilla. "Spread out, but try to stay in sight of your comrades!"

On the trail, Jasper's thick fingers worked quickly, prodding the female elf's leg. At the same time, he told the other townsfolk to watch the trees and stay low. Two men ignored his advice and helped him stop the elf's bleeding.

"This'll hurt," the dwarf said as he gritted his teeth and pulled the arrow out. The elf cried out and fell back into the arms of one of the men. "Not too deep. Nothin' too serious."

"See to the pilgrims first," she pleaded.

The dwarf muttered, "Fine. I'll get right back to you. Press down on the wound," he said as he moved toward the injured men. "An' keep your head down!"

"This'll hurt," he repeated twice more as he pulled arrows from the men's arms. Blood flowed freely from one man, and Jasper held his hand over the wound, closed his eyes, and mumbled something in his native tongue. The words weren't necessary for the spell the dwarf was invoking. They merely helped him focus his thoughts. He reached deep inside himself, visualizing his heart, concentrating on his heartbeat, feeling a warmth spread from his chest and down his arms, centering on his hand and flowing into the wound. "The power of the heart," Jasper whispered. Goldmoon had been teaching him to nurture his healing power.

"Not too good at this yet," he told his patient. The words came haltingly as he continued to concentrate on the enchantment. His hand was warm and sticky with the man's blood, warmer still from the energy of the spell. He deepened the enchantment and felt the heat leave him and radiate upward from the wound. "That should do it."

Slowly Jasper opened his eyes and saw with considerable satisfaction that the wound had closed and the man was breathing regularly. "Rest," he said. "An' keep your head down." He pushed himself to his feet and tended to the other man's arm. Then he cast a glance at the trees. "Don't know where those knights came from, but it's a good thing they came." Or we might all be dead, he added silently. He closed his eyes and felt for the warmth.

* * * * *

The knights continued to thrash about in the woods, spreading out and searching for the archers. Camilla snatched up an arrow and inspected the ground for tracks. The frozen ground was too hard for the attackers' feet to leave an impression. She cursed softly and started scanning for broken twigs, disturbed leaves, any signs of the attackers' passing.

Willum, a skilled tracker, was having no better luck. "Trevor saw someone—or something." He stopped his nervous humming to call to her. "He's gone after it!"

She knelt by the exposed roots of a ginkgo, found a small piece of fur. "Which way did you go?" she breathed. "And who are you?"

* * * * *

"Stay still, Mr. Andersen," Jasper urged. "Almost finished." He felt the warmth radiating from the second man's wound, could tell without looking that the flesh was mending. "It'll be sore for a while, but it shouldn't bother you too much. You'll be good as new soon." Much softer, he added, "If Goldmoon was here, she'd fixed you up like nothin' had happened." He returned to the female elf and frowned when he saw her blood-stained dress. He shook his head as he knelt at her side. "Told you to keep pressure on it."

I did, her eyes told him.

"Will she be all right?" asked the man holding her.

"Tell us she'll be well." This came from the man at her other side. There were more words of concern from the rest of the townsfolk.

The dwarf nodded reassuringly, then admonished everyone to continue to keep their heads down. There had been no more arrows or spears coming from the trees for several minutes, but the attackers could still be out there.

"Relax, Iryl," he said, attempting to make his craggy voice sound soothing.

"But you've got to see to Gair," she protested.

"He's next," Jasper said, closing his eyes and searching for his inner spark. "Only one patient at a time, an' you're my patient now. Relax. 'Sides, he's a healer, too."

* * * * *

"Nothing!" Willum stomped through the brush toward Camilla, his face red from the cold and from exertion. "No trace. No tracks. Ground's hard as—"

"I know." She thrust the arrow and bit of fur at him. "If there were snow on the ground, we could follow their tracks, determine their numbers. At least we chased them off. I'm going to see to those people. Some of them were hurt. We'll have to take them back to town." She headed west toward the trail. "Gather the men and follow me."

* * * * *

"There," Jasper pronounced, drawing bloody fingers away from Iryl's closing wound. "Wrap somethin' around that to keep it clean. Lost some blood. You'll be a little weak, but . . ." A moan from Gair cut him off. "Next patient.

Jasper was at the male elf's side by the time Camilla came out of the woods, headed in their direction. The dwarf glanced only briefly her way, then dropped to his knees and devoted his full attention to Gair. "Thought you said you were all right. Said see to the others first. Said you could heal yourself."

The elf's face was even paler than usual. "Are the others all right?"

The dwarf leaned over Gair's face. "Yeah, they'll be

fine." He frowned when he saw how much blood the elf had lost. It pooled on the ground around Gair, soaking Jasper's trousers. "How'd you manage to catch an arrow, too?" There was one in his calf.

"Just lucky, I guess. It hurts."

"I'll bet it does. Hurt too much for you to concentrate. No wonder you couldn't heal yourself. Just lie still."

The elf offered a weak smile. "Can't move," he whispered. "I'm . . . I'm dying, Jasper."

"Quit arguin'."

The elf coughed, and the dwarf winced when he saw a trail of blood trickle down Gair's lower lip. The elf was indeed dying.

"You'll be fine. I'll fix you up like new." The dwarf's tone lacked confidence. He heard the lady knight approach, her armor clanking above the muted conversations of the townsfolk, heard her announce that the attackers had been chased off, but they should stay down a little while longer to be certain.

Jasper concentrated on his heart, listened for the rhythm that helped him focus his mystical energy.

The lady knight was expressing concern for the injured people, surprise at their mended wounds, asking them what had provoked the attack, did they see anything. None of them could provide any information.

He heard more clanging of metal as another knight approached. "Commander, Trevor went chasing after something. He doesn't answer."

"Find him!" she barked. "I want no one out there alone!"

"They're searching for him now!"

"Help them search. Everyone within eyesight. No one alone!"

The dwarf heard thrashing in the brush again as the knight returned to the woods, heard the *clink-clank* of the lady knight's armor as she came closer. More words swirled around his head, more questions from the knight about the unknown assailants, questions from the townsfolk about Gair's condition.

Jasper thrust the noise to the back of his mind, listened for his heartbeat, heard it grow loud enough to drown out the buzz of questions. Louder. Warmer. Capturing the warmth with his mind, he directed it down his arm. Not as warm as before, though he prayed to the missing Reorx that he could find the energy to stoke the heat. The dwarf was exhausted from healing the others, cursing himself for not seeing to Gair sooner and for not realizing just how badly the elf had been wounded.

Suddenly the heat was in his hands, the healing energy Goldmoon had taught him to use. Jasper moved his fingers to Gair's shoulder, felt the shaft of the spear. Not too deep. With one hand, he tugged it free, heard the elf groan softly in pain, and swore at himself for not cutting it out. The jagged stone tip tore the flesh. The other hand he held over the wound and focused the heat.

"So much blood." The dwarf said the words aloud, though he hadn't meant to.

"Dying," the elf repeated. "It's okay, Jasper. I'm not afraid. I'll be like Riverwind. Just wish it didn't hurt so much."

"Don't die on me!" the dwarf cursed. "I need someone to argue with. Delirious, that's what you are. Foolish talk. Don't you dare die." He fought to keep his concentration on the spell, focused on his heartbeat. Beneath his fingers, he felt the elf's heart beating weakly. Gair's breathing was shallow and irregular, and the elf had started to sweat despite the cold.

Suddenly the lady knight was kneeling next to the elf. Through squinted eyes, Jasper saw her take Gair's hand.

She was saying something to him, words of encouragement, a prayer to Kiri-Jolith. "That's it," Jasper told her. "Keep him occupied. Stop all this talk of death."

Camilla stared into Gair's violet eyes. "Hold on," she said. "We'll get you to town." She felt him grip her hand tighter as he coughed again. More blood trickled over his lip. "You'll be all right."

The dwarf felt faint as he continued to pour his healing energy into Gair, stanching the flow of blood from his shoulder wound. His fingers drifted over the elf's chest and down his leg, finding the spear there.

"Need some help," the dwarf said. He heard feet shuffling over the ground and hands grabbing the haft. "Don't pull it out! It's barbed. Break it off. Close to his leg. It's all the way through an' into the ground. Use his sword if you have to."

Jasper directed his fingers lower and found the arrow in the elf's calf. He tugged it free and sent his healing energy into that wound. He felt the elf's whole body tremble.

"Shock," the dwarf pronounced. "Someone put a blanket on him. Keep him warm."

He couldn't risk many more words. His hold on the spell was becoming tenuous, and he feared he didn't have the energy to start it over. He needed to direct all his concentration on the power of his heart.

"Not . . . not afraid of dying," Gair whispered. "Riverwind. Not . . ."

"Don't talk." Camilla squeezed the elf's hand. With the other, she brushed the sweat-damp hair from his eyes. "We'll get the wagon and take you back to town. It's just down the trail." She continued to stare into his dark purple eyes, glazed with pain. She lifted his head when one of the townsfolk thrust a blanket under him. Another blanket was placed over his chest. "The dwarf seems quite capable."

"Jasper. . . ."

"Do what the pretty lady says, Gair. Don't talk! An' don't interrupt me."

Several pairs of hands wormed their way under the elf's leg and lifted, pulling him off the broken spear haft. Gair clamped down on his lower lip to keep from crying out, only succeeding in muffling his cry. In the background, there was talk of the dead townsman. Camilla released his hand, intent on helping the dwarf.

"Don't go," Gair whispered. His hand found hers again.

"Easy!" Jasper ordered as the hands lowered the elf's leg again on the other side of the broken spear haft. The dwarf's fingers hovered over this wound now, and he summoned all of his mystical strength, pushing himself further than he ever had before and feeling himself grow lightheaded and dizzy, slipping toward unconsciousness, his hold on the enchantment slipping quickly with him. "C'mon! C'mon!" The words were to encourage himself. "C'mon!" Suddenly the dizziness passed, and the dwarf felt a wave of intense warmth radiating outward from his chest, racing down his arms and legs, invigorating him and spreading into the elf. "That's it!" The warmth continued to pulse through him for several moments. He felt the wound closing, and he eased back on his haunches and opened his eyes wide.

The elf's chest was rising and falling steadily. Blood had soaked through the blanket and soaked Jasper's pants legs and shirtsleeves, but Gair had finally stopped bleeding. All the wounds were closed.

"Magic," Camilla breathed. She was still holding the elf's hand. "You healed him without the gods."

"Well . . . spiritualism, mystic sorcery," the dwarf said. "An' whatever it is you call it, mine's not the best. I'm just learnin'. Though today was quite an education." He rose to his feet, steadied himself, and continued to eye his patient. The blood on the dwarf's hands was so thick it looked like a glove. "I don't want him movin', not for a while. Gotta get the wagon back. We'll put him on it."

"How did you do it?" Camilla was amazed, yet skeptical. She glanced at the two men who'd been wounded by arrows. Both were up and moving around, as was the female elf who'd taken an arrow in the leg.

The dwarf gave her a "that's a long story" look.

"Thank you, Jasper," Gair said.

The dwarf dismissed it with the wave of a hand. "I should be thankin' you, Gair. If you hadn't pushed me out of the way, I'd be the one skewered, an' you'd be the one doin' the healin'." The dwarf watched as Gair's eyes fluttered closed and Camilla placed his hand on his chest. "Personally," he added with a wink, "I'm not sure you could've pulled it off. I've been at this a little longer'n you. Y'know, I tell you to take more chances in your life, my elven friend, but I didn't mean for you to do somethin' like that. You rest now, Gair." He turned from the elf. "You got some water? I'd like to clean up a bit."

The female elf hurried over, her wound forgotten, fussing over Jasper with a waterskin and blanket. The townsfolk gathered around the dwarf, the air buzzing with questions and words of congratulations and thanks.

The knight stood and used the edge of her cloak to rub the blood off her hands and the metal plates on her calves. "Camilla Weoledge," she said by way of introduction as she approached Jasper. "Commander of the Solamnic Knights now stationed on Schallsea Island."

"Jasper Fireforge," the dwarf returned, extending a clean, but cold and wet, hand. "My injured friend there's called Gair Graymist." He pointed to the female elf. "An' this's Iryl—"

"Songbrook," Camilla finished.

"We've met?" The elf turned her heart-shaped face toward the knight.

Camilla shook her head. "I walked by your hostel in town."

Iryl smiled warmly and her eyes sparkled with pride. "The Cozy Hearth. It was most fortunate for us, Commander Weoledge, that you were traveling this road. If you hadn't driven the attackers off, perhaps none of us would be alive. . . . Poor Harrald." She cast a glance at the man who lay dead. A woman was draping a blanket over him. "We owe you our deepest thanks."

The Solamnic knight shook her head. "You owe us nothing. It is our responsibility to keep the residents of this island safe." She shifted her weight to the balls of her feet and stared, unblinking, into Iryl's eyes. "Have you any idea who attacked you?"

"No." The other townsfolk echoed her answer.

"Or why?"

Another chorus of nos.

"Who lives around here?"

"There are tribes scattered on the island," Iryl said. "The Wemitowuk and the Qué-Nal, but neither would be responsible for this. They're peaceful people, and I'm a close friend of the Qué-Nal chieftain. They trade in town sometimes."

"Anyone else around here?"

"There's a village of farmers not too far away, Heartspring, but I don't believe they have weapons."

"Bandits, then," Camilla mused. "They thought perhaps you carried something valuable on your wagon that might help them through the winter."

"The wagon!" someone hollered. "It's there down the road. Let's get it!"

"Well, I suppose it would be considered valuable," Iryl returned. "Blankets and flour, oil, all manner of building supplies."

The knight cocked her head as a thrashing came from the trees. Camilla whirled to see Willum and five of her knights returning. Three of them were carrying the body of Trevor. Arrows protruded from gaps in the unfortunate knight's plate mail.

Camilla's face reddened in anger.

"We didn't see who killed him, Commander," one knight began. "We knew he was chasing something. He slipped between some trees and we lost sight of him."

"Found him under an evergreen," Willum huffed. He doubled over, chest heaving, and put his hands on his thighs. "Looks like whoever killed him tried to hide the body. Took us a while to find him." He finally caught his breath, hummed in his throat a moment, then straightened. "Orders?"

"I've lost a man, Willum," she said softly, her gray eyes sad. "Not here but two days, and I've lost a knight already." She nodded toward the north, in the direction the clatter of the wagon was coming from. Two townsmen had turned it around and were guiding the horses. "We'll put Trevor on the wagon, with the dead townsman and the wounded elf, and head back to town immediately. The elf needs bed rest, Trevor needs to be buried, and we need a larger patrol to scour the countryside for the bandits. I want to interview each of these people." She swept her hand behind her to indicate the people gathering around the wagon. "Perhaps one of them saw something that can give us some clue to the bandits' identity. And then—"

"Excuse me, Commander." It was Iryl Songbrook. The elf nodded respectfully to each knight. "We won't be going back to town."

"We have to get these supplies to the settlement," Jasper finished.

"But the dead man—"

"Commander, we can bury Harrald at the settlement," Iryl said. "He would have wanted that. Harrald wasn't from Schallsea. He came here from Caergoth to see Goldmoon."

"The settlement of mystics." Camilla's tone was even, her face rigid.

Jasper nodded. "That's where the supplies are goin'. About a day an' a half to the north, at the Silver Stair."

"My charges," the knight said to herself.

"Anyway, we need to be leavin' now." The dwarf extended his hand. "Thanks for helpin' us."

"The elf needs attention."

"He'll get it at the settlement." Jasper turned toward the wagon, noted with satisfaction that the townsfolk were putting Gair on the back of the wagon. Harrald, shrouded in blankets, lay next to him.

"Aren't you concerned the bandits will strike again?"

The dwarf shrugged, then scowled. "I certainly hope not." He trundled off toward the horses and grabbed the reins. "I'll keep an eye out for 'em, of course, but I'll worry more about gettin' this wagon to the settlement. Goldmoon's expectin' it." Iryl offered the knight a departing smile and joined him.

"Orders, Commander?" one of the knights asked.

"Lethan, Earl, Chadwik, and Grant, take Trevor's body back to town and bury him in the Sentinel plot—full ceremony. I'll write a letter to the Solamnic Council and his family expressing our sorrow at his loss when I join you at the Sentinel next week. Willum, you and I and Nate"—she nodded at the remaining knight—"will escort these people to this settlement, since they seem so determined to continue. Keep alert," she warned, casting a last glance at the pines.

Chapter 4

Hunting Party

"Six months, my beloved. Six months to this day we've been here now, and I still am not certain I'm doing the right thing." Goldmoon squared her shoulders and wrapped her cloak tightly about her. She watched the small pine cones blow across the ground, chased madly by the wind. "It's not that I'm questioning the course my life has taken since the gods left us. Mine has been truly a good life. But perhaps I am attempting too much at my age."

She followed a meandering, narrow path through the woods, toward the east and the Barren Hills, where an almost imperceptible rosy glow in the otherwise gray sky signaled that the sun was coming up. Goldmoon strolled at a leisurely pace through a copse of hickory trees, pausing occasionally to gather fallen nuts and stuff them in the pockets of her tunic. It had started to snow. Large flakes swirled merrily in the wind.

"I know the gods may never return, that we may well be on our own forever. I know that many people have little faith." She sighed and shook her head, cupped her hand over her eyes to keep her long silver-gold hair from whipping into her face. "The people here at the settlement have faith, but sometimes I think they have more faith in me than in what we're trying to accomplish."

Goldmoon shivered as a particularly bracing gust washed across her. She wrapped herself tighter in the folds of her thick cloak. The path narrowed as it wound up a rise where the hickory and walnut trees were closer together and where much of the ground between them was covered with bare thickets. Her boots crunched over walnut shell husks, and she walked hunched over to keep the branches from catching her hair. It took her several minutes to reach the top, where the trees thinned out.

"Will I live long enough to see the citadel built? Should this Citadel of Light be the dream of someone younger? Perhaps one of my students should take over." Her cloak fluttered away from her, threatening to tangle itself in the low-hanging branches as she made her way down the other side of the rise. "Perhaps I should . . ."

Her words trailed off and she spun and squinted, searching the path behind her. There, by the dead oak . . .

"Who's there?"

Nothing. Perhaps it was a trick of the shadows. She stared again. No, there was something there. A shadow hesitatingly separated from the darkness of the trunk.

"Good morning, Goldmoon! What a surprise to see you." The elf quickly caught up to her, moving silently and gracefully up the path, though it was evident he was favoring the leg that had been injured a few days ago. In his black clothes, he looked stark against the falling snow.

"No surprise at all, Gair. You were following me."

He scowled and shook his head, started to disagree, then thought better of it. "All right. Yes, Goldmoon, I was following you. I didn't mean to intrude. But I . . . I wanted to talk to you."

"You don't have to follow me off into the woods to talk to me."

"I wanted to talk to you alone. Away from the—" he gestured with a long arm back to the west—"away from all those people and our Solamnic visitors."

Goldmoon offered the elf an understanding smile. Gair Graymist was perhaps her most eager student. His capacity for grasping the intricacies of mysticism was remarkable, his curiosity insatiable. She thought of him as she thought of this morning's breeze—relentless and unable to be ignored. She had sensed his persistence the first day she saw him, when he'd walked calmly into the Qué-Shu village in northern Abanasinia, introduced himself, and announced that he'd traveled hundreds of miles just to study at her side. Goldmoon accepted him on the spot, and when she took on a few more students and decided it was time to leave the tribes behind and establish a center for mysticism, he had insisted on following. She enjoyed his company and had come to think of him almost as a son. He tried hard—too hard sometimes—to please her.

"Talk to me about what?" she asked, shaking her mind loose from her musings. "What could possibly be so important that you had to follow me way out here without a coat? You've hardly had time to recover from your wounds."

"Jasper healed me well enough . . . saved my life, in fact. You finished the task and made me whole again. I feel fine, truly. My shoulder's not even stiff anymore."

"But not even a coat? Don't undo our healing." Her eyes softened. "So what is it that is so important?"

He studied the toes of his leather boots for a moment, then slowly drew his gaze up again to meet her stare. "Riverwind."

Her mouth fell open in surprise. She thought he meant to ask about learning another spell. Riverwind had been Goldmoon's husband of nearly three decades until he died at the claws of the red dragon Malystryx several years ago.

"I know you talk to him," Gair said. "Every day. Some of the others . . . when they hear you talk to him, they get confused. They know you miss him terribly, but they think that you're . . . touched, talking to yourself. They don't think any less of you. They admire you—everything you've done and are doing, like I admire you, but . . . they think you're getting—"

"Senile," she finished for him. She closed her eyes and sighed. "Addled by the years. So this is why you wanted to talk to me alone. Gair, are you telling me that you agree with them? Do you think I'm . . . touched? Senile?"

He studied his boots for a moment more, brushed at some snow on the ground, then vehemently shook his head. "You're not senile. You're the sanest person I know, and I think you really are talking to Riverwind, or at least to his spirit. Can you see him? Is he here now?"

She cast a glance over her shoulder, then reluctantly nodded.

"I want to talk to him, too." He dug the tip of his boot into the ground. "Well, not necessarily to Riverwind, but I want to talk to the spirits of the dead. This is very important to me, you must understand. I would've asked you earlier. I had intended to ask before we ever left Abanasinia, but the time never seemed right. You were always so busy. But I guess you'll always be busy."

"And so you're asking now?"

"Yes."

"No." She sadly sensed Riverwind's presence depart.

"Goldmoon, I desperately want you to teach me this. I've wanted it a long time. When I almost died a few days ago, it became even more important to me." He paused, searching for the words, studying her face, which looked uncharacteristically impassive, then plunged ahead. "I just thought this was the right time to bring it up. We're alone. Riverwind's here."

"Not anymore. He's gone now."

"To where? I want to know, Goldmoon. What is after this life? Is it full of happiness? Is it filled with misery? You could teach me to—"

"Absolutely not." Goldmoon started walking to the west, back toward the settlement. "You're not ready for this."

"When were you ready?"

She ignored the question.

He walked beside her until the path narrowed and he was forced to walk behind her. "Goldmoon, this truly is important to me."

"Healing people is important."

"I heal people. Goldmoon—"

"The dead are dead. They've no impact on the living, Gair."

"But Goldmoon . . ."

She stopped abruptly and whirled to face him, her eyes boring into his. "You are not ready."

His jaw was rigid. The veins in his neck stood out, but he kept his voice soft and even. "Why, Goldmoon? When were you ready? You've been talking to the spirit of Riverwind for as long as I've known you."

Her eyes narrowed slightly. "So you've followed me before?"

He rubbed his chin. "Listen, Goldmoon," he went on, "don't be upset with me. I meant no disrespect. I mean you nothing but respect. I'm curious, that's all. Talking to spirits must be fascinating. What could be the harm? It doesn't matter if it's difficult. I could master it. I know I could."

"It could master you," she returned sharply. She squared her shoulders. "Gair, speaking with spirits is the dark side of mysticism. Think of it as a door, one that is best left closed and forever locked. One that I hadn't intended opening myself. It just . . . happened."

"There's nothing dark about you, Goldmoon. There will never be anything dark about you."

"I am an old woman, Gair, and—"

"Not so old," he cut in. "The years have been very kind to you, Goldmoon."

"I am old and I miss my husband. I talk to Riverwind and only to Riverwind."

"Could you talk to other spirits if you wanted?"

"I suppose so, if I wanted to, but I've no intention of opening this door any wider."

Gair scowled, his expression grim. "I don't think I can learn it on my own."

"No," she admitted. "Fortunately, I don't think you can."

"You know I will bring this up again."

"And I will say no . . . again," she answered.

He sighed, then grinned, though his countenance couldn't hide his disappointment. "Want an escort back to the settlement? I'm sure breakfast is cooking somewhere." He extended his arm. "It's getting cold out here."

"I told you you should have worn a coat." She reached out a hand to take his arm, wet from melting snow. She paused and cocked her head to the side, sensing something.

Gair turned to the north, hearing it, too. "Sounds like boars," he observed. "I can hear them snorting. Good thing I did follow you, Goldmoon. You could get hurt out here alone. No one should be out alone, not after the bandits." His hand drifted to the pommel of his sword. "Something doesn't seem right."

Gair opened his mouth to say something else, but Goldmoon had turned from him, already starting toward the faint sound. Quietly she picked her way through the hickory trees, her breath in the cold air feathering away from her face like a lacy fan. Gair sighed and followed, rubbing his hands together in a futile effort to keep them warm.

* * * * *

There were eight in the pack in the small clearing, two of them males. One of the males was especially large, with long, wickedly curling yellow tusks that were stained brown at the tips from blood. Their thick bodies were shaggy with winter fur, and they were rippling with fat from the food they'd been storing the preceding summer and autumn. The boars seemed nervous.

"That big one has to be seven hundred pounds," Gair whispered, keeping his voice low. "An old fellow to be certain, and one I'd not want to anger. He's one I'd not want to hunt, either—too dangerous, and his meat would be too tough. Ah, but those others . . . If I weren't so cold and in a hurry to get back to the settlement, I'd scatter the pack, and I might chase after one of the smaller ones. That one over there, for instance." He nudged her shoulder. "Something is making them nervous, but I can't tell what. Maybe it's the sound of the wind in the branches. Can we get out of here now?"

She shook her head no.

The elf huffed and resumed watching the animals, cursing himself for not bothering to grab a coat this morning. When he'd seen Goldmoon leave the settlement, he was in a hurry to follow her.

Gair and Goldmoon lay side by side on their stomachs, faces peering through gaps in a clump of dead ferns. She seemed indifferent in her curiosity to the cold ground. Gair, his teeth chattering, glanced enviously at her wool cloak.

The boars were pawing at the earth, snorting irregularly, their breath puffing from their wide snouts like smoke from chimneys. They were in no mood to forage, despite a plentiful supply of fallen nuts and pine cones on the forest floor. Instead, they milled uneasily and sniffed the air, eyes darting in all directions, waiting for something. It was as if they were afraid of something.

"They can't smell us," Goldmoon whispered, her words almost softer than the breeze. "The wind is from the wrong direction. They smell something. . . . I think they're ready to bolt."

"I will calm them," Gair offered.

Not waiting for her reply, he closed his eyes and touched his slender fingers to his temple, a gesture he used to help himself concentrate. His lips moved as if he were talking, though no sounds came out. It was an enchantment to calm wild beasts, one of the first Goldmoon had taught him in an effort to help calm his capricious spirit. He focused on his heartbeat until he heard its rhythmic thrumming above Goldmoon's steady breathing, then above the wind rustling through the branches overhead, and finally above the loud snorts of the boars. He slowed his heart, then sent the thrumming outward, like a wave rippling from him to the pack. This spell, like many others, came easily to him, requiring little real effort and practically no time. He knew it was successful even before he opened his eyes and spotted the boars crunching nuts and rooting beneath the thin layer of snow. Even the largest was at ease.

"Done," he pronounced softly and started to inch away. "They are calm now, and at least with all that fur, they're staying warm. Watching them has made me even hungrier. Let's go get something hot to eat."

Goldmoon remained quiet, her eyes fixed on the pack. She reached out a hand and touched the elf's wrist. "Wait," she whispered. "Maybe you shouldn't have . . ."

Gair cocked his head and he squinted through the trees beyond the animals. "I think I see something. There's . . ."

A high-pitched squeal sliced through the air, coming from beyond the pack, which, still soothed by Gair's spell, continued to forage. It was followed by another squeal, then another that ended shrilly and abruptly. Birds shot from the treetops, startling the elf and streaking to the south. They heard the sound of branches cracking and rustling, indicating something was headed this way.

"People," Goldmoon suggested. "Hunters."

"And I've unwittingly provided them with easy prey," Gair whispered, looking at the calmed pack. "Perhaps I could try another spell. I could agitate them, give the hunters a real challenge."

Before Gair could act, the crashing in the woods crescendoed, and three more boars burst into the clearing, followed by hunters, but not human ones. The elf gasped in surprise.

The hunters were manlike, but in form only. Indeed, they walked on two legs, but there most of the resemblance to humans ended. There were three of them, with heads that resembled hyenas and slavering jaws filled with sharp-looking teeth. Their skin was a mottled green-gray, fuzzy, like moss growing on a stagnant pond, and it was dark at the muzzle, almost black. From the tops of their heads sprouted brushy white manes that ran down their necks and disappeared beneath the collars of the ragged tunics they wore. One, with a thick, barrel-like chest, wore a cape, and it was this that made Gair's eyes widen even more in disbelief. The cape, a tattered flag, flapped wildly in the wind. From the design, the elf guessed it was from a ship that had sailed for Cuda, a port city in which he'd wasted nearly two years. During those long, tedious months, he'd never seen creatures like these who were scattering the boars in the clearing.

One of the hyena-men wielded a lengthy crude spear from which fluttered tattered strips of colorful silk. The one wearing the flag carried a dagger in each of his pawlike hands and had more strapped about his waist. The third was the most muscular of the lot. He waved a cutlass in the air and was the first to charge the boars.

The soothing effect of Gair's spell on the boars was shattered as the creature's cutlass bit deep into the side of the smallest male. The boar squealed sharply, so high it made the elf grit his teeth, and the other animals answered in a chorus of piercing squeals as they tried to flee from the clearing in all directions.

Goldmoon pressed herself into the loam as a female boar charged madly by, close enough so she and the elf could smell its rank breath. Gair inhaled sharply as another passed near enough to him to brush against his leg. He prayed that the hyena-men wouldn't follow and would be content with the boars that remained in the clearing. His fingers stretched toward the pommel of his sword, just in case, and his eyes drifted to Goldmoon, who was intently taking in what was transpiring.

Gair wanted to do *something*, but Goldmoon preferred to let everything run its course. He would respect his teacher's lead, which seemed to consist of, at the moment, doing nothing.

"What are those things?" he asked in a voice so soft he could barely hear himself. "Products of the Chaos War? Might they have overrun the Blood Sea Isles, and news hadn't yet reached here? And how did they make it from there to Schallsea Island?"

The one with the spear, the tallest of the hyena-men at well over seven feet, dropped to his knees in front of a fleeing boar and swung his weapon in a wide arc, whacking the beast in the snout and grunting in satisfaction. The animal paused, stunned for a moment, and the hyena-man took advantage of the opportunity, twirling his spear and jamming the tip down between the boar's shoulder blades. The strength of his thrust pushed the spear all the way through the boar and into the ground, pinning the animal as a collector might pin a butterfly. The animal's legs twitched a moment, then grew still.

"The one with the spear," Gair whispered. "Whoever attacked us on the trail used spears."

"And bows, you said," Goldmoon returned softly. "These creatures do not have bows."

Vaulting from the ground, the hyena-man howled and abandoned his spear, leaping at another fleeing boar. He wrapped his long arms about the beast's midsection and howled still louder. Gair watched in horror as the creature sank its teeth into the boar's side again and again, barking excitedly when the animal cried in terror and pain. The boar's stumpy legs churned over the earth, then waggled madly in the air as the hyena-man rolled to his back, clutching the boar to his stomach. It tried desperately to free itself, its squeals so shrill they sounded like a whistle. With one arm firmly around the animal's middle, the hyena-man lifted his free hand to the boar's head and wrenched it sharply, snapping its neck.

Goldmoon remained impassive, her eyes locked onto the other two creatures. The hyena-man with the daggers was astride the large old boar, riding it as a man might ride an unbroken horse. He was jabbing the twin daggers into its sides, his flag cape billowing behind him like a sail. The boar was so large that the blades hadn't yet found a vital mark, though they obviously had caused the animal considerable pain. It was doing its best to dislodge the hyena-man, its head thrashing from side to side in an attempt to gore its tormentor's arms and throw him. The hyena-man locked his legs tighter and stabbed repeatedly. He let loose a string of hideous-sounding growls and snarls, and as if in response, the hyena-man with the cutlass backed away from the one he'd just slain and ran toward the gyrating old boar.

Unable to expel the tormentor on its back, the old boar angrily charged the third hyena-man. Its feet pounded over the ground, sending a shower of nuts and snow and dirt in its wake. It lowered its head beneath the swing of the cutlass and drove forward, its tusks sinking into a green-gray thigh as it barreled into the hyena-man and drove him to his back. The boar continued its assault, trampling over the creature's stomach and goring his chest. It thundered over the body and spun, returning to gore the downed hyena-man once more.

All the while, the creature on its back continued to plunge the daggers into the boar's sides. The hyena-man looked like a fat bird, his arms rising and falling rhythmically like wings, blood arcing away with each sweep.

On its third goring pass over the fallen hyena-man, the boar let out a long wail that drowned out the wind and the squeals of the rest of the boars, who were escaping from the clearing. It stopped and snorted, shook its great head, then shuddered and collapsed. Its bloodied rider threw back his snout, howling to the sky. Finally the creature pushed himself off the dead giant's twitching body and glanced about.

Snorting and barking, the hyena-man thrust the daggers into sheaths on his hips, bent, and tugged at the great boar's body. The muscles under his green-gray skin rippling, he managed to pull the massive carcass. He snapped and growled at the hyena-man with the spear.

In response, the other dropped the spear and reached to his side, tugged free a length of thick twine, and fell to lashing the three smaller boar carcasses together. Finished, he shuffled toward his downed companion and sniffed.

The gored hyena-man made a whimpering sound and placed his pawlike hands over his stomach and chest, as if that might block the flow of blood. He struggled to get up, looking to the one standing over him for help. All he received was a snarl and several hard kicks in the ribs to finish him.

The hyena-man bent to retrieve his companion's cutlass. He tugged the scabbard free from the downed creature's waist and quickly strapped it on. Proudly brandishing the weapon, he turned and joined his barrel-chested fellow with the flag. Together, the two pulled the dead boars from the clearing.

Goldmoon and Gair lay silent for many long minutes, feeling the cold of the ground and the air and listening intently. The snow was falling faster now, wetting their hair and faces.

The elf studied Goldmoon and determined she had cast a spell, no doubt one that was extending her senses into the plants or animals nearby, wanting to know where the hyena-men were heading. He could effect such magic, too, but he was content to rely on his teacher's findings and save his energy. At last her expression relaxed.

"Gone?"

She nodded. "They're far enough away now. And I don't think they'll come back."

Gair was on his feet quickly, still favoring his leg. He

brushed the snow from his shirt and extended a hand to assist Goldmoon. She was slow to rise and worked a cramp out of her calf before she edged by the elf and padded into the clearing.

Small pools of blood dotted the ground, and the earth was churned up from the great boar's feet. She threaded her way to the hyena-man and knelt by the body.

"One of the pilgrims mentioned rumors of dog-faced raiders who were attacking hunters and trappers," Goldmoon began.

"And maybe attacking people on the trail to the settlement."

"I thought the story was a product of too much ale. I should have given the tale more credence, perhaps."

Gair bent over her shoulder. "I would say someone who saw a creature like this could be driven to drink. I wish his companions would have left him alive, though. I would've liked to question him if I could have found some way to understand him. I want to know if these were the creatures who attacked us a few days ago. I wonder where he came from. I don't think he's native to Schallsea. The one with the cape—"

"It was a flag from Kothas or Mithas."

"Kothas. Cuda, to be precise."

"A Blood Sea flag. The creatures are definitely not native to this island," Goldmoon agreed. "I've never seen their like in all my years on Krynn." She paused and examined the hyena-man from muzzle to clawed feet. "He's not dead. Not yet."

Gair's keen eyes narrowed, and he noticed with surprise that the hyena-man's blood-soaked chest faintly but irregularly rose and fell. Blood continued to seep from the deep gouges on the creature's stomach and chest, dyeing what was once a dun-colored tunic a deep scarlet.

"But he is dying," he observed.

"Yes." Goldmoon closed her eyes and reached inside herself, focused on her heartbeat, as she had taught Gair and Jasper and her other students to do, ignoring the elf's continued speculations about the creature. Her heartbeat was all she heard now as a comforting warmth rose in her chest and extended down her arms, made her fingers pleasantly tingle. She placed her palms on the creature's chest and coaxed that warmth to flow from her into him.

"What are you doing?" Gair stepped back, amazed. True, he wanted to question the creature, but he wouldn't have wasted his energy healing him. The creature was a monster, and if the tale Goldmoon heard was correct, he'd been killing Schallsea's trappers and therefore didn't deserve to live. He might even be the one who killed Harrald and the Solamnic knight. "Better to show him mercy with a swift stroke of my sword. His fellows certainly gave him no mercy. Monsters. We can find out about them another way, by speaking to this one's corpse. You could talk to it, just as you talk to Riverwind."

Goldmoon didn't reply. She couldn't hear him. She was listening only to her heart, and to the hyena-man's, which was growing stronger with each passing beat. A faint glow covered his chest, radiating out from her fingers. Pale gray like the sky, it intensified slightly above the deepest of the monster's wounds.

As Gair watched, the gouges started to close. The elf marveled at Goldmoon's ability. Healing magic was relatively easy for him, but he doubted that even his most potent spells could mend wounds this severe and this quickly. He made a mental note to press her for information about this nurturing glow she'd created. Perhaps it was how Jasper had healed him. He wanted to learn this advanced mysticism almost as much as he wanted to talk to the spirits of the dead.

The creature made a gurgling sound, coughing up blood and spittle. His eyes flew open and locked onto Goldmoon's, and he started to struggle, to push her away. Her eyes held his, and she used all her strength to keep her hands on his chest.

"Don't move," she said. Words could interrupt her spell. "Don't move." She said nothing else.

The hyena-man lay still, staring unblinkingly at Goldmoon, growling softly as the glow covered more of his body and healed more of his wounds. Several minutes passed, and the healer's breath became shallow and her shoulder's sagged. Just as the glow brightened, she pitched forward against the creature's chest. The glow disappeared.

Gair darted in to pull her back, keeping a wary eye on the creature. Her long tunic and leggings were covered with the monster's blood, and the ends of her hair were matted with it. Gair dabbed at a streak of blood on her cheek, then returned his attention to the creature. It lay still, regarding them.

When Goldmoon was breathing more deeply and regularly, Gair tugged her to her feet. "Are you all right?"

She nodded yes. "The creature will live."

The creature made a guttural barking noise, then repeated it and raised a hairy eyebrow.

"I think maybe he's talking to us," Goldmoon suggested.

"Well, unless you have some mystic enchantment that will let us learn his language, I think it's likely to be a one-sided conversation," Gair pointed out. "I don't speak hyena."

"Do you have a name?" she asked.

He growled a word.

"Orvago?"

He struggled to prop himself up on his elbows.

"Orvago?" she repeated. "Is your name Orvago?"

He nodded and his eyes narrowed warily.

"Well, Gair, it looks as if he understands us." Goldmoon was leaning against the elf for support, still weak from the powerful healing spell she'd invoked. "It appears you can talk to him after all."

The elf stared at the creature for several moments. Goldmoon took a step away from him. The blood on her tunic had soaked through to her skin, and the wetness was chilling her. Gair edged forward and squatted, eye-to-eye with the hyena-man. Where to begin? What questions first?

"What are you?"

The creature's gaze drifted back and forth between the elf and Goldmoon, resting longer on her.

Gair sighed and rocked back on his heels. "How did you get here?"

The creature nodded toward the boars.

"I can see that you followed the boars. That's not what I mean. Goldmoon, this is getting us nowhere. Maybe he can understand us. Maybe he can't. He's an animal, and a dangerous one, at that." The elf groaned and stood, paced in a tight circle, then whirled on the creature, who, still in some pain, was gingerly getting to his clawed feet. "Did you and your fellows attack us a few days ago? Have you hurt others? How did you get to the island? And where did you come from? How many of you?"

The creature cocked his head. A string of spittle edged over his lower lip and dripped to the ground.

Exasperated, Gair ran his fingers through his hair. He pivoted to face Goldmoon and gestured with his head toward her, concentrating to retain an even, polite tone. "She healed you, creature. She saved your life. Because Goldmoon saved your life, you should answer my questions."

The creature nodded toward Goldmoon, then brushed by the elf and slowly walked in the direction his companions had dragged the boars, limping on his leg that had been gored. A heartbeat later, he had disappeared into the trees.

Gair drew in a deep breath and shook his head. He stared into the woods, hoping to catch another glimpse of the creature. "We should go after him. He can't move very fast with that injured leg. We could force him to come with us, take him to town. The authorities there might get something out of him. Maybe we should—"

"Let him go?" Goldmoon's eyes gleamed, and her lips edged upward slightly, giving away her amusement. "Join me for breakfast?" She turned and started back toward the settlement. "I don't know about you, Gair, but I need to wash up and change clothes, and I'm hungry. No reason to stay out any longer and catch a cold, or worse. There's no reason for you to undo all of Jasper's hard work. I think I'm going to sit by a cookfire for a while and warm up. Perhaps I'll have a chat with our Solamnic visitors. Coming?"

Still flustered, he hurried to catch up. "I wanted to find out about that flag," he muttered softly to himself.

Chapter 5

Gray Tidings

Gair padded silently through the woods, tracing roughly the same path that Goldmoon and he had followed early this morning. This time wisdom prevailed, and he wore a heavy coat that draped to his ankles and brushed the top of the snow. Dark green, it helped to conceal him among the trees, a shadow among shadows. Like the shirt and trousers he wore, it was relatively new and exquisitely made. Only his boots were well worn, kept because of their comfort. However, he made a mental note to buy another pair on his next trip to town and start breaking them in.

The elf had a significant cache of steel and gems, an inheritance from his family. And while he had given a more than generous amount of it to Goldmoon for her citadel and various other causes throughout the past several years, he still had plenty to indulge his pleasures—fine clothes and good food—for a long while, likely for the rest of his life.

As the woods became thicker, blocking out the early evening starlight, he focused on his heightened senses. His keen eyes separated the shadows so he could continue on his way without slowing his pace. The snow helped to brighten the area, reflecting the light of the stars and the moon where it penetrated gaps in the pine canopy. He mused that the stars sparkled like the lady knight's eyes. Gair found himself thinking of her again and wondering if he should be spending time with her rather than on this macabre errand. He admitted he was captivated by the face that had hovered over his when he was injured by the spears. Perhaps he would visit with her in the morning.

He was as careful as possible where he walked, avoiding passing beneath certain trees where the crunch of his boots on fallen nuts and pine cones might give him away. Were the snow harder, he would worry about the crunch of that, too, but the snow, which had fallen most of the day, was downy soft.

Though he wasn't particularly worried about others being out in the woods at night, he didn't want to take any chances of being discovered. He didn't want to be followed by any of Goldmoon's curious students, and he didn't want to be discovered by any green-furred creatures such as he and Goldmoon had encountered this morning or by any bandits. He shuddered when he recalled his brush with death several days ago on the trail to the settlement.

Gair moved almost silently, listening carefully for wild boars, wolves, anything that might pose a threat. He wanted to be about his business, then return to Goldmoon's camp before his absence had been noticed.

The wind had died down considerably, or so it seemed in the thick woods. He breathed deep. The scent of pine needles was pleasant to one who had spent much of his early life in the forest, and he detected a trace of rotting wood from a few dying trees. These were the earthy smells of winter, and they reminded him of his home so far away along the southeastern coast of the elven country of Silvanesti.

Stepping off the path and striking off deeper into the woods, he came to a grove of willows, huge trees half-dead from age and errant lightning strikes. Some had carvings on their trunks, symbols he tried to commit to memory and hoped to decipher later. The oldest of the carvings—the bark had grown to nearly cover the scars—showed a half sun, and under it a stick figure carrying a spear. There were smaller symbols around the figure, words perhaps, much of it not readable anymore. The more recent carvings looked like masks with empty eyes, with more symbols around them. He knew several languages, but nothing here was familiar. He traced one of the symbols with a bit of charcoal and a piece of parchment he'd brought along, then thrust them deep into his coat pocket.

He turned north and followed a trail he had missed on his first few explorations of these woods in the early fall. Other eyes would have continued to miss it, but Gair's years in the forest had taught him to look for branches artfully trained to touch the ground. When the leaves began to thin with the fall, he noticed it. They were hiding a narrow trail, one not often traveled, at least on this end, and one certainly not intended for the uninvited.

The elf ducked beneath the limbs and walked faster now, listened more carefully. He'd placed a few branches across the path on his last visit, and they were still here and unbroken, indicating this part of the trail had not been traveled in the past few weeks by people or any animals of significant size.

The trees were so dense here that they blocked the mild evening breeze almost completely. They helped to lessen the cold, too, though his breath still huffed out in a vaporous cloud. There were more symbols on trunks here, none of them recent. Gair made another tracing of a few more symbols, then continued on his way.

The elf felt a mix of excitement and apprehension. He was heading toward what he believed was a sacred spot. Why else would someone hide the trails and carve symbols into trees along the way?

Finally he came to edge of a circular clearing. In the clearing was a series of earthen mounds, radiating outward from a pebble-dotted center. The mounds nearest the center were the oldest and therefore the most worn, weather and time eroding the dirt and stones and the various objects on top of them.

He crept quietly up and down the paths, slipping from mound to mound and hurriedly brushing the snow aside so he could inspect them more closely. The elf had been here twice before, both times briefly and at night. Each trip had added to his knowledge. He was certain the mounds with the smoothest, flattest stones covering them contained the remains of people of importance. Many of these stones had intricate carvings on them. Words, perhaps. On this trip, the elf pocketed one of the more elaborately carved rocks and rearranged the others so it would look as if nothing was amiss. His fingers trembled from the cold. He intended to take the stone into the port town, with the rubbings of symbols he'd made, to the scribes there. Perhaps they could be translated.

Some of the mounds had only small rocks scattered atop them, and Gair decided these graves were for commoners. The smallest mounds were likely for children or animals and had the fewest decorations. A mound near one edge of the circle was fairly recent, made within the past month, since the earth had not yet settled. He brushed away more snow. There were mounds decorated with shells and rotted nets—for fishermen, he suspected. Those graves with daggers thrust into the earth were undoubtedly the resting place of warriors. Arrowheads artfully arranged were likely for hunters. He stopped and his breath caught in his throat. Arrowheads. He dropped to his knees and tried to tug one free of the mound. The frozen earth resisted his efforts, and he resorted to pulling out a small knife from his belt and working the arrowhead free. It was made of stone, with the same jagged edges of the spear tips and the arrowhead had that found their way into him several days ago.

"Who is buried here?" he said too loudly for his liking, and instantly turned his thoughts to a whisper. "Iryl Songbrook said the natives of Schallsea couldn't have been responsible for the attack, that they are peaceful." Gair ran his fingers over the arrowhead, wincing when a sharp edge drew blood. His leg seemed to throb in response, and he shuddered. "It wasn't bandits who attacked us. Bandits don't bury their dead in elaborate graves. So this arrowhead proves Iryl was wrong. It was natives, and I must show this to her and Goldmoon." He stood and pocketed the arrowhead, then frowned. "If I show them, I'll have to tell them where I got this. Do I want to do that?" He stared at the remainder of arrowheads on the grave. "Perhaps I should say nothing. They might never attack us again."

Deciding he would give the matter more thought tonight, he padded toward the opposite edge of the clearing, passing by one mound in particular that had caught his eye on his first visit. He knelt beside it now. It seemed to be one of the oldest graves, and almost reverently he brushed the snow off it. The rocks atop the mound were so carefully arranged and so deeply embedded into the earth that they seemed to form an intricate mosaic. The pattern meant nothing to Gair, though he studied it intently in the light of the moon, trying to commit it to memory. He worked one of the larger, more intricate stones free and pocketed this too.

When he returned to his tent later, he would sketch the mosaic on the grave and see if someone in town could tell him what it signified. Perhaps the man beneath the stones had been a king or a chief. Definitely someone important, as more work had gone into this mound than into any others here, and it seemed as if it were still being carefully tended. Gair's fingertips traced the pattern of the stones, and he concentrated on the feel of them, on the various textures.

"One more attempt," he whispered. "Who are you?"

He focused on his heartbeat as Goldmoon had taught him to do with healing magic, and he raised a hand to his temple to help him concentrate. He felt his heartbeat slow, sounding rhythmic and soothing in his ears. Warmth pervaded his limbs, chasing away the cold of winter. He reached out now with his senses as he had done when he calmed the boars. This time, though, he reached down, down into the earth. He sensed the coldness of the dirt, the age of the stones atop it. He sensed a hint of life—insects wintering beneath the ground. He concentrated harder, listened more intently to his heart, listened, searched. He imagined a man beneath the earth, perhaps wrapped in regal, ceremonial burial garb, imagined that what was left of the man was only a skeleton covered with scraps of rotting cloth.

"Nothing." He rocked back on his heels, frustrated. The elf could not sense the body in the mound nor in any mound he had approached on his previous trips, but he was certain there were bodies here. It was a burial place.

He simply could not sense the spirits of the dead.

"I have to know. I must." Gair had hoped his nearness to the dead in this place would help him to contact spirits. He'd certainly had no luck trying to contact spirits from inside his tent. "It seems it won't be tonight. Maybe not ever."

Reluctantly he rose and carefully inspected the ground, brushing at his boot prints to conceal them. He retraced his steps, covering all of his tracks, and stood at the edge of the clearing, staring at the circle and realizing that if anyone happened by, he would know the snow on the graves had been disturbed.

"One more try." He knew he should leave, told himself that he shouldn't stay here one minute longer and risk discovery, but he was here, and the dead were here. Who else would come to visit them on such a cold winter night? Winter, he mused, a season of death. It was appropriate that he was here at this time of year. "Besides," he whispered, "It would be for the good of the settlement if I can learn about these people, whose descendants almost certainly attacked us."

He knelt at the most recent mound, a small grave at the edge of the clearing, a child's grave, by the size of it. The elf splayed his fingers over the snow, above where he guessed the body's heart was in life. Again he concentrated on his heartbeat, let his senses drift into the frigid, hard-packed earth, sensing the husks of insects, stones, twigs, bones. Bones! He let out a long breath and tried futilely to dig his fingertips into the earth. He sensed the bones of someone who had lived on this island!

His mind was feeling them, not imagining them, guessing their length—indeed it was a child, a child who had lived to be perhaps ten or twelve. Bones were covered by flesh and muscle partially eaten away. Long hair was braided with beads and shells. Young . . . recently dead. Of what? Disease? Disease that perhaps Goldmoon or he could have cured? An accident? His senses revealed no broken bones. So young. So very few years on Krynn. Beads and shells and braids . . . a clue to these people.

He felt sadness for . . . her. Somehow he knew the child had been female, but he felt a twinge of pleasure at the same time. A smile played along his lips. He had sensed no spirit, but he had sensed *something*, and that was a minor victory of sorts. Perhaps if he kept at it, he thought, if he came back here again, worked longer and harder. Perhaps then he might finally be rewarded.

"Find the door," he whispered. "Find the door and open it." From that door he would reach the spirits he was seeking to talk to.

"Jasper says I don't take enough chances." He stifled a laugh. "I will take a chance with this, and I will speak to Goldmoon again. I have to make her understand."

He tried to smooth the snow back into place as he pulled his mind away from the child's grave. Perhaps he needed to concentrate on the recently dead. That could be the answer. Perhaps their spirits were closer to their bodies and to this world, and perhaps that would make them more receptive to his senses.

"What lies in wait for us after life?" he whispered. He continued staring at the graves for the better part of an hour, lost in his thoughts and oblivious to the cold. "What is all of this for . . . life? You struggle to better yourself, to help others, to gain some measure of status. For what? In the end, someone will bury you and forget you. Is that all there is? With the gods gone, is there not even a promise of redemption? Certainly Riverwind's spirit exists. And if Riverwind's spirit exists, so must others. But what existence?" His eyes locked onto the child's grave. "Is whatever follows life better than life itself? Or is it some hellish shadow of life? When we die, what awaits us?"

Carefully Gair retraced his steps. Several minutes later he was on the path that led back to the settlement. He walked slowly, still lost in thought. Only when he heard voices as he approached the settlement's camp-fires did he stop thinking about spirits, and then only to think about finding Goldmoon.

He, Goldmoon, and Jasper arrived on Schallsea Island a little more than six months ago, carrying nothing with them except blankets and a few treasured possessions. Since that time, Goldmoon's followers in Abanasinia had made the trip here, bringing building supplies, tents, seeds for future gardens, and more. From three blankets on the ground around a single campfire, the area around the Silver Stair had grown into a thriving tent town that most certainly would grow even larger come spring.

Nearly a hundred tents and lean-tos stretched east of the Silver Stair toward the cliffs that overlooked the Straits of Schallsea. Some were elaborate, with trinkets hanging on the outside that jangled pleasantly in the wind, or with names and home towns painted on the exterior canvas. In the light of the day, the multihued tents looked quite cheery. The elf imagined that from above, the camp looked rather like a big patchwork quilt. It would be getting bigger, he knew.

The number of Goldmoon's followers continued to increase as word of the settlement spread throughout the southwest part of Ansalon. Many of those who came here were single individuals, wanting to make a difference in the world by learning Goldmoon's mystical healing powers or her philosophy. Others were families who had come to be near the famed Hero of the Lance and who hoped to find inspiration in a world absent of gods. Some were curiosity-seekers, intrigued by the Citadel of Light Goldmoon intended to build, or mystified by the Silver Stair. Finally there were the townsfolk who came out to visit, many of whom ended up staying to join the community. The latest addition was a miller named Roeland, who had sold his shop to join the ragtag community.

Dozens upon dozens of pilgrims, as they were calling themselves, were living in the port town, where the accommodations were better. This had resulted in the building spurt and in the "no vacancy" signs in nearly every inn's window. Iryl Songbrook was doing her best to house as many newcomers as possible in her hostel, some of whom had spent every coin they owned for passage to Schallsea Island. They made monthly pilgrimages to the stair and to visit with Goldmoon. Iryl herself conducted most of the tours.

And then there were the settlement builders. Heavy hide tents ringed by stacks of crates stood at the far edge of Gair's vision. These belonged to the dwarves, who came a few weeks ago and who, under Jasper's instructions, were beginning construction on the citadel. A few of the dwarves sat around a campfire. They appeared to be drinking.

Gair stood and took it all in, listening to the musical notes of someone's wind chimes. There were a few small perimeter fires to help the sentries see and to warn away any wolves. Toward the center of the tent town, a large cookfire still burned. Someone was eating late—venison, the elf's nose told him. He slipped in past the first row of tents. To his far right, a Solamnic knight walked with one of the settlement's sentries. More knights were expected soon, and more soldiers as well.

To the east, the Silver Stair rose above everything. He stared at the mystical creation. Someone was walking down it, though Gair was too far away to see who it was. Goldmoon? He wanted to talk to her. Gair edged closer, staying concealed by the shadows of the tents. No, it was not Goldmoon. It was the Solamnic lieutenant named Willum, his plate mail reflecting the shimmering of the steps. Jasper stood at the base of the stairs, waiting for Willum. The dwarf had climbed the Celestial Ladder a half-dozen times since their arrival.

"Perhaps I shall try soon," Gair breathed.

The elf moved deeper into the community, slipping

from tent to tent. He wasn't entirely sure why he was staying hidden. Goldmoon's tent was near the cliff, as the healer enjoyed looking out at the Straits of Schallsea toward Abanasinia. His tent was several dozen yards away to the north.

Gair thrust his hands in the pockets of his coat and hurried toward her tent. A light was burning inside. She was still up.

"Goldmoon?" He paused outside her tent, waited patiently for her to draw back the flap. No answer. He risked poking his head inside and discovered no one there. "Where are you?" Determined to find her, he started pacing away from her tent, nearly bumping into Camilla Weoledge when he turned the corner around a large lean-to.

"Good evening, Mr. Graymist," the knight said.

"Gair," he corrected her. "Only Jasper is so formal to use my last name."

"Gair, then."

"Weren't you able to sleep either?"

She shook her head, her breath clouding around her face in the cold air. "I was just going to turn in, after one last stroll around your settlement."

He extended his arm. "Then allow me accompany you, lady, and let me thank you again for comforting me when I was so grievously wounded on the trail by the"—he stopped himself, swallowing the words that might give away his trip to the burial ground— "by the bandits."

As the elf escorted Camilla toward the cliff, it began to snow once more. The full moon, though partially hidden by wispy clouds, illuminated the start of a dock far below them. The pilings were in place, the planks on the shore covered by a snow-dusted tarp. Stakes wedged into the cliff face suggested the path a set of stairs would take.

"Like stars falling to the earth," Camilla stated.

"What?"

She was watching the lacy snowflakes spinning slowing down, disappearing into the darkness of the water below. "That's what my father called snow."

"The snow is lovely," Gair returned, "but not so lovely as you."

She blushed and looked away, studying the distant dark water and removing her arm from his.

"You truly are lovely, Camilla."

The elf's keen eyes noticed her face redden. He knew she was not elegant and graceful like the elven women of the Silvanesti woods that he used to dream about. She was as tall as he and muscular, not the dainty woman on his arm he'd always pictured. She wasn't someone he had expected to be drawn to, but he was drawn to her nevertheless.

"Don't turn away," he said softly.

"I . . . I hardly know you."

"Then you must get to know me better." He took Camilla's hand, and she did not protest. He led her around the perimeter of the settlement.

"Where I come from, Gair, relationships aren't rushed."

"Where I come from," the elf countered, "people follow their hearts, and I think you've captured mine."

They indulged themselves with idle conversation about the port town and the Solamnic order, and when the conversation turned to his Silvanesti homeland and his family, he deftly changed the subject—to her mysterious eyes, her curly hair, her milky complexion.

"You remind me of Goldmoon," he said and failed to notice that she bristled at the remark. "Daring, strong, admirable . . ." He added to himself, and I believe that is why I am so taken with you.

She turned her gaze from his. However, she did not

shy away when he moved closer, released her hand, and draped his arm around her shoulders.

"I am a Knight of the Sword," she told him. "My heart belongs to my order, and this—" she stared at the ground and brushed at the snow with her boot heel—"this is too fast. We've known each other only for a few days. This is—"

"Don't say it's wrong," he interrupted. "Please, give me a chance."

She looked toward a tent where Willum, wrapped in blankets, stood at the flap. Her pace increased as they walked past him and headed toward another tent, which the knight occupied.

"Gair, I do not believe in this settlement. I think what Goldmoon is doing is wrong, and therefore I think you're wrong in following her."

"Then why are you here?"

"I am here only because of my orders. I am a knight, and my heart—"

"Let just a little of your heart belong to me." He stepped back and stared at her eyes. Impulsively he darted forward and kissed her on the cheek. "Just a little," he repeated as she slipped out of his arms and ducked into her tent.

Gair returned to Goldmoon's tent. This time he found the healer at home. She poked her head out between the flaps to talk to him when he called softly.

"It's late," she said simply, but she was not dressed for bed. She was still wearing the deerskin tunic and breeches she'd put on after the incident that morning with the creature and the boars. And she had her cloak on, still wet from melting snow.

"Goldmoon, I . . ." The elf closed his eyes and sighed. "You know how much I want to talk to spirits. I—"

She shook her head firmly. "Gair, I will not teach you dark mysticism. I told you that this morning."

"I've thought about it all day." The elf was clearly exasperated, but he tried not to show it. "Goldmoon, I know I push you sometimes, but I've never misused what you've taught me, and I wouldn't misuse this. You talk to Riverwind. That's where you were earlier, isn't it? Talking to Riverwind?"

She didn't answer.

"There's someone I want very much to speak to." He lowered his gaze to the ground, studied the tips of his boots for several moments. "If you don't teach me this, I'll have to stumble along on my own, trying to contact the dead. Maybe I can't learn it on my own, but I won't stop trying. I have to know that my family still . . . exists, that there is something beyond this life. Maybe once that knowledge is within my reach, I'll be satisfied and can move on, and then this won't consume me."

She stared at him, his silver-white hair shimmering in the moonlight, lips set in a determined line. Suddenly her eyes showed that she had made a decision. "All right, Gair. Against my better judgment." She ran her fingers through her hair and shook her head. "Maybe if I wasn't so tired and you weren't so persistent . . ."

"When?" he pressed.

"It had better be now," she answered softly, "before I change my mind."

She beckoned him inside her tent. He felt his heart racing, his palms sweating. Her tent was sparsely furnished, with a bed raised above the ground atop some sturdy-looking crates. A small chest near the bed held the possessions that she'd brought with her from Abanasinia. An oil lamp rested atop the chest, bathing the interior of the tent in a soft glow. A large crate stood in the center of the small tent and served as a table. Two chairs abutted it, the only real furniture in Goldmoon's tent—given to her by a farmer as thanks for healing his sick wife and son. Goldmoon told the elf there would be time for furniture after the citadel was built.

It was much warmer inside the healer's tent than Gair expected. She'd hung thick blankets up against each wall to help keep out the cold. Taking off his coat, he carefully laid it across the back of a chair and sat, steepling his fingers on the table.

She sat opposite him, looking pale in the soft light. "The first thing you must do is clear your mind," she said slowly. "I hope this gives you some measure of peace, and that I am not doing the wrong thing." She studied the elf's face; his brow was knitted in concentration.

"This process is not unlike reaching the minds of animals," she began, "but this is sensing a different type of . . . life. You must look elsewhere for it."

For the next hour, she showed Gair what were mostly rather familiar mystical concepts, but with some peculiar twists. The elf realized he had been close in his attempts to communicate with the dead at the burial ground tonight, frighteningly close. There were just a few differences in approach.

Under her direction, Gair closed his eyes and let his senses drift. In his mind, he could see the features of Goldmoon's tent and see her sitting across from him. The sensation was heady and a bit unnerving, as he was perceiving the world unconventionally. Rather, he was searching for things not of this world. In the back of his mind, he saw shadows all about him, fleeting images of insubstantial people, but no one he recognized.

"Search a little longer. Picture a different land," she told him. "Picture different shadows, ones recognizable and familiar."

"Father . . ."

Goldmoon moved to stand behind the elf and placed

her hand on his shoulder for reassurance. The healer had discovered this path of mysticism accidentally years ago when she was grieving for her husband. When her senses reached out and touched his spirit, she was at first startled, then overcome with joy. Since his death, she had felt so alone. To contact him again, she had to mentally retrace all the steps. There had been many failed attempts before she finally found him and the secret again. Ever since, contacting him had been relatively easy, and she often found herself talking to him without even realizing she'd opened the door.

Until this evening, the healer had never taught anyone this mystical ability. Her doubts about doing so now vanished when she saw a calmness come over Gair, his brow smoothing and his breathing deepening. This student would be the exception.

"Father, I wasn't there when the dragon came. I should have been with you, not sneaking off into town when you had ordered me to stay home. If I hadn't been so young and foolish, if I hadn't disobeyed you . . ."

Goldmoon stepped back. She didn't want to eavesdrop on his conversation, and so she reached for her cloak and padded from the tent, leaving Gair to his visit.

"I couldn't stay in the forest afterward," Gair continued. "There was nothing for me there. . . . You . . . my sisters . . . all gone. I sold the estate and took the emeralds. I made a few investments for the future. I'm sorry, Father. . . ."

Goldmoon strolled toward the end of the community where the dwarves had their encampment. Jasper had joined two other dwarves, who were nursing mugs of ale and hovering close to a low-burning fire.

"Can't sleep?" Jasper's voice was uncharacteristically thick, evidence he'd been drinking.

Goldmoon nodded and sat on an overturned crate and warmed her hands by the fire.

"Tomorrow we finish the foundation." Jasper glanced at the moon. "Well, later today, actually. Told you my friends work fast. We'll start buildin' in a day or two. Listen, don't be surprised if . . ." The dwarf's words trailed off, and his eyes narrowed. He had spotted Gair leaving Goldmoon's tent.

"It's all right, Jasper."

Then his gaze drifted from Gair to the construction site. "Always concerned about you, Goldmoon. Always . . . what in the name of Uncle Flint's beard is that? . . . A monster!" he hollered, reaching for the hammer that always hung at his waist. Jasper's short legs propelled him toward a large pile of building supplies, and Goldmoon followed. The other dwarves threw down their mugs and trundled awkwardly after them.

"Monster!" Jasper's cries alerted the sentries, who ran toward the construction site. Here and there lights were blinking on inside tents. "Monster!"

Gair's long legs carried him quickly through the settlement toward the noise. He was at Goldmoon's side, long sword drawn, before the sentries had reached her.

"There's the monster!" Jasper waggled his hammer, pointing at a dark shape hunkered down behind a pile of lumber. He stalked toward it, Gair towering behind him. One of the inebriated dwarves grabbed a rock and skirted around the other side.

Jasper and the elf raised their weapons, intent on striking the trespasser, who hadn't moved. The elf's eyes narrowed, and his hand shot forward just as Jasper was drawing his hammer back to throw it. Gair grabbed the handle and yanked it from the dwarf's stubby fingers.

"It's not a monster," the elf said. "Not exactly, anyway."

"Orvago!" Goldmoon breathed from behind them both.

The creature edged away from the pile, holding out a long hairy arm to keep the drunken dwarves from coming closer.

More lanterns blinked on. People draped in sleeping clothes and blankets emerged from tents and lean-tos, some bearing torches. Camilla clanked forward, still in her plate mail. Willum, wrapped in blankets and hoisting a sword, was at her side. Footfalls sounded across the dry ground of the settlement. There were sounds of weapons being drawn.

Goldmoon whirled to face the others. "He's a friend," she explained. Her stern expression stopped all but Camilla from coming closer. She made a gesture, and those who had weapons out sheathed them.

More torches. The construction site's shadows were being chased away, revealing the green-gray form of the creature. His tunic was stiff with dried blood, and matted blood stuck here and there to his fur.

"What manner of creature is this?" someone sputtered.

Iryl Songbrook made her way through the crowd, eyes wide, mouth opened at first in a yawn, then open wider in amazement.

"He's nothing but a monster!" an elderly man shouted. He wriggled a crooked finger. "A demon from the Abyss!" The woman at his side gaped at the creature as her husband continued, "He's not human. He's a creature of Chaos!"

"*I'm* not human!" Gair cut in, "and *they're* not human." The elf pointed to the dwarves. His sword was held protectively now, letting the settlement folks know he was defending the creature.

"It's a creation of some foul wizard," the old man went on.

"Look at all that blood on that thing!" another cut in. "It must have killed someone, it did. We've got to kill it. It's probably part of the band that attacked you and killed Harrald!"

"He didn't attack us!" Gair returned. His free hand was in his pocket, feeling the arrowhead. "It wasn't him."

The creature growled softly. A trace of spittle edged over his lower lip and ran to the ground. He growled again. It seemed as if he were trying to say something.

Several settlers gasped. "A demon for certain!" someone cried.

"Goldmoon, save us from the dog-beast!" a young woman cried. She clutched the hands of two young boys. "Save us!"

Cries of "Save us," "Demon," and "Dog-beast" echoed around the camp.

The healer padded toward the growing throng and tried to calm them. Behind her, Gair sheathed his sword. Jasper's inebriated friends took another look at the creature and swayed unsteadily on their feet.

"It's all right," Gair said to the creature, who grunted and brushed by the elf, heading toward Goldmoon. The crowd backed away instantly. The old man stabbed his finger at the air, pointing at the creature and leering.

Goldmoon shook her head. "Shame on all of you!" she said. "I don't judge any of you by how you look." She held a hand out to Orvago, and the creature took it with his clawed paw. "Gair and I met Orvago earlier today. His clothes are bloody because he fought a boar."

"The monster's not staying here!" This came from a young man standing next to the elderly couple, one of the tent town's more affluent members.

"He's not a monster," Gair said.

"I believe he's a gnoll," Camilla said suddenly. The knight's face was grim, and her hand was tightly clenched around the pommel of her sword, though it remained sheathed. "What in the name of Kiri-Jolith is a gnoll doing on Schallsea Island?"

"A gnoll?" Iryl found her way to the knight's side. "What's a gnoll?"

"I never saw one before," the knight was quick to reply. "Only pictures, and I've heard tales, but I don't really know anything about them, other than the fact that they're not native to anywhere around here. According to Solamnic records, Lord Toede captured gnolls and used them as servants."

"Well, whatever he is, he's welcome to share my tent tonight," Gair said, stifling a yawn.

"There," Goldmoon said. "The matter is settled. Orvago will stay with Gair as long as he likes."

She didn't notice the elf's wide eyes.

"Orvago can stay," she continued, "just as anyone here can stay as long as he likes. If you cannot abide by this, then this place is not for you." She stood defiantly amid the throng, listening to their whispers. Some seemed to accept her words, while others seemed merely curious. Still others seemed frightened. Finally the crowd began to disperse back to their tents.

Goldmoon watched the creature follow Gair toward his tent, then motioned to the sentries. One would be stationed near Gair's tent for the rest of the evening, just in case some of the people in the tent town opted not to abide by Goldmoon's decision.

Gair ducked through the low tent flap and stepped inside. The gnoll stepped forward, his head catching the top of the tent. The creature howled as canvas billowed around them, and then the tent collapsed.

It took the elf nearly an hour to set it up again.

Chapter 6

A New Threat

Orvago woke with a start, snarling loudly to get Gair's attention. The elf glanced at the floor, where the gnoll had fashioned a makeshift bed out of blankets, and rubbed the sleep out of his eyes.

"What are you howling about?" the elf grumbled. "I haven't had more than an hour or so of sleep, and . . ." Then he cocked his head. The gnoll wasn't howling; it was the wind, and the tent was flapping threateningly. Gair jumped to his feet, stuck his face outside, and instantly pulled it back in, sputtering and blinking furiously.

The wind keened furiously, a great low whistle that drowned out everything except the flapping of the canvas. The elf hurriedly searched through his clothes for his warmest pants and shirt, then struggled into them as the canvas continued to flutter madly and the center pole began to wobble. Orvago growled softly and edged toward the tent opening, cautiously crawling on his hands and knees, a ridge of hair standing up on his back.

Gair continued to hop about, pulling on stockings, then one boot, then another, all the while cursing in his native tongue. "We've got to get outside," he said as much to himself as to the gnoll. "I think this tent is about to . . ."

Before he could get the rest of the words out, the smaller poles tugged free of the ground and the center pole tipped, bringing the beating canvas down on the elf—but only for a moment. The wind continued to batter the tent, pulling it loose from its stakes and sending it flying away. Blankets and books followed it. Gair gave a shout as his cot spun over, banging into the back of his legs. He made a mad grab for a red leather-bound book, and the cot turned end over end away from him to disappear in the snow.

Howling, the gnoll crawled out of the path of Gair's tumbling belongings, then pressed himself into the snow as more objects passed quickly over his back. Orvago propped himself up on his elbows, only his face above the thick blanket of snow, and cupped a hairy hand over his eyes and tried to get a better look around.

The world was totally white. Snow was driven practically sideways from the south, reminding the creature of the fierce storm at sea he had endured more than a year ago. Through the nearly opaque whiteness, he saw faint shadows moving about slowly. It took several seconds to realize the shadows were people from the settlement. Above the terrifying wind, the creature heard the shouts of men and women and the frightened whinnies of horses. He heard Goldmoon. Orvago crawled on his hands and knees toward her voice.

Gair clutched his precious book to him, thrusting it inside his shirt and buttoning the shirt up to his neck to keep the book safe. The elf's teeth were chattering, and he reached out his mind to his father while he fumbled in the snow for his green woolen coat.

The elf closed his eyes against the threatening snow,

bundled his coat tightly around himself, and thrust his hands deep into the pockets. "Father, can you see through this?" He concentrated on the mystical ability Goldmoon had taught him but a few hours ago, opened the door to the realm of the dead, and heard an answer in his mind, though it was difficult to understand with the roar of the wind around him. "If this snow is nothing to you, then guide me through it, Father," he implored. "I must find Goldmoon and Camilla."

The spirit, unhampered by the blizzard, unerringly guided his son around chests and crates too heavy to be tossed by the wind but hidden by growing drifts of snow. Slowly he directed Gair in the direction where Goldmoon's tent used to be.

The gnoll and the elf arrived at nearly the same time, finding the aging healer bundled in blankets, surrounded by a few dozen men, women, and children, and calling out to the rest of her followers. Some of the people were hysterical, unable to find loved ones in the blizzard. The healer was trying to gather everyone close and was counting heads.

"Jasper!" The word was lost in the wind. A dwarf at Goldmoon's feet, looking like a tree stump covered by snow, shouted that she hadn't seen Jasper since last night.

Orvago pushed himself to his feet, draping an arm across his brow in an attempt to keep some of the wind and snow out of his eyes. He leaned into the wind and headed toward where he'd hidden himself last night at the construction site. The scent of the dwarves would be strongest there.

"My baby!" A woman huddling near Goldmoon cried. "I can't find my baby!" The woman made a move to dart away, but a man held her fast and Goldmoon tried to calm her.

"My wife!" a young man blurted. "She was right next to me when we were awakened by the storm, but then we became separated on the way here. Help me find her." He, too, was entreated to stay put.

"We've got to stay together!" It was Iryl Songbrook's voice. "Call out and the others will find us."

"Amanda!" the woman wailed.

Goldmoon began calling out names again, and others joined her chorus. Their words began to cut through the wind. Camilla and Willum appeared at the edge of the group, bundled in cloaks and blankets and carrying a rope. Camilla tied it about her waist, handed the end to Willum, and headed out in search of people lost in the snow.

At the same time, Gair chatted softly to his father, confident the wind and the people's cries would conceal his conversation. "Help me find the children," he urged. "They must be brought to safety first."

There is one nearby, his father replied, and the spirit began guiding his son. Gair kept his eyes closed, wrapped his coat even tighter around him, and trustingly followed the voice in his head ever closer to the cliff.

The elf softly cursed the island as he went, so hot in the summer, so cold in winter. And this blizzard! Despite his travels, he'd never been caught in something so fierce and so cold. His teeth chattered uncontrollably, his face stung horribly, and he imagined his skin was as red as a cherry. He paused for only a moment when something tumbling along in the wind struck his legs and almost made him lose his balance. He plodded on through the deepening snow until he heard the rush of the waves beating the rocks below and heard his father practically scream in his mind for him to stop.

Careful. Kneel down, the elder Graymist instructed. *Be*

very careful. The edge of the cliff is only inches away, and a child is just . . .

"Over the ledge," Gair finished, shouting to hear himself over the wind. "I think I can hear her. Barely." The elf knew it was his acute hearing that allowed him to detect something over the pounding water and the howling wind. "Must have fallen over the side. Couldn't see in this storm." *I can't see in this storm either,* he added to himself.

He crept forward, his bare fingers painfully cold in the snow, feeling for the edge of the cliff.

That's it! his father encouraged. *Off to your right. Just a little farther! That's it . . .*

The elf lay on his stomach, the spine of the book beneath his shirt pressing uncomfortably into his chest. He found the ledge and pulled himself to it, until his head and shoulders hung over the edge and were buffeted all around by the blast of cold and snow. He was certain he heard the girl crying now, soft and desperate for her mother. He called out to her and relied on his hearing and his father's directions to find her.

She was on a shelf several feet below the ledge, and Gair leaned over as far as he safely could, until only his hips and legs were anchoring him against the edge. "Child!" he hollered as loud as his voice could muster, sputtering when the wind whipped snow inside his mouth. His tongue felt thick and stiff from the cold. "Child!" he repeated. The crying stopped, and he felt something brush his fingertips, achingly sore now from exposure. "Grab my hand! I'll pull you up!"

He felt the faint brush of her fingers, then heard wails of "I can't . . . reach it." The elf turned his thoughts inward to his father, whose presence hovered in the elf's mind.

She will not climb up the rocks. She is too frightened. You must leave her, Son. Together we will search for others whom we can save. Her death will be swift, and we will welcome her into our realm. The cold is claiming her even now.

Gair hesitated and opened his eyes slightly. He knew the cliffs were steep, with few handholds in most places, and he couldn't see anything to grab on to. He could see only the never-ending sheet of bone-chilling white. It would be risky.

Too risky, my son. Don't take the chance.

"My friend is always telling me I don't take enough chances," the elf replied as he maneuvered around until he lay parallel to the cliff edge and carefully swung himself over the side. The rocks bit into his fingers, slicing into his skin as the elf struggled to hang on. His feet flailed about along the cliff face until he found a lip of rock so narrow it accommodated only the toes of his boots. He found another handhold and worked himself farther down. The rocks were coated with frost and terribly slippery, but somehow he managed to hold on until he had worked himself down to a shelf. The crying was louder here.

Slowly he inched his way toward where his fretting father said the child cowered. A heartbeat later, a small pair of arms wrapped around his leg and held tight. The crying eased a little.

Gair's fingers walked down the rock, over trails of ice, steadying himself until he could kneel without slipping. He drew the girl into his arms in the same instant he reached inside himself and searched for his mystical strength. He felt his heart, heard it beating even as he heard his father's worried words, sent the thrumming outward to wash over the child and to calm her as he had calmed the boars.

She was trembling from fear and from the cold, and Gair shuddered when he felt around her to make sure she hadn't broken any limbs. He discovered she had on only heavy socks and a nightshirt. He fumbled at the buttons of his own coat and wrapped it around her like a blanket.

"You'll be all right," he said firmly, his mouth against her ear. "I'll get you out of here. What's your name?"

A whisper.

"Amanda? That's a pretty name. I'll get you out of here safely, Amanda."

He closed his eyes again to shut out the white. With one arm, Gair cradled her to his chest, and with the other, he began searching for handholds in the rock. There were small cracks here and there that his aching fingers found, but they were too narrow to get a good grip. He barely felt his fingers as he continued to grope about.

"Damn!" he swore softly. "Father!"

The elder Graymist's words swirled in Gair's head, encouraging him to keep searching. The spirit said he perceived the cliff, but seemed unable to judge a precise path up and could not make out enough details to help with handholds. The elf's sisters joined in the spirit chorus, murmuring that Gair must not give up and that it was not yet time for his essence to join theirs in death.

"Help! Goldmoon!" He hollered loudly, realizing instantly that there was no way the healer or anyone else could hear him. Gair had no idea just how long he'd been gone from the camp. The intense cold and driving snow made it seem like hours. He held his eyes clamped shut, since they were useless to him in the whiteout. "Please," he whimpered to the departed gods as he continued to feel about.

When his sense of touch had all but abandoned him, he found a horizontal crevice just above his head large enough to squeeze most of his hand inside. He did so and pulled himself up slowly, scrambling to find footing against the cliff face, his boots scraping against rock and ice and finding nothing. He lowered himself back down, still clutching the child tightly. "It will be all right, Amanda," he said into the folds of his coat. There was no answer, and he pressed his face into the gap of his coat and opened his eyes. The child looked at him mutely, her lips a ghastly bluish tint and trembling. "My magic can't warm you," he said. "Perhaps Gold-moon can help, but I've got to get you out of here first."

He gritted his teeth and focused all of his strength into his right arm, flexing it and pulling himself up until his chin struck the edge of the crevice and his wrist. He hung there, trying to find something to wedge his boots into, but the leather was too thick and only scraped against the rocks and ice. "Nothing," he cursed as he dropped back down and stared at the cliff. Through the whiteness of the blizzard, he saw only the shadow of the rocky cliff face. He closed his eyes again.

Don't do this! his father warned. *It is not yet your time! Leave her here! Use both your hands to save yourself! Don't do this!*

"I've no intention of dying," Gair told him, as he struggled out of his boots and gasped when the frigid air hit his stocking feet. He tucked the boot tops under his belt at his back. "But I am getting both the child and myself out of here." He clamped his teeth together and again searched for the crevice, wedged his hand into it, and his fingers gripped the rocks. His muscles bunching, he slowly pulled himself and the child up. He flailed his feet around, searching for even the slightest of outcroppings, something he could sense with his toes. The rocks cut through his stockings and slashed at the flesh beneath, the pain keeping him alert and making him more determined.

He continued to wriggle about until his fingers felt numb and he feared he would lose his handhold. At last he found something to wedge his toes into. Plaster-ing himself against the rock face and whispering words of comfort to the child, he cautiously released her, holding her body between his chest and the cliff. He searched with both hands now, finally finding another handhold. He held her again with one arm and pulled himself higher.

At last at the top, he lay down, gasping for breath. Even through the coat, he felt her shiver against his chest, and he struggled to pull his boots back on, all the while cradling her. Finished, Gair slammed his eyes shut again, blotting out the hateful white, and forcing himself to his feet.

"Father!" he yelled, though he knew the spirit could hear his thoughts. "Guide us back! Hurry!"

The elf stumbled along, falling more than once to his knees when he tripped over objects that had been scattered about by the wind. Each time it was harder to get to his feet, which had lost nearly all sensation and continued to move through the snow only because of Gair's force of will and his father's urging.

The wind continued to whistle unmercifully and tauntingly, stinging his face beyond feeling. *Where, Father?* His questions were inside his head now, his lips so horribly chapped he didn't want to move them. *Where?*

The spirit of his father continued to guide his son until Gair heard the cries of Goldmoon's throng and could find the way on his own. *Are there any more lost children?* Gair demanded of his father. The spirit reluctantly told his son where, and Gair thrust the child at Iryl Songbrook and disappeared again into the swirling snow.

* * * * *

Nearly a hundred yards away, Orvago found Jasper. The dwarf was hunkered down behind a large crate, which was shielding him from the worst of the wind. Jasper's eyes were closed and his snow-covered body was drawn together into a ball. The gnoll had to feel around to find the dwarf's arms.

Jasper's eyes popped open wide and he blinked furiously, trying to see through the snow. The dwarf let out a howl when he spotted Orvago's snow- and ice-covered visage. The gnoll rocked back on his haunches, the snow drifting up to his waist. The dwarf howled again and fumbled in the folds of his cloak until his hand found his hammer.

He tugged it free, but suddenly Orvago's paw shot forward, long fingers closing around the head and yanking it away. The gnoll rocked back again and waited, and Jasper blinked once more and finally calmed down.

"Orvago?" The gravelly voice was a whisper in the blizzard. "You startled me."

The gnoll leaned forward, returning the dwarf's hammer and taking his arm. This time Jasper didn't resist. Following the gnoll through drifts that were nearly waist-high for him but came almost to the top of the dwarf's head, he allowed himself to be led to Goldmoon's gathering. The gnoll left the camp again immediately to search for more dwarves, who had a strong scent and were easy to find.

*　*　*　*　*

The blizzard stopped shortly before noon, and Goldmoon and Iryl counted heads. About a dozen people were missing, but a thorough search turned all of them up. Many people were suffering exposure and needed tending. However, despite the fierceness of the storm, there was only one fatality, an elderly man who had frozen to death in the remains of his tent.

The snow seemed impossibly deep. Only the tallest of the building crates reached above the drifts, and though here and there chair legs, tent poles, and cooking pots and pans poked above the snow, the drifts had all but obliterated signs of the settlement. Camilla and Willum searched where their tents had been, looking for their armor. Nearby, the dwarves grumbled that they couldn't find the section of the foundation they'd finished.

By midafternoon, Goldmoon and her followers had retrieved the settlement's horses, uncovered the wagon, and cleared away a swath of snow around it. The gnoll had gathered wood, which, with considerable effort, was coaxed into flame. The settlers gathered close to the fire, thawing out their limbs, murmuring about lost possessions, and offering prayers for the elderly man who died. Jasper fussed over Gair, bandaging his cut hands and chastising him for not wearing warm enough clothing.

"Undoin' all the healin' I did," the dwarf sniffed. "I got better things to do than patch you up all the time. Where's your coat?" More softly, he said. "Heard you saved that little girl on the cliff. Turnin' out to be quite the hero, you are, Gair Graymist. I'm proud of you. An' I guess I'd better stop lecturin' you about takin' more chances. Just don't take too many, okay?"

Gair tried to hide a grin, thanked the dwarf for his ministrations, then headed toward where his tent used to be. He started digging in the snow, looking for his treasured books and any pieces of clothing he could put on to help keep him warm.

Iryl was directing some of the stronger men to pull the settlement's wagon toward where the trail used to be and hitch the horses to it. They finished the task and had started knocking the ice out of the wagon wheel spokes by the time an armored Camilla approached.

"Iryl Songbrook," the Solamnic commander began, "my men and I will help you load the weakest individuals on the wagon and will lead the way back into town."

Willum tromped through the snow behind her, fastening an icy breastplate as he went. Another knight followed in the path he was forging in the snow.

Iryl looked at her curiously. "I don't understand, Commander."

"I said we will help you escort these people back to the port. We can house some of them in your hostel, the rest at the Sentinel. There's a large fireplace, and—"

"I'm the only one leaving," Iryl said. "Everyone else is staying here."

Camilla stared at her.

Goldmoon joined the women. "Commander, Iryl has volunteered to return to town and gather more supplies and to send word to the mainland that we need more—more of everything, I'm afraid."

The knight glared at the healer. "You can't be serious! You can't expect these people to stay out here." She waved her hand at the throng gathered around the fire that the gnoll was continuing to stoke. "Not after that blizzard. You were foolish to be out here in winter to begin with. They'll die of exposure."

"We'll stay together and manage to keep warm. It will be all right."

"These people's lives are in danger here. I won't have it!"

"You have nothing to do with it," Goldmoon returned evenly. "You do not command these people, Lady Weoledge. They are free to do as they wish, and they wish to stay here at the settlement. We've already discussed the matter."

"What settlement, Goldmoon? The blizzard destroyed everything." The knight bristled and took a step forward. Willum grabbed her arm to hold her back. "I don't approve of your mysticism, Goldmoon," Camilla said. "Healing without the gods is preposterous. Blasphemous. I don't approve of this settlement, but these people are mine to watch over, and I'll not have them dying out here because they are too foolish to see that what you are doing is wrong. I have remained civil to you up to this point, since my orders are specific, but my orders do not include allowing these people to die because of your absurd dream."

Jasper approached the confrontation, careful to give the two women room.

"These people are staying," Goldmoon repeated. "I will watch over them."

"Like you watched over the old man who died?" Camilla paused to let her words sink in. "I am returning to the Sentinel." She squared her shoulders. "I am taking all of these people with me." She tramped away from the healer, heading toward the throng gathered around the fire. Jasper moved quickly out of her way just in time to avoid being trampled.

The knight strode purposely into the center of the gathering, glowered at the gnoll, and pointed to the wagon. "The oldest and the youngest of you will ride on the wagon. The rest of you will walk behind it. Gather whatever possessions you can find, and be ready to leave within the hour."

A woman stepped forward, holding the small girl Gair had rescued. "Commander, I appreciate your concern, but I'm staying here." Amanda, still wrapped in Gair's coat, nodded vigorously.

"I don't think you understand," Camilla continued. "I'm not giving you a choice. You are all coming with me."

The woman shook her head. "No. I don't think you understand."

Other voices were added to hers.

"The blizzard was only a minor setback," the woman's husband said. "We'll find our tent and have it up before nightfall."

"Won't take us more'n a few days to clear all this snow away," another man offered.

"We'll pile the snow up around the tents to keep warm." This from a woman who looked like a walking pile of blankets. "All this snow was a blessing in disguise!"

"Won't take us long."

"You can't force us to leave. This is our new home."

"Goldmoon will help us."

"The winter won't last forever."

"Goldmoon will guide us."

"You're welcome to stay with us, Commander. There is room for everyone."

"We're not going anywhere," the woman holding Amanda added firmly.

The knight seethed but managed to keep her temper in check. "This is foolishness," she said finally, the words hissing out between clenched teeth, "and I want no part of it." She paused and caught her breath. "Any of you who are sensible enough to return with me to town, gather your things now."

She whirled, bumping into Willum, who'd moved up behind her. He lost his balance and fell into a snowdrift. He floundered in the snow, trying to get up but succeeding in only burying himself deeper. Camilla groaned in frustration and helped him up, all the while quietly cursing Goldmoon.

"You can't mean that you're done with them," Willum said as he followed her. "Our duty—"

"Our duty is to watch over Goldmoon and these misguided fools. I know what our duty is, Lieutenant, and I'll not shirk it. But I've a letter to write to the Solamnic

Council about Trevor's death, and another letter to write to Trevor's parents. I will send some of the soldiers and a half-dozen knights here to help, and I will follow in a few weeks after I've attended to some other matters. By then perhaps Goldmoon's followers will have tasted more of Schallsea's winter and will have changed their minds. Keep watch over these fools while I am away."

Camilla waited several minutes, standing thigh-deep in the snow. When it became obvious no one would accompany her into town, she turned to the south, where the trail was obliterated by drifts. She ignored the gnoll's wave good-bye and began to trudge through the snow down the trail toward town.

Carrying an armload of snow-covered books, Gair spied her leaving. He hurried to follow, pausing when he drew even with the gnoll. "Orvago, listen. I hope you can understand me."

The gnoll cocked his head.

"These are books, prized possessions that I have a burning desire to read again and again, things you will never understand. I need you to take care of them for me. Please." He thrust the books at the gnoll and reached for a blanket he'd tied like a sash around his waist. Flapping it to chase the last of the snow out of its folds, he tied it about his neck like a cape. "Please. Do you understand?"

The gnoll grinned, a trail of spittle easing over his green-gray lips and freezing before it could fall from his chin.

"Goldmoon!" Gair shouted, turning to get the healer's attention. "I'm going in to town. I'll help gather some supplies, and I'll be back before the week is out." With that, he trundled after the knight, following as fast as his legs would carry him in the path she'd made in the snow. Despite not having to break a path, it took him several minutes to catch up with the Solamnic. When he did, he was quite out of breath.

"I don't require an escort, Mr. Graymist. I am perfectly capable of taking care of myself."

Her pace, fueled by her ire over the entire situation, was demanding, and he labored to stay even with her.

"If I needed an escort, Mr. Graymist, I would have brought Willum along."

"But *I* could use an escort, Lady Camilla," he huffed, "a little Solamnic protection."

"Suit yourself." Her voice quavered, and she slowed her stride.

"There could be bandits in the woods." His fingers drifted into his pocket, feeling the arrowhead he'd taken from the grave. "Though this snow seems a greater threat. No matter. I really have to go into town, and I don't care to travel alone."

You are not traveling alone, my son. Gair's father had opened the door. *I will always be with you.*

* * * * *

At the snow-covered settlement, Jasper made his way slowly toward Goldmoon, practically swimming through the snow. An unaccustomed frown was etched deeply into his broad face.

"Goldmoon," he began as he closed the distance, "the foundation's covered by a mountain of snow. Covered our timber, nails, hammers, everythin'. We can't work in this . . . this . . ." He waved his stumpy arms about as if he were trying to take flight. "This stuff!" He pointed toward a middle-aged female dwarf. "Redstone and I have been talkin' it over, an' we've decided we'll have to wait until spring to do any more buildin'. Until all of this . . . this . . . stuff has melted." Jasper paused to catch his breath. "Spring. Better workin' conditions. Much, much better."

The healer squatted, her lined face even with his. "If you don't want to work under these conditions, I understand, Jasper," she said softly.

The dwarf breathed a sigh of relief. "I told Redstone you'd understand. This blizzard made a mess out of the settlement. Maybe we should follow the knight back into town."

"You can ride on the wagon with Iryl. She's getting ready to go."

"What'll you do? When'll you join us?"

"I'm staying here. I will find others to lead the building project and we will continue in your and Redstone's absence," she added. "I'm an old woman, Jasper, and I've little time in my life to wait for the snow to melt. or to wait for anything else, for that matter."

The dwarf's eyes popped wide with surprise.

"I will find someone else to replace you," she repeated. Her voice was firmer, her eyes clear. "The building project will go on."

"You can't be serious! This blizzard—"

"Brought snow, and snow can be brushed aside. I'll not let the weather stop me. The Citadel of Light will be built." She rose and trod through the snow toward the wagon, where Iryl was checking the horses.

Jasper slapped the heel of his hand against his head. He whirled on his stumpy legs and waved at the dwarves. "Everybody start clearin' away the snow! We've gotta get back to work. Now! Anythin' too wet to use, take it over there by the fire so it can dry out."

At the fire, Goldmoon's followers continued to warm their hands and make plans for putting up their tents again—this time closer together and anchored with more stakes. A few men threw more wood on the fire. Orvago shuffled closer to the flames, the people parting so he wouldn't touch them. He stared at the fire for a few moments, then tossed Gair's books on it. The gnoll grinned wide when he saw that he'd added to the blaze and had helped keep these people warm. "Burning desire," he remembered Gair saying.

Iryl and Goldmoon stood by the wagon. "I'll catch up to Gair and Camilla soon enough," Iryle told Goldmoon, a lilt of laughter in her voice, "though it's going to take a good while to ford through this snow. On second thought, maybe I'll dawdle here a few more moments. Give them some time alone. In town, I'll take whatever I can from the hostel, get the merchants to donate supplies, send word out on whatever ships are in the harbor. I shouldn't be gone too long."

"Be careful," the healer cautioned, motioning for two of the settlement's sentries to accompany her. Goldmoon traced a deep scar by the wagon seat, where a spear had ricocheted off it. Her face was etched with worry. "Be very careful, my friends."

Chapter 7

Reflections

Red Street was neither red nor a street. At best, it could be considered a narrow alley lined with gray cobblestones that ran behind the biggest warehouse off Schallsea's burgeoning merchant district and ended at a stone wall. The three buildings that faced the alley—a leather shop, a tailor's, and a weaver's— were neatly shingled in brown with various shades of yellow, white, and blue trim respectively. There wasn't a shade of red to be seen anywhere. The three buildings that faced away from the street, whose back doors opened onto the alley, were all owned by the same businessman, one Lenerd Smithsin, who also owned Schallsea's newest stable. These buildings were being used as residences for the town's new-comers, who were filling Smithsin's pockets with steel, which he already had plenty of. Smithsin had inherited his buildings from his father, Markus.

Red Street had tickled Gair's ever-present curiosity, and so he sought out its origin, even as he sought out the goods sold along it. He told himself he needed something to occupy his mind other than Lady Camilla, who was busying herself with "Solamnic concerns." So through a string of carefully worded and persistent questions, the elf learned that several decades past a stream had cut through the middle of the port town, which was then little more than a barbarian village. The stream was called Red Creek, named after a Qualinesti elf who homesteaded along its northern bank and who seemed to get along well with the natives. No one Gair chatted with could remember the elf's name, as it was long and difficult to pronounce. They knew that, according to the island's history, the elf dressed only in shades of red, which the natives at that time considered odd for an elf, since the few other elves in the area favored hues of green. Hence, for some reason known only to those long-dead folks, the natives named the stream Red Elf's Creek. It was shortened through the years and slips of the tongue to Red Creek.

As more years passed, and the land changed with the addition of buildings and people who'd moved here from Abanasinia and Southern and Northern Ergoth and elsewhere, the elf moved on to the northern end of the island, and the creek dried up–at least on the surface. Below ground, the water still ran from a crystal-clear spring. So the well outside of the building at which Gair now stood pulled water from what was once Red Elf's Creek. The brightly clad elf who unknowingly had the alley named after him was said to have died roughly a dozen years ago, killed during a misunderstanding with a hunter. Gair considered using his newfound skill to attempt to contact the deceased elf's spirit, and perhaps the spirit of Lenerd Smithsin's father, so he could learn firsthand what the village was like decades ago. He would indeed do just that—but not today. Gair had too many other things to accomplish today.

Gair strode into Logan's Bootery and Leather Shop

and inhaled deeply. The scents of leather and polish pleasantly filled his nostrils. Carefully tooled shoes and boots gleamed on shelves from floor to ceiling along the right-hand wall, embroidered belts and satchels hung along the back on either side of a counter, and leather trousers and shirts were carefully folded on shelves along the left.

"Good day to you sir!" The balding proprietor beamed at the elf. "What can I help you with?"

"Boots, trousers, a few belts." Gair rattled off a considerable list while the proprietor measured his feet and selected a few pairs for the elf to try on. "And a very large belt—something that would go around me two . . . no, make that three times."

His choices made, Gair paid the man generously, then added a tip. "Could you have them delivered? To Smithsin's stable? I've obtained a cart there to transport my purchases."

The man set about accommodating the generous elf, nodding politely as Gair exited the shop and strode to the weaver's across the alley. Here he purchased three dozen blankets, all exquisitely made and practically the weaver's entire stock. He made little fuss about his choices, as they were meant to be hung inside his tent—and inside the tents of the dwarven builders and the Solamnic Knights and soldiers—and so they did not need to be of any particular color. They just needed to be thick. Again he had them delivered to the stable.

His last stop was to the smallest shop, where an elderly man custom-made garments. The elf suspected the owner could have easily afforded more expensive space in a better district. He charged enough for his clothes, and for good reason. The man was an artist with scissors and thread, and the elf envied his talent. Gair pressed him why he stayed on

Red Street when he could certainly increase his sales elsewhere. The man answered that he simply liked it here. It was quiet. He lived upstairs with his wife, worked when he wanted, made a reasonable living— better now with the influx of people coming here to see Goldmoon and the Silver Stair. He had no desire to run a shop in a busier part of town, where he himself would be therefore busier and would be forced to hire others to work for him to keep up with the demand. Too much bookwork, too few days off—and a bigger store meant there would be more snow to clear away from the front door and walk. Gair immediately liked him.

"I need a cloak," the elf began. "Better make that two cloaks."

"Colors?"

"I don't suppose it matters. They just need to be long . . . very, very long."

"You want it to drag on the ground behind you? A fashionable thing, though not very practical, especially in the winter."

"It's not for me," the elf sighed. "It's for . . . an acquaintance. He's nearly seven feet tall, broad shouldered. I'd say twice as thick as I, a trifle more. Make sure it's plenty big. A tunic, too, with very long sleeves. No, make that two of them. And trousers. Make them baggy, to be safe—and make them long."

"Your oversized friend can't come here for a fitting?"

The elf shook his head. "It wouldn't be . . . practical. How soon can you have them done?"

"A few days," the old man replied.

The elf reached into his pocket and extracted an oval-cut emerald. It gleamed enticingly in the light that spilled through the window. "Today?"

The old man's eyes widened, realizing the gem was

worth more than all the garments and fabrics he had on display, probably worth as much as the entire building. "I could alter some garments already finished. Get my wife to help, but to be honest, I still couldn't promise them before sundown."

"Make sure the cloaks have hoods—large hoods. If you've any shirts that are very big, I'd like those, too."

"Certainly, sir."

Gair drifted away to the shelves, pulling down a few cloaks that were roughly his size and a coat to replace the one he'd wrapped around Amanda. He felt the fabric to select the warmest ones, then brought them to the counter. He tugged off the blanket that he'd tied around his neck, passed it to the shopkeeper, and put on one of the cloaks he selected.

"Deliver everything to Smithsin's stable. I've a cart there. And—"

"Yes?"

"Do you know where I might purchase some wax?"

The old man looked at him quizzically.

"My . . . acquaintance . . . has a terrible problem with snoring. Therefore I'm in terrible need for something to stuff in my ears, some strongly scented lamp oil, and some perfumed soap."

* * * * *

"Ah, Father," Gair mused as he left Red Street behind. "The wind that used to race through the Silvanesti Forest pales beside the winter wind that blows here. This wind brings with it only scents of the sea, not the sweet smells of the deep woods."

He followed the main road that ran down to the harbor and listened through the rhythmic rush of the sea against the docks and the cries of hungry gulls to hear the phantom voice of his father.

"Nothing to slow the wind here, you say?" Gair shook his head. "The buildings here are thicker than Silvanesti's oldest trees, Father, and still they don't do much to take the edge off the wind. But spring . . . ah, I suspect spring here will be beautiful. There will be flowers in the spring, everywhere, I'd guess. And I will pick bouquets for Camilla."

The elder Graymist glided at his side and encouraged Gair to look elsewhere for female companionship. *Humans do not live long enough*, his father said. *There is the elf, Iryl Songbrook, to consider. She is pretty, and a Silvanesti besides.*

"How long is enough?" Gair asked. He ignored the stares of a few passersby who thought he was talking to himself. "Long enough to love? I don't know if I love Camilla, but I'm truly smitten with her, Father. I can't get her face out of my mind. I can still feel the softness of her cheek against my lips."

She will join me in the spirit realm before you've a hint of gray in your hair, my son. Humans count their lives in months and years, not decades and centuries. She gives all her wealth to the Solamnics. Foolishness. Look elsewhere.

Gair changed the subject and continued through the town's pristine streets, dashing around the snow swept into piles on corners, chattering endlessly to his father, and ignoring the stares of townsfolk who cast curious glances his way. Goldmoon is not mad, as I am not mad, he mused. My teacher and I simply enjoy conversing with the dead.

He stopped at a bathhouse, where he indulged himself for nearly an hour, discussing the world with his father, all the while thinking about Camilla, and ending his session with a haircut. After a sumptuous late lunch, he made a brief, unplanned stop in a weaponsmith's when he spied an ivory-pommeled broadsword in the window. It wasn't the elf's blade of choice—he favored the more elegant long sword on his hip—but the pommel was exquisite, covered with carvings of pegasi and other fantastical winged creatures, decorated with inlaid platinum and large opals. It was nothing he expected to find in this town, and he intended to hang it in his tent and admire it as one might admire a painting.

Gair's path took him to a silversmith whose shop had just opened this week, and eventually to a scroll merchant. After purchasing rolls of parchment and ink for Goldmoon, he tugged the leather-bound book out from beneath his shirt and opened it. The rubbings he'd made from the trees by the burial grounds were folded neatly inside, as was the sketch he'd made of the mosaics on the elaborate mound. He carefully removed them and spread them out, his fingers avoiding the charcoal so he would not mar the tracings.

"What do you make of these?" he prodded.

The pot-bellied merchant drew close and carefully studied the symbols. "There are translating costs, you realize," he said. His voice was soft, like a harsh whisper.

"Everything costs. How much?"

"One steel. You might think that too high, but . . ."

Gair placed three steel pieces on the counter. "I'd like to know what they mean by day's end."

The scribe laughed and waggled a thick finger at the elf. "You can push all the steel at me you want— I'd certainly like to accept your money. It takes time to do research on something like this, and no amount of coins will cut the hours I'll have to spend digging through my notes and books. I can tell you they're Qué-Nal. That I'll give you for free."

"Qué-Nal," Gair said softly. "So they are indeed the ones who attacked us. But why?"

"Pardon, sir?"

He placed the arrowhead on the counter. "Qué-Nal, too?"

"I deal with words, not weapons, lad. But the Qué-Nal use stone arrowheads and knives. They don't like steel."

"What can you tell me of the Qué-Nal?"

The man exhaled slowly. "They've lived on the island a long time," he began. "Came here from Abanasinia. Most folks around here call 'em barbarians. There's nine main villages on the island, mostly along the east coast, a few small ones inland at the edges of the Barren Hills. A tribe used to live near Castle Vila and—"

"Where's that?"

"North of the Silver Stair. It's nothing but ruins now. Nobody lives there. Anyway, the Qué-Nal are peaceful folks. Don't bother anyone."

Gair edged three more coins toward the man and placed a stone next to the parchment, the one he'd appropriated from one of the burial mounds. He added to it a piece of the carved mosaic from the elaborate mound. "Please translate these as well. How soon?"

"Hard to say. Two, maybe three weeks. I've dozens of orders . . . folks visiting Goldmoon's settlement wanting letters sent back home and such. So I'll have to juggle my time. A little information would help my work, though." The scribe searched beneath his counter for a quill, brought up a piece of parchment, and took down Gair's name. "Where are the symbols from? Locations are important with Qué-Nal writings. Were there other symbols with them?"

Gair didn't reply, pretending not to hear and to be engrossed in the framed, ornate letters on the man's walls.

The scribe scratched his head, leaving a trace of ink on his age-spotted skin. He raised his voice, thinking his customer hadn't heard him. "You see, young elf, a few of the tribes here on the island put precious little to paper. Written language just isn't important to them. Even their history is held in stories. Where are these tracings from?"

Gair shifted back and forth on the balls of his feet. "I am from Goldmoon's settlement," he said finally. "I take my walks to the north, beyond the Lake of Swords and into the woods. I came upon a burial ground in the vicinity." He expected the man to lecture him about the folly of trespassing. The scribe's answer surprised him.

"Interesting places, cemeteries. I find myself studying the stones in the cemetery east of town— made a few rubbings from the small mausoleum there. My wife's buried in that cemetery. If you're into studying such things, there're some interesting gravestones in that cemetery, especially on the south side, where the oldest markers are from the first settlers from Abanasinia. Of course, they're all easy to read, except for the very oldest. The weather's beaten those stones something fierce. Only a handful are Qué-Nal, though more'n enough of 'em died around here, but there's a marker for 'em down by the harbor. Sailors'll point you to it. Don't need to purchase my services for that information either." He continued to study Gair's symbols. "Fascinating. Two weeks, three at the most." He took three coins, pushed the other three back at the elf. "You pay me the rest if I'm successful. You coming back into town? I don't deliver."

"You may take three weeks," Gair said. "I will not be back until then."

*   *   *   *   *

The cart was the sturdiest to be had in the town, and it was practically filled to overflowing with clothes, blankets, food, a few expensive bottles of Porliost wine for himself, a keg of ale for Jasper and Redstone, and various supplies. A carefully wrapped bundle contained a woolen shawl he'd spotted in a window that he thought Goldmoon would like. A similar shawl rested about the shoulders of a woman who'd been admiring it in the shop at the same time, but who didn't have the coins for it. Gair told her to consider it a gift from Goldmoon's settlement. Her thanks made the elf feel surprisingly good. Another bundle tied with colorful ribbons was for one of the settlement's healers who was celebrating a birthday next week. Several small bundles held spices and sugar for the cooks among Goldmoon's followers, and there was the small package in his pocket.

The cart was pulled by a large draft horse with a shaggy coat. Gair intended to give the horse to the farmer's village in the spring to help with the plowing. The dwarves could have the cart, as the elf didn't intend to buy so much again for quite some time. If he did, there were other carts to be acquired, and there was the large wagon at the settlement.

He waited patiently at the horse's side, glancing to the west, where the sun was starting to set, and talking to his sisters. "Where are those clothes?" he mused aloud. He strolled a dozen yards away, toward the docks, glancing often over his shoulder to make sure the cart remained undisturbed. "I wanted to be on my way well before dark. Iryl won't be leaving for two more days. I suppose I could wait for her, but—"

But you want to return to the burial ground? His father intruded on his thoughts.

"Well, yes, and to the ruin of the castle the scribe mentioned."

Neither will be going anywhere, Son. Leaving tonight or tomorrow will make little difference. There is something in town you've yet to see.

Gair huffed, watching his breath rush away from his face in a misty cloud. "The Qué-Nal marker," he said.

Yes. The marker. You should go pay your respects.

A few sailors directed him to it. One lingered beside the marker with him and wiped at some dirt and sand that had become wedged in the crevices of the carved letters and brushed the snow off the top. Even the sailors of Schallsea were fastidious.

"Horrible thing," the sailor began.

Ask him what is so horrible, Gair's sisters urged. The elf had inadvertently opened the door wider.

"The deaths of the Qué-Nal?"

The sailor nodded and scratched his chin. "Horrible thing. Never cared much fer the barbar'ns. They come inta town once in a while. Not often, though. I always steer clear of 'em. Odd ones, ya know, wearin' feathers an' beads, keepin' ta themselves. Not that I blames 'em really. What do we got ta offer 'em?"

"How did they die?"

"Die? They was all massacred."

For several long minutes, Gair pried the sailor with questions, and he listened intently to the answers. Many decades ago only the Qué-Nal and a handful of elves lived on the ground that was to become the port town. According to the few barbarians who still came to town today to trade, it was in the process of becoming a thriving, cooperative village. All of that changed during the War of the Lance. The dragon-armies moved in and slayed all the Qué-Nal they could catch, tying them to boulders and dropping them into the bottom of the deep bay. The dragon-armies then settled in, using the island—and the port in particular—as a staging area for their military campaigns to the east and west.

The sailor pointed to the Sentinel southeast of the last dock. "'Twas the Blue Dragonarmy what built the docks. Some of 'em are still used today. Built that stronghold, too, an' the tower hooked ta it. Never quite finished it, though, 'fore they moved out. There's talk the Solamnic Knights what moved in might hire some dwarven engineers ta finish it."

"The Qué-Nal never returned after the war?"

The sailor shook his head. "Nah. The ones what survived the massacre all headed north and south and west and scattered into a buncha villages along the coast. Town here was taken over after the war by settlers from Abanasinia, New Coast, some from Southlund, I guess. A coupla folks are from Southern Ergoth. An' Goldmoon's people are from all over, I unnerstand. The Qué-Nal are a superstitious bunch, an' maybe rightly so. They wouldn't come back here ta live 'cause they say the bay's haunted with the spirits of the men, women, an' children who were drowned by the dragonarmies. They say the spirits are restless on account a how horribly they died. At least the spirits haven't bothered me none. Don't seem ta bother the fishin' neither."

The sailor moved on, and Gair stared at the stone marker. *In Memory of the Qué-Nal, Whose Lives Were Cut Short by Darkness.* The voices of his sisters faded, leaving him alone with his thoughts for several minutes. He stretched out with his mind, even as his fingers reached out to touch the carved letters.

"Who were you?" he asked. "Are you truly restless?" His senses floated away from him, touching the stone and stretching to the ground beneath his feet, then flowed toward the bay. He crept toward the edge of the shore until the tips of his boots touched the water. He stared down at his reflection, distorted by the rippling water. "Are your spirits tied to the place where you died? Will you speak to me?" The elf's heartbeat slowed to accommodate the spell, and his keen ears shifted their perception of the world around him. He continued to work the magic tentatively, unsure of what would happen and uncertain if he could contact spirits whom he had never met in life.

He persisted. Concentrated. Directed more energy into the enchantment. Nothing . . . There! Finally he heard something, so faint he thought it was the winter wind whistling around his ears. He focused on it. Screaming, soft at first, as if it were far away, then growing louder and more horrifying. Dozens upon dozens of screaming voices. He closed his eyes to help him concentrate and separate the sounds. Unnoticed, his reflection in the water became grossly distorted as the ripples increased. Gair focused on the distant sounds, picking out the cries of terrified children, the pleas of men to spare their families. He heard dozens upon dozens of last gulping breaths, heard mental prayers to the gods who were still in the world at that time but never answered the Qué-Nal. He saw faces sinking beneath the water—men, women, children so young they could barely walk. They *could* die. All of them could, and did, die.

He tried to contact them, any of them. It wasn't at all like talking with his father. Perhaps they couldn't see him or hear him. Maybe he needed to know their names to really establish contact. The elf intensified the spell by forcing all of his energy into it, determined to reach one of them, and steadying himself when his limbs grew weak. Then suddenly he felt a heaviness on his chest, the burning feel of tight ropes about his wrists and ankles. He sensed himself being pulled into the harbor with them, and he gasped for breath.

"Gair!" an unfamiliar voice called.

"You wish to talk to us?" the wind seemed to say. "Join us!"

"Stop! I can't breathe! Who are you? Don't do this! Who—"

"Gair!" the call repeated, intruding on his spell and rousing him. "Gair Graymist!"

The elf snarled as the spirits he'd been so close to rushed away and his senses returned to the present. He tried for an instant to regain contact, but the moment was lost.

"Sir! Oh, sorry to bother you, Mr. Graymist. I . . . uh. . . ." The stableboy looked uncertainly at the elf. "Your last order just arrived, sir. When I saw you walk down here a few minutes ago, I kept the stable open to watch for it."

Gair's expression softened. "Thank you for your attentiveness."

He followed the boy back to the stable. The sun was an orange sliver against the choppy bay by the time he and the youth were able to effect the considerable amount of pushing and rearranging required to make the large packages of garments fit inside the cart.

He felt wetness on his hand, a melting snowflake, and looked to the sky. It had begun to snow again, fat, wet flakes. The sky was darkening with the coming of night and the thickening clouds. The elf's expression darkened, too.

"I don't want to be caught in another blizzard," he growled softly.

"Sir? It's just a few flakes."

"It could herald worse to come." He let out a deep breath and handed the reins of the horse to the stableboy. "Stable the horse for me, please," he said, "and stow the cart and belongings. I will leave in two days with Iryl Songbrook. Perhaps fair Camilla will let me sleep in front of that fire she mentioned. Perhaps she will share it with me."

He turned to study the Sentinel.

I *thought you wanted to be on your way*, the elder Graymist intruded again. *You've seen the marker. Nothing else holds your interest here.*

"You pointed out there is no hurry. The burial grounds is not going anywhere."

You are looking for an excuse to visit with the human again.

"Yes," Gair said simply, ignoring the bewildered look of the stableboy. He felt in his pocket for the small package resting there. "Yes indeed."

Chapter 8

Darkhunter

The winter wind prowled angrily through the tower chamber, howling at every corner and bringing a biting cold on its tail. There were no motes of dust for it to chase. The room was spotless, and there was little furniture for it to slip under and whistle around—only a desk, stark in design, a straight-backed chair that offered no hint of comfort, and a narrow bed with a quilt so tightly in place it could toy with only a few frayed threads.

There were no rugs on the stone floor, no pictures on the walls, no knickknacks or sentimental remembrances of youth—nothing that could be disturbed by the wind, and nothing that could distract the room's occupant.

Camilla stood alone at the window, seemingly mindless of the frigid breeze that played across her face and teased her freshly washed hair. Her slender fingers were wrapped around the edge of the sill, and her gray eyes, which mirrored the shade of the early morning sky, were narrowed in contemplation.

She inhaled sharply at the rap on her door, turned, and nodded as a primly dressed woman entered, balancing a silver tray on one hand.

"Mornin', Lady Weoledge," the woman chirped. She hurried to the desk, set the tray down, and arranged the silverware precisely upon a linen napkin. She hummed as she moved to the window and pulled the shutters closed, leaving the blinds on one side open just enough for some light to spill in. "That wind! Don't want your breakfast to get cold, do you, lady? Sausage and shirred eggs, fixed just the way you like them, with a bit of sharp cheese. Sugared grapes, too. Do eat. Please, Camilla." This last she added softly. "At least somethin'. Usually you only pick at your plate—except for these past two nights when your young gentlemen dined with us. He should sup with us every night. So polite. And handsome."

"Judeth . . ." Camilla warned.

"Well," the woman huffed, throwing back her shoulders and sticking out her ample chest. "I worry about you, lady. Someone has to."

Camilla offered her a warm smile. "I don't need to be the object of anyone's concern, Judeth. People should be concerned, instead, about Goldmoon."

"Isn't your young man from Goldmoon's settlement?"

Camilla frowned. "He's not my young man, Judeth. He's one of Goldmoon's students. I was simply extending him the courtesy of a warm place to sleep."

Judeth slyly winked. "Courtesy," she tittered. "And you hold hands with everyone you let sleep in front of our fireplace? In all the years I've known you, Camilla, I've never seen you so taken with someone."

The knight blushed.

"I think he fancies you, too," the woman continued.

The knight's fingers fluttered up to her neck, where a thin silver chain and a heart-shaped charm dangled. "A heart, as you've stolen mine," she recalled Gair telling her last night as he fastened it around her neck.

"Indeed, he fancies you quite a bit," Judeth needled. "It's about time there was something in your life other than your order." She poured a cup of tea. The steam rose in a twisting spiral in the chilly room, releasing the scent of orange peel. She stepped back, smoothing her apron with her hands. "Fancies you quite a bit, he does. Pity he said he'll be leaving soon. Within the hour, he told me. Will you be going with him to the settlement?"

She shook her head. "I'm sending a dozen soldiers with him for reinforcements."

"I would think you'd want to make sure they get settled." Judeth winked at her.

"I've other concerns."

The servant drew herself up to her full height, still a head shorter than Camilla. "Well, then, I do hope he comes back. Can I get you anything else, Lady Weoledge?"

"Thank you, no, Judeth."

Camilla sat at the desk, speared a piece of sausage, and watched the woman bustle out of the room, closing the door behind her. Camilla studied the meat as Judeth's footsteps receded down the stairwell beyond, actually considered eating it, then decided against it.

"Goldmoon." She uttered the word as a curse. To mollify Judith, Camilla stirred her eggs to make it look as if she'd at least nibbled at something, dropped the fork, and pushed away from the desk. She returned to the window and opened the shutters to stare down again at the town. Her fingers tightened on the sill until her knuckles grew white, the muscles of her neck knotted tightly with tension.

At the docks, she spotted a carrack raising its sails. It had arrived yesterday from the city of New Ports, far across the bay to the west, bringing in its belly more than a dozen people who'd sold their worldly goods and intended to build a new life here on Schallsea

Island. The ship was returning to New Ports or some other mainland coastal city, and Camilla knew it would come back again—with more people and with all manner of supplies for Goldmoon. Iryl had spoken with the captain a long time this morning, and there would be other ships. Schallsea's harbor was too deep to freeze over even in the coldest of winters.

"Blasphemy," Camilla muttered. "What Goldmoon's doing is blasphemy. Her magic of the heart will only push people away from the true gods, though they are absent. Someday the gods will return."

She whirled and paced the length of the room, her boot heels clicking rhythmically over the stone. Passing by her desk, she paused to snatch up the cup of tea, which was growing tepid. She held it briefly, stared at her reflection in the pale brown surface. She let out a long breath, watched the ripples in the tea disturb her image, then downed all of it in one long gulp. It soothed her throat but did nothing to ease her ire. "Blasphemy." She resumed her pacing.

"People coming here, using their last steel pieces to do so. People camping in the snow, freezing to death in blizzards. Misguided, foolish people. Healing without the gods. Blasphemy." Camilla's fingers fluttered to her hip, closed about the pommel of a sword that hung there. "I cannot let Goldmoon build this citadel. I cannot let her ruin so many people's lives."

She returned to her desk, pushing aside the breakfast tray. Tugging open a narrow drawer, she retrieved a bottle of ink, a quill, a length of black ribbon, and a sheet of fine parchment watermarked with a rose wrapped around the blade of a sword. Camilla carefully considered each sentence she put to the paper. Her handwriting was painstakingly meticulous, the letters like soldiers marching clearly and evenly across the page. Finished, she cleaned the quill and replaced it

and the ink in the drawer, blew on the parchment—
even though the chill wind had already dried the ink—
then carefully rolled it and tied it with the ribbon.

She rose and pushed the chair in close to the desk.
"Goldmoon will not build her Citadel of Light on this
island," she said. "It's blasphemy."

* * * * *

Goldmoon stood next to Gair at the construction site,
watching the dwarves hard at work erecting support
posts on the outside of the building. The posts would
help strengthen the structure so additional floors could
be placed on top of it. The harness of Gair's draft horse
had been attached to a rope and pulley system, and the
animal was aiding in raising beams to the second floor
by walking forward on command.

Most of Goldmoon's followers were helping, as Gair
had been, too, until he allowed himself this brief break.
They were trimming boards and stacking lumber that
would make up the walls and ceiling of the second
floor, and they were earnestly doing their best to follow
the dwarves' instructions.

Within a day, two at the most, the basement and first
floor of the building would be finished enough to move
many families into it. A thin woman who used to sell
bait in the port town was applying a thick resin
between the outer boards. The mixture, Redstone's
devising, would keep out the wind and seal the structure and at the same time help protect the wood from
warping because of moisture. On the roof, what would
become the floor of the second level, twin brothers who
used to run a butcher's shop in Solace were spreading
more of the resin. Their faces, red from the cold, were
identical except for a scar on the left cheek of the man
who claimed to be a minute older. They hollered down

a good morning practically in unison to Goldmoon and continued their work.

The building looked boxy, but was large and impressive, bigger than the new stable in town, and according to Jasper and Redstone, built much better, despite much of it going up during freezing temperatures. With the spring, it would be trimmed and finished properly, the female dwarf explained, adding proudly that the final touches would be truly impressive.

Already people were inside working on rooms. A family of six, all blond, hinting that they came from the island of Christyne, busied themselves applying a plasterlike mixture to the walls. They sang as they worked, the youngest off-key and loud. Also inside a trio of dwarven brewers from Thorbardin sanded the floor and softly grumbled about the child's singing, though they did so with a hint of amusement in their gruff voices.

"What about a winder?" A stocky man in a threadbare coat wandered inside. He had a thick piece of charcoal in his hand, and he paced about nervously. "Can't plaster ever'thing iffen yer gonna have a winder in here. I can draw it in fer you." The man claimed to be an artist from Solace who had fallen on hard times and had decided to throw in his lot with Goldmoon's followers. Sketches of the people he'd drawn hung in several tents. "I'll make a round one, nice'n pretty."

"No 'winders' in this building," one of the Thorbardin dwarves told him. "At least not on this level."

The man shrugged and thrust the charcoal in his coat pocket. "Can't spread resin," he said as he stood over the dwarves and watched them work. "Stuff makes my hands itch. Can I help you here? I wanna do something."

One of the dwarves tugged on the man's coat, indicating he should kneel. He passed the fellow a sanding stone and whispered, "You can help us as long as you'd like. Just no singing . . . okay?"

The sound of hammers drifted up from the basement. Fishermen from the Schallsea port town were boxing off more rooms down there. They had volunteered to help because they said the weather was too cold to take their boats out onto the bay. They were a cheerful lot, though not the most talented with hammers and nails, and they were closely supervised by one of Jasper's friends.

Two young girls threaded their way into the building, passing biscuits to the dwarves and the artist, setting a plateful in front of the family from Christyne. They carried more to the people downstairs. On their way out, they dawdled as they watched a burly woman working on stairs that would lead to the upper floors.

Outside, a dozen men were hard at work making the walls that would be hoisted up to the second story and nailed in place. They were a varied lot: men young enough that some would call them children, old men that age had bent and who favored clothes that looked as worn as themselves. Everyone worked at his own pace, resting when he needed to and never complaining. Even a patrician with rings on every finger worked hard, outfitted in fur-trimmed boots and a sealskin coat. He was at the shoulder of Roeland, the miller who had given up his shop to join the assembly. Roeland never took a day off and worked until he was too tired to lift a hammer, and though his clothes were not the warmest, he never complained about the cold.

The largest worker wore a blood-red woolen cloak that hung to his ankles and shadowed his face. The boots on his feet were new, a rich brown leather, the tips of which had been cut off and replaced with the ends of heavy wool socks, or else his hairy gray-green feet would never have fit inside. His tunic was a dark purple shade, gathered at his waist with a thick tan belt. The sleeves were of a purple a few shades lighter, and except when they were pushed up to his elbows, as they were now, they covered all but the ends of his claws. His trousers, which fit surprisingly well, were forest green, with deep pockets roomy enough to hold hammers and nails.

Orvago presented an all-too-colorful picture for Gair's tastes. The tailor had provided quite a bundle of oversized garments, many of which were reasonably color-coordinated, given the short notice. However, the gnoll favored things that clashed, reveling in putting together outfits that were visually disturbing.

Orvago had growled about the clothes for the first two days. However, after a stern but gentle lecture from Gair, the gnoll seemed more accepting of the outfits. The people in the settlement didn't stare quite so long when he was dressed in the human garb, and the occasional visitors from town, which prompted him to roll down his sleeves and retreat into his hood, simply thought he was a very big man.

Goldmoon's followers were gradually getting used to the gnoll, and even those who initially opposed his presence had to admit he was useful to have around. His exceptional hearing and sense of smell made him a natural sentry. He could carry as much as three men, which made him a boon at the construction site. Unfortunately, he was also sometimes as clumsy as any three men, and hence everyone gave him a wide berth when he was toting logs. He was not such a bad sort after all, they decided.

"Watch out!" Jasper hollered.

Orvago had plucked up a stack of finished boards. As he carried them to where Jasper pointed, he inadvertently clunked three dwarves in the head along the way. The builders rubbed their noggins and glared at the oblivious gnoll. Jasper made apologies for Orvago as the gnoll retrieved a second stack of boards and accidentally knocked over Redstone, who was trying to assist him.

Jasper mouthed "I'm sorry" to her as she struggled to her feet, then motioned where the gnoll should put this load. Orvago was quick to comply, dropping the wood with a clatter. He cocked his hairy head, looking for new instructions. His upper lip curled back and he snarled softly. A ridge of hair stood up on the top of his head, and his nose quivered. He padded toward the edge of the construction site, eyes locked onto the pines in the distance. Jasper followed him, his hand on his hammer.

The situation was not lost on Goldmoon and Gair. They watched the gnoll move closer to the trees, with Jasper following, the snow practically thigh-high on the dwarf.

Suddenly a hawk cried and rose from the pines, scattering other nearby birds. They flew over the settlement and dropped down over the cliff toward the sea. The gnoll cocked his head again and sniffed the wind, growled louder, and he eventually returned to the construction site, accidentally knocking over a kender who was carrying a sack of nails.

"I wonder what that was all about?" Gair mused.

Goldmoon's face showed concern. "I don't know," she answered, "but I'm going to double the sentries tonight, just in case."

The elf returned to planing boards, something he wasn't especially good at. He quickly covered his smile when he spotted the gnoll dropping a log on the foot of an unsuspecting dwarf. "Orvago," the elf whispered. "When the gods created gnolls, they must have—" Gair scowled as an internal voice interrupted his train of thought. "I like the creature well enough, Father."

Like a boy enjoys the company of a pet dog. The elder Graymist had opened the door and intruded on his son's ruminations. *He is an animal, and you share your tent with him.*

"I'm curious about him, that's all," Gair replied. The elf didn't see Jasper looking quizzically at him, so he continued. "I want to know where he came from and how he came to be on this island. And I want to know about that flag one of his fellows was wearing. . . ."

And you think you will gain that information by sharing your tent?

Gair shrugged. "Possibly. Besides, I doubt that anyone else would take him in."

You are too kind.

* * * * *

"Another shipment." Camilla stood on the docks, watching workers unload crates and bins, all destined for Goldmoon's settlement.

"Any word, Commander?" the young knight at her side was attentively watching the activities on the dock. "It's been nearly four weeks since you sent that letter to the Solamnic Council."

She shook her head.

"It shouldn't be much longer, Commander," he offered cheerfully, "and then Goldmoon will be gone, and you will rest easier. You won't have to come to the dock every day and watch for ships, and we can concentrate solely on protecting the people in this port."

She folded her arms across her chest, covering up part of the sword etching on her breastplate and continuing to stare out across the water, watching a white speck on the horizon. It grew to be a tiny flag, signaling the arrival of yet another ship that she feared carried more fanatics who wanted to see Goldmoon and the

Silver Stair. There was little room left for newcomers in town, though the carpenters were much closer now to finishing the new row of houses, working feverishly in spite of the weather.

"Shall I return to the Sentinel, Commander?"

She didn't answer. She was watching the ship that was closing on the harbor. It carried a Solamnic flag.

* * * * *

It had been four weeks since Gair had taken his etchings to the scribe in the port, and the elf was upset that he had not been presented with the opportunity to return to the town. Everyone had been consumed by the building project. Still, he intended to head back tomorrow and see if the man was finished—and visit Camilla. He had hoped she would have returned to the settlement by now.

Tonight he had another destination. The elf stole away from the construction site, where work was progressing on the third story. He headed straight northeast, not following any trail this time. He had planned to visit the burial ground before now, but Goldmoon had been instructing her students in the various nuances of mysticism in the evenings—after work ceased on the citadel. By the time her classes ended, he was tired, his muscles sore from sanding and cutting, and turned in, but there were no classes this night. The aged healer was spending the evening chatting with the dwarves, and though his muscles were still sore, his curiosity was at fever pitch.

"What do the spirits think of Goldmoon and her Citadel of Light?" The elf scowled. His father's spirit would not answer. Neither had he answered Gair's most pressing and oft-repeated questions: Where do spirits dwell? Is your existence like life as dwellers of

Krynn know it? Or is it better or worse? Do all spirits drift in the same realm?

Gair tried another tack as the campfire lights from the settlement grew smaller. "Do you know Riverwind? Goldmoon talks to him often." To this, his father finally answered no.

It had started to snow again. The flakes were large, and without the wind to drive them, they drifted down lazily, settling on the backs of Gair's hands and melting instantly. His breath feathered away from his face, which he turned up to glance at the clouds overhead. It was a beautiful night, and not as cold as the past few had been. He allowed himself to enjoy his surroundings as he moved farther away from the settlement.

"Do you miss the feel of the snow, Father? The feel of the breeze? Can you smell the earth? What is your misty realm like? Are all of the spirits who in life walked on Krynn in your same misty dimension, Father? Are the spirits of dragons there, too? The gods—do you sense any trace of them?"

As before, he received no answer to any of those questions, and so he continued toward the Qué-Nal burial ground, chattering, unanswered, to his father about his current activities as a carpenter, his captivation with Camilla, and the advanced healing magic he was studying. As he drew near the circle, he stopped talking, not wanting to alert any living Qué-Nal who might be nearby.

Again I am being too cautious, he told himself. This was his fourth late-night visit to the grounds, and he'd never encountered any living souls there. "Perhaps the barbarians believe the place haunted at night, foolishly thinking spirits roam only when the sun goes down."

Only some spirits are more powerful then, his father said.

The elf paused. "What do you mean?"

No answer.

Gair crouched at the edge of the clearing, watching the snow come down, a little harder now. "What do you mean, Father?"

Again nothing.

"So you only talk to me when it suits you? Just like when you were alive, dear father." Sighing, Gair unbuckled his sword belt and laid his weapon against a tree, removed his new heavy coat, and draped it over a branch. He wanted to move with less encumbrance, and it wasn't quite as cold tonight. Indeed, the snowflakes melting against his skin invigorated him. He slipped into the circle and crept from mound to mound, noting that there had been no new additions since his last visit. The Qué-Nal were very unlike the Abanasinian barbarians from which they sprang, the elf had learned by questioning some of Goldmoon's older followers. The tribes on the mainland built walled burial chambers to house their dead. The Qué-Nal kept the bodies of their people closer to the land they cherished. They saved the buildings for the living.

The elf knelt by the old stone-covered mound, brushing away the snow and tracing the mosaic patterns. "Who were you?" he whispered to the mound's occupant. "Why is your grave more impressive than any others here? Father, can you sense this spirit? Was he a king? A queen? A chieftain?"

The elder Graymist offered no reply.

"Well, perhaps now I can sense who rests beneath."

Gair placed his hands where he suspected the body's heart rested. It was an unnecessary gesture, he knew, but he did it nonetheless. "Who were you?" he repeated as his senses slipped from his mind down his arms and into his fingers, into the etched stones, and then into the cold, cold earth. Deeper they went, past the husks of insects and past the pebbles that covered a shrouded form. Only bones were beneath the cloth. His mind sensed brittle, yellowed bones that were cracked in several places. Was the individual a warrior who died in battle? Were the bones splintered in a fight? His mind probed further, examining the tattered cloth that clung to the bones, ornate for a barbarian, embroidered with symbols. Was the individual old? Had the cruel years broken his body?

"Who were you? *What* were you? What were your dreams, your hopes? Did you die after fulfilling your plans? Did you die too soon? Were you old? Sick?"

He sensed no presence, no energy as he had when he first contacted his father and his sisters. Nothing.

"I am coming to believe this 'dark mysticism,' as Goldmoon calls it, works only on those you knew in life," he whispered.

Frustrated, he decided to at least do a little exploring while he was here. He directed his senses to drift beyond the bones beneath him to nearby mounds, seeking to learn if these corpses were also ornately garbed. Through the cold, heavy earth his mind wandered, briefly touching bodies in various states of decay. All were wrapped in cloth, some of which was thick and brocaded, as if it belonged to a merchant or an entertainer from the port town, likely meaning it was something the person in life had traded for or purchased. None were so embroidered with symbols as the cloth around the form that lay beneath the elaborate mound.

"Who were you?"

His mind stretched to other mounds, and he touched bits of simple jewelry here and there and focused on them. Primitive, he decided, but some were beautiful despite their primitiveness—hammered silver bracelets etched with leaves and stick-figure animals. A deer. A flock of birds in flight. He was amazed at the details he could absorb through his spell. Of course, he'd continually made adjustments to the magic since Goldmoon had taught him how to contact spirits, as he was interested in their realm, not just in the spirits themselves. He had not counted on the magic revealing so much. It was as if he could see through walls, through years, through worlds. He just could not contact strangers.

Gair looked closer, spotting what amounted to a jeweler's mark. It was on the inside of a bracelet worn by what had been a tall young woman. All of the Qué-Nal were on the tall side, lean and muscular, according to the descriptions of them he'd gotten from the folks in port. That would fit with their Qué-Shu counterparts. However, this woman had been especially tall. Around her neck was what appeared to be a silver necklace so thick it looked like a collar. There were tiny holes along the bottom of the necklace, and from them dangled rotting strings of leather, and in turn from them dangled moldy feathers. He imagined what her face had looked like: high cheekbones, a proud expression. Somehow he knew she was a chieftain's daughter.

"Beautiful," he hushed. "Did any of your dreams come true when you walked this land? What had you hoped to accomplish in this world? Was yours a good life? Were you loved? Happy?"

No answer.

Again his mind drifted, this time to the most recent mound, the one that on his previous visit he determined held the form of a child. Perhaps this time he could tell what she died of. His senses floated over her body, over her skin, which he knew had once been tan and unblemished, over her face, down her neck. There! He detected a swollenness that had nothing to do with a corpse bloating or decomposing. A sign of illness, one that should have been curable, a childhood malady.

"Had they no healers? Or had the disease simply spread throughout the child's body before someone sensed its seriousness and tried to do something?" he mused aloud. There was a strange substance on the skin, the remnants of a poultice, he finally determined. "So someone had tried to treat the child, but he was unsuccessful. So young to die."

The features he pictured were truly amazing. He continued his mental explorations, never leaving the side of the mosaic-covered mound. Some in the clearing had died of old age, which somehow made death a little more palatable to the elf. Some died from harsh diseases, a few from what Gair assumed were falls; necks or backs were broken. One died from a sword thrust to his chest, the splintered ribs telling the tale. Another had two arrowheads resting amid the bones. The wooden shafts of the weapons that killed him had rotted away.

"Who killed you? Do their bones rest here, too?"

No answer. There never would be an answer, he sensed, because he hadn't known them.

There were three whom he could not begin to guess at what they succumbed to, though he suspected he could eventually determine that he could if he spent enough time and mystical energy here. Neither could he tell what had killed the man in the ornate mound. Perhaps he would focus all of his initiative here.

"Who were you?"

Darkhunter, the spirit replied.

Gair's heart soared. He had contacted a spirit—the essence of someone he had not known in life, a complete stranger. The door was opening wider for him, he knew. Next he would talk to the elf of Red Creek, to Lenerd Smithsin's father, and to the Qué-Nal who drowned at the hands of the Blue Dragonarmy in the Schallsea harbor, perhaps now able to shut out their screams and hold a reasonable conversation with them. He would ask them all about what, precisely, rested beyond this life, and about what their lives on Krynn were like. If his father would not give him the answers, perhaps strangers would.

I am Darkhunter, the spirit repeated, *and you are Gair Graymist, puppet of the healer Goldmoon*. The spirit pulled the names—and more—from the elf's mind. *My people hate the Qué-Shu. My people will drive your mentor from the land or drive her to her death, her spirit to be tormented forever. Do not get in their way or you will fall with her.*

The questions instantly drained from Gair's mind, and he felt chilled, the sensation not at all a result of the cold. A shiver raced down his spine and his eyes snapped wide open. Calm yourself, he scolded. "The spirit cannot harm me, nor will it frighten me. The spirit is of another realm. Goldmoon is safe."

From the dead, she is safe, the spirit continued. *But not from the living.*

The elf concentrated on his breathing, then focused all his efforts on the mound beneath his fingertips, searching the form more closely, discovering bits of jewelry against the bones of the wrist, semiprecious stones on the numerous heavy bracelets. Jade and—he studied them more intently—jade and moonstone, garnet and onyx. More jewelry lay about the neck, silver and gold chains, not of Qué-Nal make, elaborate, such as would be found in the large cities of Palanthas, Silvanost, and Solanthus. They were covered with gems—mostly garnets, but pieces of agate and peridot, too, stones not naturally available on this island or from Abanasinia. A bit more at ease now, the questions started returning.

"Your necklaces and bracelets were gifts? Gifts to an important man? Purchases?"

Conquests. I took them from those I vanquished. As Goldmoon will be vanquished. If you wish to save her, puppet, make her leave the island.

Gair shivered again and focused on the jewelry.

141

The jewelry was valuable and would have netted a tribe considerable food and goods in trade. But the tribe had buried them with the man—because he was so important. A warrior. A chief? A king?

They buried them with me because they feared to take anything from me, even in death.

"Perhaps," the elf conceded. "All powerful men are feared and respected, but they honored you by wrapping your body in this embroidered cloth and covering your mound with these carved stones."

One of which you stole.

Gair's mouth fell open. So the spirit had been aware of his son's activities on his previous visit. Were all the spirits here so aware? he wondered. All the spirits everywhere? Were the eyes of a hundred dead men on him now? I should end this, Gair thought.

End this? But there is so much left of the night.

The air around him felt thick, and where the snow fell directly in front of him, it did not melt. The elf couldn't see the man, not as he could see images of his father and his sisters, and not as Goldmoon could see Riverwind, he was certain. Yet he sensed the spirit was right in front of him.

Do you fear me, young elf? Do you entertain thoughts of leaving because you are afraid?

For some reason, the elf did. Nevertheless, he said, "No."

You should be afraid.

"I have nothing to fear from the dead." He tarried over the mound. "Still, I should end this soon," he said, "and get back to the settlement, but not just yet. Just a little longer. Another question or two of this Dark-hunter."

His mind drifted up to the skeleton's face, and he pictured what the man had looked like in life. If the spirit would not show himself, Gair would use his mystical senses to gain an image. Broad-faced, he had a long, straight nose and dark eyes.

Eyes that Gair felt were directed at him.

"Why do you hate Goldmoon, Darkhunter? You do not know her. You died before she came to this island."

Before she was born. She is a Qué-Shu, that much I have pulled from your mind, and that is enough reason to hate her. There are living who hate her, too. Their blood boils at her presence.

Gair focused harder on the remains. Darkhunter had eyebrows that were thick and muddy brown, like the shaggy mane of hair that had once covered the man's head. Blood-soaked beads and feathers were braided down its length along the sides of his angular head, and from the ends of the braids hung polished shells. His lips were thin, set in death as if they were in a perpetual sneer.

Gair felt as if the corpse was sneering at him.

"Goldmoon means no one harm."

But my people mean to harm her. I sense their thoughts, as I sense yours. I sense their anger, and I know their plans. Shadowwalker leads them.

"Enough!" Gair felt the spirit move closer still, felt a chill so intense and unnatural that he gritted his teeth. "Enough! No more questions. I will have no more to do with you!" The elf spat the words as he pulled his hands off the mosaic stones and stepped away from the mound, slamming shut the door between this world and the realm of spirits. "Enough of my curiosity this night. Some doors are better left closed," he said, repeating Goldmoon's words. His breath was ragged, puffing away from his face and melting the snow before it could touch the ground, but on Darkhunter's mound, a thin coating of new snow remained, as if it were colder than the other mounds.

He hurried to the edge of the clearing, still feeling

unnaturally chill. He sensed that a bit of Darkhunter's foulness had settled itself in the pit of his stomach. He felt dirty. "Footprints." He cursed himself and retraced his path, remembering to cover his tracks and grab his coat and long sword. "No more visits here," he admonished himself. "I'll keep my conversations to the spirits I know—at least for a while. Father?"

Even that spirit was distant now, the door firmly closed and locked. "All right," he said, needing to hear his own voice. He forced his heart to slow, his breathing to become regular. He used the enchantment Goldmoon had taught him to calm himself. "I'll talk to you later, Father. I'll open the door just a crack when I'm far from here and a few hours have passed."

He left the clearing by backing away, keeping his eyes on the mounds and checking one more time to make sure his tracks had been covered, and then he raced toward the settlement. He paid little heed to the ground he traveled over now, not caring if his boot heels crunched over crusty snow or on fallen nuts or twigs. It was, he'd guessed, five miles or so between the burial ground and the construction site. He'd be back in his tent well before dawn, and with luck, Orvago would be sleeping soundly.

I need time to think, he mused. I must tell Goldmoon about the Qué-Nal—that it was they who attacked us weeks ago. Warn her that someone named Shadowwalker means to somehow do her harm. What should I say? How should I tell her I know all about this?

The questions whirled in his mind as he continued headlong toward the settlement, guided by the central campfire, which was especially large for such a late hour.

"They must be celebrating something," Gair said. "Perhaps I'll join them and take my mind off spirits." As the elf neared, his thoughts of merriment turned to horror. It wasn't the central campfire he'd spied. It was the construction site. The building that everyone had labored so diligently to complete was on fire.

Chapter 9

Ashes

Gair raced forward, churning through the drifts until he came upon a path that seemed to head straight toward the blaze. As he ran, he took in the shouts and cries filling the air, the crackling of the flames. The entire settlement was awake, and panic ruled.

He could distinguish no one voice, which was what he was trying to do in hope of locating Goldmoon. So many people were shouting, arguing, screaming. Children were wailing, and parents were too preoccupied to silence them. Only a few words managed to rise above the din, and these seemed to be shouted orders. The elf closed with the crowd and slowly began pushing his way through it closer to the center of the chaos. As he went, he felt the air become warmer from the heat of the fire. His boots sloshed in snow that was melting.

Three stories of flames illuminated the evening sky. Like an orange-red waterfall, the fire seemed to pour from the roof and down the walls, sparking and snapping angrily as if it were some great, wrathful beast.

Those with tents closest to the citadel were taking them down as quickly as possible, fingers madly fumbling in the canvas, arms locked around valuables and dragging them away.

"Everything!" one woman moaned as she sank to her knees. She was one of the first who had moved into the building, Gair recalled. "Everything I own has been lost!"

"Not everything," said a man trying to comfort her. "You still have your life."

Gair blinked furiously. The heat was pushing outward, stinging his sensitive eyes. He brushed at his face, finding it smudged with ashes that filled the air. Gray snow, it looked like. He cast his gaze about, searching for Goldmoon.

His eyes locked on the shining armor of the Solamnic knights. They were carrying people away from the burning building, their exposed faces black with ash. Some of the soldiers were keeping the panicked crowd back. Others were at the edge of the burning building, calling out to see if anyone was trapped inside.

"Goldmoon!" the elf shouted as he continued to move forward. He shook the shoulders of one of the Solace twins. "Is Goldmoon in the building?"

The man shook his head. "Other side o' the fire!" he barked, his voice raspy. Gair noticed his hands were blistered, and part of his sleeves had been burned away. "She's with Roeland and my brother."

The elf made his way around the blaze, dodging people dragging their belongings farther away from the conflagration, getting out of the way of a dozen men who'd loaded up pieces of tarp with snow. They were running forward, and Gair watched as they hefted the tarps and flung the snow at the fire. The flames seemed only to laugh at them and glow more brightly.

Smoke poured from one of the citadel's doorways, and through it Gair saw dark shapes. People indeed were trapped! The elf paused in his search for Goldmoon, edged closer to the building, and breathed a sigh of relief as the three fishermen from the port stumbled out, coughing and patting their clothes. Two Solamnic knights were behind them. A pair of the Thorbardin dwarves rushed forward to tug the fishermen away from the building—and just in time. There was a great flapping sound as part of the roof came free, spiraling down, flames licking madly in the air. It landed where the fishermen had paused a mere heartbeat ago. The knights joined the crowd and began plucking pieces of their armor off, revealing blistered skin beneath it.

Gair continued his way around the massive inferno. He spotted Iryl Songbrook. She was taking stock of the followers, and by concentrating he picked out a few of her words. It seemed she was trying to determine who else might be inside.

"No one, I hope," Gair said as he continued to press himself through the hysterical throng. "Nobody else is going to make it out of there." He was knocked to the ground as another snow regiment thundered forward, futilely trying to fight the fire by slinging more tarps full of snow at it. Gair knew there was little water available. Since the snows came, everyone had been melting it for water rather than continuing to dig wells.

Still, there was one functioning well at the far edge of the settlement, and the elf could tell that a bucket brigade had formed. The line of humans and dwarves, adults and children alike, was working quickly, shuttling pots and pans, helmets, and even a few actual buckets toward the blaze.

The fire was too big, burned too quickly. "The resin," Gair muttered as he picked himself up and continued around to the far side of the citadel, finally spotting Goldmoon. "The resin's fueling it." He could smell the odd mixture of tree sap and oil that the builders had been diligently applying for days.

He turned the corner and saw that the healer was perilously close to the flames, Roeland at her shoulder, his hands clenched on her cloak to hold her back. Orvago was behind them, fur tinged black with soot and obviously singed, as if he'd been inside the building when it had caught fire.

"What started it?" Gair called as he waved to Goldmoon and weaved his way toward her.

Shadowwalker's clan. The elder Graymist had opened the door.

Gair stopped in his tracks, staring mutely at the flames that continued to pour down the sides of the citadel as if they were liquid. The heat this close was nearly unbearable, and it had melted the snow far back from the building, turning the top layer of the once-hard ground muddy. Shadowwalker, Gair thought. Darkhunter had mentioned the name.

"Let me go!" Goldmoon started to struggle with Roeland. He had his arms wrapped around her now, keeping her from bolting.

"So you can die, too?" Roeland's voice was firm. "You yourself said no one else was to go in there."

Gair swallowed hard and pushed himself through the last several people to reach Goldmoon's side. "I went for a walk," he began, for some reason believing he needed to supply a reason for his absence. "I saw the fire as I was returning, and—"

"Jasper's inside." Goldmoon's face was ashen. She was smudged with soot and tears. Her hair was plastered to the sides of her face with sweat, the edges of her cloak singed.

"Everyone else made it out," Roeland said, "but Jasper—"

"And Redstone," Goldmoon breathed. She sagged against the former miller.

"They were helping to get the last ones out," Roeland

continued. "People were sleeping when it started, and—"

"Suddenly part of the roof caved in."

Goldmoon dropped to her knees, her head in her hands and her shoulders shaking. Gair had never seen her look so old and frail, so broken. He knelt at her side, brushing the hair away from her face, his fingers adding to the gray smudges.

"Maybe he got out on the other side," he offered.

You know that's not true, Son.

"Maybe . . ." Gair left the sentence unfinished, unable to come up with another even half-convincing prevarication.

The healer pressed her hands into the slush and sent her senses forward into the fire. "Jasper," Goldmoon whispered. "I'm sorry, my friend. By the memory of Mishakal, if only I'd—"

A growl cut her off, angry and loud and coming from the gnoll. He tore off his red cloak and charged forward, hairy arms in front of his face. Gair was on his feet in an instant, reaching out to stop him. The elf's fingers closed on air.

"No!" Goldmoon shouted.

"Orvago, don't!" Gair's words were lost in the crackling of the flames.

The gnoll leapt through a smoky doorway, growling and disappearing behind a wall of flames. The building groaned, seemingly in response to the hairy intruder. Sections of the roof tumbled down, burning and sending stinging ashes into the crowd.

There was a gasp from the other side of the citadel, followed by something like a moan. The noise grew, and there were cries of "Run!" There was a loud crash. Gair didn't need to be there to know that one of the walls had collapsed.

"Orvago is searching for them," Goldmoon's voice was soft. "He can't see them. They're in the basement.

No, he's looking up."

Black smoke was billowing into the air now, thick and choking and forcing the crowd back. Over the sound of gasps and groaning beams, the elf heard the sizzling splash of water being uselessly thrown on the citadel.

His eyes were watering from the heat and the ashes, and he rubbed at them.

Sentimental, his father observed. *Are they tears for your dwarven friend, or for the animal that shares your tent?*

"Can you see inside?" Gair knew he was inches from Goldmoon, that the healer might realize he was talking to a spirit. "Like you saw through the snow?"

"I can't see anything," Roeland answered, thinking the elf was talking to him. "Just fire and smoke. Goldmoon wouldn't let us go in after them. She said it would be suicide, but she would've gone if I had let her."

A stalemate of wills. Fire and smoke and a foolish hairy beast who has given up on the upper levels and is heading for the basement.

"The basement?" Gair repeated.

"As far as we can tell, the fire started on the top floor," Roeland said. "Maybe the roof. Can't see how, though."

The basement, the spirit said. *The dwarves fell through to the basement. I think the beast can smell them somehow.*

* * * * *

Inside the inferno, Orvago blinked furiously. Water streamed from his eyes, and his breath came in ragged gasps. He couldn't smell the dwarves. All he could smell was the thick smoke and the overpowering acrid scent of burning wood and resin. Through the smoke and the flames, he saw a gaping hole in the floor. He was rapidly running out of places left standing on this level, so he leapt through it.

The smoke was thick in the basement as well, though

the heat wasn't quite as bad. The cold of the earth offered a little protection. The gnoll flailed about with his arms, finding broken and burning beams and yowling when the flames caught at his tunic. He batted them out and shuffled forward, peering into the smoke and shadows, using the light from the fire to see bits and snatches of things.

Pots and pans were strewn on the floor, scattered by the people who'd managed to escape. He saw burning blankets and smoldering chests that held someone's cherished possessions. He felt a broken doll beneath his foot.

Above him, he heard the crackling grow louder, then heard a thunderous *whoosh*. Wood was groaning far above, sounding almost like the timbers on the ship on which he'd been enslaved. He found a wall and pressed himself against it, held his breath, and cringed when the groaning grew in intensity, punctuated by a great crash. Just as the ship's mast had broken through the deck, support beams from above came hurtling down. The flames licking along them leapt out to catch more dry tinder ablaze in the basement.

The gnoll coughed, then found he could scarcely draw in another breath. He fought for air, taking in smoke instead. He fell to his knees, cutting himself on shattered glass and pottery, and tried to inhale more deeply. There . . . a breath. His face close to the floor now, he crawled forward, arms still out and paws searching.

The gnoll had almost given up when the tips of his fingers brushed coarse hair. He groped about, finding a beard, short and singed, a broad face. He felt the dwarf's chest, barely moving—but it was moving. His paws fumbled about and found the dwarf's belt, and he locked his hairy fingers under it.

Continuing to crawl, Orvago dragged the dwarf's body with him. The gnoll was searching for the stairs now, remembered where they were from his many trips bringing lumber inside. His free paw continued to grope about, pausing only when coughs racked his body. The gnoll was breathing so shallowly now that he felt faint, but he pushed himself onward. He was nearly there when something barred his way.

His fingers moved across a lumpy shape. He felt tattered clothes, thick, short limbs. He put his head to the lump's chest and sniffed. Another dwarf. This one he cradled to his chest as he nudged himself forward, finding the stairs at last and not bothering to see if this second body still breathed. The steps were hot to the touch, brittle like summer twigs, and smoke was pouring down them so thick he couldn't see through it.

The gnoll slammed his eyes shut, took a last gulp of air against the basement floor, and drove himself upward.

* * * * *

"No magic," Goldmoon sobbed. "Not one enchantment to stop such a blaze."

Gair held her close.

"Someone set this fire," she said. "In my heart, I know it. Why? Who?"

The elf opened his mouth to say something but was cut off by words dancing in his head.

You mean you'll tell her it was the Qué-Nal?

The elf nodded.

And that you discovered this by talking to the spirit of a man long buried? Misusing the magic she taught you so you could talk to me?

"I have to," Gair whispered.

And that you've known it was the Qué-Nal for quite some time? That you could have said something to her weeks ago and possibly prevented this?

The elf stopped and pulled Goldmoon farther away

from the flames. The building was groaning more loudly. Great gouts of smoke poured out. Suddenly there was a shape darker than the smoke, large and moving erratically.

"It's the gnoll!" Roeland cried. "He's got the dwarves!" The big man rushed forward, others following closely at his heels.

The gnoll fell, his tunic and hair in flames, the clothing of the dwarves burning, too. Roeland tugged his coat off and batted at the flames even as more pairs of hands were darting in and tugging the gnoll and dwarves away from the building.

"Jasper's alive!" someone cried.

"Redstone, too!"

Roeland continued to slap at the flames, discarding his coat when it caught fire and ripping off his shirt to use that. The former miller persisted until the last of the flames had been snuffed out. Someone else started beating his cloak against the gnoll as the creature continued to be tugged away from the building.

Goldmoon was on her feet, pushing away from Gair and hurrying to the dwarves' side. "Help Orvago," she said, her voice so soft Gair could hardly hear it above the constant crackling of the fire. The elf was quick to oblige, turning the gnoll onto his back and cringing when he saw how badly the hair on his body was burned and how raw the split and bubbling skin underneath looked.

Gair splayed his fingers wide over the gnoll's chest, which was still painfully warm from the fire. He concentrated on his heart, calling forth the mystical energy he'd so recently been using to communicate with the dead. Out of the corner of his eye, he saw Goldmoon, and his breath caught in his throat.

The aged healer had one hand on Jasper, the other on Redstone, and she was using her magic to heal two individuals at the same time. The elf had never seen such a feat but did not doubt Goldmoon's ability to handle it.

He returned his attention to his own patient, working hard to find the healing spark and coaxing it to grow like the flames grew behind him. For an instant, he wondered if he possessed the ability to heal the gnoll, the creature being so different from a man. Then he recalled Goldmoon healing Orvago after the incident with the boars. He focused on that memory, pictured it in the back of his mind as the warmth radiated from his chest and down his arms into the gnoll. At the same time, the air grew warmer still from the fire.

Behind the healers, the citadel shuddered one last time. The flames, sucking the last of the life out of the building, rose ever higher, then erupted outward in a great show of sparks as the last few walls collapsed into the basement. Screams of terror and shouts of anger cut through the night as the settlers watched the flames finally begin to grow smaller.

A crowd formed around Goldmoon and Gair. Roeland was telling of the gnoll's heroic rescue of the dwarves. Others were crying over their lost possessions, some over the weeks upon weeks of work that had been for nothing.

"What started the fire?" It was Amanda's mother.

"Someone set it, that's for certain." It was one of the Thorbardin dwarves. "Redstone's resin. A barrel of it was dumped around the foundation."

"To feed the fire," another dwarf added. "Someone doesn't want the citadel built."

"Who? And why?"

Gair kept quiet, focusing on his spell and trying to shut out their words.

* * * * *

Dawn found the dwarves and Orvago in new clothes and with less hair. Jasper was speculating if he would have to shave off what little was left of his beard. He looked forlornly at the gnoll, who appeared much the worse for wear.

"Saved us, you did," Jasper stated, slapping the gnoll gently on the back. "Didn't think anyone would come down to get us."

"No one should have," Redstone cut in. "You could've been killed, Orvago."

The gnoll grinned sheepishly and scratched at the bandage on his chest.

Goldmoon hovered around them, and Gair stayed in the background, listening to his father and pondering whether he should reveal his knowledge of a Qué-Nal named Shadowwalker.

"Guess this means we're not buildin' again until spring," Jasper said. He wrapped his stubby fingers around a steaming cup of tea and stared sadly at the charred remains of the once-impressive building. Occasional wisps of smoke still curled upward from the site, disappearing in the gray sky overhead.

Goldmoon shook her head. "We start again tomorrow, my friend, though I don't want any of you three lifting a nail until you've properly mended."

"Tomorrow!" Jasper gasped. He nearly dropped the tea. "Goldmoon, you can't be serious! It's obvious someone set the fire."

"And therefore obvious someone does not want the citadel built," she added.

"Exactly."

"All the more reason it must be built." She turned and walked toward the charred ruins. "We start again tomorrow."

Jasper let out a deep breath and looked back and forth between Redstone and Orvago. They were silently watching the healer.

Chapter 10

Obsessions

Gair insisted on going to the port town for Goldmoon to arrange for more building supplies to replace everything that had been destroyed in the fire. He didn't tell the healer that he had planned the trip anyway, intending to stop at the scribe's. Willum accompanied the elf, determined to inform Camilla of the sabotage against the settlement and to ask for a larger garrison. They rode horses to cut the time of the journey considerably.

Gair thought that he might tell the knight commander about the Qué-Nal and Shadowwalker, since he had not yet mentioned either to Goldmoon—or to Iryl, who claimed friendship with the Qué-Nal. Camilla might not think to press him for information about how much he knew. The elf worked at being pleasant and plied Willum with questions about Camilla to keep his mind off the fire and his dilemma.

"Why don't you ask her yourself tonight?" the lieutenant said as they neared the town's gates. "Over dinner. You'll be my guest."

Gair accepted, of course, and was exceptionally amicable company, silent only when Willum discussed the tragedy of the citadel. Camilla politely expressed remorse for the fire, then astonishment that Goldmoon would consider proceeding.

As the evening wore on and the subject finally changed, she found herself eating everything placed on her plate, and at the elf's encouragement, having a second helping of plum pudding. The Solamnic commander's eyes drifted often to the elf, then quickly stared at her plate each time others noticed her. As soon as dinner was finished, she excused herself. "Letters to write," she told Gair and her men.

In her tower room, she paced in front of the desk, glancing at a letter that had arrived for her on the Solamnic ship still anchored in the harbor. It was in reply to one she'd written a little more than four weeks ago, asking the Solamnic Council to give her the authority to oust Goldmoon from Schallsea Island. She read the reply again and again then paced some more.

She let an hour drift by. As the stars winked into view, she strode to the window and looked out over the city. She peered toward the harbor. The full moon reflected off the waves, illuminating the docks and the Solamnic ship moored there, and illuminating Gair Graymist. What was the elf doing up so late? Couldn't he sleep either?

* * * * *

Gair sat on the dock, wrapped tightly in his heavy wool coat and staring at the water. The waves danced with color, the black of night, the bright yellow splashes of light reflected from the residents' windows, the iridescent white of the mirroring moon. His fingers were stretched over the frosty rough planks, and his senses extended deep into the harbor, where he'd detected slivers of human bones, broken skulls, pieces of rusty chains, and the boulders that were used to drown the Qué-Nal.

The spirits weren't screaming at him this time. He was picking through them, as his keen eyes picked through the shadows, and he was listening to the musings of those who had lived the longest and had the most memories to share. Sadness, vengeance, fear, hope—the emotions were so strong they nearly overwhelmed him. He fought to remain in control and continued to sort through the words and feelings, attempting to put faces to them, trying to reach them and communicate. He almost talked himself out of coming here, since his experience with Darkhunter had so unnerved him. Darkhunter's was a tainted soul, and these spirits could not possibly be so malevolent.

The elf focused his efforts on only a few of the voices, urging at least one of them to talk to him. "Nothing! Why can't I contact them? When I was here weeks before, I almost . . ." He slapped his forehead with his hand in frustration. "I sensed someone reaching out to me then! Are there too many, Father? Is this beyond my reach?"

Not beyond, his father answered supportively. *Just more difficult. Don't give up, Son.*

Gair filled his lungs with the frigid salt-tinged air, searched harder, and opened his mind wider to the harborful of thoughts, allowed himself to drown in them. In a vision in his mind's eye, his surroundings melted around him, his father disappearing, the dock beneath him disappearing. He was swimming in the water with the spirits, who appeared as ghostly waves. Now he was diving to the bottom, the surface of the harbor far above his head. The spirits didn't carry the images of their living selves, but at least he could see them now— diaphanous clouds in the water. He strained his senses to their limits and began to talk to the ghosts.

And they began to answer.

No longer were they randomly talking to each other;

they were talking to him! The elf was at once both fascinated and horrified, and all trace of fatigue disappeared as he continued to speak with the dead. He learned that not all of those who drowned here left spirits behind. The essence of some of them had moved on to a place he couldn't reach. Also, he discovered the spirit of a Blue Dragonarmy general who had lost his life in a battle fought in this bay. This spirit rose toward the surface, and the elf's senses followed it.

Gair felt himself floating on the surface of the harbor now, the spirits of all the others sinking away from him. Only the general remained close by. He'd been a powerful man, like Gair's father, the elf could tell, and he was angry still, despite the decades that had passed, that his men had been bested here. The spirit's rage was excitingly palpable, and Gair focused on it and the man until a hazy black image formed in front of him. Like a black silk curtain, it hovered two-dimensionally over the water, begging the elf to give it more form.

"Could I?" the elf mused aloud. "Could I give the general form?"

Please, the spirit replied.

Should I even dare try? Gair wondered. The elf was still leery after his scare at the Qué-Nal burial circle, but he hadn't been harmed then, only spooked. Spirits couldn't harm the living, could they?

No, his father answered. *We have left this world long behind. Only our shadows remain, but you could give those shadows substance. You have the ability.*

"What harm, then," Gair said.

It would be another test of his mystical energies to give the dead some semblance of life. Only good could come of improving his magical skills, he told himself. He could apply it to other areas, perhaps helping those very close to dying.

He paused. "Who am I kidding?" he whispered. "There is no good to this. There is only feeding my own morbid curiosity."

Then feed your curiosity, his father encouraged. *You do not take enough chances.*

"I've heard that somewhere before," the elf mused. "And I suppose you are right, but how to go about it?

He looked to his heart, to the strength Goldmoon taught him was there, felt the power surge through his chest and down his arms, through the cold wood his body was still sitting on and over the water to touch the black silken image hovering there. Gair concentrated as if the general were a patient he was tending to and directed his efforts to healing that patient.

He stared at the image, which seemed for a moment to become blacker than the water, a touch thicker. "Much thicker," he implored. The silk wavered, began to fold in on itself, and the general's wispy form disappeared.

"No!" Gair croaked.

The general's thoughts remained strong, however, and they urged Gair to try again.

"I can't," he said finally. "I don't know how. Even if I did, I haven't the power to give you substance."

You have the ability, his father repeated, *but you do not have the power—here.*

"I know better than to ask Goldmoon for help. I suspect she wouldn't approve of how I'm using her mysticism. It's why I haven't told her about the Qué-Nal and Shadowwalker."

Do not give up, my son. You could get the power, his father encouraged, *oh so easily.*

The elf pushed himself to his feet and thrust his cold hands into his pockets. "No, Father, I will not ask Goldmoon."

You do not need Goldmoon. You need something that bris-

tles with energy. You could steal a bit of it. Gair, your sisters had but a few years on this earth. If you could give them form and substance as you almost did the general . . . What a gift!

Gair's eyes widened. "The Silver Stair surges with power," he breathed.

Yes, his father answered. *The Silver Stair. You are a bright son.*

The elf's heart beat faster. "It could just work! Goldmoon sometimes relies on the magical medallion she wears, pulling energy from it to heal the gravest of injuries. There is a tremendous amount of energy in the stair. I felt it when I first touched the steps!"

You could use that energy.

"Of course! I will leave first thing in the morning and . . . damn! The scribe. The shop doesn't open until midmorning. Well, that simply won't do." Gair hurried from the dock.

The city was exceptionally quiet this night. Outside of the lights spilling from the windows of homes, only the light from one tavern still burned. The cold and the hour were keeping the townsfolk inside. No light burned in the scribe's shop. Gair pounded on the door, loudly rattling the pane of glass in it. He pounded again and again until the door threatened to break.

"See here!" The voice came from the second floor.

Gair looked up into the irate face of the scribe.

"You! Come back tomorrow, elf. Be on your way now, or I'll call for the watch."

Gair scowled and dug into his pocket, pulling out an emerald. "Will this open your shop?"

The scribe squinted and shook his head. He couldn't see what the elf was holding. "Come back tomorrow."

"It's an emerald, a valuable one," Gair said, "and neither it nor I will be here when you open tomorrow."

The scribe pulled back into the room, closing the window. A moment later a lantern blinked on downstairs. Dressed in a long woolen nightshirt, with thick socks on his feet, the scribe opened the door and yawned.

Gair thrust the emerald at him. "The Qué-Nal rubbings . . . what do they mean?"

He waved the elf inside and to the counter, lit a second lantern, and pulled out the parchments Gair had given him. He stifled another yawn.

"Well?" The impatience was thick in Gair's voice. "What do they say?"

"These are tribal symbols only," the scribe began, "They tell you—that is, if you're a Qué-Nal—which tribe lays claim to the land. Sort of like a no trespassing sign, I guess, unless you're considered friendly to the tribe, and then you wouldn't be trespassing."

"The stone and the mosaic chip?"

The scribe let out a low whistle. "Now, those are interesting pieces."

"Well? Be quick about it, will you? I'm in a hurry." The elf's tone was harsh, and he instantly apologized.

"The etching on this stone is only a part of something larger, like a couple of words out of a phrase. As far as I can tell, this mark here means 'shield' or 'safe,' or perhaps 'protected' or 'blessed'—something like that. The mark on this chip is similar, but it seems to mean the opposite—'treachery,' 'violence,' 'danger,' 'evil,' 'corruption,' something dark."

"Darkhunter."

The man yawned and cocked his head.

"And. . . ?"

"That's it. These are only a couple of pieces, like out of a puzzle. Bring me more of the puzzle and I can give you more information." He looked at the emerald in his palm. "Bring me more and there's no charge. You've paid me more than enough."

Gair took the Qué-Nal stone and the mosaic chip and

left. He found his way back to the Sentinel and was able to catch a few hours of sleep before being roused for breakfast. He nearly declined the meal, wanting to be on his way back to the settlement and the Silver Stair, but there was the company of Camilla Weoledge to consider. The elf genuinely liked her.

"So you will be coming with me to the settlement?" Gair's voice sounded hopeful. His eyes sparkled and locked onto hers.

Camilla broke free of the stare and fixed her gaze on a spot over his shoulder. "Yes. I am leading a garrison of soldiers to your settlement for added protection."

Gair looked incredulous. "An entire garrison? Then who will remain here to man the Sentinel and look after the town?"

"More soldiers and knights will be arriving within the week." Her voice carried a hint of disappointment as she thought of the letter on her desk. "The Solamnic Council has decreed that Goldmoon's citadel project be protected at all costs. No more sabotage to her Citadel of Light, no more raids on the trail. The Solamnic Council wants her guarded for as long as she desires to remain on the island." She swallowed hard. "Guarded so that she can spread her mysticism."

She stirred her eggs. "If we're fortunate, the settlement's problems will stop with the presence of my men. I would just like to know who is responsible . . . who the enemy is."

Gair felt for the stone in his pocket.

* * * * *

Gair stood at the base of the Silver Stair. Dawn was only a few hours away, the sky already lightening. His legs were numb from the cold; he'd been standing here that long, trying to gain the courage. Once more snow was falling, deepening the cover already on the ground and soaking his hair.

"Stars falling to earth," he mused aloud. "That's what Camilla calls snow."

You think too often of her, my son.

"When I am not thinking of spirits, I am thinking of her. I can't get her out of my mind, Father. She makes the air seem sweeter, the winter bearable. I hated leaving her side tonight, but I dare not press myself on her. She is hesitant, does not want to be here. I think she fights her feelings for me, as I do with Goldmoon."

Then forget her.

"If only it were that easy. I think I am obsessed with her."

You use her now as an excuse for staying on the ground. Pining for the human woman when you have important things to do.

"I'm not afraid of the Silver Stair," he said softly.
He'd said that more than an hour ago when he first came here, after he'd made sure everyone was sleeping except the sentries and a handful of Camilla's soldiers. Both were on the far side of the settlement at the moment.

What is keeping you? his father prodded. *Your friends climb this regularly, you've told me. Why not you? The power is here.*

"I love magic," the elf said, "but this . . . this is overwhelming."

Too much to take a chance on?

"I've been taking more chances, Father. A great many more." The elf sucked in a deep breath and stood on the lowest step. He quickly climbed up the first dozen and peered toward the camp of the Solamnic soldiers. Nearby stretched what was left of the citadel, a gaping black hole in the ground, with bits of charred timbers sticking up in all directions. The workers had started clearing everything away, but it would be days before they were ready to start building again.

It does not matter if anyone sees you, Son. They will merely see one of Goldmoon's faithful climbing the Silver Stair.

He continued up, the air growing colder as he went. The elf bundled his cloak so tightly about him he entertained the notion that he might smother himself. He slowed his gait as the campfires grew smaller. The steps were narrow and terribly steep, and there were no handholds.

It is heights you are afraid of, my son, isn't it? Not the power of the Silver Stair.

"How does Goldmoon do this? And Jasper with his short legs?" Gair's words were muffled by the folds of his coat. "What do they see at the top?"

Several dozen steps later, he asked, "Where is the top? There's no end in sight."

The snow had stopped and a gentle fog had settled in, its tendrils wrapping about the elf as he continued his journey. He was grateful for the fog, as it helped to mask him. He had no intention of making it to the top step and receiving a vision this night, though he didn't want any passing sentries or knights to know that. Not that either would question his not climbing to the top, he suspected, as they likely knew little about the magical site anyway. They would simply believe he had changed his mind, or like others among Goldmoon's students he got too tired and stopped.

When he was high enough, certain that the light fog and his distance from the ground concealed him reasonably well, he sat upon a narrow step and curled his fingers over the translucent edge. It was far colder here than on the ground, and his teeth chattered, so the elf directed his healing energies to warm himself a little. He concentrated, feeling the arcane energy that coursed through the Silver Stair, and he urged it to course through him.

Gair closed his eyes and forced all thoughts of Camilla from his mind. The air was not so sweet now, and his breath was shallower. He seemed for some reason to breathe deeper when he was near Camilla, perhaps wanting to capture the scent of her inside of him. He focused on the chill air, then he pictured the silver stairway twisting up and out of sight, imagined that the energy that ran the entire length of the stairway was rushing toward him. The elf directed all of his thoughts to this latter notion, slowed his breathing and felt his strength drain from him, felt himself slip toward unconsciousness, felt his fingers loosen their grip on the step. He felt himself slump forward, and for a heartbeat he worried that he would fall from his perch and plummet to his death. His legs felt numb and he couldn't feel his toes. He felt terribly weak all over.

"Faith," he croaked. "I must have . . ."

Just as he felt the blackness of unconsciousness rush up to meet him, he also felt a rush of warmth, greater than that he had nurtured with his simple healing spell. The tingling heat roused him, rising from where the tips of his fingers touched the step, reaching up through his arms and into his chest, then down into his legs. It felt like the Raging Fire—the hottest summer month in Abanasinia. It felt incredibly powerful and wonderful. His physical strength was not returning, but his magical strength, what Goldmoon called the power of the heart, was increasing dramatically.

Gair slowly opened his eyes and brought a finger to his temple. "Nura . . . Arale." They were the names of his young sisters. He repeated their names over and over, opened the door to their misty realm and sensed them waiting. Like the ghost in the Schallsea harbor, they hovered before him, looking two-dimensional, like floating shadows.

"I will give you form. We can be together again, after all those years we missed."

No, the girls said, their forms retreating.

Surprised, Gair's mind stretched out to them. "Nura, Arale, you died too young, missed too many years. I can give those years back to you. I am certain of it. I have the power of the Silver Stair. Who will be first?"

Neither of us. It is wrong, they replied, retreating farther still.

He could see them now only as wispy images the size of his fist. They were growing smaller with each heartbeat.

"It is wrong you died so young," he entreated. "Don't go! I've gone to so much trouble!"

Let them go.

"Father?" Gair peered into the darkness of the spirit realm. With the power of the Silver Stair boosting his enchantment, Gair was able to delve deeper into the misty dimension, could see his father much more clearly now, as clearly as when he was alive in the Silvanesti woods.

Let them go, Gair. I wanted them to live again, as you did. I thought you might be able to persuade them. But they have accepted their deaths and want to stay here. So young. . . . such a pity.

"And you, Father, do you accept your death?" Gair still felt the power of the Silver Stair pulsing through him, felt the step beneath his fingers crack as he drew more arcane energy from the ruin. "I want so to use this power. Such power within my grasp, Father. You can't imagine the energy. I wanted to give my sisters back some semblance of life. Since they refused, would you allow me to give you substance, Father?"

The elder Graymist's spirit floated closer.

"Father?"

Gair frowned when the elder Graymist shook his head, too. "All this power within my grasp—"

No, my son. There are others more worthy of life than I. Look around. Can you see them?

"No. I . . ." The words caught in the elf's throat as he saw other shapes coalescing around his father, some elven, and some of those recognizable from his time in Silvanesti, people his father knew and whom he vaguely knew. He was so young then. Had they died in the dragon attack also? The others were a mix of humans of various nationalities. There were barbarians among them, Qué-Nal perhaps. A dozen shapes, then two dozen, nearly three. Their insubstantial arms, which were growing more tangible with each passing heartbeat, reached out to Gair. Their eyes, once hollow, now glowed softly white like stars. . . .

"Stars fallen to earth," the elf whispered.

They glowed brighter now with energy, with the arcane power he was pulling from the Silver Stair and passing to the spirits. He kept one hand on the step, raising the other to rub his temple, helping him to concentrate. "All . . . this . . . power." He began to work the healing spell Goldmoon had taught him, the one he tried on the general in the harbor. Could he heal a spirit enough to return it to some semblance of life? Would his spell give it a corporeal body as fleshy as his own? If he could accomplish it on one of the images here, perhaps he could do so to Riverwind. Goldmoon would be so happy.

He centered his efforts on the closest form, a man in scant clothing who wore beads in his hair. "Breathe," the elf urged as more energy flowed through him and into the misty dimension. "Live." He continued to keep one hand on the stair, using the last of his physical strength to grip it. He couldn't risk falling now, not when he was so close. "Live!"

Another form moved closer, this one somehow familiar, a human with dark skin and long black hair. Shells were woven into the man's hair. Jewelry hung about his neck and wrists, the gold glittering like stars as the arcane energy continued to pour from the stairway.

"Stars fallen to earth," Gair repeated.

The man with the gold jewelry moved closer still, his form thickening, his eyes glowing so bright the otherworldly light was uncomfortable to Gair. The spirit's lips edged upward into a smile, and his glaring eyes, through the doorway to the misty dimension, locked onto Gair's.

The elf felt the crack in the step beneath his hand widen. A piece the size of his thumb fell away. Taking energy from the ruin weakened it, the elf noted. He would be careful and not use this same step the next time. "Darkhunter."

Yes, the spirit answered.

Gair shivered, though not from the intense winter cold, and directed his thoughts away from that spirit. The Qué-Nal still inexplicably bothered him, though they were far from the burial circle where his bones rested. The elf would offer his father life again rather than use this powerful magic on a man he had never known.

"I will not use this magic on you," he whispered.

Gair Graymist, the spirit of Darkhunter pronounced. The words seemed more intense inside the elf's head than the words of other spirits. *Gair Graymist of Silvanesti*. The words swirled in the fog around the elf on the Silver Stair.

"No," the elf decided. "It is indeed time to end this."

He would try again tomorrow night, contacting only his father, perhaps his mother, perhaps Riverwind. Imagine how happy Goldmoon would be to have a tangible, breathing Riverwind walking at her side! Yes, tomorrow he would contact Riverwind and direct this spell at his spirit, not at the spirit of a Qué-Nal who made his skin crawl.

Gair dropped his hand from his temple, brought his other hand to his lap, and steepled his fingers. He inhaled deeply and focused on the chill night air, thrusting aside his thoughts of the Silver Stair and of the spirits on the other side of the door. "Camilla," he whispered. He thought of her, pictured her smooth face and hesitant smile. "Camilla," he repeated more strongly.

He felt the pulsing arcane energy slowly leave his body, seeping back into the stair. The warmth left him, too, and he found himself shivering now from the bitter cold. There was an icy coldness inside of him, as if the winter had settled in the pit of his stomach. It was like the iniquitous feeling he had at the burial ground, a darkness growing inside himself, as if he'd planted a seed that was taking root.

"No more!" Gair firmly closed the door to the spirit's dimension, and with that felt a bit of his physical strength returning, though the chill he sensed in his stomach remained. The fog still swirled around him, and through gaps in it, he could barely make out the torches of the sentries far below.

"Like stars."

Such a romantic.

The elf shot to his feet, nearly losing his balance. He steadied himself and looked all around, instantly fearful that an acolyte had somehow followed him up the stairs.

He could see no one.

A mystic such as yourself should not waste his time on women, especially human ones. Your father is right. He should concentrate only on his considerable magical talents.

"Who . . . who are you?"

Darkhunter, the voice replied. *Your magical talents are indeed impressive.*

Gair's feet took the stairs two at a time. Falling wasn't his worry now. The elf wanted to get away from the spirit who, he realized, had slipped through the door before he closed it.

Why run from me? the spirit persisted. *You wanted me free! You removed a link in the fence that bound me to my grave. You removed a stone. It is still in your pocket. Now finish the task! Make me whole!*

The elf felt about in the pocket of his coat as he continued to run. His fingers found the carved mosaic stone from the burial ground. I must tell Goldmoon, he thought as he raced toward her tent.

Tell her what? the spirit interrupted his thoughts.

Gair couldn't see the Qué-Nal, but somehow he knew the spirit was at his shoulder.

Finish the task!

"No!" I must tell Goldmoon.

Tell her that you dabbled in something she had oft refused to teach you? Tell her that you abused the skills she shared with you? Tell her you've breathed life into a ghost? What would your teacher think of you?

The elf's feet pounded over the snow-slick ground and he rounded a corner. He blinked his eyes furiously against the snow that had started to fall again. Goldmoon's tent was only yards away now. He'd tell her about the spirit and the stone, take the stone back to the burial circle in the morning. Maybe she could cleanse him.

Tell her that your magic is greater than hers? That you were able to pull someone through what you term a doorway? That you can raise the dead?

Gair stopped.

Tell her nothing, Master.

"Master?" Out of breath, Gair nodded to a passing

sentry rather than return his greeting. He walked by Goldmoon's tent and allowed his hammering heart to slow. Within moments he was inside his own tent, then beneath the covers. Fortunately the gnoll was asleep, he thought, and fortunately for once he wasn't snoring.

Orvago slivered his eyes and saw that his tent mate hadn't even bothered taking off his boots. The gnoll yawned, opened one eye, noted the oddity, then drifted off back to sleep.

Neither saw the pair of softly glowing white eyes move inside the tent and hover near the elf's bed.

Chapter 11

Discoveries

"The fire changed everything," Gair explained. "The new citadel will be more complex. Some of the dwarves have gone north and are mining crystal to use, and—"

"You believe in all of this, don't you?" Camilla interrupted.

He took the knight's hand and led her down one of the several paths that had been cleared through the thigh-high snow. The paths led from tent to tent to the main cookfire to the old building site, which was completely free of snow because of the heat of the recent fire. Only a light dusting from the new snow tried to conceal the rubble.

The eldest of the builders was already at work clearing away more of the debris. He was none too pleased about the weather and was cursing the snow that was still falling. "It doesn't snow inside Thorbardin," he muttered loudly enough for Gair and Camilla to hear.

"This section will be—" the elf paused, drawing his lower lip under his teeth as he searched his memory for the new plans he'd only bothered to glance at—"part of what will be called the Healing Lyceum. We're standing in what will be its very center." He led her toward the edge of the old site, where bits of charred wood still remained, and he pointed down into a deep, snow-dusted basement. He tugged her back when he discovered how slippery the ground was. "Careful," he warned, pointing at a patch of ice that looked dull-gray in the pale dawn light. "According to Redstone's and Jasper's plans, the lyceum will have five floors, and part of it will cover this."

The Solamnic commander shook her head in disbelief. "I can't believe Goldmoon isn't giving up."

Gair smiled wistfully. "I don't think she knows how."

"I wish I knew who was working against you. The ambush on the trail. The fire: it's not bandits—they wouldn't destroy, they'd steal. Maybe Knights of Takhisis, sent here to vex Goldmoon, though I thought they had some measure of honor and would have attacked openly. I just don't know." She ran her fingers through her tight curls. "I might not agree with what's going on here, Gair—Goldmoon's mysticism and everything—but these attacks against you must stop. I've sent word to the council that I need skilled scouts. They should be here in a few more weeks, and with them we'll get to the bottom of this."

"Are you warm enough for this?"

She nodded. The red wool cloak the knight wore this morning, coupled with the thick padding under her armor, kept the cold at bay. "I just wish I knew who the dastards are. An enemy you know is easier to fight."

Gair decided to change the subject as he steered her past Jasper and Redstone at the dwarven tent community. Both had their hair trimmed oddly short, and their skin was still terribly blistered from the fire. The smell of roast pork and the crackling of eggs cooking was rousing all the builders. They were chattering in their gravelly voices, seemingly oblivious to the human and elf.

"Jasper's going to build a tower for the knights you intend to station here. Maybe you should talk with him to make sure it will be big enough."

Her eyes flashed with a hint of anger. "Is all of this really necessary?" She closed her eyes and exhaled slowly, then opened them again and took in the camp. Though the tents and lean-tos were much closer together now than before the blizzard and the fire, it still looked the same: a ragtag community of dreamers who had bundled up their hopes and worldly possessions and who had hitched themselves to the aging Hero of the Lance. "Why would someone of Goldmoon's age undertake something like this? She used to be a priestess of Mishakal. This"—she waved her hand to indicate the settlement—"this goes against the gods, and it goes against all my principles to protect her."

"But that's what you're doing—protecting her."

No answer. Her eyes were fixed on two bundled-up boys doing their best to add extra tent stakes to their canvas home. They were fighting with the frozen ground, and neither showed any indication of giving up.

Gair shrugged. "Camilla, I believe in Goldmoon. But maybe I don't always agree with her. I would have given up after the blizzard."

"This image you're painting of multiple buildings is most disturbing. Imagine how long it could take to construct them. Imagine the cost! The steel could be better spent helping the poor, rebuilding towns devastated by dragon attacks, paying soldiers in an army, funding . . ." She spun until her face was inches from Gair's. "Don't you realize this is all a frivolous waste of resources? If Goldmoon isn't senile, she must surely know that people, not this new order of mysticism, could make far better use of the money and effort."

Camilla scrutinized the elf. He looked like a two-legged bear in his hooded coat. She sighed and started to draw away, but he pulled her closer. "Gair, Goldmoon could have at least waited until spring when the weather was better. All the money and effort will be doubled if there are more fires and—"

"And perhaps the citadel will never be more than a dream," he said, "especially if this sabotage keeps up." He moved his face closer still until he could smell a hint of rose, something she washed her hair with. "If things get too bad, Camilla, maybe Goldmoon will take her project somewhere else. Then you'll have nothing to worry about."

"Will you go with her?"

The elf brought his slender fingers to her cheek, his thumb brushing her lips.

"Mornin', Commander, Mister Graymist," Willum interrupted as he hurried past toward a growing rank of soldiers. He drilled them each morning, though there were fewer today because several had accompanied the dwarves. "Cold one this mornin', isn't it? Cold enough to make your eyes freeze open."

The moment lost, Camilla stiffened and turned to watch the men.

"Good morning, Commander!" a tardy soldier chirped as he crisply saluted Camilla and rushed to find his place in line. The knight's eyes narrowed. She would reprimand the young man for his lateness when she returned this evening.

Gair tugged her away, noticing that she relaxed a little when they passed a high drift and the men were lost from view. He reached his hand to her face again as they slipped around another drift and were nearly knocked over by Orvago.

The gnoll grinned as he trundled by, growling a greeting to her and the elf. He was shuffling through the deep snow, making his own path and angling toward the building site, his bandaged arms wrapped around a bundle of wood dowels. Two shaggy mongrels followed him, light enough to scamper on top of the drifts. They barked and playfully nipped at each other's tails.

Camilla had seen the dogs before, hanging around the docks in town, though their ribs showed more prominently there. Even the four-legged strays had found their way to Goldmoon's settlement, she mused.

The gnoll barked at the dogs, and they barked back. One darted in front of Orvago, and he stumbled. Dowels went flying everywhere, landing in the snow, most of them sinking as if they were arrows shot from a bow. The gnoll howled, the dogs joined his chorus, and tardy risers poked their heads out of their tents to see what the ruckus was about.

"Hard to be alone here," he said too softly for her to hear.

"Wherever did this notion to build the citadel arise? Did you and Goldmoon spend months planning it?"

The elf gave a clipped laugh. "This Citadel of Light started as a vision," Gair began as he took her arm and steered her toward the main cook tent, where he was given a large basket of dried fish. "Goldmoon came up with the idea after she climbed the Silver Stair. She said she had a dream of dormitories for her students of mysticism, chapels, halls, lodging for visitors, stables, shrines, a great garden in the center, and in the very center of that the Silver Stair. Perhaps a moat around the entire complex, and . . ."

"And . . . ?"

"I guess the whole thing is pretty overwhelming."

"Sounds like a nightmare, not a dream."

The pair struck out toward the east now, plodding through the snow and making their own path as the gnoll had tried to do. It would take them perhaps a few hours to reach Heartspring walking through these heavy drifts. Without the snow, the trip of a few miles took little time.

"It's my turn to visit the village," Gair had told her. Someone from the settlement went to the farmers' village once a week or so to check on the families and to see if anyone needed healing. The blizzard and the fire had interfered with that routine. "I'm glad you agreed to come with me. I wanted to talk to you, to spend some time with you alone, and—"

"Gair!"

The elf turned to spot Iryl Songbrook plodding through the snow toward them, two Solamnic knights behind her. She was wrapped in a coat practically the color of the snow, her dark hair whipping out of the folds of her hood providing a sharp contrast. She was almost out of breath by the time she caught up to them.

"I was worried I'd missed you."

Gair gave her an impatient look.

"I'm going to Heartspring, too." She jangled her coin purse. "I need too see if the farmers have any more wool blankets to spare. Many of ours were lost in the fire. The ones you brought back with you from town helped, but—"

"I can do that for you," the elf volunteered.

"Nonsense!" she objected. "You'll be too preoccupied tending to the sick."

"You've brought these men to carry the blankets?"

She smiled at the elf. "Willum sent them. He said no one goes anywhere without protection. There's safety in numbers. He would've sent more, but he thought the commander would be satisfied with two."

Iryl brushed by the pair, taking the lead and forging the path through the snow. The lithe elf struggled in places, but he didn't sink as deep as the others and made a little better time. The knights fell in behind Gair and Camilla.

"So much for some time alone," Gair muttered under his breath.

The land between Goldmoon's settlement and the village of Heartspring was relatively flat, with a broad open stretch between two stands of pines and oaks. The snow that had blown to obscure the gently winding path gave character to the area, the drifts rising and falling like white waves captured on canvas with an artist's brushstrokes.

Gair mused that it seemed a shame to mar the landscape with their boot tracks, yet that is what they continued to do by plodding onward. They'd traveled several minutes when the sun broke through the gray sky and painted the snow a delicate pink. As the sky brightened further, the snow turned a glistening white, cut through at the edges of their vision by the blue shadows of the tall pines. A breeze was blowing from the south, dusting flakes across their path.

By midmorning, Heartspring came into view. The village was quaint, though not as tidy as the port of Schallsea. There were fewer than two dozen homes, all of them a mix of large fieldstone, mortar, and logs, none of them looking quite the same. The roofs were thatch, patched here and there with sod, and all had chimneys puffing merrily away. Outside each home was a collection of tools: plows, axes, bins, and others in various states of repair. These gave the village an old, cluttered look. Added to that were barns, some with roofs sagging under the weight of the snow, most with peeling paint, some with doors standing permanently ajar because the wood had warped. The fields extended to the east and south of the village, blanketed with white, though it was obvious Heartspring was spared from the worst of the blizzard that had struck Goldmoon's settlement many days ago. In the distance, a shed leaned into the wind, its door banging back and forth with each gust of wind. Behind it, an ice-covered lake reflected the sun's rays like a mirror.

The people who came out to meet the elves and knights seemed to match the buildings. Homesteaders who chose the fertile lands inland from the coast, they were all human. Many were in rumpled, mismatched clothes decorated with patches. The adults had weathered skin from the hours they spent under the sun in better climes. Some had hammers and other small tools sticking out of their pockets. The children wore clothes that looked either too small because they were outgrowing them or too large because they hadn't yet grown into the hand-me-downs. Only a few children had clothes that seemed to fit right. Nearly all of them wore smiles, and they were obviously happy to see Gair.

The children ogled the knights, rubbing grubby fingers over the silver armor and oohing and aahing at their wide-eyed reflections in the leg plates. The knights obliged the youths by answering questions about weapons, fighting, and life beyond Schallsea Island.

The visit in Heartspring was not unpleasant, but it had the feel of a ritual, with Gair presenting the dried fish to the village leader, a crusty old man with a voice as gravelly as any dwarf's. Iryl visited with a man who raised sheep, and Camilla could tell from the delicate elf's expression that she had secured more blankets.

Gair stopped at each home, taking time to ease the fever of an elderly farmer, mend the arm of a young child who slipped on the lake, offer reassurances to a pregnant woman. There was tea at one home, hot biscuits at another, kind words exchanged at all of them. Camilla silently watched, amazed at Gair's mystical talent—and troubled by it.

It was late afternoon before Gair had finished his

rounds, turning down invitation upon invitation for dinner and promising that someone would return next week.

"Home, m'lady?" Gair said, extending his arm to Camilla.

"The settlement is *your* home, not mine," she replied. She volunteered to carry some of Iryl's blankets, keeping her arms occupied.

The entourage made better time on the return trip, following the trail they'd blazed in the morning. The knight noted that they would be at the settlement by sunset, in time for the evening meal and in time for her to patrol the grounds with Willum again before turning in. The wind had picked up considerably, blowing the topmost powdery layer of snow across their path and nipping at their fingers. The sky had quickly turned gray again.

"I'm looking forward to spring," Gair said simply. "I think—"

"Down!" Iryl dropped, hands and legs flying out, bundled body hitting the snow with a muffled *whuff*.

"What is it?" This came from one of the knights who'd been toting blankets. The other was fast to follow Iryl's example, landing atop his pile of blankets and driving them into the snow.

"Get down!" Iryl repeated.

Gair reflexively crouched, pushing Camilla into a drift just as a spear whizzed past from the north, slicing through the air where the commander had been standing a heartbeat before. Another spear came from the south, striking the sluggish knight's armor with enough of an impact to rattle him. He pitched forward, blankets flying like big, spooked birds.

Gair pressed himself into a drift, then rolled to face to the north, his fingers splayed across the snow. He was stretching out, magically, with his senses. He cursed himself for paying so much attention to Camilla that he hadn't noticed anyone lying in wait. He knew Iryl's natural senses, not so distracted, had warned her heartbeats ago that something was wrong. He reached inside himself and coaxed his mystical power to grow and flow outward.

My son, take care. Gair's father had opened the door. *There are barbarians on both sides of the trail. Qué-Nal. A deadly ambush.*

"I think I saw something move!" Iryl called. "Too far away to make anything out. Can't tell how many!"

Gair swallowed hard. "Qué-Nal," he said softly. "Why didn't I say something about their involvement before now?"

Your words would not have prevented this.

The elf saw an unending blanket of white, cut through here and there by scraggly bushes. In the distance stood some evergreens, but the spear-throwers would not be that far away. Hiding behind one of the drifts, then.

"How many of them?" he asked as his senses flowed over the snow like running water.

Seven, the elder Graymist replied. *To the north. Hidden by deep drifts.*

"We're halfway between Heartspring and the settlement, too far from either to be seen," Iryl said, her voice low and panicked. "A perfect spot for an ambush. Why? Who would do this? We've nothing of value!"

"Except blankets," Camilla muttered.

Gair glanced over his shoulder to make sure Camilla was all right. She was extricating herself from the drift he had pushed her into and was now crouched in the narrow path they'd been making, edging her head up and looking to the south.

The elf returned his concentration to his spell and felt a tingling warmth in his fingertips, though his exposed skin was cherry-red from the cold. Directing the warmth away from him, his senses grew even more acute. He smelled the faint scent of pine, carried from the distant row of evergreens, smelled rotting wood where a bush had died and the snow was decaying the dead branches, smelled the snow, which had a clean, almost mystical scent. And he smelled wolves, mixed with the scent of men, the scent of the latter being more prominent. Men were wearing the skin of wolves for warmth, he decided. Indeed, there were seven to the north. To the south? He directed the warmth away and behind him, where he heard the shush of steel as Camilla drew her sword, then more whispers of steel as her two knights followed suit. Next he heard a fluttering noise. Camilla released her woolen cloak so it would not hamper her.

I can direct you out of here, the elder Graymist said. *Alone, you would have a chance to escape. The barbarians would concentrate on the knights.*

"Out of the question," Gair hissed.

Save yourself.

The elf blocked out his father's insistent urgings, not bothering to shut the door, since the effort to do so might disrupt his other enchantment. His senses continued flowing farther to the south, where he discovered more men, wearing the skins of wolves and beavers. His acute hearing picked up their hushed conversation, but it was of a language he could not comprehend. The group was about thirty feet from the trail, well hidden behind snowdrifts and crawling closer. From the west, one large figure was approaching.

"Camilla," Gair whispered. "There are six to the south, seven to the north and one coming from the west."

"How . . . how do you know that?"

"Magic."

Camilla growled softly in her throat. "Badly outnumbered," the knight said, "and they've got us pinned down."

"Maybe we can crawl back to the settlement," Iryl suggested. "It's not dignified, but—"

"We stay put. They'll have to come closer if they want us," Camilla said. "Everyone stay alert."

"Unless they intend to freeze us out," one of the knights whispered.

The wind continued to chase the snow across their path, blowing stronger now. Gair squinted and cupped a hand over his eyes to keep the snow from getting in them. He noticed a white mound moving a little closer, and he dropped his hand to his belt, tugging free a knife. His other hand reached for the pommel of his long sword. His fingers were so painfully cold. Still, he kept his concentration on the spell so he could follow the barbarians' movements.

"What do you want?" Gair called out to them. "We've no coins with us!"

"The elves!" a strong voice from the north called. "The knights can go on their way."

Listen to me, Son. I can find you a path out of here.

Gair gritted his teeth.

"What is this all about?" Gair challenged. "We've done nothing to you!"

"You defy the gods!" This a softer voice from the south. "You and all in your settlement, all of you must die!" A spear followed the words.

"I can see them!" Iryl chirped. "By the blessed memory of Habbakuk, they're Qué-Nal!"

Gair swung his gaze to the south. There were six barbarians, standing on a stretch of hard-packed snow, white and gray wolfskins and dark brown beaver furs covering their tall forms. The one in the lead carried a shield made of deerskin. There were symbols painted

185

on it similar to those the elf had seen on the trees near the burial ground.

The shield-bearer spoke. "Silver knights! Our fight is not with you."

"Then leave us be!" Camilla called out.

"We will fight you if we have to," the shield-bearer continued, "unless you surrender the elves from the settlement, and unless you promise to leave the cursed settlement forever. We offer you life."

Son, there is still a chance I can direct you out of here! Listen to me!

To the north, Gair heard the sounds of more snow crunching, watched seven wolf-clad forms rise from behind a drift. Thirteen Qué-Nal altogether, plus whoever the large figure was, were advancing from the west. The barbarians readied spears.

Listen to me!

The elf closed his eyes, tilted his head until his chin touched the snow. He released the enchantment he'd been holding and focused on another, and on the snow beneath him, reaching out with his thoughts to the north to sense the snow beneath the seven warriors' feet.

"Peace," Gair whispered. "Peace, warriors. I have peace in my heart. Find the peace in your hearts, too." It was a mystic spell similar to the one he'd used on the boars. He sensed their rapid pulses and tried to slow them, chattering comforting words as a mother would to calm an upset child. He directed all of his energy into trying to convince the men to be calm and to drop their spears. "There is no reason to threaten us," he murmured. "We do not threaten you. Find peace inside your hearts."

The elf discerned that four of the seven relaxed. Their fingers quivered, and they dropped their spears. Their breathing slowed. "Peace," they murmured, almost in unison.

Their fellows snapped at them and shouted that sorcery was at work. Gair continued to concentrate, and the quartet remained at ease, did nothing to regain their weapons. "Peace," the elf repeated. The word was echoed by the four barbarians. "Friends."

There were other words swirling amid the blowing snow—unintelligible words from the barbarians to the south, who were moving closer, words of concern and disbelief from Iryl Songbrook, orders from Camilla. There was a crunch of snow as the Solamnic knights stood to meet the challenge.

Listen to reason, Gair. Save yourself. It is not yet your time to die.

Gair used the last of his mental strength to reach out to the other three barbarians to the north. "We are no threat," he repeated emphatically. "Let me be your ally, not your enemy."

"No threat," two finally parroted. They dropped their spears. "Allies."

Iryl gasped. "Camilla, Gair's spellbound. . . ."

"No!" bellowed the last of the Qué-Nal warriors. Gair touched the man's mind and was instantly repulsed. His will was strong, and he was angry. That ire was a shield that kept the elf's soothing words at bay. The barbarian cursed to his companions, who continued to stand docilely. Then the barbarian bolted toward Gair.

The elf struggled to get to his feet, but his coat tangled in his legs and cost him precious seconds. Behind him, the knights advanced to the south to meet the charge of the six approaching barbarians.

"Take the woman knight first!" one of them roared.

"I don't want to kill you," Camilla hissed through clenched teeth. To Iryl, she said, "Keep yourself down and watch for more."

Gair managed to make it to his feet just as the angry

Qué-Nal warrior was upon him. The elf held his sword parallel in front of him, using it to fend off the barbarian's attack. The Qué-Nal was young, perhaps only fourteen or fifteen. The scattering of blood-soaked beads in his hair clacked together as he dropped to a crouch, thrusting up with his spear.

"They don't sink into the snow!" Gair reported, studying the odd, wide boots his attacker wore. It distributed the youth's weight and kept him on the surface. The elf easily parried each jab, while at the same time, he kept a corner of his mind focused on the six submissive warriors to the north. He needed to keep them calm so they would not join the fray.

"No!" It was Camilla's voice, and Gair risked a glance behind him.

One of her Solamnic knights was staggering, hands clutched in front of him. He fell onto his back, a spear protruding from his throat, and beneath the weight of his plate mail, he was quickly swallowed by the snow.

Still parrying the young warrior's frantic attacks, Gair noticed that Iryl had retrieved a miscast spear. She held it in front of her, evidencing that she knew how to use it, and kept her eyes glued to the west, where a shadow on the horizon suggested the large figure was closing.

Camilla and the remaining knight were back to back, thigh-deep in snow. The two knights were exchanging blows with the six attackers who had ringed them and were at a disadvantage because of their lower position. Still Camilla managed a lucky blow, her sword cleaving deep into the leg of one of the barbarians. He fell, howling, and the Solamnic commander brought her sword down hard, finishing him off.

"This is senseless!" Iryl spat. The lithe elf had discarded her voluminous cloak and was heading toward the knights, plodding through the snow and waving the spear back and forth in front of her. "The Qué-Nal are peaceful. My friends, stop this!"

A young warrior broke away from the knights and charged Iryl. "Friends! Only the weak Qué-Nal befriend outsiders," he proclaimed with a sneer. "Only they ignore the trespassers at the stair. Not Shadowwalker's clan!"

"Shadowwalker!" Iryl declared. "By the blessed memory of Habbakuk!"

She used her spear to knock away his first thrust, whirled in the snow, and fell prone as his second attack passed over her head. She rolled to the right as he moved in and jabbed downward. Covered with snow, she managed to get to her feet and continued to parry the warrior's attacks.

To the north, Gair tried to reason with his foe. "I have no desire to kill you!" he said.

The youth laughed. "Zebyr Jotun does not trouble my mind with such concerns." He drove forward, pressing the elf back and jamming his spear down, trying to impale the elf.

Gair moved at the last possible moment, hurling his knife at the youth and striking him in the stomach. The young warrior continued to cackle, tugging the bloodless knife free. His furs were so thick, it was as if he were wearing armor and the blade was too small to find its way through. Knife in one hand now and spear in the other, he advanced on Gair again.

"You give me no choice!" the elf shouted. Softer, to himself, he added, "I can't afford to dally with you when Camilla is in danger."

The elf darted in, swinging hard to the right and splitting the youth's spear. Without pause, he lunged in and swept the blade again, cutting through the thick skins and finding flesh beneath them. The young warrior struggled back a step, gasping in surprise and pain.

Nearby, Camilla crouched in the snow, making herself a smaller target. Then a heartbeat later she rose, and feinting to her right, sliced forcefully under the barbarian's shield. The blade bit through his fur and deep into his stomach. The startled Qué-Nal grunted and fell back, his hand pressing against the growing line of red staining his pelt, then dropping the decorated shield.

"Kill the woman knight!" This was a new voice, and all eyes swiveled to the south to spot an ancient man yards away, his long hair as white as the snow and blowing wildly about a deeply lined face. "Kill all of them!" He raised his hands, thumbs touching, fingers spread wide.

"Shadowwalker!" Iryl moaned. She was still locked in a fight with a Qué-Nal warrior.

Another blow, and Gair dropped his foe.

The remaining four Qué-Nal continued to jab at Camilla and her knight. Blood stained the snow around the latter, and his slow movements showed he was seriously wounded.

Gair! The elder Graymist intruded again. *You and your friends cannot win this battle. Not now. Hide!*

"Never!" Gair cursed as he plowed through the snow to the south, slowed only by his indecisiveness of whether to help Iryl or the two knights.

The four around Camilla and her knight increased the tempo of their attacks, thrusting with the tips of their spears, then bringing the other ends around as if their weapons were quarterstaffs.

Far behind them, the old man was humming, the droning sound cutting through the clamor, unnerving Gair.

He has magic, Gair's father surmised. *That's why you cannot win. Run while you can, Son! We've much work to do together. Do not throw your life away for these people.*

"These people are my friends," the elf growled.

Several blows glanced off Camilla's armor, but one struck the side of her head, momentarily stunning her. She sagged back against the other knight, who was faring worse. A spear had found its way between the plates in his armor just as he had managed to land a serious blow against one of the barbarians.

Another glance told Gair that Iryl was holding her own, so he darted toward the knights, feet flying over the snow and sending a shower of white in his wake.

"Orvago!" Iryl hollered. "It's Orvago!"

The shape coming from the west was the gnoll. He was running, jowls wide open as he howled.

"Orvago! Help us!" Iryl called to him. "Hurry."

As the gnoll closed the distance, Shadowwalker clapped his hands together, the sound booming like thunder. The wind gained more strength, whistling fiercely and whipping snow into the eyes of the knights and the elves. The snow seemed not to bother the Qué-Nal, who continued to worry at the knights.

A grievously wounded warrior dropped his spear and threw himself on the male knight, bearing him to the ground and pitching him into Camilla in the process. Camilla struggled to stay on her feet as the other three warriors thrust their spears at her.

Gair wasn't yet close enough, and one of the Qué-Nal spears found its mark. It skewered the commander from behind.

"No!" Gair cried.

Despite her injury, the Solamnic knight moved quickly. She brought her sword down on the arm of an attacker in front of her, cleaving it and sending a shower of blood everywhere. With the spear still protruding from her back, she whirled and swept her sword high, slicing through the hides of the already wounded barbarian who was atop the other knight.

The youth cried out once, then fell lifeless.

"Only three left," Gair chattered to himself as he closed the distance. "We can prevail here yet."

You can't, his father hissed into his ear, *and now you can't run.*

The wind became even more fierce, like the blizzard of a few weeks ago. The world turned white. "Did he cause that storm, too, Father?" Gair hollered to hear himself above the wind. "Was the old man responsible?"

I do not know, the elder Graymist replied, the spirit's voice a mere whisper.

Camilla's chest was heaving from the exertion, her breath puffing away from her face like a chimney being stoked and melting the flakes that swirled in front of her. Her back burned, and she felt the blood running from her wound and soaking the padding beneath her armor. She couldn't see more than inches in front of her and concentrated on listening to the swishing sound of the Qué-Nals' feet over the drifts. There was one in front of her! She rained a succession of harsh blows toward it, hearing a sharp crack when her sword cut through a spear.

Three Qué-Nal, two of them weaponless, danced around her as if the snowstorm was not there. One darted in and picked up the fallen knight's sword, then brought it up to parry Gair's swing. The elf was not relying on his eyesight but was listening to his father tell him where the barbarians were.

Crouching, the elf feinted, then rose up and rammed his sword forward and felt it sink into someone in front of him. "Keep me away from Camilla!" he called to his father. "I don't want to harm her by mistake." Nor do I want her to harm me, he thought.

Away from the pair, Iryl clutched the spear in one hand, and with the other tried to bat away the snow so she could see. She felt a rush of air and leapt to the side, feeling the brush of fur as the Qué-Nal charged where she had been a heartbeat before. She felt another brush of fur, this more coarse, and heard a deep-throated growl.

"Orvago!" She let out a sigh of relief. "Thanks be to the memory of Habbakuk!"

"Kill them!" the old man continued to shout. "For Zebyr Jotun! Kill them!"

"A beast!" the Qué-Nal nearby Iryl cried. "Shadow-walker, they have monsters on their side!"

Chaos continued to rain in the swirling snowstorm. The clang of Gair's and Camilla's swords rang out against the spears of their foes and the soft thuds of the blades striking the thick hides of the barbarians. A muffled cry cut through the wind, Camilla's, followed by a series of thuds and clangs as an incensed Gair retaliated.

"Camilla's down!" Gair called out, hoping that Iryl still lived. "Father, how many left?"

Still three, the elder Graymist answered. *One is sorely injured.*

"Tell me where they are, Father!"

More blows rained.

Somewhere in the wicked whiteness, the old man continued to shout, "Kill them all!"

Near Iryl, the gnoll was wildly slashing at a barbarian who was doing his best to crawl toward Shadow-walker. The gnoll's hood was thrown back, revealing his doglike face, spittle flying and freezing as he continued to claw at the man.

Camilla was face first in the snow and struggling to push herself up. The knight was faint from cold and the loss of blood, her fingers practically frozen.

Gair was wounded, too, from spear jabs that penetrated through his defenses and punctured his legs, but none of the wounds were serious. He stepped in front of Camilla, following his father's directions, thrusting his sword forward like a spear, driving it through one of the remaining barbarians.

Two left! The elder Graymist's voice finally showed a hint of optimism. *The monster you call your friend has finished another, and the old man is retreating!*

The gnoll's victory cry cut through the chaos, sending a shiver down Gair's spine.

The two remaining are fleeing, too, his father continued. *The monster has unnerved them! It was fortunate your beast was worried over your tardiness and came looking for you. The monster is good for something after all.*

The gnoll was snorting and growling, trying to find his way through the snow to pursue his quarry.

"Let them go, Orvago!" Gair shouted as his father explained what the gnoll was trying to do. "Over here! I need you!" Then the elf slumped to his knees, as if the effort of shouting took the last of his strength. "I should have told Goldmoon and Iryl about the Qué-Nal, Father." His voice was soft, cloaked by the sound of the wind-driven snow.

No, his father corrected. *You were right to keep the knowledge hidden. It would not have prevented this.*

"Camilla!"

There was nothing but the persistent shushing of the snow and Orvago's growls.

"Where is she, Father?"

Lost to you, Son. Mortally wounded, I'm afraid. She is slipping toward my realm. I will welcome her for you.

Gair shut out the rest of his father's words and groped furiously with his frigid hands, desperately trying to find Camilla. She was lying on her side, a layer of snow atop her, a spear lodged in her back. He felt her face, his fingers dancing down her body until they encountered the warm stickiness of her blood.

Gair blocked everything else, focusing on his heart, trembling from fear of losing her, calling forth his healing spell.

The magic was dead within him. He was exhausted, physically and mentally, too spent to nurture a mystical spark.

"Please!" the elf whimpered as he concentrated harder, felt himself grow colder as all his energy was directed inward. His breathing became ragged, and he slumped over her still form. "Please!" He could sense his heartbeat, weakening himself further as he tried to draw energy from it. It thrummed irregularly as he gave up the last of his strength in an effort to find his mystic center. The penetrating cold, and a blackness that came up from nowhere and everywhere, swelled to surround him, and he felt himself lose his grip on consciousness and spiral downward. "No!" It was a hoarse whisper of protest. "I won't give up yet!" Just as he suspected he might fail himself, he found a last bit of energy left in his limbs, and the elf felt something stir within him, something inexplicable, a faintly mystical pulse.

He pictured it as a flame, and he crouched over it, protecting it from the wind and blowing on it gently to give it more substance. The image became more real in his mind until he could feel the warmth of the fire he was building. It was chasing the cold from his limbs, melting the snow all around him. He continued to tend the flames, fingers scrabbling over the dry ground he was mentally painting, gathering twigs and dead leaves. These he shoved into the fire, and it grew.

The elf pulled back from the image now, registering himself draped over Camilla. The warmth from the fire in his chest was surging down his arms and into her unmoving form. The waves were strong, as he'd felt them moving into himself when Jasper healed him on the trail in what seemed so long ago. He stoked the fire higher and was rewarded when he heard her gasp, felt her move slightly.

Still focusing on his healing wave, he reached around to her back, where the spear was lodged. It was not too deep, and he tugged it out, pressing his fingers into the wound and coaxing his mystical warmth inside.

She moaned softly.

"You'll be all right." Guided by Orvago, Iryl had found her way to the knight commander's side. "Gair is healing you."

"No!" The word was firm. She tried to push herself away from the elf's hands, but Iryl held her down, and Camilla hadn't the strength to handle the slight elvish woman. "Take me to town, please. There's an herbalist at the Sentinel. She'll see to me. No magic."

Gair's fingers fluttered across her arm, where he felt a broken bone. He couldn't set it, though he knew Goldmoon or Jasper could handle that task. He could stop the bleeding and ease her pain. He directed the warmth to flow into the arm.

Camilla was growing stronger, and Orvago helped keep her from squirming.

"I don't want this!" The words were almost lost in the still-blowing snow. "None of this mysticism. None of it. Let me die . . . or take me to town."

"I won't let you die, lady knight," Gair said. "And the port is days away." He turned his attention back to the spell and directed the last of the healing warmth into her. Thoroughly spent, he fell back into the soft snow, gasping and clutching his cold fingers to his chest.

"Willum," Camilla moaned. She was feverish, ranting. "Willum, don't let them heal me. None of their mysticism. None of it."

Iryl smoothed the knight's hair and cradled Camilla's

face in her lap to protect it from the wind. "Everything will be all right, Commander Weoledge. Rest now."

The miniature storm died several minutes later, leaving behind snow that had all but covered the bodies of the slain Qué-Nal and the two knights. One of the latter lived, barely, and Gair somehow found just enough mystical strength to stop his bleeding. The elf plucked at the fastenings of the armor and tugged it off the man.

The gnoll padded over, removed his own cloak, wrapped it around the wounded knight, and hoisted him gently over his shoulder. Orvago glanced to the west. He had followed their tracks to get here, and the storm that came from nowhere covered up all trace of them.

Iryl brushed the snow from the slain knight, ran her fingers across his eyelids to close them, and offered a quiet prayer to the departed Habbakuk. Finished, she joined Gair, who had removed Camilla's armor and was wrapping her in one of the blankets, then lifted her in his arms. The knight was as tall as the elf and at least as heavy, but Gair somehow managed to carry her.

"We'll have to return for the armor and the rest of the blankets," he told Iryl. "Too heavy to deal with now."

A blanket under each arm, she nodded and took the lead, her eyes darting to the north and south, fearful of spotting more Qué-Nal. "I did not believe the Que-Nal capable of this," she said. She shook her head in disbelief. "As a whole, they are a peaceful people. I apologize."

"For what?"

"I was blinded to the truth of the real nemesis. If I'd had a clue that Shadowwalker was involved, I could have prevented this," Iryl declared.

"Prevented it?" Gair sucked in his breath. "How?"

"Shadowwalker's a renegade. The chieftain of the Qué-Nal, Skydancer, is a close friend of mine. I could have said something to him. He and his people could have stopped Shadowwalker, stopped all of this. Shadowwalker's mad, my Silvanesti friend. You heard the young warriors mention Zebyr Jotun? That's one of their gods. You might know her as Zeboim, queen of the sea. Shadowwalker believes the gods are still here and thinks that his power comes from her. He's mad . . . and dangerous. He's probably behind the fire at the citadel, the attack on the pilgrims. All these deaths, Gair—the fire, everything—they could have been prevented if only I'd known."

Not another word was spoken as Orvago, Gair, and Iryl forged a new path through the snow.

It was after sundown by the time they reached the settlement. They went straight to Goldmoon's tent, where the aging healer and Jasper tended to the knights. Camilla's protests to their mystic ministrations were ignored.

Gair padded from the settlement when he was confident Camilla would live and that she was resting comfortably. "Could have prevented this," he muttered to himself as he passed by the Silver Stair, just winking into view with the stars. "Well, I will put an end to all of this. Darkhunter will tell me where to find this Shadowwalker, and I will deal with the old man." And then I will return to Goldmoon and beg her to cleanse this darkness I feel growing stronger inside me, the elf added to himself.

Chapter 12

The Whisperers

The gnoll stood stoop-shouldered inside the tent, too tall to stand completely upright without tearing the tent stakes loose, something he'd done several times already. He was admiring the ornamental broadsword Gair had hung just inside the doorway. When the light hit it just right, as it was doing now, he could see his eyes reflected in the blade.

He grinned, a trail of spittle edging over his lip. He wiped at it with a hairy paw, rubbed the paw against his pants leg, and reached up to tug the sword loose from its fastenings. He ran his clawed fingers over the carvings of pegasi and made a sound reminiscent of a cat's purr. Almost reverently he placed the sword on Gair's cot, admiring it a few more moments.

Next the gnoll slipped out of his red cloak and bright blue tunic. He tugged his boots free and carefully placed them and the socks on the end of his bed. Naked except for his loose-fitting trousers, which he rolled up to his knees, Orvago snatched up the sword again and stepped out of the tent, nearly barreling into Goldmoon.

"Good evening, Orvago." She smiled up at the gnoll.

"Aren't you cold?"

He shrugged, wrinkled his snout, and glanced toward the sun, which was starting to set.

Her eyes drifted to the sword. "Isn't that Gair's?"

The gnoll nodded sheepishly.

"You're borrowing it to go hunting? I'm sure he won't mind, though I wish I knew where he was. I haven't seen him since last night."

The gnoll shook his head and shrugged his shoulders.

"I'm sure he's all right."

The gnoll smiled broadly, revealing a double row of sharp teeth. His eyes glimmered with the same excitement she'd noticed when she saw him hunting the boars. He demonstrated to her how the blade reflected like a mirror.

"Tired of eating our cooked food?"

He nodded again.

"Well, good hunting, my friend," she offered as she turned and headed toward the settlement's main cook-fire.

The scent of roast deer and the sound of friendly conversation drifted across the settlement. His keen ears picked up Jasper toasting the memory of Reorx the Forge, whom the dwarves considered the greatest of Krynn's gods, and he heard Camilla and Iryl discussing the renegade Qué-Nal.

The pads of his feet were cold against the snow, but he considered it a pleasant sensation as he ran toward the north, toward where the River Shard met the Lake of Swords. He had grown so used to wearing boots that he'd almost forgotten what it was like to feel the snow beneath his feet. The biting cold put him on edge and made him more alert, and the wind teasing the green-gray hair of his chest was invigorating. The sun was halfway swallowed up by the horizon, painting the ground a pale orange and making the edge of the broad sword gleam as if it had just been pulled from the forge. He sniffed the air, searching for prey, no longer picking up the scent of roast deer. The woods loomed ahead, and he raced toward them, quickly losing himself in the shadows of the thick trees.

He ran a little farther then dropped to his knees and traced a depression in the snow. There were other tracks nearby, under the spread of a massive willow—a large elk. Orvago followed the elk's trail, pausing occasionally to check his position and sniffing to keep track of its spoor. He dropped again, noting more tracks, tracing their outlines and sniffing. Abruptly he turned to the west now, following a different set of tracks.

The sun had set, and the woods were growing darker. The gnoll's dull red eyes separated the shadows. He could see well in the dark, but these tracks were difficult to follow, since they'd been covered up here and there.

The last of the light was fading, making the air even colder. Orvago traveled another hour, then another. The stars were winking into view, illuminating a trail made narrow by thickening trees and spreading ground cover. The tracks were fresher here.

The sound of voices drifted to him from ahead, beyond a thicket of trees. The gnoll recognized one of them. He picked out six distinct voices, all whispering in low, raspy tones. He crept closer. Eyeing the trees, he noticed several had carvings on them. He selected one with a hollow trunk and hid the broadsword in it, approaching weaponless.

Orvago drew himself up to his full height and walked forward into the clearing. His lips curled up in a smile at Gair, and he waved a hairy paw in the air in greeting.

The elf was standing in the center of a clearing filled with snow-covered mounds, bright to the gnoll's eyes against the black of the tree trunks, and against the black of the *things* that seemed to be talking to Gair.

There were six of them, manlike in shape and somehow blacker than night. They floated above the snowy mounds, speaking in voices that sounded like coarse whispers. Their hair, if it could be called such, looked like trails of smoke waving madly away from their mouthless faces, and their eyes . . . these were what set a ridge of hair standing up on the gnoll's back.

Their eyes burned white, unblinking and looking hot as coals. All six pairs were focused on Orvago. His lips curled back in a snarl. What passed for their black chests did not rise and fall. He could not smell them, and they did not breathe.

A menacing growl rose in Orvago's throat. The gnoll took a step back, and then another. A chill ran down his spine as he saw two of the black creatures separate from the group and advance toward him. They moved slowly, like clouds floating across the sky, their eyes seeming to burn white-hot. The other four remained in a semicircle around the elf.

What manner of creature are you? one of them asked in its coarse, whispery voice.

"He is called a gnoll," Gair supplied.

A gnoll, it repeated. It cackled then, a sound like glass shattering. *A living thing. We hate life*, it continued. *We will end the gnoll's life.*

The others cackled, too, and Orvago threw his paws over his ears and backed away faster. The laughter was physically painful.

We will end your life, the second parroted, *and we will make you one of us. You will thank us for your death.*

They shot forward with a speed that amazed the gnoll. Impossibly black arms grew claws and reached out, slashing at Orvago's chest. He waved his hairy arms in an effort to fend them off.

The cackling continued, and two more spirit shapes floated forward. Four of the things circled the gnoll now, taunting him, darting in and scratching him with nails as sharp as any sword. The cuts were not deep, but they hurt terribly. Each swipe brought with it a freezing jolt. Their touch was colder than the snow!

Orvago retaliated with his own claws, but to little effect. His arms passed right through the black bodies and made him feel as if he'd thrust his arms into an icy pond.

We'll make you one of us! another tittered. The sentiment was quickly repeated until the coarse whispers drowned out his snarls. *Make you dead!*

Make you dead! The words became a chant that was echoed around the clearing. *Dead. Dead. Dead.*

"No!" The voice was Gair's, and it gave the creatures pause. "Leave the gnoll alone!"

The black creatures still hovered around the gnoll, darting in and out, eyes burning. The gnoll continued to bat at them as he backed away, glancing around. The hollow tree where he'd hidden the sword wasn't much farther away.

"Leave the gnoll alone," the elf repeated, moving forward even as Orvago continued to back away. "I want to talk to him."

The gnoll continued to back away as he tried to look beyond the black bodies to see his friend, carefully looking him over to make sure the black creatures had not injured the elf.

Gair understood the gnoll's concern. "I'm all right. They haven't harmed me."

We would not hurt him. Only help him. The master summoned us and gave us life, one of the black creatures explained.

Orvago's heart thundered in his chest, and his thick eyebrows rose in bewilderment.

Intensely glowing eyes moved to within an inch of the gnoll's face. They exuded a frigid wave, and they took on a reddish cast that grew steadily brighter. The gnoll's teeth chattered, and he backed away faster now. He was at the edge of the clearing now, nearing the hollow tree.

"Orvago, don't leave." It was Gair's voice again. "We need to talk, you and I. Well, I suppose I have to do the talking, and you have to listen very carefully."

The gnoll's eyes darted back and forth between the black shapes, vigorously shook his head and motioned frantically for the elf to come with him.

"That wouldn't be a good idea—not right now, anyway." Gair's tone was terse. "I need to stay a while longer with my new friends."

Orvago howled mournfully, and he desperately motioned to the elf once more to come with him. The woods had closed completely about Orvago now as he had maneuvered himself farther down the trail. The black creatures were still following him, passing through trees and effortlessly keeping pace.

Kill him? one asked in its whispery voice. *Can we kill him, Master? Then we can go to your settlement, drink the life there.*

Gair shook his head. "Not the citadel grounds. Goldmoon is there."

Not the citadel, Master. As you wish. But this animal? Let us drink the life from this animal, Master. You summoned us to do your bidding. Please let that bidding be to kill this creature.

The gnoll glanced through a gap in the icy black bodies, met Gair's stare.

"I summoned them, Orvago, just like the spirit said." The elf was keeping pace too, but he remained behind the black creatures, sticking to the center of the trail. "I used a spell that Goldmoon taught me, and because I summoned them, I am their master." He paused and threw his head back to look at the stars, inhaled deeply, then dropped his gaze to the gnoll. "I owe Goldmoon much for this enchantment, Orvago. She uses her magic only for the living. I simply made a few adjustments and called upon my father and Darkhunter for help. I choose to use my magic on the dead now."

Orvago was close to the tree now. Just a few more steps. The gnoll raised his hairy arms, trying to bat the creatures away.

The black things cackled. It sounded like breaking glass to the gnoll's sensitive ears. Gair was laughing, too. "Orvago, it takes more than that to drive them away. Indeed, I don't think I could make them go away even if I wanted to." His eyes narrowed. "Which I don't."

Suddenly Orvago's back was against the tree. He was feeling behind him for the hollow spot. There. He was working the fingers of his right hand inside the hollow trunk, stretching them lower.

"I know you consider me your friend, Orvago," Gair began.

The gnoll nodded his head animatedly.

"I'm not sure I can trust you. I know you can't talk, at least not in my language, but you can get your point across when you want to. I don't need Goldmoon finding out about my dark companions, my loyal wraiths."

Can we kill him now, Master? the largest of the black creatures asked. Its eyes consumed Orvago's vision. *He reeks of life. Let us drink the sweetness from him.*

The gnoll's red eyes grew wide and he swallowed hard. That word "Master" again.

Can we, Master? the large wraith repeated.

"I suppose so . . . yes, Darkhunter. You may kill him." Orvago howled in disbelief.

"You may kill him," Gair continued, "but do so

quickly. I do not want the gnoll to suffer for long."

The large wraith moved to Orvago, touching its icy chest to his hairy gray-green one. The gnoll yowled in agony at the painfully frigid sensation. The undead creature persevered, and Orvago slid to his rump, sobbing and twitching, growing weaker by the moment.

The gnoll's paw fumbled behind him, his fingers moving erratically. The pain was becoming even more intense, threatening to render him unconscious.

The wraiths' whispers grew louder, filled with promises that the gnoll would die but not die, that he would be raised at the behest of their elven master to walk with them. *Stronger than the living, more powerful in darkness.*

Behind them, Gair's voice grew irritated. "I told you to finish him quickly. There will be others to kill at your leisure!"

Tears poured from the gnoll's eyes, both from the pain that wracked his body and from the knowledge that his elven friend was ordering his death. His fingers continued to fumble about in the opening as one of the creatures thrust its intangible hands into his thighs. The icy sensation was almost more than the gnoll could bear, and he screamed, his voice sounding practically human in its pain.

"Enough of this, I said!" Gair spat. "Kill him now!"

With his free hand, Orvago tried desperately one last time to bat the creatures away. His hand passed through them again, adding to his icy agony. But when his claws raked at the eyes of the creature in front of him, the one called Darkhunter, the thing backed away. If he couldn't harm their ghostly forms, maybe he could hurt their eyes. And if he could hurt them, maybe he could kill them, or at least make them return to wherever they had come from.

The clawed fingers of his right hand finally closed

about the carved pommel of the hidden sword. He drove Darkhunter back with the other by poking at the creature's eyes. Another spirit darted in under the sweep of his shaggy arm, its claws out and digging into his side.

The gnoll's sharp cry pierced the night, and the creatures howled in glee.

Do not fight the death we offer. Join with us, Darkhunter said. He floated just beyond the gnoll's reach, letting his fellow creatures dart in and out for the attack. *Join with us. Join with us.* The words became a ghostly refrain picked up by the other five. *In death gain life. Join with us. Join with us.*

The gnoll growled fiercely, summoned the last of his strength, and pushed himself to his feet. In the process, he passed through the forms of two wraiths, the sensation insufferable and threatening to send him to the ground again. He gritted his teeth and forced back a howl, then doubled over in pain as one of the spirits passed a hand into his chest. He withdrew the broadsword and swung it in an awkward arc, slicing into the large wraith called Darkhunter.

The wraith screamed, the noise so high and shrill it nearly caused Orvago to drop the blade. The other wraiths paused in their attack.

"Orvago, where did you get my sword?" Gair shouted.

Orvago gasped and swung the blade at Darkhunter again, driving it deep into where its belly would be. The scream was inhuman and long, and it trailed off into a snarl as the wraith flew backward. Darkhunter floated behind Gair, moaning from his unseen wound and cursing the gnoll.

The blade is enchanted, the wraith muttered.

"A magical sword?" Gair waved his hand, beckoning the five other wraiths to resume their attack. "So the man in town sold me a magical sword. Most certainly he didn't realize what he had, or he would have charged me much more. I didn't realize what I had. Do be reasonable, friend Orvago, and put it down. It is not yours, after all. I promise you this will be over swiftly."

The gnoll bellowed and charged forward, swinging the blade to the right and slicing at the waist of the nearest undead. The gnoll's muscles bunched; dragging the sword through the creature was like dragging it through mud. He sliced again, and the wraith howled and fled, even as he brought the weapon around to jab at another. This one, too, retreated.

Only three were left to face him. The elf's eyes were narrow slits, his lip curled upward in a sneer. Orvago had never seen him look like this. The elf's expression caught him off guard and bought his undead opponents an opening.

The nearest spirit suddenly disappeared into the ground, coming up beneath the gnoll to grab his ankles. Icy pain shot through Orvago's legs, and his knees buckled. The gnoll pitched forward, straight into the second wraith, whose claws clutched at Orvago's heart. The third had somehow gotten behind the gnoll and was clawing at his back.

The gnoll screamed and rolled on the ground, still refusing to drop the blade. He swung it clumsily and ineffectually, his opponents able to dodge his erratic movements.

The elf's expression softened as he regarded his friend. For a brief moment, he considered calling off the wraiths, but Darkhunter was at his side, demanding revenge for the pain the gnoll had inflicted on him.

Kill him, Darkhunter urged his fellow wraiths.

"Finish him," Gair pronounced. "Now!"

The three uninjured wraiths wrapped themselves around the gnoll like an inky blanket. Writhing on his back, it was all Orvago could do to raise his arm and try to feebly swing the sword.

The gnoll bit down hard on his lower lip, hoping this new pain would help him concentrate. It barely registered, though he could taste the blood in his mouth. Focusing his energy into his next swing, he lashed at his own leg, slicing through the wraith on top of it and digging into his own flesh.

The gnoll and wraith cried out simultaneously, and the spirit floated away. Two left. Orvago drove the blade down again. The tip bit into his abdomen, sending another jolt of agony into him. He tugged the weapon free and swung again. Another ghostly scream cut through the air as a second wraith fled. One left.

The gnoll was able to push himself to his knees. A few yards away, Gair was urging the injured wraiths to move forward, to surround the gnoll. "You should have finished him when I told you to," he lectured. "See what you've done by toying with him?"

There was a chorus of coarse-whispered apologies. The wounded undead continued to beg their master's forgiveness as Orvago stood shakily and faced his remaining opponent. He avoided looking at the things' eyes, which continued to unnerve him. Instead, he swept the sword back and forth in front of him, glancing sidelong at the elf.

The gnoll took a step forward, purposely giving the wraith an opening. The black creature took it, darting in and raking the gnoll's bleeding abdomen. Orvago felt numb, whirling only by sheer will and slashing at the creature before it could move away. The blade passed all the way through the wraith, and Orvago spun about and sliced at it again and again.

The wraith's brief scream drowned out the cries of its fellows as it dissipated. Bits of blackness, like rain, fell on the snow, then disappeared.

Orvago was weak and bleeding profusely. Still, he squared his shoulders and snarled defiantly. He waved the sword again in a serpentine pattern he'd seen the men use on the ship that brought him close to Schallsea Island.

Darkhunter was conferring with Gair, the whispery words too soft for the gnoll to hear. The other four wraiths were behind the elf, nursing their unseen wounds and glaring at Orvago with their ice-hot eyes.

"I can't let him return to the settlement," Gair said. "Not now. No matter what. Goldmoon would question him about his injuries. Perhaps she could use a spell to pull the information from his small brain." With a gesture, he waved the four wraiths forward. Darkhunter remained at the elf's side.

Orvago spread his legs and bent at the knees, jabbing forward, sending the blade into the lead wraith's chest, then dragging it up through its mudlike form until the blade sliced through its neck. The creature screamed and disappeared, raining blackness on the snow. Not pausing, the gnoll aimed a blow at the ground, where one of the wraiths was coming up between his feet. The sword cleaved the thing's head in two. More rain.

The elf called the remaining two off, but Orvago pursued them. He slashed to his right, narrowly missing one, then turned and brought the sword down to his left, slaying a third. He shuffled forward, sweeping the blade left and right until he connected with the last of his foes.

Behind Gair, Darkhunter sought safety by seeping into the ground. The elf backed up, warily watching Orvago, who was stumbling toward him.

"You're hurt," Gair said. "I could heal you."

Orvago snarled. "I do not trust you," the gnoll said, the words guttural but clear.

"By the vanished gods, you can talk!" The elf drew his sword. It gleamed faintly in the starlight. He continued to back farther into the clearing, and the gnoll continued to follow him. "You're good with a sword," Gair said. "I'll warrant you that, especially with a magic one—my magic sword—but I'm the better swordsman."

"Maybe," the gnoll grunted.

"I don't want to kill you, Orvago."

"Liar."

The elf spun and darted down the trail, kicking up snow as he went. He dashed into the middle of the clearing, down a path between a row of burial mounds. A black shadow—Darkhunter, the gnoll guessed—rose from a mound and followed him.

Orvago did not pursue. He didn't have the strength. He turned and staggered southward, the magical sword in one hand, the other hand pressed as firmly as his strength would allow over the deep wound in his abdomen.

* * * * *

Dawn painted the snow a pale pink—like Camilla's lips, Gair mused. The clouds overhead were the color of her eyes. The elf was sitting deep in the Qué-Nal woods on a rotted log. Wrapped in his cloak, he stared at a spot on the snow-covered ground.

The Solamnic knight commander was probably lost to him now, he suspected. He doubted she would understand or condone his dealings with the dead. Perhaps he could contact the spirits of some famous long-dead Solamnic knights. That might impress her. He could give them form as he had to his wraiths, and maybe he could convince them to reason with her.

"Goldmoon?" he whispered. "She might forgive me on her own. Forgiveness is in her nature. She'd probably accept me back into the settlement, but she certainly wouldn't teach me any more mystical spells." He thrust his sword into the ground between his feet. "She'd try to stop me from using dark mysticism, and that I could not tolerate."

A shadow moved away from him and clung to the trunk of a thick willow tree. It was Darkhunter. The wraith was still recovering from the wounds Orvago had inflicted with the magical sword.

The elf allowed himself a wry smile. "My sword. With my sword that damnable gnoll dashed an entire day's worth of work—slaying five spirits I painstakingly brought through the doorway. One was my father, and that is a spirit I will bring back again."

Would it be easier the second time? he wondered, or harder, given that the elder Graymist had been slain by an enchanted weapon?

"By the vanished gods, why did I leave that sword hanging up in my tent where the gnoll could get it?"

No matter. He would try to get the sword back. He had to return to the Silver Stair sometime anyway, since he needed to use the energy that coursed through the ruin to bring back his father, and more. Perhaps on that trip he would liberate the sword. He had purchased it, after all. Perhaps he would kill the gnoll with it.

He dropped his head into his hands and sobbed.

"What am I saying? What's wrong with me? Kill Orvago?" The elf's shoulders shook. "I only intended to deal with the dead, not to add to the dead. What's happening to me?"

You are becoming stronger, the shadow of Darkhunter whispered.

* * * * *

It took the gnoll several hours to make his way back to the settlement. There was little life left in him when he collapsed at the base of the Silver Stair. His chest rose and fell raggedly, and his eyes fluttered closed.

It was dawn before he was discovered.

The entire settlement was ringed around him. Camilla stood over him, talking to Goldmoon and to Willum. Orvago couldn't make out the words. He hurt all over, and he felt terribly cold and weak. He couldn't move his arms or legs, couldn't feel them.

Goldmoon's face appeared above his, ringed by a fur-trimmed hood. He vaguely registered the feel of her hands on his chest. He sensed a warmth in those hands and in her smile. The dawning sun touched a few stray locks of her hair, making it glisten like gold. In the early morning light, she looked younger to the gnoll, beautiful for a human, and she made him feel warm. She was taking some of the hurt away.

The healer concentrated, focusing the power of her heart on Orvago. He was injured far worse now than when he had been gored by the huge boar. She prayed fervently to the memory of Mishakal that she could find the power to heal him.

The medallion about her neck tingled. Magical, she began drawing on its power. The warmth continued to surge from the necklace, from her heart, down her arms and into her fingers, into Orvago. In strengthening him, pouring all of her energy into the effort, she was weakening herself.

The gnoll moaned, and his chest began to rise and fall somewhat regularly now. The wound on his abdomen started to heal.

He heard Camilla above him. She gasped in surprise as his wounds closed. He heard Willum and the others who had gathered exchange words of amazement. He heard words of concern from Goldmoon's students and the dwarven builders, and this pleased him. The people of the settlement seemed to actually care about him. They were frightened *for* him, no longer frightened *of* him.

"Goldmoon," Orvago croaked. "Goldmoon . . . thank you."

"He talks!" This from Redstone, who hovered nearby. "When did he learn to talk?"

"Goldmoon . . ."

She shushed him to be still, and he felt blankets being draped across him. Something soft was being edged under his head by the dwarf, Jasper. Goldmoon's hands remained on his chest, continuing to warm him. He could breathe deeper with her here. The ache was lessening.

"Stay quiet," she said, drawing back. "You will be all right, but I don't want to move you for a while. I want you to get a little stronger first."

Jasper edged closer and placed his hands on Orvago's chest. The dwarf took over for Goldmoon, continuing to mend the gnoll's wounds. "We'll move you to your tent in a little while," the dwarf said. "You'll have to stay there for a few days. What did you run into that chewed you up like this?"

"Indeed. What happened?" It was Camilla's voice. "Who . . . what . . . did this to you?"

"Gair," he croaked. "Gair and the whisperers did this."

Chapter 13

The Shattered Door

They were shadows against shadows, deep in the Qué-Nal woods. The wraiths, recently given life by Gair, slipped across the drifts and clung to the darkened tree trunks, chasing their prey toward the ruins of Castle Vila and reveling in the fear the men radiated.

The elf followed the wraiths, moving almost silently across the hard-packed snow and down the winding path of a frozen stream. Darkhunter was at his side, his father floating somewhere above them beneath the spidery branches of dormant maples.

"They stood their ground longer than most men would," Gair said. "Knights are like that, uncharacteristically brave. I know two of them."

You knew *them*, Darkhunter corrected. The wraith floated through a tree stump that Gair had to step around. *You knew them when you were with Goldmoon and her doting disciples, but you are beyond them now, as far beyond them as the stars are above the face of Krynn.*

A part of Gair shuddered at the thought, the part that was being smothered by the darkness still growing inside him. That small part regretted his hand last night in killing a half-dozen Solamnic knights who had been sent to search for him, and that small part had suspected that sweet Camilla, concerned about him, sent the men. The darkness within the elf had relished watching the knights die.

The darkness helped Gair understand Goldmoon better now than he ever had before. She was too caring and sympathetic. She put other people's welfare before her own, and all of that made her emotionally weak. The night that she taught him to open the door to the realm of the dead—because she believed it would give him peace—he sensed that he had forged a bond with her. He wondered if she sensed the link as well. He could somehow tell when she was thinking about him, which she was now. However, he hadn't yet been able to divine precisely *what* she was thinking.

"That will come," he said to himself. "I will strengthen our bond, Goldmoon, use the magic in the Silver Stair. I will learn what you are up to and if—and how—you intend to stop me." He realized it was a newfound obsession, this wanting to know what Goldmoon was planning. "Perhaps I will question these men about Goldmoon's plans and about where she takes her walks now with Riverwind."

The elf continued to glide along after the wraiths, talking to Darkhunter. The trees were thinning out, giving way to scrub and small oaks bent by the weight of the snow on their branches. The sky loomed dark to the west, with only a smattering of stars poking through the clouds. Gair strained his eyes and saw a finger of blackness prodding up from the flat expanse of snow-covered ground.

Castle Vila, Darkhunter announced, *where we chase our prey.*

"Camilla's knights and Goldmoon's men. You will help me become as powerful, magically, as Goldmoon." It was more of a statement than a question.

No, Master, the wraith hissed. *I will make you more powerful.*

"When I am, I will face her. I'll kill her, and I'll capture her spirit as I've captured yours. She will serve me. I cannot have her remain alive."

Slay her, Gair's father agreed. The wraith fluttered down to float at Gair's other side. *She might be the one person who could stop you. Her citadel must fall, and she with it. And then, my son . . .*

"And then I will raise the spirit of every Qué-Nal who died on this island. When I am finished with that, every Dark Knight, every farmer, every one of Goldmoon's followers, Smithsin's father, the elf of Red Creek . . ."

Schallsea Island will become the realm of the dead, Darkhunter finished.

The elf slowed his pace and watched the wraiths dart around the fleeing men, all of them shadows against the snow. The wraiths circled the men, though they did not yet know their path to Castle Vila had been cut off.

"The tallest is Roeland Stark," Gair said, his voice as soft as the small icicles gently clicking together on the branches in the breeze, "a miller from the port town. He came out one day in the early fall to meet the famed Hero of the Lance. Goldmoon impressed him, as she impresses nearly everyone. He went back to town the next day, closed his shop, gathered his belongings, and joined the settlement. He is strong-minded, just learning the rudiments of healing magic. I like . . . liked . . . him."

He shall die swiftly, Darkhunter pronounced. *His body shall feel little pain.*

"He'll not die until I've spoken to him. Do you understand?"

You've left that life, the spirit argued. *You've no need of their company, no need to talk to them.*

The elf chuckled. "I need only the company of the dead?"

Darkhunter's eyes seemed to glow a little redder.

"I only want to question him," the elf explained, "and then he will die. Yes, kill him quickly. That would please me. You may take your time with the others."

And then they will join us, his father's spirit whispered, *all of them*.

Made stronger in death, Darkhunter said.

The words were echoed by the elder Graymist and repeated in the distance by the other wraiths until they swelled into a chant. Darkhunter flowed away from Gair and moved to join the other undead.

* * * * *

In Goldmoon's tent, Camilla faced the healer across her makeshift table, sitting stiffly, as if she were at attention. Orvago sat on a crate near Goldmoon's bed, yawning and watching both of them, idly rubbing his heel in a small pool of spittle on the ground. He hadn't left Camilla's side since the fight with the Qué-Nal band. He had hovered around both women throughout dinner, had followed them in here even after Goldmoon had said she needed to talk to Camilla alone. However, she finally relented and let him stay. He listened closely to their conversation.

"I did not ask for your healing," Camilla began, "though I suppose I should thank you for it. You probably saved my life, but I will not allow you to use your mysticism on me again. I truly want no part of it."

"As you want no part of this settlement," the healer added. "Commander Weoledge, I understand that you do not want us here. More precisely, you do not want me here. However—"

"However, the Solamnic Council does not share my

opinion." Camilla fixed her eyes on the top of the healer's head, avoiding meeting her gaze. "The council is elated that you are building a center dedicated to your new mystic order. They have doubled the number of Knights of the Sword and soldiers under my command and have instructed me to protect you at all costs and afford you whatever other assistance is possible. Now that we know the threat is from a band of renegade Qué-Nal, we can better defend you."

Camilla continued to stare, unblinking. "I understand from Iryl that the Qué-Nal still revere the old gods, though they call them by names unfamiliar to us."

Goldmoon smoothed her hands on her tunic. "Let us hope I can make my own peace with the Qué-Nal in the spring. I want no discord between them and the settlement. Commander, do you feel well enough for a walk?"

The women walked shoulder to shoulder, presenting a sharp contrast—Camilla young and very much the warrior, walking stately, though she was without her armor, the aging Goldmoon clad in soft browns, soft like her hair and expression and tone, her cloak shushing about her feet. Orvago followed several paces behind them.

The sky had darkened overhead, with clouds obscuring most of the stars, and the tents farthest from the few fires that burned loomed in a row like the bony spine of a great black beast.

"Have you walked the Silver Stair, Commander? The visions I've received there are quite illuminating."

She shook her head. "I have no need of visions. My own faith serves me well enough."

Goldmoon's path took them by each tent in the settlement, then around the construction site, where a dozen dwarves and humans continued to work by the light of a few large lanterns. Jasper and Redstone were putting the finishing touches on a doorframe, and they slowed their work long enough to nod their greetings and eavesdrop a little. The healer noted that Camilla made eye contact with each person in the settlement, as if she were constantly measuring them.

They passed by the row of closely spaced tents belonging to the knights and soldiers. Willum saw them and said he'd heard nothing yet from the search parties of knights and volunteers that had been sent out after Gair and his "whisperers." The men who went to collect the armor and the blankets on the trail to Heart-spring had also come up empty-handed.

Goldmoon finished the tour at a small bay southeast of the tent town, taking Camilla down an overgrown path that led to an imposing cliff.

Camilla let out a long breath between her teeth, making a soft whistling sound. "Pelican Cove," she said, looking down at the water. "I was here with Gair not too long ago." Pilings rose above the choppy surface. "So you'll build a dock here when the weather breaks, which means you won't be needing the docks in town."

"This will be for visitors' use. The cove is not nearly deep enough to accommodate ships of much size. Materials can't be unloaded here." Goldmoon pointed down the cliff face. "In the spring, we'll build steps here."

Camilla glanced across the cove to the Straits of Schallsea and to the New Sea beyond. The water looked as black as ink, and the light from the few stars that showed in the cloudy sky was too faint to reflect on the surface.

"I know you do not want me here." Goldmoon finally brought up the subject again.

"It is because I do not agree with what you are doing."

"I am offering my students hope, teaching them to heal others."

The Solamnic Commander shook her head. "You teach them magic that comes from within."

"The power of the heart."

"Magic comes from the gods, Goldmoon. You were a priestess of Mishakal, and so you of all people should know that."

"You truly don't understand, do you, Commander? The power of the heart is from the gods, the last gift they gave men before they left to wherever Chaos bade them go. Mysticism, some call it. It is still god-magic, and I still believe in the gods. I am a priestess of Mishakal, to my last day."

Camilla's gaze softened. "I thought—"

"That I had forgotten the gods? I revere Mishakal with each breath." The healer sighed and drew Camilla back toward her tent. They paused outside a lean-to, where a family inside was singing an old elvish folk tune about the forest, some of the words mispronounced by their human tongues. "There is something you must know . . . about Gair Graymist."

Camilla pursed her lips, her brow furrowing. She followed Goldmoon back inside the tent. Orvago was quick on her heels, failing to duck in time and rattling the tent pole when his head hit a support. He scowled and offered an apologetic grin. He tried to right the pole, and in the process, he knocked down one of the blankets that was hung to keep the tent warm. He bent to pick up the blanket, butting heads with Camilla. Goldmoon stepped out of the way and patiently waited for the pair to repair the damage.

"Camilla, Gair came to Schallsea Island because of me. It is because of me that he consorts with the dead." The healer's shoulders sagged noticeably. "I am to blame for what happened to Gair. I taught him how to speak to spirits. I thought it would give him peace. The deaths of his father and sisters troubled him greatly."

"According to Orvago, he seems to have gone beyond speaking to them," Camilla returned, a slight edge to her voice.

"Gair somehow misused what I taught him. I'll teach no one else how to open the door to the spirit realm. Camilla, I should not have taught him this dark side of mysticism. It was a door best left closed to him . . . and to everyone."

The commander paced in the small confines, careful not to bump into the gnoll, who was standing, crouched, by the table. "If my knights and your followers find him, can you—"

"Heal him?"

Camilla's gaze was fixed on the design of a blanket that hung against the interior of the tent wall.

"I hope so. That is my intention, anyway."

Silence held sway for several moments. Even the gnoll breathed softly, careful not to make a sound.

"Three search parties we've sent," Camilla finally said. "One of them should find him. My knights, your followers . . . good people who know what they are up against."

"No." The word was a growl. "Men do not know at all. Men will not come back." Orvago shuffled to the tent flap and looked outside. "Whisperers will kill men."

Goldmoon watched the gnoll leave, certain by the shuffling outside that he was walking around her tent on a self-imposed patrol. Her face looked pale in the glow from the lone lantern on the table.

"Do you think the gnoll is right?" The knight showed concern on her young face.

"I will pray to Mishakal that he is wrong," the healer said softly, "but . . . I can see if the men we sent out are safe."

The healer sat, shoulders rounded, fingers steepled against the coarse wood. She closed her eyes and decided for the first time in her life to contact a spirit other than Riverwind's. Inside her mind, her husband urged her to try another tack, but Goldmoon paid his warning little heed.

"It will be all right," she told him. "I'll be careful."

Camilla looked curiously at her.

"I will try to contact the spirit of a man with a good heart. If I cannot reach his spirit, dear Riverwind, I will be grateful that he is not dead. And I will go myself to search for my people—and Gair—come morning."

She laid her hands flat on the table now, her thumbs drawing imaginary circles. The flickering lantern made her hair gleam like thin chains of silver and gold and made the shadows dance behind her.

"Roeland Stark," Goldmoon said almost inaudibly. "Are you in the realm of the dead, my friend?"

* * * * *

The moonlight edged from beneath a cloud and revealed that four men were still standing, two of them Solamnic knights. An equal number were lying face-down in the clearing, the blood from dozens of deep scratches on their bodies tinting the snow a dark red. Gair lurked at the edge of the clearing and watched, virtually mesmerized, as five wraiths danced around the men. Behind them loomed the ruins of Castle Vila.

The wraiths were the spirits of the Solamnic knights and soldiers who had made up the first search party to find Gair Graymist, their natures corrupted through the magical process the elf had used to raise them. Once kind and generous and honorbound, they were now sinister and hateful of life. They toyed with the four remaining men, darting in and slashing at the woolen clothes that covered those from Goldmoon's ranks. Icy-black claws cleaved through the thick material as if it were paper and sliced into the skin beneath. Insubstantial claws reached through the silver mail of the knights, raking deeply into the knights' chests.

Blood dripped onto the snow and brought peals of hideous laughter from the unseen mouths of the wraiths.

More powerful in death, the five chanted.

One of the men screamed as claws raked at his face. Another had come up from beneath his feet and clawed at his legs, shredding his pants and ripping through skin and muscle. He fell to his knees, and a wraith rose up through him, poking its black head out his chest, the feel of the icy dead creature sending numbing pain through the man's broken body. The wraiths left him, for the briefest of moments, retreating as if to offer him the slightest measure of hope, then darted in again, one sinking its claws into the man's shoulder, the other scratching at his eyes.

The man's screams were so shrill they hurt Gair's ears. The elf gritted his teeth and watched as the two wraiths slowly finished the man. Gair tried to place him. The elf had seen him around Goldmoon's camp before, but he couldn't remember the man's name. It wasn't important, Gair decided. He could learn his name later when he brought his spirit back from death.

The other three wraiths, now joined by Gair's father, cavorted around the two knights.

The tall one with no armor, the elder Graymist directed. *He is last. My son wishes it.*

"What are you?" the tall man howled at the inky figures. He brandished a club, which passed harmlessly through the bodies of the undead.

Gair smiled at Roeland Stark. Had the man been facing living foes, he likely would have dropped three or four of them by now. The two knights were also armed, one with a long sword, the other with twin daggers, his long sword lost somewhere in the woods. None of the blades gave the undead pause. They were no threat.

The men could do nothing to stop the wraiths, though one of the black creatures cried mournfully each time a weapon passed through it, pretending that it was being hurt. Gair sensed that the wraith savored offering false hope. Finally the wraith fell to the ground, a pool of unnatural icy blackness. It flowed like spilled ale under the boots of the knight with the long sword, then ran up the man's legs and clawed brutally at his stomach through the plate.

"What manner of creature are you?" Roeland howled again as he watched the knight writhe. Clenching his right hand tighter about his club, he swung it in an effort to keep the creatures away. With his free hand, he tried to peel the creature off the knight. The wraith laughed at the futile gesture and sent a bone-chilling wave of cold into Roeland.

Gair stepped forward just as the knight with the long sword succumbed under the assault of the elder Graymist.

Roeland's eyes locked onto the elf. "You! We came out here looking for you!"

"A pity that you found me." The elf displayed a suitably smug impression, cringing noticeably when the knight with the daggers cried out. "Camilla will not cry when she faces my minions," the elf whispered.

Gair's father dragged his claws along the length of the last knight's right leg, shredding the flesh beneath the armor. He fell, twitching in the snow.

Roeland glanced between the dying knight and Gair, then swung his club futilely. The wind whistled from each inconsequential blow. He hadn't been hurt much—just some claw marks on his arms and face, nothing deep, but he was frightened. His lip quivered, and his hands shook in terror.

"These c-c-creatures," Roeland stammered. "Gair, what are they? Do they hold you? Are you their—"

"Prisoner?"

Roeland nervously nodded. Tears flowed from the big man's eyes as he watched the knight twitch and moan and imagined the horrible pain he was feeling.

"That's what you'd like to believe, Roeland, that they hold me spellbound." The elf took a step closer; the wraith of Darkhunter moved at his shoulder. "Dear, gentle Roeland, I am not their prisoner. I am their master."

Master. Master, the wraiths chanted in unison. *More powerful in death. The master made us more powerful in death.*

"They are people you knew, Roeland. Knights stationed at the settlement. Gregory, Leland, Markus . . ." The three creatures darted in at the introduction, swiping at the downed knight as they went and scattering his daggers far from his grasp. "Bernard and . . . let's see . . . yes, Bolivar. You remember Bolivar? He got along so well with Jasper."

The shortest of the wraiths came near to Roeland, the intense cold of its body making the big man shiver uncontrollably. Roeland's eyes were wide with dread and disbelief.

"You killed them, Gair?"

"Well, not precisely. I *had* them killed. I didn't really have a choice, Roeland. I didn't want to be found."

"Goldmoon will find you."

Roeland stepped back, bumping into a crumbling wall of what used to surround Castle Vila as the spirit of Bolivar reached forward to touch his stomach. The mere contact with the undead felt like a hammer blow.

Roeland's knees shook, and he did his best to steady himself.

"Goldmoon will find me when I want her to."

"She'll stop you."

Gair shook his head.

Nothing can stop the master. It was the elder Graymist, the wraith crouched over the downed knight, poking a jagged black claw into his ear.

"Call off your creature!" Roeland barked. "Take me, Gair. We were friends. Take me and let the knight go. He's not dead yet, but they'll kill him if you don't stop them."

More powerful in death, the wraiths chanted in unison.

"He is in such pain," Gair said, forcing his voice to sound compassionate. "They *will* kill him, Roeland. It's just a matter of how soon. I can have them end his misery now."

"Do it!"

"Ah, that requires a little cooperation on your part. Tell me about Goldmoon. What is she doing now? You said she'd find me. How? How hard will she look?"

Roeland vigorously shook his head. "I'll tell you nothing!"

The elder Graymist had his claw all the way into the downed knight's ear. The wraith was saying something, but its whispery words were drowned out by the man's screams.

"Look at the pain he is in, Roeland! Look what you are allowing him to endure. Squirming so. Very unbecoming for a knight. Camilla will not squirm."

Gair's father chose that moment to thrust his thumbs into the knight's eyes.

Roeland fell to his knees, sobbing, pulling his gaze away from the knight and the malicious wraith. "Gair, please . . ."

"Tell me about Goldmoon."

The big man's shoulders shook. "No."

The knight was whimpering now, no longer having the energy to scream. He lay still, only his hands and feet twitching.

"Tell me."

"No!"

Gair nodded, and his father and the other wraiths fell on the knight, insubstantial claws reaching through the armor to tear at the flesh the way a rabid animal might tear apart its prey. The knight was dead long before they stopped their rending.

The elf moved closer, being careful not to step in the blood and soil the soles of his boots. "Your turn, Roeland," he pronounced. "Tell me what I want to know, and your death will be swift. I'll even let your spirit rest. I'll not turn you into one of my minions."

Roeland's voice froze. Whatever words he was trying to say came out as a string of unintelligible gibberish.

"Come now, my friend." Gair knelt in front of him, took the club from his quivering hands. "I admired you. I venture to say I even considered you a friend once. I'll give you the grace of staying dead."

More powerful in death, the wraiths chanted.

"I'll let your spirit wander about the misty realm beyond the doorway. Maybe you'll even meet River-wind, Goldmoon's dead husband."

Sweet death.

Roeland numbly shook his head.

"Just a little information. That's all."

His lips moved, but no sound came out.

"I can get it from you after you're dead, you know, but the words will not sound so pretty, your voice not so deep. Maybe the knights know, but you are one of Goldmoon's students. Were, that is. You would have more information than they. Cooperate, Roeland."

"Go to hell." The former miller drew on the last of his

courage and found his voice. "Go to hell!"

"Father . . ."

The elder Graymist was a shadow on the ground, moving slowly and inexorably toward the elf and Roeland.

"Roeland . . . one last chance."

* * * * *

"Roeland . . ." Goldmoon pictured a doorway in her mind, the one she had seen when she first became aware of Riverwind's spirit. There was darkness beyond the doorway, a black sky cut through here and there by wisps of fog.

Riverwind floated beyond the doorway in the fog, looking tall and handsome and young, as she remembered him from their first meeting. She probed further, seeing other people, some she vaguely recalled from her youth—great-grandparents, nameless aunts, her parents' friends. Goldmoon inhaled sharply. They looked so real, yet when she glanced away, out of the corner of her mind's eye, they looked as insubstantial as ghosts, as if they were part of the mist. They *are* ghosts, she reminded herself. It was the first time she had tried to contact someone other than Riverwind.

Her mind stretched out, picturing Roeland Stark. Of the men she'd sent with Camilla's knights looking for Gair, she was closest to him. She prayed to the spirit of Mishakal that she would not find him here.

"Roeland . . ."

* * * * *

Roeland screamed as the elder Graymist drew a claw from his sternum to his waist. Roeland's coat and tunic fell from him like a peel of a fruit. A second slash cut the skin beneath. A line of red formed, and blood started dripping on the snow.

Gair moved back a bit, not wanting his garments soiled.

"Roeland. It's only a little information I'm looking for. I want to know what Goldmoon's intentions are toward me. Will she leave me be? Does she intend to send more searchers? Will she come for me herself? Does she talk about me? The Silver Stair . . . does she climb it often? Does she pull power from it as I do? Or . . . perhaps she does not know that she can."

Roeland spat at the elf. "She'll stop you! She'll—" His words ended in a high-pitched scream as the elder Graymist reached into his chest and squeezed his heart. The man slumped forward, dead.

"Father, I was not finished. I wanted to talk to him a little more."

More powerful in death. His father's whispery voice was sonorous.

More powerful in death, the other wraiths joined in.

Speak to him in death, Darkhunter suggested.

Gair made a tsk-tsk sound and stared down at the broken form of Roeland Stark. "I've no choice but to talk to him in death now," he replied.

The man's voice would not be so interesting to listen to. Roeland had possessed a rich voice, and in life his laughter sounded like a pleasant song. In death, it would be raspy and sound only like a harsh whisper. All the wraiths sounded the same to Gair. The elf circled the body, finding a spot to stand next to it where the blood hadn't seeped out to tint the snow.

Nearby, the wraiths tugged the other bodies away from the ruins of Castle Vila. The elf knew they would play with the flesh a little while before Gair raised the dead men's spirits.

"Roeland." Gair knelt, almost reverently. He closed

his eyes and imagined the doorway. The door was never closed anymore. He'd shattered it with a thought. The elf's mind moved easily now between the world of the living and the dead. He fancied himself a part of both realms, and soon he would be master of both.

He saw other spirits hovering in the wispy realm, some of their visages repulsed by him, some horrified, some pleading, wanting to be given some semblance of life again.

"Roeland," he repeated. He glanced at the body, used the man's club to turn it over so he could gaze at the face. The man's eyes were open, the mouth open as well in a final scream. Gair pictured them closed and serene. Handsome. "Roeland."

Mist always pervaded the realm of the dead. Roeland formed out of part of that mist, transparent at first, then gaining substance and color. He looked like a miller again, wearing the trappings of a merchant, as he had the day Gair met him.

The elf stretched out a hand as if to shake Roeland's in a simple greeting, but the image of the miller tried to retreat. Gair shook his head and stoked the heat in his chest, sent the warmth from his heart into his arms and fingers, pictured his fingers glowing red like Dark-hunter's bright eyes. A magnet, his fingers began pulling Roeland to him, closer to the shattered door-way. The elf began uttering a string of words, frag-ments of part of an ancient spell that Darkhunter taught him, old magic he had corrupted and coupled with Goldmoon's enchantment that required no words. Qué-Nal and elven words mixed, powerful words that would not permit the spirit of the miller to flee.

"Roeland . . ." Gair beckoned.

* * * * *

"Roeland . . ." Please do not be here, Goldmoon pleaded silently. Please be alive and whole, be on your way back to the settlement with Gair in tow. "Roeland . . . gods!"

He was there, in the misty other-realm, looking as he had the day he first strolled into her camp. On the young side of middle age, jaw firmly set, eyes filled with curiosity. He'd come to meet her, as he'd been brought up on stories about her and the other Heroes of the Lance. She was a hero on a pedestal to him, and he wanted to see her in person, to shake the hand of a legend.

Goldmoon had been cordial to him, had welcomed him as she had the others who'd journeyed that day from the port town of Schallsea. She shook his hand and said she was pleased to meet him. She had meant it, and his heart skipped a beat. A hero in the flesh.

She showed him around the settlement, told him about the plans for the citadel, about giving Krynn hope. She made it clear that this was all about helping people and restoring a sense of purpose in a dragon-devastated world. Roeland wanted to be part of that. He wanted to be something more than a miller, and he badly wanted to make a difference in the world.

Goldmoon. His eyes took on a sadness, and a lone tear fell shimmering from his eye, disappearing into the mist. *Where am I?*

She was instantly puzzled. Where was he? Didn't he understand?

He does not know, Riverwind told her. *His spirit just arrived.*

Her face grew ashen. Just died? She watched the mist swirl around him, heard dozens of voices in many languages, all of them speaking words of welcome and explanation, flooding her senses.

She watched his handsome face grow stern, as if he

were instantly filled with a purpose and understanding. *I am dead, aren't I,* he said. It was a statement, not a question.

She nodded, a tear edging down her cheek. "Gair?"

He walks with the dead, Goldmoon. He's sent men to your worldly realm, slaying for no reason. He takes spirits from this realm, willing and unwilling ones who serve him, or who at least pretend to. Giving them half-life, denying them rest. The spirits slew me. Such pain. The image of Roeland paused. *They slew the Solamnic knights, too, and he's drawing their . . .* Roeland's face contorted, wavered.

"Roeland?" Goldmoon reached a hand out, but she was in her world, not his, and her fingers brushed Camilla's arm.

. . . spirits. Not letting them rest. The knights—

"What?"

Taking them.

"Roeland?"

Taking me. No! Goldmoon, no! By the will of Solinari and all the vanished gods, don't let this—

"Roeland!"

The image of the former miller seemed to fold in upon itself, and the images of men and women around him recoiled and disappeared in the mist, which now writhed angrily, like a storm-worried sea.

They're taking me!

"Roeland!"

* * * * *

"Roeland Stark." Gair stood and brushed the snow off his pants.

A sheet of blackness hung before the elf. It shimmered in the light of the moon and began to shape itself. A head with a wild mane of spiderweb hair sprouted; eyes glowed palely white, then red. Arms thrust out of the blackness, and hands and claws grew from these. Legs emerged, with feet that hovered above the ground.

Master, the specter of Roeland Stark said in its whispery voice.

More powerful in death, its brothers chanted. They had returned from rending the bodies.

"Now," Gair began, "you will tell me about Goldmoon."

The specter laughed hauntingly. *I do not know her plans regarding you. In life or in death, the answer is the same. I do not know.* Its laugh was long and eerie, sending owls shooting from the branches of trees. *Her plans are her own. Nothing shared. Perhaps she has none.* The wraith laughed deeper, whispery-coarse, no longer musical.

"Is it possible Goldmoon has no plans regarding me? Was I that inconsequential to her? Impossible." Perhaps he would concentrate solely on this mysterious link between himself and Goldmoon, probe her mind and get all of his questions answered that way. "When does she use the Silver Stair?"

If there's a pattern to it, the newly birthed wraith said, *I don't know it. But someone climbs the stair almost every night the moon is out, searching for visions.*

"Only in the moonlight does the stair reveal itself," Gair admitted.

So someone will climb the stair tonight, the wraith of Roeland continued. *Shall we go there, Master? Slay the one who seeks insight from the Celestial Ladder? Let me take the climber's sweet life.*

Powerful in death, the wraiths chanted.

"It is a long way to the Silver Stair," the elf mused aloud. "Too far to travel tonight when I must be inside this castle come the morning."

Not far to us. Darkhunter was at Gair's side again.

Master, may we show you?

The small part of the elf not yet corrupted was apprehensive, but the chill touch of Darkhunter seemed to bolster him. He nodded. The wraith of the Qué-Nal took his left hand and the wraith of Roeland took his right. Together the undead lifted Gair from the ground and flew him toward the southeast.

Much more powerful in death, Darkhunter whispered.

* * * * *

Goldmoon buried her face in her hands and wept. All of the men she and Camilla had sent looking for Gair were dead, and all by his hands. The once-gentle elf whom she considered her most promising student, so gifted and intelligent, so filled with curiosity, so obsessed, so . . .

"Corrupt," she said aloud. "Gair's dark magic has thoroughly seduced him, and ultimately I am to blame. I showed him the door."

Orvago poked his head inside the tent, stooping low this time to enter. He carefully regarded the women.

Camilla was silent for several minutes as the aging healer composed herself and busied herself finding glasses and a jug of bitter cherry wine. She poured a glass for each of them and revealed what she'd experienced. The healer drank her wine slowly, worrying her thumbs around the edge of the glass, staring into its dark surface at the reflection that stared back in the lantern light.

"He must be stopped," Camilla said finally. She forced herself to appear stoic, thrust to the back of her mind all the happy thoughts of Gair she once indulged in. It was silly anyway, she told herself, to entertain a notion that a knight might find room in her heart for romance. She took a deep swallow of the wine. Then another.

"Roeland said weapons couldn't harm the whisperers," Goldmoon said. Her voice was weak. She dabbed at her eyes and returned to worrying about the lip of the glass. "My magic, perhaps, might. I want nothing to do with this . . . sort . . . of mysticism. It's dark magic, but maybe it's the only way to stop Gair."

The gnoll drained his mug and wiped his snout on the sleeve of his tunic. He tugged the sword free from his belt, laid it on the table, and reached for the jug of cherry wine. "Whisperers, dead by this sword."

Goldmoon ran her fingers over the edge of the blade. "This is a magic weapon, Orvago."

He nodded.

The healer looked into his big eyes. "Why did you wait so long to talk to us, my friend?"

The gnoll gave a shrug. "Did not have anything important to say." He stared at his reflection in the sword, then met the gaze of the women.

Camilla drained her mug, and the gnoll courteously refilled it, spilling only part of the jug's contents on the table. "I've a magic sword in the Sentinel. It belonged to my brother. I've never used it. Maybe I was saving it in case he ever came back for it." She took a long pull, felt the warmth of the bitter wine flow down her throat. It felt like it was starting a fire in her belly. She barely felt the ache from the wound in her side that Goldmoon finished healing a few days ago. Her broken arm had been mended magically, too. "I'll leave to get the sword in the morning. It will give me a chance to check on the Sentinel and the town and to bring more soldiers here."

Orvago filled himself a third mug and handed the empty jug back to Goldmoon. She stoppered it and set it under the table. He wiped his hairy arm across the table to clean up what he'd spilled. His elbow smacked the lantern and it teetered precariously.

"I have a staff," Goldmoon said. It was wrapped in

blankets at the side of her bed. "One I used a long time ago." During the War of the Lance, she added to herself.

"Maybe you won't have to use this dark mysticism of yours after all," Camilla said. "Maybe we can deal with Gair and his whisperers a more direct way."

"Gair is my responsibility," Goldmoon said to herself.

"He was." Camilla finished her second glass and stood, balancing herself by holding the table. The knight was not used to drinking. "This island, and everyone on it, is mine to watch over. He's my responsibility, too."

The gnoll looked back and forth between the women and tucked the short sword protectively into his belt.

Chapter 14

Solamnic Visions

"They said Vinas Solamnus had visions." Camilla
stared at the translucent silver steps that spiraled up
and out of sight. Like gossamer, they didn't seem at all
real, shimmering strips of fabric that she would slip
right through to the ground if she tried to stand on
them. She bent to touch the bottom step. "Solid," she
pronounced, holding on to it for support. She felt
slightly lightheaded. "I guess it'll hold me." She slowly
stood and let out a long breath that fanned like a puff of
smoke away from her face. "It'll hold me better than I
can hold wine."

Camilla glanced upward and felt a wash of dizziness
as she tried to spy the top step. "Of course, without the
wine I probably wouldn't be standing here. False
courage. Or foolishness. I wonder if the people who
make it to the top really do have visions?" The knight
found herself on the first step and then the second. She
wasn't thoroughly aware she was climbing the stair
until she glanced down and discovered that she was
higher than the tallest tents. "Oh my." She felt instantly
dizzy again. She closed her eyes and steadied herself.

The winter wind played around her, teasing her red

cloak, which was threatening to become entangled in her feet. With a quick tug, the cloak fluttered to the ground, stark in the faint moonlight against the snow. Camilla opened her eyes and gave her garment a quick glance, as if she were making a note of where she left it. She returned her gaze to the spiraling steps in front of her, and she told herself again she wouldn't be doing this if she hadn't been polite and joined Goldmoon and the gnoll in a drink.

"Polite," she grumbled as she climbed higher. "Politeness had nothing to do with it. I let down my guard, indulged in a bit of melancholic ruminations, and . . . oh, my."

Camilla glanced down again. She felt herself swaying on the step and spread her legs as much as possible to gain better balance. There were a few lights below, around the construction site. She knew men and women were still working. A few of the tents glowed softly, as if lanterns were burning merrily inside of them, their occupants unable to sleep.

Taking a deep breath, she resumed her climb. "Don't these stairs ever stop? To think Goldmoon regularly climbs them, at her age." Camilla had witnessed truly elderly folks take the climb, hobbling up with canes, and the dwarves from time to time, their stubby legs finding this a real challenge. Jasper had climbed it again just last night.

Their legs? She touched her thighs. Her legs were aching. Camilla considered herself very well conditioned. If she was having trouble with these steps, how did the common folk in Goldmoon's settlement handle them?

Higher and higher. Still there was no end to them. The knight considered climbing back down. This was a waste of time. The chill air had helped to sober her, bringing with it more thoughts that this stunt was absurd. She had no reason to climb these stairs. Foolish though it may be, she decided, it was now a matter of triumphing over this insubstantial-looking relic. She needed to reach the top just to prove that she could do it. She would reach the top and then instantly climb down.

"In the name of Kiri-Jolith," she breathed, "do these stairs indeed reach to the stars?"

Her side ached. The air was thin, and she gulped it in raggedly. Her teeth were chattering from the cold, and when she reached down to touch her legs again, the leggings she wore felt like ice. A mist rose around her; she suspected it was the low-hanging cloud she'd spied from the ground. She stopped to catch her breath and toyed with the notion of sitting here for a moment.

"Just a moment. Sit in the cloud and think and rest." Camilla had no idea how long she had spent in Goldmoon's tent or how long it had taken her to climb this high. If morning came before she was finished, the steps would vanish from sight. Would she plummet to the ground? Disappear with them? Or were the steps always here but you could only see them in the moonlight?

Faster, she urged herself. She climbed above the mist, climbed so high it looked as if she were standing amid the stars. "Stars fallen to earth," she whispered, remembering her stroll with Gair. "So beautiful."

Camilla saw no top step, but suddenly when she thought she didn't have the energy to go any farther, she was standing on it, balanced like a dancer on a gossamer strip of . . . what? Just what were the steps made of? She breathed only faintly, worried that too much motion might cause her to topple. "Foolishness," she whispered. "Foolishness and cherry wine."

"I much preferred ale, dwarven if I could get it." The voice was strong and rich, coming from in front of her and behind her at the same time.

Forgetting for an instant just where she was, she pivoted and found herself in an oak-ringed glade. It was late spring or early summer, judging by the leaves on the trees and the wildflowers that grew in clumps here and there and at the feet of a towering elderly man in ornate plate mail.

His long gray hair and drooping mustache were teased by a breeze that felt pleasant and warm. All trace of Schallsea Island's winter had vanished in a heartbeat. A long sword and a shield, both gleaming in the midafternoon sun, and a great horned helmet were propped against a large block of black granite.

"Vinas Solamnus," Camilla said in disbelief.

"Ah, fate has sent someone to fast with me" came the rich-sounding reply. "Come!" He crooked a finger at her, beckoning her closer.

She didn't hesitate, didn't consider that she was on the very top of the Silver Stair and that one step, which she was taking now, and another and another, might send her hurtling through the air. She wasn't falling, wasn't thinking about the ruin. She was thinking only about the great man several yards in front of her, and she was walking on solid ground. It had rained recently, and the mud was sticking to the soles of her boots. The grass felt fresh with the moisture.

He smiled kindly at her, took her hand, and led her to the granite slab. "You have me at a disadvantage," he said. Again the wonderful voice. Mesmerizing. "You know who I am, but I've no clue who you are, beautiful lady."

Beautiful? He called her beautiful, but she wasn't beautiful, and she wasn't really here. She was only dreaming.

"Your name?"

"Camilla," she said, her name nervously catching in her throat. "Camilla Weoledge."

He scratched his chin with his free hand. "A familiar name."

Up close, she noticed that he appeared gaunt, as if he hadn't eaten in days. There was a line of stubble along his chin and cheeks, and his hair was tangled at the ends. His boots were worn and dirty, hinting that it had taken him a while to journey here.

"Where are we?"

"Sancrist Isle, beautiful Camilla. Join me?" He knelt at the rock, and she knelt nearby, but a few feet away so she could study him.

"What are we doing here?"

"Fasting, praying, looking for guidance."

"Praying to whom?"

"Kiri-Jolith."

He closed his eyes and a serene expression came over his rugged features. He looked so much like the Vinas Solamnus of the paintings and sculptures she'd seen— the man who had founded the order of the Solamnic knights so long ago and who she idolized above all others. It couldn't be him. He would be bones and dust now, and she couldn't be on Sancrist Isle. She was on Schallsea Island. Wasn't she? On the Silver Stair?

Her stomach growled, and she noticed that the afternoon sun had turned to evening. Morning and evening flashed before her again and again until her belly felt like an empty pit and her lips were cracked like a dry riverbed from lack of water.

It was daylight again, and she was still kneeling, as was the image of Vinas Solamnus. She was hungrier than she ever remembered, so terribly thirsty. She tried to say something, but her throat was so dry, no sounds would come out. Foolishness, she thought to herself. Time to end this dream. She made a move to leave, but her legs felt like tree trunks rooted to the spot. The sky darkened again and the stars came out. Constellations that were familiar to her before the Chaos War. Constellations of her youth, representing the gods Habbakuk, Paladine, and Kiri-Jolith.

The stars shimmered and began to fall like snowflakes, grew and formed transparent images of three humans in shining plate mail. They shimmered more brightly, solidifying before her eyes. The gods were taking human form—the historic vision of Vinas Solamnus.

The celebrated event was played out before Camilla's wide eyes. Vinas rose and was touched by each god image, was instructed to create a knighthood such as Krynn had never known.

"It will last for generations," the image of Habbakuk said.

"Three separate orders will there be." This from the image of Paladine. "Each shall uphold our ideals, and together the knights shall unite the lands."

"The knights will carry on your concepts of goodness and honor," Kiri-Jolith finished.

Honor, Camilla repeated in her mind. Honor. Honor.

The god images vanished, became stars again that climbed to the heavens. Their light reflected on the surface of the black granite slab, which was shimmering and growing taller and narrower, paler and brighter. Camilla gasped as it was transformed into a pillar of white crystal.

The pillar, according to Solamnic history, signified the gods' pact to watch over the orders of the knighthood. If the knights strayed, the pillar would crumble. It was standing to this day, Camilla knew.

"Time to leave, beautiful Camilla." Vinas was facing her, hands extended to help her to her feet. His shield was strapped to his back, his sword in his scabbard, his great horned helmet firmly atop his head.

She shivered and accepted his hand, stared up into

his face, which was shimmering as the stars and as the granite block had shimmered, shimmering and melting and reforming into another image—a younger man in the armor of a Knight of the Crown.

"Kastil!"

"Dear sister, it is good to see you."

The years vanished in a heartbeat, and Camilla's tunic and leggings melted from her like hot butter, replaced by a flowing blue gown. The holy symbol of Kiri-Jolith hung on a silver chain about her neck. She was little more than a child, an acolyte at the temple.

As she blinked in amazement, her surroundings melted too, replaced by the austere halls of her father's manse. She and her brother stood looking out a window at a rolling meadow. In the far distance was a temple of Kiri-Jolith.

"I wish this could be under better circumstances," the image of Kastil continued, "but life rarely gives us the best of circumstances." He smiled, his eyes gleaming mischievously, then drew his lips into a tight line, and a bit of the light faded from his eyes. "I'm leaving the knighthood. Too rigid for my tastes, dear sister. All this duty is nonsense, sheer drudgery. I'm completely bored. I certainly can't deal with giving all my coins to them. This is poverty!"

"This is madness. You can't leave the knighthood!" she protested. "You took an oath."

"*Est Sularus oth Mithas*," he said flatly. "My honor is my life."

She nodded. She was familiar with the Oath. It was ingrained into her very being. Her great-grandfather had been a knight, her grandfather, her father until an injury took his right arm and with it his fighting heart.

"The knighthood is not *my* life. It was something expected of me. Dear Cam, don't hate me for failing to live up to expectations." He handed her his sword and backed away, his boots clicking on a stone hallway that melted beneath him, becoming instead the scrabble of a worn trail. In the distance, the temple became a garrison, and Camilla could see knights keeping watch from atop a barbican. Kastil was backing away from them, as he had moments ago left her. His mouth moved, and she caught his whisper on the breeze.

"Do not hate me, Cam. I will always treasure you."

"You're abandoning your post!" she called to him. Camilla thought she saw him smile faintly, though his image was too far away now for her to be certain. "You're abandoning your post!"

She was young when he left the knighthood and disgraced the family. She was an acolyte who was finding the rituals and studies of the temple not to her taste. She had not backed away from the temple, not until the day she was told that he had fled from the garrison, dishonoring himself. She wouldn't have left the priesthood even then had an elder not suggested that her heart lay elsewhere and that there was no dishonor in pursuing another honorable calling.

The last she heard of Kastil, he was making his way across Ansalon by singing bawdy tunes in taverns.

"My honor is my life," she whispered.

The garrison vanished, and the sky turned a brilliant blue. The grass that appeared beneath her feet, each blade carefully trimmed and carrying a hint of dew, was darkened by the shadows of dragons flying high overhead. There were knights on the field around her, one holding a sword and touching it to her shoulder.

She was being welcomed into the Solamnic Order on the day a battle of dragons in the middle of the dragonpurge raged amid the clouds.

"*Est Sularus oth Mithas*," she stated solemnly. "I do not hate you, Kastil. I just wished I would have told you so."

"You didn't need to." He was suddenly there, behind the knights, smiling proudly at her. "You never needed to. Use my sword well, dear sister. There's a good bit of magic inside."

Again the scene changed, and the top step of the Silver Stair came into view beneath her feet. A blast of winter-cold air hit her like a slap, and she put all her effort into steadying herself. The stars were spread out like a blanket all around her. Breathtaking and frightening.

Was it the wine? Or was there indeed such magic in this ancient construct? The vision seemed so real. Her brother's face, his words.

Turning carefully, she picked her way down the steps. There was no ache in her side or legs now, and the warmth of the alcohol was a distant memory. The stairs did not seem so high on her downward trip.

Safely on the ground now, she looked for her discarded cloak. She remembered leaving it behind. She made a note of where it fell. Nothing. That's odd, she thought. The snow was brushed as if her cloak had been dragged across it. The marks led away from the stair to the north, as if someone had covered his footsteps. Or as if an animal had grabbed her cloak and dragged it away to make a warm bed of it. A wolf, likely, or a big fox.

She had a few other cloaks in the Sentinel, though none so colorful, the one bit of brightness she had allowed in her wardrobe. "I hope it keeps you warm," she mused as she made her way back to her tent, "and that you need it more than I."

"It will help me to think of you," a voice replied after she was well out of earshot. "It carries your delicate scent."

Gair rose from behind a bank of snow and silently crept toward the Silver Stair. It was so late, he suspected no one else would climb tonight. Late and cold, the settlement, for the most part, was asleep.

He skittered up it like a monkey wrapped in Camilla's warm red cloak. Shadows followed him to either side—his father and Darkhunter.

You still think of her too often, his father scolded in his dead, whispery voice. *A human . . . her life is too short, but if she were dead, she could be with you forever.*

Gair stopped and cocked his head in the direction of her tent. He was about twenty feet above ground, and with his keen elven vision, he could see a faint glow in Camilla's tent. He stared at it, imagining her inside, lying in bed. He wondered what she had seen on the Silver Stair and decided that she was probably at this very moment thinking of him, as he was thinking of her.

"I'm obsessed with her," Gair said.

Then slay her, Darkhunter suggested. *Make her one of us. By your side.*

Forever, Gair. No longer would I call you foolish for being smitten with a human, his father added.

"Father, you would have me in love with a spirit? One who has no soft flesh to touch and who does not have flower-scented hair to smell?"

Love is more powerful in death, my son. I know this. I love you more now than when I breathed.

Darkhunter nudged the elf with an icy claw, encouraging him to climb higher and out of sight of any passing sentries. *Gair Graymist, are you not already in love with death*? the Qué-Nal posed. *Shall I slay the human for you to keep your conscience clean?*

"I have little conscience left," Gair said with a sneer. "She will die eventually."

He stopped when he was more than fifty feet above the ground. With Darkhunter's and his father's black bodies to shield him, no one would notice him. If, by chance, someone elected to climb the stair so very late, there was always room for one more wraith in his growing army.

The elf's fingers gripped the frigidly cold step, and he concentrated on the energy pulsing in the magical site. So strong! His senses heightened under Darkhunter's tutelage, he was able to picture in his mind the shifting bands of arcane power that ran the length of the ruin. Sometimes dozens of feet long, sometimes hundreds, the ruin seemed not to have a precise height. The elf suspected it varied based on the individual climbing it. The stronger the man—or woman—the higher the stairs went.

The Silver Stair would likely stretch to the very heavens for him if they were to present a challenge, Gair guessed. He was becoming stronger and more magically aware with each passing day. The steps would have to stretch beyond the stars! He did not need the visions, and therefore did not have to climb to the top step. He only needed their power, and that he could get right here.

He focused on the bands of energy and pulled them toward him, felt the arcane aura surge into his hands and arms, stoke his chest as if it were a caldron. His feet felt as if they were on fire; his chest felt as if it might explode.

"More," he coaxed. "I need more."

He felt the step crack beneath his fingers, a spiderweb of fine lines racing away beneath his palm. A chunk of whatever material it was made of fell away, and then another, and he scrabbled down to a lower step to pull still more energy. Another step damaged. And then another.

"More!"

The elf's body shook, mildly at first, then as if he were having a seizure. He wondered if Goldmoon had thought to use the ruin in this manner. He pictured her in her tent.

She was trying to sleep! *What are you dreaming of?* he asked. In a corner of his mind, he saw her eyes flutter open and her mouth gape in surprise. "I woke her up," he told the wraiths.

Were you dreaming of me, Goldmoon?

"Gair!" she gasped.

Or were you dreaming of Riverwind? I could make him a creature of half-life, too, Goldmoon, if I draw enough energy from these stairs. I've tried before, you know, to solidify his spirit here, but he's very willful and wants to remain very dead. He's just beyond my grasp—but not if I gain more power. He could walk at my side, Goldmoon. He could be unreachable to you until you, also, walk at my side.

He saw her stand. In a woolen nightgown and bare feet, she walked to the flap of her tent and pulled it back, looked in the direction of the stair, but he knew she could not see him.

You realize I am on the stair. You can sense me, as I sense you. Good. The link is stronger; the stair did that. I'll use the link to learn all your secrets. I'd best hurry now, Goldmoon, since I sense you're planning to summon the soldiers. I cannot have you interrupt me, and I cannot have you catch me. Gair withdrew from the healer's mind and returned his full concentration to the stair. So hot. The energy made the steps feel as if he were sticking his hands into hot coals. "Just another moment more. Power. Give me all your power."

Darkhunter's icy dead fingers grabbed one arm. His father took the other. The power flowed into them, too, and they soaked it up like inky sponges.

"More!" Suddenly he felt as if his entire body were engulfed in flames. The sensation was too much for him to handle. The fire so hot. So . . .

He awoke on the ground at the base of the gossamer

spiral, the blackness of his father and Darkhunter hovering over him.

We carried you here, Darkhunter explained. *You would have fallen. We saved you from death. It is not yet your time to join us, Gair. You must make more of us first.*

Many more. Enough to rule the island, the elder Graymist insisted.

Gair shook his head as if to clear his senses. A small part of himself was scrabbling for control, forcing the darkness back. "Why would I want to do that? It would be wrong, evil, to bring more spirits into this world. I have already done enough damage. It would be wrong. And—"

Don't you want us to rule the island? Darkhunter's red-hot eyes bore into the elf's. *At your behest? More powerful in death. Don't you want us to have power, Master? Don't you want us to serve you? Forever?*

Master? Gair mouthed. For some reason, the word sounded good to the elf, and the red of Darkhunter's eyes was somehow warming and comforting. Master. The wraith of the long-dead Qué-Nal seemed to make sense. "But Camilla—"

Will join us in death soon, Darkhunter continued. *She will call you Master, too. She will be more powerful in death. Don't you want her to be more powerful?*

The elf nodded. Everything was clear again. He was more powerful, too, had pulled the energy from the Silver Stair. He knew he was weakening the steps. If he kept it up, perhaps he would destroy the thing. He'd have to take much more power from it before it collapsed, enough to raise the spirit of every man who died on this island and in the sea around it, perhaps the spirits of dragons as well. "If the stairs truly did collapse in the process?" he mused aloud. "It would only be fitting. It would be keeping the magical energy from Goldmoon, and then she would not have the power to stop me."

The spirits helped him to his feet.

"Goldmoon," he said plainly, "I will destroy your Silver Stair, step by step, and then I will destroy you." Goldmoon would die, as Camilla would die, and they would be with him forever.

He padded to the northeast, letting Camilla's long cloak drag on the ground behind him to wipe away his tracks. There was still a touch of darkness left this night-time to raise a few more spirits from his favorite Qué-Nal burial ground before the spirits flew him back to Castle Vila.

* * * * *

Camilla stifled a yawn as she started toward the port just as the sun was rising. The snow had been beaten down enough into a trail now that it would not be difficult going. Four knights clanked along behind her, all on horseback, and behind them was a rustling sound that was out of place. The knight commander swiveled in the saddle to glance over her shoulder. She groaned softly. The gnoll was following them, running fast enough to keep up with the horses.

"Good morning, Orvago," she offered as the gnoll picked up his pace and made his way around the knights' mounts. He seemed to have little trouble keeping up with the horses.

The gnoll bobbed his head. He was dressed in a flowing yellow-orange cloak with a voluminous hood that covered up his hairy snout. Bright purple sleeves extended from its folds as he shook both her hands. He had on gloves, too, the first time she'd seen him wearing any. They were colored green, and they didn't at all match the baggy forest green trousers that clashed with everything. His feet were covered with a combination of heavy gray socks and brown boots with the toes cut out of them.

"So are you along because you think we need some extra protection, or because you want to see the town?"

The head bobbed vigorously.

"All right, but keep your head covered at all times."

Beneath the voluminous hood, the gnoll grinned.

* * * * *

The gnoll was dumbstruck when the entourage passed through the town's gate. He'd never seen anything like this, had only spotted towns from a distance when he was on the deck of the pirate's ship.

He stopped every few steps, ogling at the colorful buildings, sniffing the people passing by, growling appreciatively at the smells coming from the bakery and from all the chimneys that puffed away, sending a variety of scents into the air. It was fast approaching dinnertime, he could tell.

They were nearly at the Sentinel when the gnoll put a gloved hand on her knee. He pointed toward a row of businesses, all of which had the snow cleared away from the sidewalks, as if the merchants were refusing to accept the winter. A trio of Qué-Nal barbarians was coming out of a limner's shop. They were chattering and pointing in windows. The tallest was admiring a decorative leather tunic.

The gnoll growled softly.

"I'm going to talk to them," Camilla said, sliding from the horse's back. "Maybe they know something about this Shadowwalker." She strode toward them, head high, the other knights holding their position, but Orvago following. The gnoll's paw drifted to the pommel of the broadsword in his belt.

"Sword Commander!" the tallest barbarian began. "Is not that a fine garment?" He hadn't turned to greet her. He saw her reflection in the window. "It would look good on me, but I have not the goods to trade for it today. Maybe my next trip."

"Do you know of someone called Shadowwalker?" She came right to the point. She wasn't about to engage him in pleasant conversation about clothes.

"Shadowwalker is an old man and would not look as good in that garment as I." His fellows sniggered. "Shadowwalker's face is full of wrinkles, and he is not handsome like me. My next trip, I will buy this, or one like it if it is gone."

"Are you with Shadowwalker's clan?"

He shook his head, the beads in his hair clacking together.

"But you know him?"

"Maybe the Sword Commander would like to buy me that garment. Call it a trade. Information for the leather."

"I haven't the steel."

He sighed and turned away from the window to finally face her. "Shadowwalker is old, Sword Commander, but he is full of fire. You ask about him because you protect the Qué-Shu woman. The Qué-Shu and Shadowwalker's clan are not friends."

"Do you know where I can find him?"

"If I did, I would not tell you. I do not like Shadowwalker, but I like the Qué-Shu even less."

She carefully regarded him. The beads in his hair were carved in the shapes of owls and hawks. None were blood-soaked like the beads of the men who had attacked her.

"Is there anything else, Sword Commander?"

"No. Thank you for speaking with me."

"A pleasure, Sword Commander. When next we meet, perhaps I will be wearing a fine garment like this one."

She watched them stroll away, heading toward the

northern edge of town. The tall barbarian pointed toward a tavern, and he and his fellows slipped inside.

Camilla returned to Orvago and escorted him into the keep. One of the knights took the horses to the stable.

"We'll leave in the morning," she told the gnoll. Softer, she said, "When I have another suit of armor, my brother's sword, and a good night's sleep."

Orvago took off his cloak just as Judeth walked by. The stocky servingwoman stared wide-eyed at the creature. He grinned at her, showing all of his teeth, and she promptly swooned.

"Sorry," the gnoll offered.

Camilla knelt to tend to the woman. "Please don't go out tonight, Orvago. I don't think it would be a good idea."

The gnoll sadly nodded his head.

Chapter 15

Shadowwalker's Fire

The ruins of Castle Vila were tinged a burnt orange by the rising sun. Gair traced a deep crack that ran between the age-worn stones.

"The Qué-Shu sheep must die!"

He turned to watch the barbarians gathered nearby.

"It is only one Qué-Shu, Shadowwalker. Hardly worth your effort. Let her be."

The old Qué-Nal shaman stomped and spat at the ground, beads clacking angrily as he shook his head. "I decide if it is worth my effort, Windfisher. I decide!"

"You don't command the tribes, Shadowwalker. My brother does. He has made a truce with the elf Iryl Songbrook. You cannot command warriors to follow you on some foolish—"

"Your brother is not here."

"No. He would not dignify this gathering with his presence, but he has said the camp of the mystics is to be left alone. He gave his word."

Shadowwalker glared at the young Qué-Nal, puffed out his chest, and again stomped in the snow. The pair was in front of a spirit pole, an old tree carved with oversized Qué-Nal faces. The left half of each face was red, the right black. Four faces, one each facing east, south, west, and north. In decades past, the poles were believed to serve as homes for the spirits who watched over the village and who carried the shamans' prayers to the gods. Many of the barbarians believed the gods were still here but were turning a deaf ear.

Not Shadowwalker. He and his fellows were confident the gods were still here and very much attentive. "The Qué-Shu sheep who leads those people has wronged us by her very presence! The gods would be happy if we killed her. The spirits will rejoice."

On the far side of the spirit pole were more than five hundred barbarians, nearly the entire village of Qué-Jotun, and they were clearly divided. The youngest, by their murmurs and raised fists, sided with Shadowwalker, eager for a confrontation. The older villagers stood with Windfisher. All of them carefully regarded the two men as they shivered in the morning cold. Like the adults, the few children present were lean and muscular. Even the eldest looked graceful. All of those assembled had olive skin, which had not lightened despite the winter, and their dark hair was decorated with beads and feathers.

"You are mad, Shadowwalker. No one will rejoice if you try to kill the Qué-Shu and her people." Windfisher squared his broad shoulders and ground his slippered heel into the snow. He had an impressive array of beads, easily more than Shadowwalker, each one from a kill accomplished during a special hunt or given for some act of courage, but they were not soaked in blood like the older man's. "Our fight with the Qué-Shu was a long time ago, Shadowwalker, and it was based on an argument about the gods. Those years are gone. Let it rest."

"Rest. Pha!" Shadowwalker spat at the younger man's feet. "The gods care! The Blue Phoenix, Habbakuk,

Zeboim, and Zebyr Jotun are still here watching over us. The shamans said Habbakuk and Zebyr Jotun would have washed away all of Abanasinia if everyone on the land did not fall down and worship them, but not all of the Qué-Shu would revere them so. The fools! Perhaps they will wash away Schallsea if we do not slay the mystic."

Windfisher narrowed his eyes. "Abanasinia was not washed away, old man. Schallsea Island will not be washed away either. The Qué-Shu—"

"The sheep waged war on us."

"After our ancestors attacked them! Our ancestors thought war would force them to worship our gods."

"They drove us off Abanasinia!" Shadowwalker was red-faced with anger. "Threw us to the mercy of the sea."

"And to the mercy of the gods our ancestors tried to ram down the throats of the Qué-Shu."

"I have not forgotten that our people were driven from their homeland!"

"You should not, Shadowwalker. It is part of our history." Windfisher circled the spirit pole, scrutinizing the faces of those barbarians closest to him. The youths were angry, infected by Shadowwalker's fiery speech. His own words had done little to calm them. "Goldmoon, the Qué-Shu sheep as you call her, did not drive us out of Abanasinia. She had done nothing to you, Shadowwalker, and you will do nothing to her."

Shadowwalker whirled on the balls of his feet, sending a shower of snow at the younger man. He stomped through the assembly toward the wall of Castle Vila, where Gair stood alone.

"One madman running to another," Windfisher said softly.

The air around his head was buzzing with questions. Could Windfisher's brother—Skydancer, the leader of all the Qué-Nal—stop a war against the settlement?

Yes. Skydancer and he would stop Shadowwalker, as they had stopped his other foolish plans through the years.

Did he think the gods would swallow Schallsea Island if Goldmoon stayed?

No. There is a place for mysticism. There is a place for everything, and there is a need for such magic on Krynn.

And Shadowwalker? Could Skydancer stop him from acting alone?

The young Qué-Nal paused at this question, running his fingers over his smooth chin. Behind him, Shadowwalker and Gair held a whispered conversation.

Windfisher turned to address the assembled Qué-Nal. "Shadowwalker says whatever Goldmoon and her followers are building is a blight on the face of this island. Some of you obviously agreed with him and helped him set the fire at their camp. He says that Goldmoon's very presence is a slap in the face of all the villages. Yet the magic she practices is not so different from that commanded by Shadowwalker himself. Perhaps he is jealous of her and is trying to stir up all of you just for his own benefit.

"I cannot stop how he thinks," Windfisher added, "but my brother and I will stop him from provoking a senseless fight. There is room for the Qué-Nal and for one Qué-Shu on this island."

Windfisher led the way back to the village, unaware that several of the youngest warriors slipped away and headed to the ruined castle. Shadowwalker and Gair welcomed them inside.

There Shadowwalker continued to fume. "Skydancer could not dignify the gathering with his presence," he snarled. "He sent his brother instead. Both of them are soft."

The young warriors gathered close and hung on the old shaman's every word, cheering when he repeated that the Qué-Shu and her followers must die.

Gair edged away from them. The shadows were thick inside what was left of Castle Vila, since the narrow windows on the first floor let in little of the morning light. The stone walls were covered with dirt and the remains of moss that had died when the cold weather set in. His fingers brushed at the dead moss, crumbling it.

"Everything dies," he whispered.

There were bolts in the wall where the elf imagined grand paintings once hung, images of the wealthy people who built this place overlooking the sea. There were thick, rusting chains hanging from the ceiling from which the remnants of wrought-iron chandeliers dangled. In the center of the room, a great, rotted rug spread, and atop it were splintered chair legs. A large piece of wood, oval-shaped and molded by exposure to the salty air, had a hint of beveling at the edges; it might have been an impressive table decades ago. There was a lone chair still intact, far from the windows. Rickety, it was nevertheless still sturdy enough to hold the elf. He'd cleaned the dirt off it on a previous visit, and he eased his lanky frame into it now as he continued to listen to the barbarians.

"Skydancer is a weak chief," Shadowwalker snarled. "He does not respect our heritage. If he did, he would be ordering the deaths of the Qué-Shu sheep and her blind followers."

"Perhaps he should not be chief!" one of the young warriors shouted.

"Shadowwalker!" another cried.

Gair listened another few minutes, then slipped from the room and followed a winding staircase up to the second floor. There had been a carpet running down the center of the steps, thick and undoubtedly expensive. Gold and silver threads remained in the remnants of the age-worn nap. He paused on the landing, listening to the warriors swear to follow Shadowwalker to the death.

"Everything dies," the elf repeated as he was swallowed by the shadows of the level above.

And in death becomes stronger. Darkhunter waited for him.

The elf decided that decades ago this must have been a music room. The stone walls had been painted, and curled chips of pale yellow—had they been white?—clung here and there. He stared at strings lying amid a jumble of rotted wood. Strings from a harp, he guessed as he imagined a beautiful woman playing exquisite music to which others danced.

"A place of ghosts," he whispered.

In the center of the room lay the bodies of five knights and one of Goldmoon's students—the final of the three search parties sent after Gair. Darkhunter had promised to teach him a new trick with them.

Shadows separated from the wall—Gair's father, and the wraiths of Roeland and the other Solamnic knights. They floated forward slowly, and Gair fancied that they moved to the bygone music of this place. The air around the elf grew colder as the creatures came closer. Gair inhaled deeply and closed his eyes. He loved Castle Vila. It was as dead as its occupants.

What do you wish of us, Master? It was Roeland's spirit.

"At the moment, nothing, but soon I will need all of you—and more. With our living friends below, we will journey to the settlement."

And drink of the sweet life there, Roeland said.

"Yes," Gair replied. The elf padded from the chamber, retracing his steps to the lower level.

* * * * *

It was shortly past dawn, the Silver Stair invisible in the pale light, yet Goldmoon stood on the bottommost step. She'd found the relic by touch, and she did not want to wait until evening to climb it. She wanted to tax herself physically to reach the top—and hope that she did not plummet off, since she could not see a single step. She needed the ruin to help her find Gair. Perhaps a vision might provide a clue to his whereabouts.

She had to find him soon, before he hurt more people. Through the link she shared with him, and which she still could not fathom how she was so tied to him, she knew he was pulling energy from the ruin and that he was bent on some dark purpose. She'd discovered the cracked steps—eighteen of them—and she knew if he kept it up, he would destroy the thing. The knights posted nearby last evening to prevent him from using the stair were nowhere in sight, but less than an hour ago a soldier had spotted their tracks heading to the north. Goldmoon suspected that Gair had the knights and wanted her to know that.

Goldmoon hoped she could use the Silver Stair to shut down her link with Gair so he could not eavesdrop on her thoughts. She sensed he would rather have the Silver Stair destroyed than to have her use it. Goldmoon loathed the idea of channeling power from it to effect a spell. That was obviously how the steps became cracked, but Gair had to be found.

"Goldmoon!" Orvago was tramping across the snow toward her. He, Camilla, and a detachment of soldiers had arrived late yesterday.

She paused, as if suspended in the air, and stared down at the gnoll. "I do not need a guard here, my friend. Gair is nowhere near." She had explained the link to the commander and Orvago last night.

The gnoll left her, backing away and watching as she climbed something he couldn't see. Even when he could see the mystical site in the light of the moon, it raised the hair on the back of his neck. When Goldmoon was more than thirty feet above the earth, he turned and loped toward the knights' tents, kicking up snow as he went.

"What are you planning, Gair? And whatever caused you to stray?" Goldmoon sat on the unseen steps, high above the settlement. A pair of kestrels flew past, circling her, then continuing south.

The air was still, and it carried the scents of pine trees and breakfast and the sounds of the waking settlement. Goldmoon liked the settlement the way it was: tents and lean-tos, people existing on hope and hard work. A lot of hard work would go into the Citadel of Light. When it was finished, as Goldmoon knew it eventually would be—no matter the delays and the weather— things would be so very different. The settlement would not have the same feel, and she knew she would miss this.

"It is my fault, despite what you say." Goldmoon was talking to Riverwind. "It was my choice to teach him the dark side of mysticism. I let my emotions, not my common sense, get involved. He missed his family just as I missed you."

He would have eventually learned the dark mysticism without you, beloved, just as he's learned all manner of dark things.

"Perhaps, but I pointed him in the wrong direction and essentially gave him a shove. Now I have to stop him. How can I find him?"

I cannot help you. Each night he calls me. The door is always open for him, and each night he pulls spirits through. I have resisted.

A shiver ran down her spine. She couldn't bear the

thought of Riverwind becoming an undead creature.

The life he offers is not truly life. It is an abomination of an existence.

"I have to find some way to stop him, beloved. I have to save him. Gair—the Gair I took on as my student—would not have wanted this to happen to him."

The seed was there, Goldmoon, planted long before you met him.

She sensed him back away from her just as she sensed another presence intruding in her thoughts. Gair! She could almost see his face inside her mind, and she could hear his voice as if he were right in front of her.

The Silver Stair is mine, Goldmoon!

"No! By the blessed memory of Mishakal!" Goldmoon felt instantly faint and grabbed on to the steps.

Chapter 16

Conflagrations

Jasper pounded his ale mug down on a log that served as a table and gave a cockeyed look at Redstone across a merrily burning campfire. "Good ale," he pronounced. "The perfect finish to an evenin' meal." He patted his stomach. "An' now I need to take a walk and work some of this off. If you'll excuse me?"

She grinned politely, her thick upper lip coated with foam from the ale. The blisters on her face and hands from the fire were healing, and they didn't look quite so bad in the firelight. Behind her, great chunks of crystal sparkled, brought this morning by a team of dwarven miners, who turned right around and headed back to the mines. There was no rest for anyone. Work on the citadel had resumed in earnest again.

Jasper touched her shoulder and glanced up at the winking stars. The moon would be full tonight, he noticed as he watched it edge its way up from the horizon. "I shouldn't be gone too awfully long, Red. Just takin' a walk. An' then you can tell me all about those domes you've got on your mind." Then he was heading down the path away from the building site and toward the Silver Stair, which was shimmering into view.

The dwarf stared at it in amazement, which was how he looked at it every time the moon revealed it. "The gods summoned fireflies, I think," he said to himself as he trundled forward, touching the bottom step and sighing deeply as the energy tingled into his fingers. "Summoned fireflies and talked 'em into holdin' this pose forever." He pressed his palms against the step, as he did each time as way of a ritual rather than a confirmation that the stair would hold him. Then he took a step up and then another.

"No better place." He continued to talk to himself as he went higher. "Goldmoon was right." Talking to himself was also something he always did when he took a trip on the stair. It kept him preoccupied so he wouldn't look down quite so often. "Best place to build the citadel. Goldmoon was definitely right. An' I was silly to think we should wait until spring to begin buildin' again. Right place, right time. Still, I'm kinda tired of startin' it over and over again. The blizzard, the fire. Why can't the fates just let us be? We ain't botherin' nobody."

He tugged on his terribly short beard when a bracing gust of wind struck him. He reached up to touch a step just above his head for support. "Wonder if my Uncle Flint ever got to see this? Hope he did. Hope he got a chance to climb it. Hope everyone in Krynn comes here to see this and takes a climb. Amazin'."

He was dressed warmly, but the cold cut through his clothes as he climbed ever higher and watched the lights of the settlement grow smaller all around him. He paused and frowned when he glanced to the south, where the three-story citadel used to be. "A whole lot of sweat an' work went into that," he grumbled. "Well, the next one'll be even better." The damage the fire caused looked worse from above. The basement was an ugly black scar against the snow-covered earth, reminding him of that night. He pushed it to the back of his mind and continued to struggle up the steep steps. It seemed a little harder to climb each time.

"Maybe I'll see Uncle Flint tonight," Jasper reflected, "or maybe I'll have another vision of that ship. Mmm . . . what was it called again? *Flint's Anvil*. That's it. The ship with the barbarian cap'n who carried all the knives. I'd kinda like to see how that's gonna turn out. Can't imagine me on a ship, though, an' in the company of a kender. The ground's much better than the sea. Doesn't move aroun'. The ground an' these stairs."

* * * * *

"Take it easy, Goldmoon." Camilla Weoledge took the aging healer's hand and guided it to her forehead so she could feel the considerable bump.

The healer blinked to clear her senses. She was inside her tent, lying on her cot, the Solamnic Commander at her side and looking entirely sympathetic. She felt a little thirsty, and she made a move to get up. The knight helped her. There was a pitcher of water on her table, next to the lantern.

The lantern. It burned almost cheerfully.

"Camilla, how long have I been here?"

The knight pursed her lips. "Several hours, Goldmoon."

"You've been here with me?"

Camilla nodded. "The entire time. Gave me some time to think . . . about a lot of things. Primarily what you said about mysticism being a gift from the gods." She made a huffing sound and ran her fingers through her tight curls. "Sometimes I take a rather narrow view of things, I'm afraid. I've certainly been too harsh a judge on you, Goldmoon, when it wasn't at all my place to judge. I've been critical of the citadel, and the citadel's not such a bad idea, really. I'm sorry it took me so long to realize that."

Goldmoon found herself smiling. "What happened?" She touched the bump on her head again and cringed.

"You must've fallen quite a way," the knight replied. "Orvago started howling so loud he got everyone's attention real fast. We all came running and saw you on the ground. What were you thinking, trying to climb the stair in broad daylight? None of us could see it, but Jasper said it was there."

"It's always there. It's just unmasked in the moonlight."

"Jasper healed you, and Orvago carried you in here. You've been out for hours. You obviously needed the rest, and—"

"By the memory of Mishakal! Did you say hours?" She fought a sensation of dizziness, grabbed on to the table and stared at the lantern.

"Most of the day, anyway. Why don't you take it easy and I'll go get Jasper. He'll be pleased you're awake. I'll find some dinner for you, too."

"Dinner?"

"There's bound to be some left."

"It's that late?" Goldmoon edged away from table and focused on her heart to give her strength.

"Some cider, too, and—"

"No." Goldmoon remembered exactly what had happened. She met Camilla's gaze. "It was Gair. Somehow he made me fall off the Silver Stair. He was inside my head." She swallowed and closed her eyes, reaching inside herself. "Thank the memory of Mishakal he's not there now."

Camilla looked puzzled, but she remained silent. She watched the healer gather her cloak and wrap it around herself, then kneel beside her cot and pull out a long, wrapped bundle. She reverently untied it.

Inside was a staff, plain-looking and covered with whorls and knots. It shone softly in the light of the lantern. Goldmoon gently tugged it free. It was wholly unremarkable save for a leather thong that was tied near one end, from which dangled brilliantly colorful feathers and beads. The healer ran her fingers along a whorl.

"It's been a long time since I've used this." Goldmoon leaned on it for support as her eye was attracted to Camilla's hip. A long sword rested there, a different one than the knight usually carried. The pommel was uncharacteristically ornate for the commander's tastes. It was fashioned in the shape of a griffon's claw, the talons gold and gleaming and holding a red gem that glowed with an inner light.

"Have to get to the stair," she told the knight. There was resolve in her voice, in her expression. "I believe Gair is capable of destroying it." She fastened her cloak about her neck and brushed by the knight. "And capable of a lot more."

"Destroy the stair?"

"I believe that is his intention."

Camilla blew out the lantern and followed. "I'll station some of my men at the base—plenty of them this time. And we'll—"

A scream cut through the air, shrill and terrifying.

The healer cocked her head. "From the trail to Heartspring," she breathed.

The knight ran toward the trail, her young legs carrying her quickly across the snow-covered ground and leaving Goldmoon far behind. She motioned to Willum, who had paused to talk to Redstone. He had heard the scream, too, and had his sword drawn.

Another scream sliced through the air, and then another. A child was crying, too, the sobs distant and chilling. "The farmers!" she cried. "Gather the men!"

The staccato words cut through the murmurs swelling in the settlement.

The dwarven builders were on their feet, several with hammers in hand, looking about for the source of the screams. The fishermen were pointing at the knights, gathering at the eastern side of the settlement where the trail to Heartspring began.

Parents were clutching their children to them, looking to Goldmoon for direction. The healer was waving everyone into the center of the clearing, save for the warriors among the settlers. These she was directing toward the Silver Stair.

Soldiers were falling into line, and Willum barked orders at them as he rushed toward Camilla. "Guard the settlement!"

Then the knights were clanking down the trail, running in the direction of the ongoing screams.

* * * * *

The top step had just come into view when Jasper heard the screams. The faint clank of armor and the chatter of the townsfolk were so soft from his high vantage point that it sounded like half-imagined whispers. He took another step up and then another, thinking that the screams were part of the vision he was about to have. One step away from the top.

He stopped and scratched his nose, looking down at the mist that cloaked the ground so far below. He strained his ears. "By Reorx's beard, I think somethin's goin' on below!"

The dwarf took another glance at the topmost step, shimmering invitingly mere feet away, then he carefully turned around and started down. "Ship'll have to wait for later." He resumed talking to himself as his stocky legs moved quickly—but not too quickly—

down the steps. "Yep, somethin's goin' on. Don't have much built yet on the citadel for anybody to destroy. Got to be new trouble."

There was a shape below him on the steps, just emerging from the mist. "Turn aroun'." He waved to the man. "Trouble at the settlement. Gotta get to it. Hurry up."

The shape paused.

"Go on!" Jasper urged. "I can't get aroun' you. Get movin'!" The dwarf waved his thick arms, then slowed his pace as his frantic waving almost made him lose his balance.

"Be careful," the other figure said. "I wouldn't want you to fall, like Goldmoon did this morning."

The dwarf stopped and peered through the darkness, using the light from the steps to help him see the figure. "Gair?"

"I had hoped you hadn't forgotten me already."

A shiver raced down the dwarf's spine, and his fingers edged down to lock around the handle of his hammer.

* * * * *

Camilla raced down the trail, Willum close on her heels. Behind them ran more than a dozen knights, some who were still struggling to put on pieces of their armor. The moon was climbing higher, and that coupled with the starlight reflecting off the snow guided their way.

The trail to Heartspring still remained buried beneath several feet of snow, but there was a path through the drifts, cut by people traveling back and forth. It was narrow, and no more than two of the knights could move side by side without finding themselves in thigh-deep snow.

The screams continued, panicked and terrifying.

Willum was humming in his throat. "Must be a family," he huffed. "I think I heard a child."

Camilla nodded and picked up the pace. She spotted a figure ahead, crouched a few yards off the path, slight, probably a woman. A small form was lying on the snow in front of her, and she was sobbing over it. The screams continued farther along the trail.

The knight commander motioned Willum and two men to investigate the woman, then she and the others raced on, their breath puffing away from their faces like chimneys. Camilla saw more figures in the distance as she neared the village. There was a wagon turned on its side; people had gathered around it. Someone was screaming.

She looked frantically to the right and left, trying to spot any renegade Qué-Nal warriors who might have been responsible. Seeing no sign of any, she pushed herself and her men toward the wagon.

Dozens of yards behind her, Willum plodded through the snow toward the woman. He could make out her cries now. "My baby. My darling baby!"

"Let us help you!" he hollered to her as he nearly stumbled in the thick drift. Unlike the woman, he was too heavy to move about on top of the snow. He sank through it with each step. Two knights followed in the path he was blazing. "There are healers at the settlement. We'll take your baby there."

"My baby. She's dead," the woman sobbed. "Poor baby."

A moment more and Willum was at her side, reaching out to the small shape lying on the snow. Then a moment more and he was gasping, recoiling in terror, and bumping back into his men who were just catching up.

"My baby." The woman pulled back her dark cloak, the moonlight revealing a face more bone than flesh.

Hollow eye sockets looked out at the knights, and her jaw dropped open. "My baby."

The small form at her feet stirred, and Willum struggled to speak, but his throat had gone instantly dry.

The creature sluggishly stood. It was a child, a Qué-Nal, with beads and feathers in its matted hair. Not so long dead, there was more flesh on the small bones, but now the flesh that remained was swollen around the throat, revealing that some terrible disease had claimed her.

"My baby," the dead woman cackled as she struggled to her feet. The cloak fell away from her. In the moonlight, the bones showed through her rotting flesh, glistening like the snow.

"It's a trap!" Willum yelled as loudly as he could, finally finding his voice. He stepped forward and swung at the adult creature, slicing through an arm and sending it flying away. "Warn Camilla!" He barked to the knights behind him. "Go!"

Despite the order, only one of the knights trudged hurriedly away. The other came up to Willum's shoulder, drawing his sword and pointing it at the smaller corpse. "What manner of creatures are these, sir?"

Willum shook his head. He was humming nervously in his throat and weaving his sword in front of him. The large corpse advanced on him, cackling "My baby" and clacking her bony jaws. She reached out for the lieutenant just as he swept the blade to the right, and her clawed hand darted to scratch at his mail. A finger broke from the impact with the metal, and her hollow eyes stared at it hanging limply on her hand.

"They can't hurt us!" Willum said, his voice a shout, though the knight was only inches away. "They can't get through our armor. I'll be all right. Go warn Camilla." The knight turned reluctantly. "No!" Willum shouted. "Get back to the settlement. I think these things were meant to draw us away!"

The Solamnic lieutenant turned his attention back to the corpses. The smaller staggered forward, wrapping her arms around Willum's waist. The knight ignored her for the moment, concentrating on the larger foe.

Jaws clacking, cackling, the larger female corpse shuffled forward atop the snow, too light to sink beneath the drift. She lashed out at Willum's face, but the knight turned, and the bony fingers raked only air. At the same time, he brought his sword up through her rib cage, what would be a mortal blow to any living creature. She only cackled louder.

He pulled his sword free as she threw herself at him, arms wrapping around his sword arm and shaking hard. The corpse was strong and persistent, eventually forcing the knight to lose his grip on the pommel. The blade fell into the snow and disappeared.

"My baby!" she wailed as she brought her jaws toward his unarmored hand.

Willum clamped his teeth closed, the nervous humming in his throat louder. He brought his free hand up to her head and tangled his fingers in her hair. He groaned when he heard the fastening break on his leg plate and risked a glance down. The small corpse had sawed through the leather with her teeth, and her claws were reaching to his leg.

"No!" he hollered as he tugged hard on the adult corpse's hair. Muscles bunched as he yanked, and he was rewarded with a sharp crack. He held the dismembered head in his hand for a moment before he hurled it aside, taking a deep breath before dealing with the smaller one.

The large corpse continued to fight and would not let go of his sword arm. Although it was muffled by the drift he tossed the head into, he heard it continue to cackle.

"By the breath of Kiri-Jolith, what manner of creature are you?"

The dead girl's fingers clawed at Willum's leggings, finding the flesh beneath. The knight didn't cry out despite the pain, only doubled his efforts against the larger corpse. With his free hand, he began tearing it apart, bone by bone, and crushing the brittle ribs with his fist. At last the corpse released his sword arm, and Willum finished shredding the thing, all the while enduring the pain in his leg.

He turned his attention to the child.

Her face had been well preserved by the cold. Only a bit of her cheek was missing. Her eyes stared vacantly at him, and he prayed silently to the memory of Kiri-Jolith as he reached down and wrenched her head off. He fought with her for a few moments more, gritting his teeth as her small hands continued to tear into his leg. Not so long dead as the other, her flesh and muscles held her together more firmly, though in the end, Willum managed.

Gasping for breath, he dropped to his knees, effectively sinking to his waist in the snow. He fumbled around for his leg plate and quickly found it, then discarded it when he saw the strap was so badly mangled he couldn't reattach it. "Gods," he whispered, then dug through the snow for his sword, humming as he searched. The snow was disturbed by the fight, and several times his fingers closed about a bone from the larger corpse. "My sword," he muttered. "It's got to be around here somewhere." He persisted, refusing to be weaponless.

"Creatures of Chaos," he cursed when at last his icy-cold fingers closed on the pommel. "Got to find Camilla and . . ."

And die.

A pool of blackness slithered across the snow, looking like oil and moving quickly. It approached Willum as the knight got to his feet and started backing away. The blackness rose, forming legs and arms, spiderweb-fine hair, and eyes that glowed white like stars, then red like hot coals.

* * * * *

Camilla and her knights closed on the overturned wagon. She drew her sword and motioned for her men to spread out and to watch the snow for any hidden foes.

"We'll help you!" she cried as she rushed toward a man leaning on a wagon wheel. "We'll . . ." She stopped in her tracks. Closer now, she could make out the grisly details. The man was the village leader whom she'd met when she was with Gair, and he was dead.

"All of them are dead, Commander!" A young knight was turning over the other bodies. There were eight in all. Two families, she recalled from her previous visit. "They're clawed up pretty bad, like some big rabid animal got them. Maybe a bear. No wonder they were screaming."

Camilla's gaze dropped to the snow. There was a good deal of blood on the wagon and tinting the snow. "Tracks!" she snapped. "Do you see any animal tracks?"

The knights started searching, around the wagon and farther out. She gestured to four of them to follow her into the village. In the distance, she could see lights burning in some of the windows.

"Can't find any tracks!" she heard from behind her now. "It's dark, Commander, might be easy to miss."

She ran quickly down the center of the narrow path, kicking up snow as she went. The clanking behind her was a signal that her men were close behind. "Watch yourself!" she hollered loudly, an instruction meant for the men with her and for those still at the wagon. "Keep alert!"

Within heartbeats, she was in the center of the small farming community. Everything was eerily silent, the only sounds the ragged breathing from her and the men. She took in several gulps of air and ran toward the nearest home. A soft glow showed out from a curtained window. She pounded on the door.

No answer, and no sound came from within.

Waving to her men, they fanned out, knocking on door after door and getting no answer.

Camilla's chest heaved from running, and she leaned against the home for an instant to catch her breath and watch her men. She spun and kicked at the door and plunged inside and was greeted by a chorus of screams.

People were huddled in front of a fireplace, wide-eyed, staring at her, crying in fright. She recognized one of them, the pregnant woman Gair had tended to. She held a poker in her hand as if it were a weapon.

"It's all right," she started. "When no one answered the door—"

"The creatures came," the pregnant woman cut in. "They came and we locked ourselves in. The Hansons. The creatures got them."

"At the wagon?"

The woman nodded.

"Dead things," said a man next to her. He was cradling a trembling boy to his chest. "All bones and teeth, and they was screaming. All of 'em was screaming something awful."

Camilla pointed to a table. "Push this against door, and don't come out until morning." She rushed back to the center of the village and waved to her men. "In twos! No one alone!" she hollered. "I'm not truly sure what we're looking for, though I believe it's—"

"Undead, Commander!" The first knight who'd left Willum rushed into the village. Out of breath, he haltingly but quickly explained about the skeletal woman and child and that Willum believed it was a trap.

"They're after the settlement, then," she said. "This was a distraction to separate us. A wise ploy, and one I fell for. Still, we can't abandon these people."

She thought for only a moment more, then ordered her men to conduct a fast search of the village and the barns, ordering them to make sure every house was locked tight and that nothing was lurking in the barns.

Several minutes later, they were running back down the trail toward the settlement.

* * * * *

"Gair," Jasper began. "My friend, I—"

"Spare me your pleasantries," the elf returned. "I'm not the same man you knew when we came to Schallsea Island."

The dwarf eyed him up and down. Once Gair had been fastidious, preferring to wear only the finest of clothes, expensive and well made, always cleaned and pressed. Now his leggings were filthy, smelling of dirt and something foul the dwarf couldn't quite place at first.

"Like the grave," Jasper whispered after a moment. "You smell like the grave."

The elf's heavy tunic was snagged in the front, and several pearl buttons hung loosely on fraying threads. His face and hands were dirty, his fingernails chipped. His hair was tangled and dusted with pine needles. The only bit of cleanness about him was a red cloak, which the dwarf recognized that as Camilla's.

"What happened to you, Gair?"

The elf threw back his head and laughed. "Happened? Happened, as in something is wrong?" He slowly drew his gaze to the dwarf's, his dark eyes wide and sparkling malevolently. "I guess you might say I learned a great deal from our teacher, my old friend. She taught me some spells when you weren't around."

"Fortunate for me," Jasper numbly whispered.

"She taught me how to talk to the dead."

The dwarf swallowed and scanned the mist. There was a break in it, and through it, he could see tiny people, the size of big beetles. From the direction of Goldmoon's tent, he saw a few soldiers gathering, identifiable only because of their red tunics. He spotted someone—Goldmoon, he sensed—pointing toward the Silver Stair. He suspected that with her human eyes, Goldmoon couldn't see him up here, not this high anyway. He took a step closer to Gair.

"An' what do the dead have to say, Gair?"

The elf backed down a few steps to accommodate the dwarf and give him more room. The mist of the low-hanging cloud swirled about the elf's thighs. "They tell me many things, my friend. The spirits of the Qué-Nal tell me about the island's past. The spirits of the drowned barbarians tell me about the terrible war with the Blue Dragonarmy. Of course, there's always two sides to every story. The dragonarmy general tells me about the battle from his point of view. Then there's the Solamnic knights."

Jasper's eyes twitched.

"Not the ones at the settlement. The ones I killed, or rather had killed. They tell me about Camilla. I do so like the company of the dead, Jasper, but I miss sweet Camilla."

"You're mad!" the dwarf edged down another half-dozen steps. The elf obliged him and kept a respectful distance. The mist was swirling about both of them now.

"Mad?" Gair grinned wildly. "Maybe I am, at that, but I am also powerful."

The dwarf took another step down. This time the elf didn't budge.

"I can raise the dead, Jasper, keep spirits tied to the living world. Would you like to see your Uncle Flint again? I can manage it with the Silver Stair. And River-wind—I thought I might bring him out tonight, parade him before our dear teacher. She'd be so impressed with my skills."

Jasper's fingers squeezed the handle of his hammer so tightly they nearly lost sensation. He kept his eyes locked onto Gair's, and he slowly pulled the weapon free from his belt. There was an instant shushing sound as Gair drew his long sword and pointed it up at the dwarf.

"You wouldn't want to hurt me, Jasper. We're close, the best of friends. Think of all the secrets we've shared. I've missed you almost as much as I've missed Camilla. The undead talk to me, but they don't argue like you used to. I really miss that."

"Well, climb on down an' I'll argue with you some more." The dwarf gestured with his hammer.

Gair shook his head. "I'll stay right here, thank you." Carefully he crouched on the shimmering step beneath his feet, keeping his eyes on Jasper and the sword pointed up at the dwarf's belly. His free hand drifted down to touch a step. "I need the Silver Stair, my friend. I need its power."

"Let's go talk to Goldmoon," Jasper urged, his voice carrying a hint of nervousness. "She's been worried about you."

"Quiet!" the elf admonished. "I need to concentrate."

"She'll help you," the dwarf continued. "You don't need this kind of magic, Gair. Let her help you. Let me help you."

The elf's expression softened for a moment, as if he were considering the dwarf's words. His eyes lost some of their sparkle, and he lowered the sword a few inches. "Jasper, I—"

"Goldmoon can help, Gair. Goldmoon cares about you."

"I've done things, Jasper, things she wouldn't approve of. Dark and—"

"It doesn't matter." The dwarf's words were sincere, tumbling from his thick lips. "She'll forgive you. Let her help. We can—"

"I've killed people, Jasper. Good people. Knights. Roeland Stark. Do you remember Roeland? I wouldn't let his spirit—"

"Gair, listen to me." The dwarf noticed the bits of red gathering around the base of the Silver Stair, returned his gaze to the elf. "Put down your sword an' come with me. Everythin'll get worked out. You'll see."

"I don't think my new friends would like that. The dead ones."

"Just try."

The elf seemed to be battling some inner demon. His lip was sucked under his teeth and he was chewing on it, and the sword in his hand was lowering a little more.

"Goldmoon will help you. Let her help you. Come with me."

"Goldmoon . . ." The elf's sword arm shook almost imperceptibly. "I fear not even Goldmoon could forgive me, Jasper. I—"

"There he is!" One of the soldiers had spotted Gair, and Jasper and was pointing frantically in the air. "The elf! Tell Goldmoon he's on the Silver Stair! Way up there!"

The elf's expression instantly hardened, and he raised the sword to Jasper's throat. The dwarf backed up a step.

*　*　*　*　*

Goldmoon had gathered most of the settlers around

her, was calming them and telling them to stay together. She watched a dozen soldiers and some of her followers head toward the Silver Stair. Then she spotted more soldiers lining up across the eastern side of the settlement. There were nearly a dozen more Solamnic knights whom Camilla had not taken with her. Fully in their armor now, they were receiving orders from a lieutenant whose name Goldmoon could not recall.

"What's going on?" This from one of the Thorbardin dwarves. "We heard screams."

"From down the trail," one of the fishermen explained. "Maybe them renegade Qué-Nal again."

"No." It was Iryl. "I spoke to Skydancer. He said there would be no more trouble. He would keep Shadowwalker in line."

The fisherman scratched his head. "Well, if it ain't the barbarians, who is it?"

"Whisperers." Orvago had emerged from the building site, his clawed fingers wrapped around the ivory pommel of the broadsword. A ridge of hair stood up from the top of his head and ran down his back, disappearing into his tunic. He growled softly, a trail of spittle finding its way over his bottom lip and landing on the bald head of a man who stood in front of him. "Sorry," he added softly.

The bald man growled back and wiped at his head. He glared at Goldmoon and opened his mouth as if to say something, but his words were drowned out by high-pitched shouts coming from the southern edge of the settlement.

Goldmoon threaded her way through the gathering and saw an ancient Qué-Nal standing on a crate. The light from the dwarves' campfire showed his face was so deeply lined it looked like the rough bark on a tree. Feathers were stuck, seemingly haphazardly, in his hair, and beads dangled from a wild mane of gray-black braids, clacking as he shook his head. He wasn't wearing much, despite the cold, only a tunic smeared with what Goldmoon suspected was blood, plus furry boots, the tops of which were ringed with bird skulls. With surprising agility for one so old, he leapt off the crate and made a piercing yipping sound. It was echoed by many voices.

More Qué-Nal sprang up from behind crates and drifts of snow, from around the edges of tents that were on the fringes of the settlement. They were young and muscular, their faces smeared with blood and ashes, beads clacking. Their eyes were wild and darted to the ancient shaman, who was raising a spear in his hand.

"Kill the Qué-Shu!" Shadowwalker cried. "Kill all of them!"

The Qué-Nal surged forward, spears and knives in their hands and cries of death on their lips.

Iryl stood stunned for only a moment, shaking her head in disbelief and whispering, "Skydancer promised."

Orvago roused her into action as he brushed by, knocking her into the Solace twins as he thundered toward the shaman. The elf's eyes still held a touch of incredulity as she reached to her belt and pulled free a long knife, then rushed to join the fray.

Goldmoon was shouting for people to protect their children and for those who were able and armed to defend the settlement. Some who carried no weapons made do with makeshift ones, grabbing torches to use as clubs and pulling tent poles loose.

The soldiers on the eastern edge of the settlement were charging the Qué-Nal, not bothering to wait for orders. Swords and spears clashed, and in less than a moment there were dead men on each side.

The Solamnic knights spread out, the lieutenant

ordering them to keep the barbarians from reaching the settlers. The knights made a valiant effort, but there were too many renegade Qué-Nal. Most of the young barbarians met the knights head-on, Shadowwalker screaming to strike where the plates of armor joined. Some skirted past and directly into the path of Orvago, Iryl, and the others.

Goldmoon hesitated only a second as she surveyed the scene. There were soldiers and barbarians falling, and barbarians falling to the knights, who presented more formidable foes in their heavy armor. The gnoll had dropped three barbarians in as many swings, his magical broad sword fairly whistling through the air. Iryl was at his side, crouched and slashing with her long knife, blood dripping from the blade.

At the Silver Stair, the soldiers were pointing into the air and shouting, but there was so much noise from the battle with the Qué-Nal that Goldmoon couldn't make out what they were saying.

Another soldier fell, a spear lodged in his leg, and Goldmoon ran toward the man. She nearly trampled Redstone, who was hurling spikes from the building site at a trio of young barbarians.

"Can you use a staff?" the healer shouted to her.

The dwarf nodded. "Any weapon." Her voice gruff and breathy. "I can use anything."

Goldmoon thrust her treasured staff into the woman's thick hands. "Use this well. My other talents are needed."

The dwarf looked at her quizzically for a moment as the healer continued to dash toward the fallen soldier, then her stubby legs churned over the snow-packed ground and toward the trio, a Thorbardin battle cry spewing from her lips.

Redstone cracked the staff into the head of the lead barbarian, happily surprised that he fell with the first blow. She brought the other end around to smack into the second barbarian's stomach, felling him, too. The third looked at her through narrowed eyes and jammed his spear forward, but the squat dwarf dropped to a crouch, and as the spear passed over her head, she jammed the tip of the staff forward, nearly impaling him. He crumpled, and she drove the staff against his head to make sure he wouldn't be getting back up.

"Well indeed," she said, as she pounded toward a rank of soldiers and barbarians. "I better take good care o' this for Goldmoon. Wish Jasper could see me now. Wonder where he is?"

* * * * *

Jasper watched some of the settlers leave the base of the Silver Stair, running toward the far end of the settlement. He could hear the sounds of battle. The soldiers seemed torn between staying and pursuing the elf or joining their comrades. Within a heartbeat, some of them were running away, leaving only six behind. The six began to climb up the stair.

"What are you doin', Gair?" The dwarf's broad face was etched with anger.

"Doing?"

"The fight." The dwarf cocked his head toward the ruckus.

"Some friends of mine. Living ones. They don't care much for Goldmoon and the settlement and are bent on destroying both."

"You'll get them killed, Gair. There's knights down there."

The elf shook his head. "Most of the knights are in Heartspring. If some of my new friends down there die, I'll bring them back . . . their spirits at least."

Jasper sputtered as he climbed up a dozen more

steps, the elf following, urging him higher with the tip of his sword. The dwarf made out the tiny forms of the soldiers guardedly making their way up from far below.

"You owe Goldmoon. You owe her everythin', Gair! She took you in, taught you mysticism, saved your life on more'n one account."

"You saved my life, too, Jasper." For the briefest moment, the elf's face lost some of its harshness, and he lowered the sword an inch. "On the trail to the settlement, and then . . ." The elf shook his head, the meanness returning to his visage. "Because you saved my life, I will let you live forever—at my side. Goldmoon, too."

"No." Jasper shook his head and raised his hammer in front of him as the elf forced him upward a few more steps. "Let Goldmoon be, Gair. I'll give you my life if you only . . ." The dwarf's eyes grew wide as Gair's free hand reached to the step.

The elf began mumbling something, and Jasper saw the step crack beneath the elf's fingers. There was a faint humming—moaning?—as if the Silver Stair was protesting. The elf persisted, and the crack grew wider, scintillating slivers falling away. Minutes passed, and the moaning of the stair grew louder.

"Wh-what are you doin'?" Jasper looked back and forth between the elf's hand and his face. The eyes were closed now in concentration.

The elf continued, furrowed his brow, and mumbled something in a language the dwarf could not understand. Jasper took advantage of the moment and clambered down a few steps. He raised his hammer and brought it down toward the elf's hand.

At the last possible moment, Gair brought his sword around to block the blow. At the same time, he kicked backward with his leg, connecting with the face of a soldier who had made it up this high and sending the man hurtling to the ground far below. The elf scampered down another few steps and spun, meeting the charge of the second soldier and slicing through his abdomen. The man held his ground for a heartbeat, tried to return the blow, then toppled, screaming. Four men were left on the Silver Stair, all in single file because the steps were so narrow and all looking up, horror etched on their faces.

Gair stared at them, paused like game pieces in a row, then he spun to face Jasper, who had inched closer and was preparing to strike again. The elf crouched and leapt above the dwarf like a dancer executing a perfect aerial maneuver, landing on a step above Jasper.

Jasper turned around, a shaken look on his face.

"The stair gives me power, my old friend— physical and mystical." The elf crouched again, sword pointed down at the dwarf to keep him back, free hand against the step. Again, spiderweb-fine cracks appeared beneath his fingers. They grew, and more glistening slivers fell away. "It gives anyone power . . . anyone who dares to take it."

"You're destroyin' it!" Jasper sputtered. "Gair, stop this!"

"Stop this or what?" the elf taunted. His face was so contorted the dwarf hardly recognized him. "Or you'll kill me?" The elf laughed long and eerily at this. "You were always the better healer, Jasper. We both know that, but I am the better fighter. You and the dumbstruck men behind you haven't a prayer of besting me!"

"I don't want to fight you, Gair. I'd like to help you." The dwarf gestured behind him, urging the four remaining soldiers to climb back down.

"Always looking out for others." The elf watched the four soldiers slowly and carefully retrace their steps. "You should be looking out for yourself." Gair gripped the step more tightly, and the cracks widened still more.

The dwarf struggled up toward Gair and raised his hammer again.

"You don't give up, do you?" The elf shook his head and let his fingers drift to the next higher step, where more fine cracks appeared. "I was going to kill you last, because you saved me. I was going to take Goldmoon first, then—"

"Leave her alone!"

"Our dear teacher. I'm inside her mind, you know. The stair lets me do that. She's using all her energy to heal Camilla's soldiers. She knows I'm watching her, and she can't do a thing about it."

"No!" The dwarf swung hard, putting all his strength into the blow and aiming it down on the elf's hand.

This time Gair wasn't quick enough, and the hammer landed soundly, breaking his fingers. The elf howled and skittered higher, the dwarf pursuing. Many feet below, the soldiers saw the dwarf had gained the upper hand and reversed their course and were coming to join him.

"You dare!" Gair spat, as he climbed higher still, clutching his broken hand to his chest. His eyes were wide with fury, and he swung his long sword awkwardly at the dwarf.

"You can't fix broken bones," Jasper growled as he continued to pursue the elf. A mist was forming around them. They'd climbed so high they were entering another cloud that had formed. The dwarf squinted through it to keep his eyes on Gair. "Goldmoon shared that talent when you weren't around." He pressed the elf to move faster, holding his hammer high and threatening another blow.

"You can't beat me." The elf's words were ice. "Father!"

Something cold brushed by Jasper, colder than the winter wind that continued to play around him. He nearly dropped his hammer and lost his balance. It was a shadow in the mist, as dark as a starless sky. Two red lights shone inside the shadow, locking onto the dwarf as if they were eyes. Jasper shivered and forced himself to look instead at Gair. The shadow disappeared. Moments passed, and he and the elf found themselves above the mist, the top step of the Silver Stair coming into sight.

"Look!" Jasper pointed.

The elf, still nursing his hand, glanced over his shoulder.

"Did you ever climb all the way to the top, Gair? Did you ever take that chance? There it is, waitin' for you!"

The elf stared at the top step, shimmering invitingly. He hadn't realized they'd climbed so high, and the thought unnerved him, but only for a moment. "So close," he whispered. He found himself walking backward up the stairs, glancing between the dwarf and the topmost step. "So very close."

The dwarf carefully crept up beneath him, holding his position like a statue each time the elf swiveled his head back to check on him. The elf was moving slower, since he was going backward, and the dwarf waited until Gair was nearly to the top step, keeping his eyes on it; then he scrambled forward. He swung his hammer as hard as he could, slamming it into the elf's leg.

Gair cried out, more in surprise than pain, and whirled to face the dwarf, nearly losing his balance and tumbling off the step. Jasper's hammer was coming down again, striking the same leg and causing Gair to fall backward. The elf's sword clattered down the steps, then fell away into the mist far below. He looked to the dwarf, a pleading expression on his face.

"I've no weapon," the elf said. But the fingers of his good hand were closing on a step, and tiny cracks were appearing beneath it. "You've too much honor to strike an unarmed man."

"Don't." Jasper pointed his hammer at the elf's hand. "Leave the stair alone."

The elf looked up innocently, but his lips were moving, mumbling words that once again the dwarf could not understand. They didn't sound elvish. Jasper had been around enough elves in his life. They sounded human, but nothing he could place.

"I said stop!"

Gair's lips moved faster, and a pale glow rose around his fingers and edged up to his wrist.

"That's it!" The dwarf swung, striking the elf's knee, pulled back on the hammer, and brought it down again, even as the elf was struggling to his feet. The impact sent the elf teetering, arms flailing about in an attempt to gain his balance. Jasper struck Gair's leg again, and this time the elf staggered under the blow, his feet slipping off the narrow step. He seemed to hang suspended for a heartbeat, limbs churning as if he were trying to fly, then he plummeted, disappearing into the mist below.

More powerful in death, the wind seemed to whisper.

Jasper shook his head. "By the beard of Reorx, I killed him."

Carefully he turned and sat on the step. He caught his breath and watched as the head of the lead soldier emerged from the mist. The man was shaking, and the dwarf knew it was from fear of being so high.

"It's all right," the dwarf said sadly. "Gair fell." More softly, he added, "He never made it to the top of the Silver Stair." He gestured toward the mist. "I know there's a big fight ragin' down there, so we'd better get ourselves down to it, but take it slow. None of us will do Goldmoon any good if we don't make it down in one piece."

The soldiers complied, backing down and keeping their hands on the steps in front of them for support. They mumbled to themselves about how high up they were, that they could barely hear the battle. It sounded like crickets chirping, and then they were below the mist, and the lights of the campfires came into view. Several fires blazed, and the men and the dwarf could tell that some of the tents were on fire. They quickened their pace as much as they dared, stopping when the lead soldier slipped. Jasper darted forward, stubby fingers locking around his wrist, keeping him from falling.

The dwarf's keen vision studied the shimmering steps, noticing where Gair had cracked them by stealing their mystical energy. "Didn't want to kill him," the dwarf said to himself, "but I couldn't let him destroy the stair or hurt Goldmoon."

The closer the soldiers got to the ground, the faster they went, the one at the bottom jumping off when he was five feet or so above the ground and landing on his rump in the snow. The clang of swords was louder here, as were the cries of those being wounded. The soldiers hurried toward the battle, which was spread across three sides of the settlement, the closest near the cliff.

Jasper grabbed his side, which stung from the exertion of climbing the Silver Stair twice in one evening almost to the top step. He tried to catch his breath, and he looked around the base of the mystical site, searching for Gair's body. The snow was disturbed from the soldiers, but there was no ready sign of the elf. The dwarf knew he couldn't have survived the fall and decided to look later, after the fight was over, provided he lived through it. He thrust his hammer in his belt and ran toward the cliff, taking a path that cut between a pair of burning tents.

* * * * *

Near the construction site, Goldmoon was crawling from one soldier to the next, calling on the power of her heart to stop their bleeding. She wasn't taking the time to completely heal them—that would take too much energy and keep her in one spot too long. A Solamnic Knight stood over her, keeping her safe from the spear thrusts of the angry Qué-Nal.

"Too many of them," the knight told her.

Goldmoon didn't reply. She moved on to another fallen soldier, stifling a cry when she saw he was dead. She was on her feet and sprinting toward a man who'd just dropped, the knight fast behind her, parrying the blows of the vengeful Qué-Nal.

The healer dropped to the man's side and felt for the warmth of her mystical healing powers. "Do not die on me, Samual," she said. He was one of the first soldiers stationed at the settlement. "Do not . . . yes!" His eyes fluttered open as more of her healing energy poured into him.

Above their heads, her protector knight rained a series of blows against a stocky Qué-Nal, breaking his spear and driving the man back.

The healer stayed over Samual, tearing a strip from her cloak and pressing it against his shoulder, where a spear had bit viciously deep.

"You'll be all right," she told him. She was pulling him back, away from the fighting line, even as she was casting her gaze about the entire camp to take stock of the fight.

The largest battle was being fought at the construction site. Solamnic knights and soldiers were keeping dozens of Qué-Nal from pressing into the main part of the settlement. Only one knight had fallen, and Goldmoon intended to get to him next. Several of her students were at the edge of the fight, using the skills she had taught them to save the injured soldiers.

A second battle raged between soldiers and Goldmoon's followers on the eastern edge of the camp, near the trail to Heartspring. Shadowwalker had found his way there and was directing his fiery-tempered disciples from a safe distance. Redstone was there, using Goldmoon's staff with telling effect. The dwarf had become the target of the old shaman's ire, and he was gesturing for the strongest of his warriors to deal with her.

Near Goldmoon's tent, which had also caught fire, another contingent of Qué-Nal was struggling with the healer's followers and the gnoll. The warriors in the second rank, their backs to the sea, were using flaming arrows, though not directing them into the people but rather into the tents. The result was chaos. The elderly and the children who huddled in the center of the settlement were terrified by the fires, which were sending gouts of smoke their way and making it difficult to breathe. A handful of the older children were using their cloaks to try to put out the smallest of the fires but meeting with little success.

Orvago threw back his head and howled, then pressed forward and slashed the magical broadsword. The ivory pommel felt warm against his paw, and he swung the blade wildly as he'd seen the barbarians on the ship use their swords. The Qué-Nal gave the gnoll a wide berth, trying to concentrate instead on Goldmoon's followers, only some of whom wielded swords.

One man swung an iron skillet, managing to crack it against the skull of a young Qué-Nal. Near him, a woman was using a tent pole as if it were a quarterstaff, and she drove it forward into the belly of a tall warrior, knocking him back into the second rank and pushing a bowman over the cliff. The three fishermen were here, using gaff hooks against the warriors who had shields. The hooks cut into the hide shields, ripping them.

Jasper finally reached Orvago's side, out of breath and tugging his hammer free. He brought it up just in time to block the spear thrust of an angry Qué-Nal. "Gair's dead!" the dwarf shouted. "He fell from the Silver Stair!"

The gnoll grunted in reply and continued to slash at the barbarians, sending two over the edge of the cliff.

Suddenly a series of shrill cries cut through the air, and the gnoll and dwarf risked a quick glance toward their source. Shadowwalker, illuminated on the far side of the settlement by all the burning tents, was on the shoulders of a burly, young barbarian. He was making a keening, yipping sound and gesturing wildly toward Heartspring. His warriors parted, some disappearing into the night, as Camilla and her knights thundered down the trail and into the settlement.

The knights charged into Shadowwalker's men, bashing the warriors with their shields to keep them off-balance and to prevent them from using their spears. The presence of the knights was enough to turn the tide of battle on the Heartspring side of the settlement. Shadowwalker ordered a retreat, and his men fell back.

Camilla did not order her knights to pursue. Rather, she scanned the settlement, ordering them to join the soldiers who were still fighting at the construction site. She spotted Goldmoon and headed toward the healer, stopping in her tracks when another sharp cry cut through the din.

"More of them?" she whispered as she craned her neck about, trying to find the source. "By the will of Kiri-Jolith, we do not have the numbers to fight these."

The cry sounded again, much closer this time, and it was echoed a dozen times over. It made the Qué-Nal pause, giving the soldiers and knights openings they quickly took advantage of. As they pushed the barbarians back, Camilla reached Goldmoon.

"It was a ruse to get us out of camp," the knight explained. "Good thing I didn't take many men."

Goldmoon didn't reply. She was dressing the wounds of the fallen Solamnic Knight.

Camilla defended the healer now, using her shield to keep spears from reaching Goldmoon. The knight commander was exhausted from her run to Heartspring and back, her sword arm heavy like lead. Still she refused to quit.

Abruptly the Qué-Nal started pulling back, making a fighting retreat as the cry cut through the night again. Branches snapped and snow crunched as more Qué-Nal broke into the settlement, but these were not fighting Goldmoon and her followers. They struck out at their brothers instead.

"Skydancer!" Iryl called from across the settlement.

The Qué-Nal chieftain directed his warriors after the renegades, and within moments, Shadowwalker's men were fleeing. Heartbeats later, they were nowhere to be seen.

Iryl raced toward the chieftain.

The settlers went to work battling the fires, which had consumed half the tents. Some counted heads, and others looked to the wounded. Goldmoon backed away from the injured knight and helped him to his feet. Despite the cold, she was sweating from the strain of tending to so many people. She didn't object when Camilla put an arm around her shoulder for support. Silently the two women took in the aftermath.

More than a dozen soldiers had died, and twice that many were wounded. Only one knight was slain, and this because a Qué-Nal spear found its way between the fastenings of his breastplate. Two of the Thorbardin dwarves had also perished, and Redstone hovered, distraught, at their sides.

Orvago and Jasper, their clothes coated with the barbarians' blood, tromped over, edging through the crowd of settlers and soldiers and spying Goldmoon next to Camilla.

"Gair's dead!" Jasper called to her. "He fell from the stair. I think he brought the renegades down on us." The dwarf moved closer. "I tried to help him," he said more softly, meaning the words only for the healer. "I don't think there was anythin' good still inside him." He shook his head. "I killed him, Goldmoon, but I didn't really have a choice."

"Neither do I."

The crowd seemed to utter a collective gasp. Hovering above the center of the camp, suspended by two inky-black shadows with glowing red eyes, was Gair.

Chapter 17

Acts of Desperation

"Whisperers!" the gnoll shouted. He waved his broadsword and pushed his way through the crowd, leaping and trying to get close enough to slice at one of the undead who held the elf.

"By Reorx's beard!" swore Jasper. The dwarf clutched his hammer tightly and made a move to follow the gnoll, but Goldmoon grabbed his shoulder. She pointed to the fallen soldiers and renegade Que-Nal. The dwarf was torn for an instant between helping the men who still lived and going after Gair. He couldn't reach the elf so high above the ground, and some of the injured needed immediate attention.

"By Reorx's beard," he grumbled again. He, too, pushed through the crowd, but not toward Gair. He noticed that more of Goldmoon's students were following suit, kneeling to tend to the renegades, not just the Solamnic forces. He heard Goldmoon shouting to Gair, but he couldn't quite make out the words. There was too much talking going on among the settlers.

He knelt by a soldier whose arm was badly mangled. The dwarf was exhausted, but seeing the wounded man and the others dying nearby, forced him to summon his mystical energy. "Have to get you fixed up quick," he told the man as he searched for his inner spark. Gotta be quick, he added to himself, 'cause I might have to help Goldmoon handle Gair.

"Goldmoon!" Gair cried as the shadows lowered him just enough to tantalize the gnoll.

Orvago stood underneath them, leaping and swinging the blade.

"Goldmoon!"

The healer edged through the crowd, noting the shocked look on the settlers' faces. Some were angry, while others looked frightened. However, most were still bewildered by the night's events. Amanda was at her mother's feet, reaching up into the air and calling for the elf.

"I'm here, Gair." Goldmoon raised a hand to draw his attention.

The wraiths of the elder Graymist and Darkhunter continued to hold Gair suspended. The elf slowly regarded the healer.

"I want to thank you, Goldmoon," he began. "You showed me the doorway, and through it, I've brought these men, and more. I couldn't have done this without you."

The aging healer shuddered but kept her eyes locked on her student.

"I owe you, dear teacher, and I need to pay you back, but there's the dilemma. How? I tried to bring Riverwind's spirit through the door, to give him some substance. Just for you. But he objects to the notion. Still, you know that I am nothing if not persistent. Would you like that, dear teacher? To have Riverwind at your side, as I have these men at mine?"

"Gair, come down, please."

"Ah, that wouldn't be such a good idea. My hairy friend down there doesn't seem too friendly."

Orvago howled and redoubled his efforts, his leap taking him perilously close to one of the wraiths. They raised Gair a little higher.

"And then there's sweet Camilla." The elf gestured toward the edge of the crowd. The knight commander was slowly making her way through the throng.

"Gair . . ." Goldmoon motioned to him.

The elf scowled and shook his head, then laughed. "I'll come down when you're all dead."

A scream cut through the murmurs of the crowd, coming from the construction site. Goldmoon turned but couldn't see through the gathering. There were cries of "What's happening?" and "What in the name of vanished gods is that?" She tried making her way through the bodies, while at the same time keeping her eyes on Gair. The elf laughed louder at her quandary.

Suddenly the crowd was scattering, and Goldmoon was knocked to the ground in the panic. The elf drifted toward the construction site, Orvago following him, barking and snarling. One of them stopped long enough to tug Goldmoon to her feet.

Camilla was shouting orders to her men within earshot. They quickly formed a rank and tried to restore some semblance of order. Iryl was instantly at her side with Skydancer, both trying to help.

"Gather the people by the Silver Stair!" Camilla shouted to the pair. "There's nothing there that can catch on fire. Get them away from the rest of the tents." The knight and two of her men were moving forward, eyes on the fallen who were still being tended to by Goldmoon's students.

There were shadows dancing around the healers. At first glance, it looked as if the shadows were caused by the still-flickering campfires and the tents that continued to burn, but as the knight moved closer, she saw that the shadows had eyes . . . red ones.

"Undead!" she called, realizing it would panic the people more, but wanting them away from the shadowy things. She charged forward, nearly slipping on a patch of ice, and stepping between bodies to reach the wraiths. She nearly knocked over Jasper, whose eyes were closed in concentration.

In a heartbeat, she was at the edge of the settlement, and the black shapes were moving to meet her. They hovered above the ground just beyond the reach of her sword, darting in as if to tease her.

The cries from the settlers grew softer, indicating they'd moved away from the center of the camp and that Iryl and Skydancer were having some success herding the settlers toward the Silver Stair, but not all of the settlers were being cooperative.

Camilla had the fishermen to her right. They were swinging gaff hooks at the shadowy creatures. Dwarves were hurling spikes from the construction site at the things and were greeted by bone-chilling peals of laughter. Redstone was among them, but she was swinging Goldmoon's staff. One wraith darted too close to the stout dwarf, and she landed a solid blow with the staff. The wraith flew back, howling.

"Dozens of the things!" Redstone was shouting. "Commander, they're practically impossible to see in the darkness!"

"Cold!" shouted one of the fishermen. "Colder than snow!"

The man at his side doubled over as a wraith came up through the ground and grabbed his legs. The man screamed once, then was oddly still.

"Get back!" Camilla called to the men. She saw that the spikes and clubs, even the swords of her men were doing nothing to the shadowy creatures— but Redstone's staff! The dwarf landed another blow, where the thing seemed to have a neck. It screamed shrilly and burst into pieces of black that rained down on the snow and dissipated. "All of you, get back!"

She motioned Redstone to her side as her knights covered the settlers who were retreating. "The staff . . ."

"Goldmoon's," the dwarf huffed as she swung at a wraith coming up through the snow at Camilla's feet. The creature keened and seemed to melt into nothingness. "I think it's got some potent magic in it."

The knight leapt at a wraith flying toward her, slicing away a nest of spiderweb fine hair. The black tendrils fell like rain and sent the rest of the creature retreating. "Orvago calls them whisperers. He claims only magic can harm them."

"Wonderful," the dwarf said as she jabbed the staff at a creature trying to come up through the ground in front of her. "Your sword, Goldmoon's staff, and there's dozens of them."

The dwarf and the knight backed up toward the line of wounded soldiers and renegades, where the trees were thin and they could better see the undead.

Jasper had moved on to another soldier, and then another, furtively looking toward Camilla and Redstone and at the wraiths that slipped around them and floated toward the fallen men. He watched in horror as one fell on a wounded renegade and began to devour him.

"The time for healin' is done," the dwarf pronounced as he pushed himself from the ground and grabbed his hammer.

Gair continued to float toward the construction site, watching with fascination as his wraiths did their macabre dance with Camilla and Redstone. He was paying so much attention to the battle that he hadn't noticed the gnoll. Orvago was climbing onto a crate, then onto another that was stacked higher. As the wraiths carried Gair past him, he vaulted toward them, broadsword raised high above his head.

He swung the sword as hard as he could as he awkwardly plummeted toward the ground. He had aimed for the elf, who finally saw him when the blade glimmered in the light of the moon. Gair managed to twist his body enough so the sword cut only Camilla's cloak, but the sword also bit deep into one of the wraiths holding him.

The black creature wailed inhumanly, and as the gnoll landed, he dropped the sword and threw his paws up over his ears to lessen the painful sound. The wraith contorted for a moment more, then dissolved into black rain that fell down on Orvago, chilling him.

"Father!" Gair howled. "Father!"

Darkhunter had been unprepared for the gnoll's brash attack and nearly dropped the elf when the elder Graymist was slain by Orvago a second time. The wraith juggled the elf in midair, moving his icy hands beneath Gair's armpits to keep him aloft. The elf seemed to struggle against Darkhunter.

"Orvago!" Gair shouted. "You will die! Die!"

Master, Darkhunter whispered. *The gnoll is beneath your notice. Do not let him worry you. I need you too badly to let you get caught up in petty notions of revenge. The knights first. The woman knight. And then the old—Goldmoon.* But the wraith kept his red eyes on Orvago's sword as he chattered.

"The sword," Gair cursed, his legs churning through the air. "I want that sword first. Next we'll slay Cam and Goldmoon—whatever you want. Get the sword first!"

The wraith groaned softly but finally made a move to comply, dropping the elf lower while the gnoll continued to writhe on the ground, wounded by the dissolving bits of the elder Graymist. Orvago was making a whining noise, not unlike an injured dog, and he twitched uncontrollably in the snow.

"The sword," Gair repeated. "It's mine. The animal stole it."

While the fight with the wraiths continued at the construction site and the soldiers and knights tried to drag the wounded away from the undead, Darkhunter gently deposited the elf on the ground. *Hurry*, the wraith whispered.

Gair darted toward the sword, the fingers of his good hand outstretched. At the moment his fingers brushed the ivory pommel, the gnoll's arm shot out, beating him to the weapon. The gnoll howled and leapt to his feet, all traces of pain gone.

"You tricked me!" Gair shouted. "I didn't think you capable of such a thing!"

The elf skittered back as the gnoll darted forward, slashing madly. The blade cut deep into the elf's leg, and the gnoll continued to press the attack. Gair turned and ran, eyes skyward, searching for Darkhunter. The wraith was above him, descending, inky black fingers reaching out.

The gnoll's feet pounded across the ground behind Gair, as he swung the sword again and again, slicing through Camilla's cloak and biting into Gair's back. The elf cried out just as Darkhunter's fingers grabbed him and pulled him aloft. Orvago crouched and leapt, the magical blade swinging in a wide arc that sliced off a piece of the wraith.

Darkhunter's eyes burned hotly red as he pulled Gair higher and out of sight.

* * * * *

Goldmoon was in the midst of the settlers gathered at the base of the Silver Stair. Iryl and Skydancer were keeping everyone close. Dozens of voices were asking what was going on, was that really Gair, what are the black creatures?

She ignored their questions and edged through the

press of bodies, finally reaching the stair and starting up it. The cold wind unmercifully teased her face and hands as she climbed. Below her, she heard Iryl.

"I don't understand. What's Goldmoon doing?" the elf asked.

"Perhaps she is trying to survey the battle," the Qué-Nal chieftain replied, "a battle I must join, Iryl Song-brook, now that you and the others are safely away."

The elf protested, but clearly lost. Skydancer selected a few of his strongest warriors and separated them from the crowd. The Qué-Nal hoisted their spears and ran toward the construction site.

The aging healer thrust the voices to the back of her mind and continued up. She was practically crawling, using her hands to help support her. She was tired from her efforts healing the injured and from trying to push Gair out of her thoughts.

But that will never happen, she heard inside her head. *You and I are linked. Now—and when you die.*

Goldmoon climbed higher, feeling cracks in the steps beneath her fingers where Gair had pulled energy from the mystical site. More than three dozen feet above the earth, she gingerly sat, wrapping her fingers around the edge of a step. "May Mishakal, wherever she is, forgive me," the healer breathed.

She concentrated on the feel of the energy pulsing against the palms of her hands and tickling her fingers. She urged it to flow into her, just as if she were injured and were receiving the mystical strength of a healer. She had done something similar before, by accident, pulling energy from the enchanted medallion about her neck to assist in powering a spell to save a dying man. She had not repeated the incident, fearful that stealing energy might destroy her precious medallion, a symbol of her goddess Mishakal.

"It can't be helped," she said to herself, as she felt the

energy of the Silver Stair flow up her arms and down her chest, centering on her heart, which was at the same time nurturing the mystical spark she used to heal others.

The stair did not crack beneath her fingers.

What are you doing? Gair was inside her head.

She did not bother to answer, only concentrated harder on the energy. She felt invigorated almost instantly, her fatigue a memory and her heart beating so strongly. The stair remained strong, too, and the healer sensed she was not harming it, since her intentions were pure.

I had intended to fight Camilla and her knights first. But you're forcing my hand, Goldmoon.

The energy chased away all traces of the winter cold, making her feel almost feverish. She focused on the heat and on Gair, focused on shutting off the link that they somehow shared.

Goldmoon, no!

Then his voice was gone, and all she heard was the pounding of her heart. Faintly, from the base of the stairs, she heard the voices of the settlers, questions about what was transpiring, speculations about the battle the knights and soldiers and Skydancer's Qué-Nal were fighting. There was a cry of surprise in the mix, turned to a cry of terror.

"The black ghosts!" Goldmoon heard someone shout. "Run!"

Feet were pounding across the snow-packed ground, and Goldmoon knew that the people were running in terror—but not everyone. She heard the fishermen and the Solace twins. They were standing their ground. She heard the gruff voice of a dwarf—Redstone?—and she heard the throaty growl of the gnoll.

The healer pushed all these noises to the back of her mind, then directed her thoughts to her heartbeat and to the stair and to a doorway she was picturing inside her mind.

* * * * *

At the construction site, several wraiths feasted on the dead and dying forms of soldiers and renegade Qué-Nal whom Goldmoon's followers had not been able to pull back. A handful of Solamnic knights had succumbed to the icy touch of the undead creatures. Camilla had sent several of the wraiths back to their graves in response.

Redstone left her side only when the knight ordered her to follow the black cloud that rose above the construction site and headed across the camp. Orvago was following them, too, howling and leaping, trying to slice at the whisperers.

"Willum!" Camilla cried, when she caught sight of the lieutenant out of the corner of her eye. "I was worried about you!"

There were other Solamnic knights marching out of step behind him, all of them coming from the east.

"Hurry," she cried to him. "I need your help."

It didn't initially register to the Solamnic commander that the knight's plate mail was coated with dried blood, that Willum was lacking a sword and a leg plate. She didn't notice until the knights were practically upon her that one of them held his head at a strange angle, and that he was missing a hand.

"Willum?"

The Solamnic lieutenant stared at her with sightless eyes, chest unmoving.

"Willum!" Startled and horrified, Camilla hesitated. In that instant, a wraith darted in, his icy hand reaching through her breastplate and into the flesh beneath. The undead squeezed her heart, and she screamed.

Pain coursing through her, Camilla fought to stay conscious. She swept her sword up, piercing the form of the wraith. It exploded in a burst of black rain. She clamped hard on her lower lip and swung the blade again, this time at Willum.

The enchanted sword struck the plate mail and cut through it, shattering the corpse's ribs. Willum staggered from the blow, and from a series of blows striking his legs. Jasper had moved up behind the dead knight and was pummeling him.

"Hammer doesn't work against them black things," he huffed, "but it seems to work against these." Willum fell to the dwarf's repeated strikes; then Jasper turned to face another corpse.

Camilla glanced at her fallen lieutenant and fought the tears that welled up in her eyes. She turned her attention back to the wraiths.

* * * * *

The black cloud that continued to float away from the construction site was dotted with bright red specks that glimmered like bits of flame—twelve pairs of eyes. There had been thirteen, but Orvago had slain one of the low-flying creatures. They floated through the tops of tents, some of which still burned, slowing the dwarf and the gnoll, who had to go around the obstacles. As the cloud neared the base of the Silver Stair, they dived on the people gathered there, scattering most of them like dry leaves tossed by the wind.

A few of the wraiths toyed with the handful of men and women defiantly remaining, feigning pain when swords and clubs passed through their insubstantial forms, but most of them glided up the staircase, circling it, heading toward Goldmoon.

Redstone shouldered Goldmoon's staff, swung back, and soundly struck a particularly large wraith just as it felled one of the Schallsea fishermen. Orvago cleaved another wraith in two as he pushed by the Solace twins and reached the bottom step of the Silver Stair.

The hair rose in a ridge from the top of Orvago's head and down his back. The steps glimmered like captured starlight. He growled softly, glanced up at Goldmoon, and took a step up when he saw the wraiths close on her. The gnoll continued to growl as he advanced, his paws shaking from fright of the magical construct.

"Whisperers," he growled. "Kill the whisperers."

* * * * *

We are more powerful in death. Sweet, sweet death.
High overhead, Goldmoon felt the icy touch of a wraith, the sensation like a massive blow that threatened to knock her from her perch. She kept her hands locked on the step and made no move to defend herself, concentrating on the doorway in her mind.

"Best left closed," she breathed.
You are nothing, fleshy one.
There were pinpoints of red and white lights beyond the doorway, the eyes of spirits Gair had touched. They cursed her, and the vilest among them frightened her with visions of death. Their eyes were so bright, they made the doorway gleam. There was no door, and Goldmoon knew the vision was symbolic of her student breaking down the barriers between the realm of the living and the dead.

"Closed!" She screamed the word as another inky talon sliced into her, drawing blood and sending such a frigid jolt into her chest that she lost her grip on the step. She felt herself falling, tumbling down the steps, arms flailing for a hold.

You cannot defeat us. Everyone dies. The wraiths continued to cackle in their whispery voices. *Death makes us powerful. Join us!*

"No!" She found a step to hold on to, her legs dangling over the side of the Silver Stair. Her hands gripped the edge tightly, even as another wraith floated down to take a swipe at her back. Goldmoon slammed her eyes shut and concentrated on the step she was clinging to so precariously, concentrated on its energy, pictured the doorway, and pictured a door forming to blot out the glowing eyes of the dead.

Again talons raked her, though this time they did not hurt so badly. The heat of the stair's energy was pulsing through her and shutting out some of the pain.

A growl cut through the whispers of the creatures, loud and close. It was followed by a keening wail, then another.

"Whisperers!" Orvago shouted. The gnoll was perched on the stair. His sword reflected the light of the Celestial Ladder as he arced it above his head and drove it down into a wraith diving for Goldmoon. Black rain fell on the steps, sizzling and boiling away.

Only a half-dozen of the black creatures remained, and they backed away as Orvago slowly climbed higher. He was near Goldmoon now. Keeping one paw firmly on the sword, he carefully bent over and locked the other around the healer's arm. He pulled her up until she was lying on the steps beneath him.

"Goldmoon?"

The healer didn't answer him. Eyes closed, hands still touching the Silver Stair, she was focusing all her attention on the realm of the dead. "Closed," she said.

"Noooo!"

The new voice drew the gnoll's attention, and he looked all about to find its source. There, a dozen feet above his head, perched on the Silver Stair, was Gair. The elf looked mangled. Hand broken, leg twisted terribly from Orvago's sword blow, he somehow managed to balance himself on a step.

"How did you get here?" the gnoll asked. Orvago narrowed his dark eyes. "Whisperers."

Gair did not reply, but he hobbled closer, leading with his undamaged leg.

Orvago didn't wait for the elf to close. He swung madly at the retreating wraiths, and he edged by Goldmoon, stepping over her to get beyond her and nearer to the elf. "Whisperers!"

"I have no weapon, old friend," Gair said. He was balancing on a narrow step, favoring his wounded leg. "I cannot possibly . . . Goldmoon, don't do this!"

The gnoll growled and hesitated. Behind him, he heard Goldmoon murmuring something.

"Closed," she repeated. In her mind, she was picturing the door, growing more solid with each passing heartbeat. The eyes that were shining through it were becoming softer. Suddenly they were gone, the door thick and unyielding.

"Noooo!" Gair hollered again.

The wraiths that had been retreating from Orvago's enchanted sword vanished.

"They're gone!" Redstone shouted from the base of the Silver Stair. The few wraiths remaining there were nowhere to be seen.

Far across the camp, the wraiths feasting on the bodies melted into the ground, and the undead Solamnic Knights crumpled. Whoops and cheers echoed around the settlement.

On the Silver Stair, Gair's eyes grew wide with disbelief. "Whatever it is you did, Goldmoon, I will undo it! All my work, all the spirits I've culled." He sat on the step, several feet still above the gnoll, and he gripped the edge of the Celestial Ladder with his good hand. "I'll undo it!"

Goldmoon stirred. "Stop him, Orvago."

It was all the encouragement the gnoll needed. He locked his gaze onto Gair and continued on up the stair.

The elf was mumbling something, words that meant

nothing to the gnoll but that raised the hair on his back
even higher. Gair's eyes were glazed, tinged red, and
glowing like the whisperers' eyes.

"I have no weapon," the elf said and returned to his
mumbling.

The gnoll edged closer.

"You'd not strike an unarmed man."

"Whisperer!" The gnoll brought the sword down hard
on the hand gripping the Silver Stair.

Gair cried out sharply and shot to his feet. He took a
backward step higher to get away from Orvago. His eyes
still glowed red. "More powerful in death," he hushed.
The voice was Darkhunter's, not Gair's, though it came
from the elf's body. "I am more powerful—"

"Whisperer!" Orvago swung again, striking the elf in
the side and toppling him. He flailed about with his
arms for a heartbeat, then plummeted from the Silver
Stair. The gnoll carefully turned and hurried down the
steps, stopping only to help Goldmoon to her feet.

He leapt down the last few feet, landing in a crouch
and looking about for the elf. There, partially hidden by
the drift he'd fallen into, Gair lay like a broken doll. The
gnoll padded forward, leading with the broadsword.
Gair wasn't moving, but Orvago prodded him with the
sword to be certain. The elf's eyes were open, and in the
light of the Silver Stair, they looked dark purple, flecked
with bits of gold.

"Whisperer gone."

Goldmoon and Redstone silently joined Orvago and
knelt by the body. The healer reached to the elf's face
and gently closed his eyelids.

Chapter 18

The Citadel of Light

It was the heart of Raging Fire.

There was little left of the tent community. Nearly everyone had moved into the Citadel of Light, even though the structure was not yet finished.

Redstone was hard at work on part of the complex. She sat in front of a block of crystal and was shaping it magically with her hands, as if the material were the softest clay, and in so doing showing everyone the reason why Jasper had coaxed her here from Thorbardin. An earth mystic, Redstone was largely responsible for the appearance of the citadel, and she proudly announced that it should take only another year to complete.

Nearby, Skydancer and his Qué-Nal cleared the land to make room for the rest of the citadel.

Four domes were finished, several stories tall, huge and made of the crystal mined from the northern tip of Schallsea Island. There would be nine when the work was finished, all with a pale blue tint that seemingly reflected the sky of a bright summer day. The setting sun was hitting them now, however, making them glow like dying coals.

Altogether sparkling like a jeweled bracelet, they would ring a great garden that had started to take shape. Elves were hard at work on that, training hedges to form an elaborate maze that would lead people to the Silver Stair. Flowers were woven among the hedges, scenting the air with lilacs and honeysuckle and rose.

"I don't believe I've ever seen anything so beautiful," said Camilla. She was watching the crystal grow under Redstone's hands. "In all my travels, I can't say that anything exists to rival the Citadel of Light."

Goldmoon was at her shoulder, a wistful expression on her face. "It is beautiful," she admitted. "As in my vision. They look like gems, shining with hope."

Other earth mystics were working to form hallways connecting the domes. There was one dome larger than the others, what Goldmoon had dubbed the Grand Lyceum. There was a barracks inside for the Solamnic knights and for others who had become the grounds' guardians, though the guardians merely patrolled the land now. There had been no trouble since the night Gair was slain.

Children were playing outside the great dome, orphans from the port town and from elsewhere in Ansalon. Goldmoon sensed that several of them had mystical potential and readily took them all in.

The healer nodded to a young girl with night-black hair, then turned away and strolled toward the docks. A small ship was arriving from New Ports, bringing with it pilgrims and curiosity seekers. Goldmoon and Camilla stood at the top of the cliff, waiting to greet the newcomers. The sun had set by the time the entourage had made it up the long staircase from the bay, and twilight touched the island by the time they were all were settled in.

The healer and knight continued their rounds, their

path taking them by a cemetery, where knights, soldiers, and Goldmoon's followers who had died in last winter's struggle were buried.

One grave sat apart from the others, and it was to this one that Camilla and Goldmoon were drawn. They were among the very few visitors to this stone, and when they came it was always after sunset. The carving was elaborate, courtesy of Redstone, and the words simple: *Gair Graymist, who waits for us beyond the door.* The healer knelt and touched the earth, a gesture that had become a ritual. No flowers or grass grew upon the ground here, as they grew in profusion on the other graves. The dirt was as cold as the breath of winter, and infertile. She shivered, despite the hot summer air that wrapped around her. Camilla helped her up, and then they headed toward the Grand Lyceum, where people were gathering for dinner and stories and songs.

The stars lazily winked into view in a purple-blue sky, reflecting brightly off the domes. The moon rose above the horizon and brought with it the Silver Stair. The steps shimmered invitingly.

The gnoll stood at the base of the steps, hackles raised, a growl playing softly in his throat. He had not come close to the construct since the night Gair had unleashed his undead forces. There was something about the stair's magic that intensely unnerved him.

Still . . .

He placed a clawed foot on the bottom step, cringing as he felt the energy of the Celestial Ladder tingle against his pad. He took another step, and then another. The breeze ruffled his fur as he climbed higher, and he dared to look down only once. Far beneath him the domes glimmered like wet pearls. Faintly he heard singing, dwarvish. His feet moved up the stairs now in time with the music.

The mist swirled around him, and he growled more

loudly. Despite the fear that clawed at his belly, he continued higher and higher until the stars stretched out all around him. The gnoll scarcely breathed as he tried to take it all in, one paw reaching out as if he could catch a star between his fingers. The wind was colder here, nipping at his skin, the air filled with a myriad of scents that seemed achingly familiar, yet that he couldn't quite place.

A little higher.

The top step shimmered into view, and Orvago swallowed hard. The tingling beneath his feet was no longer pleasant. It seemed to challenge him. For the briefest of moments, the gnoll considered retreating.

He held his breath, squared his massive shoulders, and went all the way to the top. . . .

Books

THE DRAGONS OF A NEW AGE TRILOGY

Volume I	**Volume II**	**Volume III**
The Dawning of a New Age	The Day of the Tempest	The Eve of the Maelstrom

JEAN RABE

Magic has vanished. Dragonlords rule and slaughter. A harsh apocalyptic world requires new strategies and new heroes, among them Palin Majere, son of Caramon. Available now.

RELICS & OMENS
Tales of the Fifth Age
EDITED BY MARGARET WEIS AND TRACY HICKMAN

The first *Fifth Age* anthology features new short stories exploring the post-*Dragons of Summer Flame* world of banished gods and lost magic. Available now.

BRIDGES OF TIME SERIES

This series bridges the stories in the thirty-year time span between the Classic and Fifth Age DRAGONLANCE novels.

SPIRIT OF THE WIND
CHRIS PIERSON

Riverwind, the fabled plainsman, answers the call for heroes and aids the kender in their struggle against the great red dragon Malystryx. Available July 1998.

LEGACY OF STEEL
MARY H. HERBERT

Five years after the Chaos War, Sara Dunstan, an outcast knight of Takhisis, risks a dangerous journey to Neraka and confirms rumors that the Dark Knights are reorganizing. Available November 1998.

Free Newsletter

The LEGENDS OF THE LANCE™ newsletter is a **FREE** quarterly publication about the DRAGONLANCE® Saga. Inside you'll find interviews with your favorite authors, artists, and game designers, information about upcoming releases, and other fascinating items.

Your subscription to the LEGENDS OF THE LANCE newsletter opens the door for you to ask us your DRAGONLANCE questions, submit articles for publication, get the latest news of the Fifth Age, and much more!

To receive your **FREE** subscription, mail or email your name and postal address to the following address or call the customer service number:

**Wizards of the Coast
Customer Service Department
P.O. Box 707
Renton, WA 98057-0707
Email: legends@wizards.com
Customer Service: (206) 624-0933**

Legends of the Lance™
NEWSLETTER

DRAGONLANCE®
SAGA

TSR